WOLVES OF THE DAWN

Balor pointed off. "Look, Father! Sailing ships! Do you see them?"

Fomor's face was as gray as old ashes. "Aye, I have seen them. I have seen those ships in my dreams for over half a lifetime. Mark this moment, Balor. By the power of the Twelve Winds you have received a great gift. The shooting star that led you to this place was a sign, my son—a sign such as I was given when, many years ago, I too saw such a star and followed it to this very place . . . and looked down on Bracken Fen and knew that I must lead my clansmen there to dwell in peace. And now, through you, once more, the star has brought me here, where I might find a message written in the dawn. Had you not followed that star, Balor, we would have had no warning—none at all—until it was too late."

"Warning? Of what?"

"Of the wolves, my son. Of mad, vengeful man-eating wolves! They run beneath the colors of the red and black, led by a warlord known as Nemed MacAgnomain, a man who has sworn to take my head and nourish the earth with the blood of my kindred."

That day, Balor's world changed forever. . . .

WOLVES
of the
DAWN

William Sarabande

 Created by the producers of
**Wagons West, White Indian,
America 2040,** and
Children of the Lion.

Chairman of the Board: Lyle Kenyon Engel

BANTAM BOOKS
TORONTO · NEW YORK · LONDON · SYDNEY · AUCKLAND

WOLVES OF THE DAWN
A Bantam Book / published by arrangement with
Book Creations, Inc.

Bantam edition / February 1987

Produced by Book Creations, Inc.
Chairman of the Board: Lyle Kenyon Engel

ISBN 0-553-25802-8

Published simultaneously in the United States and Canada

PRINTED IN THE UNITED STATES OF AMERICA

O   0 9 8 7 6 5 4 3 2 1

To Dorothy and John, my two.

Acknowledgments

Wolves of the Dawn would not have been written had it not been for the encouragement of Lyle Kenyon Engel, who said yes to the proposed project and welcomed this author so graciously into his "family" at Book Creations, Inc. Thanks are due to Philip Rich, editor in chief, for his patient counsel at the beginning. And to Laurie Rosin, senior editor, whose keen editorial eye, insight, and grand sense of humor through it all guided the author and made certain that the "wolves" kept their howling on pitch. Thanks too to all my friends at Book Creations, and Charles Cline, who helped block out the battle scenes, and Antonita Holdren, who contributed absolutely nothing at all . . . except unflagging encouragement and friendship.

William Sarabande

There's woe in the world,
An ax age, a sword age,
A storm age, a wolf age,
Before the world crumbles,
No mercy or quarter
Will man give to man.
The sun grows dark,
The earth sinks into the sea,
The bright stars
Fall from the skies.
Then shall the Mighty One come to his kingdom.

Voluspa—*the Sibyl's Prophecy*

LAND OF THE
TWELVE WINDS

GOLDEN PLAINS

NORTH

ACHAEA

FROM TOELKE DS/

LAND OF THE
NORTH WIND

SEA OF
MISTS

ALBION

EIREANN

NARROW SEA

WESTERN SEA

TORY ISLE

LANDS END

GREAT SEA

IN ALBION:
○ PLAIN OF THE GREAT
   STONE CIRCLE
△ POINT-OF-ALE
⚓ BRACKEN FEN

©BOOK CREATIONS INC. 1985

Prologue

At the dawn of the Age of Bronze, at the eclipse of the Age of Stone, a boy-child was born to the People of the Ax. The squalling infant was grandson to Manannan, warlord of the Far Island, and son to Fomor, Wolf of the Western Tribes, member of the warrior clan MacLir. But the child was also the firstborn of the slave woman Huldre, from the country of Boreas, in the Land of the North Wind, so it was not known whether the boy-child would be a blessing or a curse to the People of the Ax... if he lived.

He was named Balor. A fitting name for a warlord's son, one that had to do with luck and power and magic; at the moment of his birth, his mother took him and held him up to the piercing light of the rising sun, dedicating him to the power of the Twelve Winds.

"This one shall be a warrior," she proclaimed.

But the father snatched the infant from her grasp and lifted him high. As the Wise One watched and the women cowered, not daring to intercede against the will of their chieftain, he turned the child thrice dawnward to undo the mother's dedication. Then he spoke the words that, some said, took away the luck of the clan forever.

"May he dwell in peace. May he not know war. May he live long and not know death in battle."

But the mother had spoken first, and her dedication would not be undone. The power of the Twelve Winds would take him. He would be a warrior.

This is his story.

1

BOOK I

1

The storm came out of the north. It came from across the Sea
of Mists, from beyond the moors and highlands, and now, at
last, it struck full force at Albion, that fabled isle that men of
later days would name and know as England. Merciless,
devastating, the storm was a great, black beast running wild
across the fens, consuming the dawn, making a mockery of
spring. Lightning snagged the sky and ripped open the belly
of the clouds as sleet-stung, wind-driven rain poured down
onto a vulnerable earth that could hold no more.

Beneath the storm-ravaged sky the small roundhouses of
the village of Bracken Fen clustered close together inside a
palisade of vertically raised timbers along the raging stream
that bisected the holding of the lord of the clan MacLir. Mud
was everywhere. As thick as pudding, as dark as clotted
blood, it spattered the houses and plank walkways as the
falling rain pounded it, pooled upon it, slaked and danced
and worked up a sound that rivaled the wind.

The rain pounded the conical, thickly thatched roof of the
chieftain's roundhouse, and the wind slapped and tore at the
clay-packed, timber-braced walls of woven wattle and daub.
It was dark within the roundhouse, and now and again a flash
of lightning illuminated the interior, and flared brightly beneath the sleeping boy's lids, but it was the wind that woke
him. It trespassed into the room, through cracks and chinks
in the walls. It moved at will, a stalking, invisible predator
that sucked the warmth from the air and put the claws of
terror to the boy's throat.

A deafening clap of thunder exploded overhead. Somehow
there was the resonance of a snarling wolf within it, a wolf as
bold and white and deadly as the lightning bolt that had
spawned it. And clearly the boy heard it cry his name.

"Balor!"

He bolted upright on his bed of piled skins and furs to find
that it was only his little brother, Elathan, nine years old and
younger by a year, who had called him. Relief filled him and
almost banished the image of the wolf. The two sons of

Fomor, lord of the clan MacLir, sat close together in the storm dark, listening to the wind and the rain, and although Elathan drew comfort from the warmth and nearness of his elder brother, Balor spoke no reassuring words to him. He could still feel the claws of the wolf at his throat. In ways that he could not name, he sensed that this storm was more threatening than any that had struck the rain-blighted fens before.

"The god is walking. . . ."

Their mother's voice came to them out of the darkness; and with it came light, soft and flickering. Balor could see her now, Huldre, his father's second woman, as she knelt before the stone curbing of the fire pit. Across the tremulous darkness of the large, circular room, he could see her pale face as she bent to blow life gently into last night's coals.

"'Tis only another storm . . . that and nothing more!" snapped Mealla, the first woman of the lord.

Balor now saw that both women of the chieftain's house were up and about. Mealla was igniting the tallow lamps, muttering to herself as she worked, as she always did when Huldre annoyed her. Soon she would have the clay pots on the fire and he would smell heated goat's fat and breakfast gruel. But now the sight of her busying herself with the makings of a new day caused Balor to relax; his father's first woman always had that effect upon him. It was auburn-haired Mealla, herself barren, who had nurtured the sons that Huldre had born to the lord of the clan MacLir. It was Mealla who had been a mother to them, who had rocked them back to sleep after nightmares and ministered to them when they were ill. Not Huldre. Never Huldre.

Yet it was Huldre who stared at Balor now, knowing his thoughts, reawakening his fear, causing him to be suddenly and painfully aware of the smells of the room: of the burning coals and smoldering marsh grass within the fire pit, of the damp earthen floor of the roundhouse and the moldering rushes that lay over it, of the moist, heavy breath of the rising storm . . . a breath that had something of the smell of an animal to it. Balor's hand went to his throat. The wolf was there again, biting deep.

His mother smiled. "Yes," she said softly, watching. "You feel his presence. Do not be afraid. The god speaks to you out of the storm . . . in the voice of the white wolf that runs always at his side."

Her words were whispers exhaled in her native tongue, a language alien to that of his own people, a tongue spoken by dwellers of the distant Northland from which Huldre had been stolen and made a slave as a young girl. It had all happened long ago. She never spoke of it, but Balor knew, from what little that Mealla had told him, that his mother had been the slave-concubine to a great and cruel lord in a far land before his father had stolen her and made her his own. This had happened in what the old ones called the Days of Glory, before Balor had been born, before his father had led the people of the clan MacLir from their holdings on a place called the Far Island to dwell here, in the fens of Albion. The storytellers said that this had been a good land then. For seven long years the clan had prospered. Until three winters ago, for reasons no man could name, the weather had begun to change.

Once again lightning flared. A clap of thunder rent the sky. There was the smell of sleet in the air. Balor drew it in, reminding himself that it was spring.

"Donar . . ." Huldre spoke the name of the god and in her foreign tongue commanded her firstborn son to listen.

Balor did not want to understand her. She had never made an effort to teach either of her sons her language; yet Balor knew it. Against his will, he knew it. It had come to him as naturally as breathing.

A violent gust of wind shook the roundhouse. Elathan shivered against it as he asked his brother what their mother had said.

Balor ignored him. He was staring at Huldre. He was thinking that she was right. Donar, her people's god of thunder and storm, of lightning and star-fire, protector of those who pleased him and destroyer of those who did not, *was* about tonight. He knew it, just as he had known days ago that this storm would come. He had not known from cloud signs or from a sudden turn of the wind or the restlessness of the livestock. He had simply known, and long before Munremar, the Wise One, had spoken of its coming. Long before the old men and women felt its presence walking in their bones, before the little children had begun to squish the worms that wiggled from the earth in search of higher ground.

It happened sometimes, as it did for his mother. He knew that something would happen, and it did. He shivered now to think of it, for it was an unwelcome gift. It marked him as her son even more than his looks did.

She crouched motionless by the fire pit, as tense and beautiful as a doe set to sprint. In the quivering illumination of the firelight, her long hair was a moon-pale aura shimmering about her face and shoulders. Yet Balor failed to see her loveliness. He saw only that she was different. She did not have the rangy, solidly built, ruddy-haired look of the clan. Huldre was as pale as a winter moon, as slender as an egret, with eyes so fragile a blue that sometimes they seemed colorless.

Her eyes were closed now as her slender right hand curled about the amber amulet that hung about her neck by a braided thong. It was the one object from her homeland that Huldre had managed to keep with her when, as a girl, she had been stolen from her people and made a slave. Always, during storms, she seemed to find comfort in rubbing it. Small, carved into the shape of a hawk in flight with a blood-red stone of carnelian glinting from its tiny, wolfish eye, it never failed to soothe her. The Eye of Donar she called it. As Balor stared at it out of the darkness, he felt a strange, cold sense of uneasiness. It was as though the eye stared back at him. It seemed to glow, as it often did when the friction of her fingers worked over it in the darkness. He did not like his mother's amulet; indeed, he did not like his mother. She was a cold and unloving woman, and the rumors whispered against her by the Wise One—that it was she and her foreign god that were turning the Fates against the clan—embarrassed and troubled him.

He swallowed. His throat felt less constricted now. The wolf had left him, but he wished that he had not been so brazen as to disobey his father by predicting, in front of witnesses, that the storm would come, before Munremar, the Wise One, had done so. It did not take much to make the old priest angry with him. Both Mealla and his father had cautioned him to keep his predictions to himself, but Balor had never found it easy to do as he was told.

He frowned. He did not understand why old Munremar disliked him so. It was not his fault that, unlike Elathan, he had inherited his mother's foreign looks, and that, like her, he sometimes guessed happenings the priest failed to foretell in his conjurings. Balor saw no reason why he should keep these things to himself—unless to keep others from pointing a finger and saying that he was too much his mother's son.

"Balor!"

His father's command startled him. He turned his gaze from his mother and her amulet to see that the chieftain was rising from his own bed of skins and furs. He towered upward, a tall, naked, yellow-maned lord with a body honed to the dimensions of pure power and a beard the color of summer-dried wheat.

As Balor stared at him, the boy forgot all about his mother. He forgot about old Munremar, the Wise One, and the hawk-shaped amber amulet, the Eye of Donar. Let the god of thunder roar! Let the god of lightning snare himself in the broad, black plain of the sky! He was not afraid. He was Balor, firstborn son of Fomor MacLir, Wolf of the Western Tribes, and grandson of Manannan, fabled lord of the Far Island, who had died a hero's death before the dawn of the Days of Glory to give honor forever to those descended from the line.

"I'll have my cloak, boy. Now and quickly!" Fomor MacLir was hastily donning his clothes: a sleeved, slipover knee-length tunic of well-tanned deerskin; leggings of rabbit fur, laced to the knee over shoes that he bound just below the ankles with thongs of sinew.

There was an unmistakable urgency in the chieftain's words. Proud that his father had not summoned Elathan to do his bidding as well, Balor was on his feet in an instant, a lean, white-skinned boy with a crop of pale, unruly hair that was too much like his foreign-born mother's to please him. Like his sire he was naked, and although the cold stirring of the wind within the room roused gooseflesh, he was impervious to it as he leaped across his father's restless terriers. The big, grizzle-haired dogs yipped in protest and snapped at his heels as he bolted over them.

The chieftain's cloak hung on a rack of elk antler to one side of the narrow, oxhide-covered entryway. Balor snatched it, ran back across the room, and held it out to his sire with hands straining not to tremble. The cloak had been sewn from the pelts of four wolves, including the paws and tails. The heads of the two largest beasts, with the lower jaws cut

away, had been stitched together to form the top of the hood.
It was a warrior's robe, unique in all the land. There was not
a member of the clan who did not know that Fomor had slain
the beasts himself, long ago. . . . He had been but a boastful
youth, fighting bare-handed against four male wolves in a
timber-lined fighting pit in one of the towns where the
Beaker Folk dwelled and kept their trading centers. Now he
took the cloak from the boy and slung it on, securing it high
at the shoulder with a large, circular brooch of carved, highly
polished bone. When he turned up the hood and pulled it
low over his brow, Balor inadvertently sucked in his breath
with pride and wonder.

As Balor looked up at his father, he saw more than a man.
He saw the Wolf of the Western Tribes, the lord about whom
wonder tales were spun, about whom the one-time warriors
of the clan MacLir spoke with nostalgic reverence. He saw
the lord who had been a warrior and a sea raider, a chieftain
on Eireann, the Far Island where the clan had lived for
generations before Fomor had led them eastward across the
Narrow Sea to Albion, the Great Island, to raid, pillage, and
uphold the traditions left to them by the People of the Ax,
the ancient culture that Balor knew had existed from Time
Beyond Beginning.

The People of the Ax had been born in the vast distances of
the Land Beyond the Sea to move westward, ever westward,
across uncharted miles and seas and rivers, taking what they
would from tribes too weak to stand against them. Among the
first to use horses in battle, to define metallurgy as an art,
they had moved as a tide across history until the seeds of
their race were scattered upon the Twelve Winds, each tribe
swearing fealty to its own lord until, soon, there were a
thousand clans dwelling in a thousand lands, each separate,
each unique, each independent.

Balor's ancestors had reached the shores of the Western
Sea and looked westward to distant islands, hungering to
claim them as their own. It was in these early days that the
clan's founder, Lir, was born, to become a warlord like no
other before him as he set himself to build the clan's first
raiding ships. His sons became known as the MacLir, and
they raised a great fortress upon the Far Island's western
shores, subjugating its native peoples until, long after Lir's
death, during the reign of Manannan, invaders came from

across the sea to challenge the clan. There was a great war, fought with magic weapons. The old men spoke of a wondrous sword forged by sorcery of a metal that the People of the Ax had not seen before.

Then came the Days of Glory in which Fomor, son of Manannan, stole the great sword of the clan's most feared enemy and named it Retaliator when he became chieftain after his father's death. Of these events there was an absence of detail. The men who fought beside Fomor were strangely silent, as were the storytellers. Balor only knew that, for reasons his father refused to explain, he had abandoned the great MacLir fortress and loaded his people, some five hundred strong, into the clan's great sailing ships and led them eastward to Albion. After many battles they had settled in this hard-won holding, in this bleak, storm-benighted village called Bracken Fen, to become herdsmen and setters of seed.

In the year of Balor's birth, Fomor MacLir, son of Manannan, descendant of the fabled warlord Lir, had turned his back on the ways of his ancestors, even having their great sailing vessels put to the torch. Long before the Wolf's youth had been spent, he had locked his weapons away and had become a man of peace. His people had praised him. And now, with starving times and sickness upon them, and the looming prospect of yet another failed harvest, for the life of him, Balor could not understand why.

"You need not go out into the storm to tend your precious cattle, Fomor."

Balor turned toward the sound of his mother's voice. She had spoken in the language of the clan, her words flowing as smoothly as if in her native tongue. There was a flat, cutting edge of thinly veiled contempt to her tone, and Balor hated her for it. He glared at her as she knelt back on her haunches. Despite the sweep of dark, curly cowhide that was her dress, he could see the small rise of her pregnancy. He wondered if this one would come to term. Most of her pregnancies did not. Perhaps she was too old to bear children. She had told him that she had seen as many as twenty-seven summers. That made her nearly as old as Mealla. Balor assumed that this must be very old indeed for a woman. Females did not live very long in the fens, and in Huldre's case, even though she was his mother, Balor was glad.

The chieftain took up a heavy hank of rope and replied to Huldre as though he had not noted her tone, "I must go out, woman, and rouse the other men. If the cattle break free from the holding circle, they will stampede into the bogs and be lost to us."

Mealla had come close to the lord, her auburn hair animate with firelight, the gray strands within it sparking silver. She proffered a beaker of cold, hastily drawn mead to her lord. As always, thought Balor, she could be counted on to offer support. The boy loved her for her kindness and warmth as she assured Fomor, "You have posted the best watchmen, my lord, and you yourself were with them until half the night was done and old Falcon insisted that he relieve you. No man has a keener eye for the ways of the cattle than old Falcon. Surely he would warn you if there were danger."

The chieftain quaffed the mead and handed back the cup. "Aye, and so. A man may already be on his way. After these past weeks of rain, I doubt if the holding circle will stand against such a deluge as this. If the cattle panic at the sound of thunder, the walls of the embankment may collapse—the earth that holds them is saturated. I dare not wait for Falcon to send alert. I do not like the stench of this storm."

"There is ice in the wind." Huldre had risen to her feet. She stood unmoving beside the fire pit, her right hand curled at her throat, her fingers slowly caressing the amber amulet.

Balor felt a hollowness within his belly fill with shame and anger. He knew that his mother's next words would be of doom, based not on true vision but ill-wishings. Mealla had told him that even during the years when the clan had prospered, Huldre had prophesied disaster for them all if they did not leave the fens and return to the ways of their warrior ancestors. It had something to do with an irrational fear of a long-dead enemy, Mealla had explained. The clan folk had pitied her at first, and for years her soothsayings had come to naught; but now there were those, including the Wise One, who said that she was to blame for the turn of the weather, and Balor loathed her for that because if it was true, then she had *caused* the luck of her lord to turn, not merely predicted that it would happen. He wondered if old Munremar, the Wise One, could be right about her.

Lightning flashed again. Huldre's hand tightened about her amulet. Was she invoking the name and power of her Northland god to stay his wrath, or was she using her talisman to call it down upon them?

"The storm speaks to you, Fomor. The ice shall blight all hope of harvest. The seedlings that have been planted with such care shall not survive the wrath of this rain. Three seasons now your people have been without a decent harvest. Your cattle sicken and die. Your people show signs of starvation— the old die, children grow wan, and infants waste away. This past winter too many babies died and too many women cast off their young unborn."

Mealla's face congested with emotion. "Form not such words, Huldre! Will you never learn that Fortune comes as it is summoned?"

Huldre ignored her. She went on, her voice a soft slur of promise and warning. "The land has turned against you, Fomor MacLir. Listen to the storm, my lord. The time has come to move on, to take up the old way of life. The Wolf was born to roam the world and eat his fill of those who have not learned that life belongs to the strong. Let your precious cattle drown in the bogs. Gather up your men. Open the battle chests. Take up your axes and your spears. Release the Retaliator. Remember the past. Know that there are settlements to the south where soft men grow fat beneath a kind sun that no longer shines for you. For the sake of your sons it is time for you to take up the ways of a warrior once again . . . before it is too late."

Retaliator.

The word, rarely heard, always exhilarating, sliced into Balor's consciousness. He had never seen the sword, which had been locked away in his father's battle chest since the last of the Days of Glory. Its imagined contours slid through his mind like a well-honed dagger into a sheath fitted just for the length and width of its blade alone; but there was no time to hold onto the image. He let it fade as he saw his father's green eyes narrow and turn as dark as a sea in a storm.

"It *is* for the sake of my sons, Huldre, that I tell you now, as I swore to you upon the day of Balor's birth, that the wolf in me has died. *Because* I remember the past, I will not be a warrior again."

Her wide-set eyes gazed steadily at him. Foreign eyes, as pale a blue as an ice shadow. "The wolf in a man never dies,

Fomor MacLir. He only sleeps until he is roused. Soon you shall see. For the sake of us all, you *must* see."

Thunder growled beyond the walls of the roundhouse. Or was it the sound of Fomor's anger as he moved across the room to the doorway and whistled for his dogs to follow? Balor could not tell.

"Wait, Father. I want to come with you."

Fomor MacLir looked down at his firstborn. "No, Balor. I must forbid it. You're yet too small for such dangerous work."

"I'm no woman to sit safe by the fire," protested the boy.

"Nor are you yet a man, my son."

"He shall never be a man...not if we stay here..." Huldre's voice was redolent with warning.

But only Mealla and the boys heard her warning; Fomor went out into the storm without looking back.

2

Balor stood at the doorway of the roundhouse, wind and rain stinging his face, disappointment heavy within him. He resented being left behind by his father. After all, he had predicted this storm. He was no baby to be left behind! He was taller than most boys his age, and although he was not as brawny, he was convinced that he was as strong. He *could* be of help to his kinsmen. He *knew* that he could. He held the oxhide weather baffle across his body as he looked out the doorway and into the storm after the chieftain, trembling with his desire to follow.

Fomor had already crossed the narrow walkway of sagging, moss-slick planking that connected each roundhouse to the great central council hall, where yellow lamplight glinted through occasional breaks in the wattled walls. Fomor made no attempt to enter; he paused as other men hurried out of their roundhouses to join him.

As lightning exploded overhead, Balor could see the men in bold, livid relief. He recognized his father's big, muscular, red-bearded younger brother, Draga. He saw Dathen and Lomna Ruad, and Broen and Echur, men who had been battle champions in the Days of Glory. Others stood with their backs to him. Tall, broadly built men and a few strapping adolescents, all hunched against the wind in heavy cloaks, anticipating the challenges of the day with ropes and prods in their hands, and in their belts, daggers, no doubt, along with their short-handled axes. They had their dogs with them, terriers in the main, versatile and voracious, large beasts, trained to worry a cow or bull back into the herd with as much enthusiasm as they harried badgers or foxes.

A bent, slim figure emerged from the council hall to stand silhouetted in the light of its low-linteled, narrow entryway. Balor knew him at once by his wild, uncombed hair and the thick, gnarled staff on which he leaned. It was Munremar. The Wise One. The boy scowled as he saw the white-haired old man lift the staff and raise it upward, shaking it, not against the storm, but against Fomor MacLir. Balor wondered what the old man had said. Probably something against Huldre, something to accuse her of being responsible for the storm. The chieftain stood motionless. Balor could sense the anger in him, and the control. For reasons that Balor could not understand, Fomor MacLir adored his second woman. He would hear no words against her. Not even from Munremar, who had been high priest to Manannan MacLir, and Fomor's chief adviser since Manannan's death had brought Fomor to the chieftainship of the clan.

Whatever the old man had said, he had no chance to repeat it. Fomor turned away from him and strode off across the compound, where another group of men, some mounted, awaited him at the open palisade gateway. One of the men who stood afoot held a huge, dark, shaggy horse at close rein—one of the few survivors of a herd that had, until the last winter, been considerable.

As war-horses they had been valuable, but to a settled, pastoral people they had proven to be of little use. Hobbling against the slow agony brought on by hoof rot and chronic lung disease, in the third year of failed harvests and endless rain the horses had deprived the more valued livestock of precious pasturage. Convinced that there was no alternative, Fomor had commanded that most of them be slaughtered and salted. But there had been those—especially Draga—who had been infuriated by the horse-killing. Balor could still remember his uncle commenting blackly that, in the midst of

continuing crop failures, Fomor MacLir had made the final
break with the nomadic life they had once led as warriors of
the People of the Ax—a life that could free them from the
starvation and disease that threatened them all if the weather
did not improve. Fomor had insisted that it was only a matter
of time before the weather improved. The majority of the
clansmen had supported him. Still, Draga had mumbled that
without horses they would be bound to the fens forever, all
destined to die in the mud of the marsh country, as his own
twin infant sons had died only weeks before.

The boy felt a momentary pang of sympathetic understanding of his uncle's resentment toward Fomor over the deaths of
his twins, but then he thought better of it. Even in the best
of times it was not unusual for babies to die before they took
their first steps. Fomor had seen Huldre miscarry many times
and bring three infants into the world stillborn. The chieftain
grieved for his brother's loss, but no more than he grieved for
his own.

Now, as Balor watched, his uncle approached the chieftain.
Words were exchanged. From Fomor's reaction, Balor knew
that they had something to do with the horses; the subject
was still a corrosive element that had destroyed their former
closeness. True, with more horses tonight's work would be
easier and less hazardous; but if Fomor and the elders had
thought the horse-killing for the best interests of the clan,
then Balor knew it must be so. Draga had no right to
challenge their decision, especially since Fomor had allowed
Draga's sorrel to live.

And now, for the sake of the clan, the herd *must* be saved.
If they lost this year's harvest, they would need every sickly,
starving animal if they were to survive another winter. Fomor,
ignoring additional words from his brother, hurled himself
onto the back of the dark horse. It was a stallion, kept for
seed by the chieftain's own decree. Already edgy from the
noise of the storm, when lightning flared just as Fomor
mounted, the horse shied back screaming, rearing and pawing
at the air.

A consummate horseman, the chieftain raised an arm, and
as Balor watched and ached to follow, Fomor MacLir led his
clansmen through the gate and into the storm-riven darkness
beyond.

The boy shivered, wondering what they would find. If the

circular earth mound held against the rain, they and the watchmen would keep the cattle calm until the worst of the storm had passed. But if the ring embankment had broken, they would be forced to pursue the stock into the wild, treacherous bogs and marshlands. Even in the best weather men avoided the bogs, and no one ever went alone into the marshes. Too many had gotten lost. Too many had never returned.

And yet Balor chose to follow. Driven by some wild, unbridled impulse, he hurried into his clothes, took up his cloak and oxhide, and ignoring the reprimands of Mealla and the noncommittal watchfulness of his mother, went out into the storm.

He had Elathan at his heels and paused to turn, swatting at the boy.

"Go home! You're too small to follow me."

"I'm only a year younger than you!"

"A year younger, a year smaller, and a year less bold!"

"Ha! We'll see about that!"

They stood on the plank walkway, halfway to the palisade. In the now slate-gray light of morning the wind buffeted them, and sleet stung their faces. Across the compound a group of boys had gathered around old Munremar, before the walls of the council hall. Balor could see his closest friend, Dianket, gesturing to him as the others stared up at the towering pinnacle of the roof. The wind had peeled back a long, wide strip of thatch.

Elathan shielded his eyes from the weather. "Look at that, would you!" he exclaimed. "If the wind keeps up, it'll soon peel off the whole roof!"

Balor frowned. Someone was calling his name. It was Munremar. He knew what the Wise One wanted: someone to scale the height of the roof and drag new thatching ropes across it while others held them taut from below. Once the ropes were secured and fresh thatch worked into the breach, the roof would be as good as new. It would be a dangerous job in the icy downpour. The Wise One was too old and crippled with bone blight to do any climbing. With the men and youths on their way to the cattle ring, there were only boys available. Along with Dianket, Balor was the eldest, tallest, strongest, and most daring.

But Dianket had never outguessed the Wise One's conjurings as had Balor, nor did Dianket bear the pale, variant look of Huldre, whom Munremar hated doubly for her own foretellings and the love the chieftain bore her. As Balor watched the Wise One's scowling glare, something deep and bruising expanded behind his eyes into a bright image of his mother... an image so like his own.

Her pale hair and eyes... were they not also his? Her long, narrow face with its fair, high brow, straight-as-an-arrow nose, generous mouth, and angular chin... did it not peer back at him when he viewed his reflection in the waters of the stream? Her tall, slender body with skin the color of newly drawn cream... did he not see it each time he undressed? When his kinsmen looked upon him, they saw her, as the Wise One must see her now.

Balor shivered. Had the old magic maker chosen him to climb the roof in the hope that he would slip from the heights and break his neck? For a moment he wondered if Munremar had conjured the storm as a contrivance to be rid of him, but then he scoffed at himself for thinking it. After all, he *was* the firstborn of the chieftain, a fact that evidently carried more than a little weight with the magician.

Dianket called out. "Balor, come quickly! The roof of the council hall must be mended. The Wise One has need of you. And Elathan, fetch rope from your father's house—more from any house that will give it to you."

Again lightning struck, this time very close. In the split second that followed, Balor grimaced against frustration. He *must* go out and help his father and kinsmen. What did he care about a roof? Let Dianket fix it! He was always boasting he could best Balor at anything they set their efforts to. Well, let him set his hand to this! Let *him* risk his neck. Balor had better things to do with his time.

He turned to Elathan and commanded: "Go ahead, make yourself useful to the others. Tell them that *I* shall bring the rope. I'm faster than you are, and I know better what is needed."

Not suspecting Balor's trickery, Elathan did not hesitate. He ran off, eager to be of service. Balor did not wait to watch him go. Totally ignoring Dianket's call and Munremar's angry shouts, he wheeled and raced back in the direction of the chieftain's roundhouse. He had no intention of fetching ropes for Munremar. It would not be the first time that he had openly defied the Wise One's wishes.

When he reached the chieftain's roundhouse, he circled it and headed straight for the northernmost turn of the palisade, where he knew of a small break in the timbers, one that he and the other boys had been instructed to mend as soon as the weather allowed. He actually laughed as he thought of it and thanked the Twelve Winds for sending the fury of the storm, for now, even though he was only ten years old, he would have a chance to prove his worth to his sire. He would make Fomor see that there had been no need to insist that he stay at home. His stride lengthened, and soon he reached the breach in the timbers. It was just large enough for a lad of his size to squeeze through. In only slightly more time than it would have taken him to walk through the gate, had he been free to do so, Balor was beyond the palisade and heading directly into the fens.

The men had a head start. Balor trotted after them, doggedly setting a pace that soon had his heart pounding and his breath catching in his throat, but he was so intent upon catching up that he barely noticed his discomfort.

Somewhere along the way he realized that he had no idea just what he would do when he sighted his kinsmen. Fomor had clearly instructed him to remain behind with Elathan and the women. And when the chieftain found out that he had yet again disobeyed old Munremar, he would be angry—very angry. He had warned Balor about his disobedience in the past. Yet if the cattle did break free from the holding ring, it was likely that even women and girls would be called to lend aid. And if the storm did let up, without a sufficient number of horses to grant the men a mounted advantage, they would be fortunate if they were able to round up as many as a quarter of the herd before dusk. The men would need him. He *knew* they would. And then, seeing that he had disobeyed only out of a desire to serve the need of his sire and lord, Fomor would not be angry with him. Well, not *too* angry.

He ran boldly onward, dodging mud wallows and quicksand. Known mires were marked: Clansmen had pounded warning stakes around them—long rods of hardwood, festooned with garlands of rabbit bones; these clicked in the wind now, each topped with a raven's feather, each a signpost of death.

Backhanding rain from his face, he slowed his step. He could make out the silhouettes of men, both mounted and afoot, moving in the distance ahead of him. Beyond them, when lightning flashed, he could make out the rising back of the ring itself.

He stopped, grateful to rest and be able to catch his breath. His thoughts strayed to Dianket. By now his best friend must be straddling the apex of the council hall, stuffing new thatch into the wind-tattered roof, fighting for balance on the sleet-slick braces. It would be just the sort of challenge that Balor would have liked to try. But he had made his commitment instead to the greater need of the clan.

He went forward, then was stopped short by a sharp, imperative cry that quivered on the brink of panic. Although his clansmen had not seen him, he could see beyond them to the ring. A man was half sliding, half stumbling down the sloping sides of the embankment. Bent and bowlegged beneath a voluminous tarpaulin, he was waving his arms frantically at the chieftain. With the wind blowing into Balor's face from the direction of the ring, the boy could hear every word and recognize the voice as old Falcon's, supervisor of the men and youths who kept the night watch over the ring.

"My lord..." The old man's words were a tumbling wheeze of pure relief. "The lad has fetched you in time!"

"Lad? What lad?" Fomor asked.

"Why, the boy Rinn. I sent him back to give warning. It's been all we could do to keep the cattle calm. The ring holds fast, my lord, but the foundation stones that hold the gateposts are afloat in mud. They will not hold if the cattle continue to press against them. I told the lad to tell you that, to—"

"We've seen no sign of Rinn," informed Draga, holding his sorrel mount in check as he was echoed by mumbling affirmation from the others.

The old man was barely visible under the tarpaulin, but all heard the exhalation of his long, shivering sigh. Rinn was his grandson. "Has he fed himself to the bogs, then?"

No one spoke. Their silence was more sepulchral than the

roll of thunder, more ominous than the wail of the wind, more chilling than the falling rain.

At last Fomor spoke to one of his men. "Echur, search for the lad as best you can." Then, to the old man: "Go with him if you wish. We must tend to matters here, and quickly."

The old man took hold of the stallion's bridle. The tarpaulin fell, and rain ran down the seams of his face and soaked his long, thin braids.

"I would only slow the search. I'll stay with the cattle, lord. I've a way with the beasts. With the lads and your strong men to aid me, I can keep'm from smelling panic in the wind. You must place your mounted men there, before the gate. If it fails, there's a small chance that well-guided horses may be able to keep some of the cattle within the ring." He shook his head, drawing in a breath to calm himself. "With so few horses to grant us a mounted advantage, if the cattle do break free, I am much afraid, lord, that we might well lose them."

Balor heard Draga's comment. "Aye. And did I not speak against the horse-killing? I warned the lord, but he would not heed me."

"And still I say 'twas well I did not!" Beneath the snarling wolves' heads that formed his hood, muscles pulsed high at Fomor's temples. "There would be few cattle left to worry over, Brother, had the horses lived to overbrowse what little pasture we have left!" He allowed Draga no time for further challenge as he kicked the stallion forward at a full gallop toward the ring.

The men followed at once, their dogs close at heel. Only Draga and three others stayed back. His broad mouth downturned, his deep blue eyes black with anger, his red beard dark with rain, Draga glowered down at the three unmounted men.

Balor recognized them. Gar and Donn and Nia. They were of his uncle's age, a few years younger than the lord, in their early twenties. With Draga they formed a sullen, quarrelsome quartet that the boy had seen often together these past months.

Again lightning stung the clouds. Draga looked up and appraised the sky. "By the power of the Twelve Winds..." The words were sibilant with frustration. "He tests me...he tests us all...."

Gar, Donn, and Nia exchanged glances. Then Gar spoke,

and the words had barbs on them. "Would you challenge his chieftainship, Draga?"

The question hung in the air a moment before it was pummeled into the earth by the rain. Balor stared, breathless, waiting for Draga to speak. But the big red-bearded man remained silent. He stared down at his comrades, absently squeezing water from his beard.

Lightning flashed again, this time directly overhead. Balor gasped and jumped, and Draga's dog, an animal as broad and surly as its master, turned its huge gray head in Balor's direction. Its eyes burned as yellow as the lightning, and its upper lip pulled back to reveal its fangs. As the dog snarled and sprang forward, Draga jerked back on the beast's tether.

"Who stands there!"

Balor, knowing he had overheard words not intended for his ears, slowly pushed back the hood of his oxhide cloak. A lump lodged in his throat. He tried to gulp it down. It would not move.

His uncle and the others knew him instantly. Draga's upper lip went back in the same manner that his elkhound's had done only moments before. His large white teeth gleamed between the brazen red of his sodden beard and mustache.

Balor's eyes met his uncle's, and his heart went cold. What he saw was dark and dangerous.

"Is that you, Uncle? 'Tis I, Balor, and am I glad to see you! I feared I was lost!"

Draga's brows came down suspiciously, then expanded outward as he nodded, accepting the lie. "If you know what's good for you, which I doubt, you'll get back to the holding, Balor."

The boy had come too far to back down now. "Please, Uncle, I'll walk with Gar and Donn and Nia and not be in the way! I swear it."

Draga shrugged. "Go back or follow along. There's equal danger to you either way. Do what you will, boy, but name me as no party to it!"

They were eager to be rid of him and sent him clambering to the rim of the embankment, telling him to stay there, out of trouble. The top of the ring was a flat, muddy pathway barely more than his own height across. He stood in the rain, resentfully looking down into the interior of the holding circle where two other youths and old Falcon walked slowly among the restless, lowing cattle. Together they mixed with the animals, touched them, talked to them. Balor knew it took pure and steady nerve to move among the high flanks and sharp hooves and curling horns. Although Falcon and the youths kept their murmuring low and soft, their eyes were unnaturally bright with apprehension. One false move or sound and they would be knocked off-balance, pulp for the crushing hooves. Each time a bolt of lightning ripped the clouds, the youths winced and spoke more quickly as they licked the dryness of fear from their lips. Yet Balor knew that he wanted to join them—and would have—but the youth who stood watch on the rim of the embankment stopped him.

"Hey, there! Where do you think you're going?"

"Into the ring. I'll not stand here doing nothing."

The youth's name was Mael. He was a snub-nosed lad of fourteen, short and blocky, and as pugnacious as a young bull. He paused before Balor, eyeing him with cocky resentment. "Nothing? Is that what you think I'm doing here?"

Balor gazed down at the cattle in the ring, then across to where the men of the clan had gathered to survey the storm damage to the foundation of the gate. "Aye," he said frankly. "Nothing when compared to what they do."

"They're men. You're a little boy. And as long as you're here, I could use another pair of eyes as I tend to 'nothing.'" He removed a collection of leather pouches from around his neck and nastily thrust them into Balor's hands. "Look for signs of slippage along the rim. If you find any, pack them as best you can with earth and stones gathered up in these pouches. Of course, if you find that 'nothing' gets to be too much for you, let me know and I'll lend a hand."

Balor shoved several pouches back at Mael angrily. "I did not risk running alone across the fen to be lorded over by the half grown and half bright! We'll do the work together or I'll not do it at all!"

Mael eyed the younger lad with grudging admiration. Balor was known to be a headstrong, stubborn boy; it would do no good to bully him. Mael accepted the pouches with a muted display of annoyance tempered by goodwill. "So be it, then," he agreed.

Balor looked up at the sky. "What happens if we can't add enough mud and stone to stop the erosion?"

"We're to call upon the men, then. We'll have to set up a

passing line—use our cloaks and tunics as sacks to gather up
as much muck and stone as we can carry. If we all work
together, we might be able to pack the breach so that it will
hold until the storm has passed. Then we can repair it
properly later. But with our luck these past few years, it
might well rain forever! Not that the lord MacLir would
notice until the floodwaters washed us all into the distant sea
to drown!" Even as he spoke he cursed himself for a fool. He
had momentarily forgotten that Balor was the chieftain's son.

Balor bristled with righteous indignation. "You'll take back
those words!"

Mael's temper flared, as much against himself as against
the boy. Still, he could not respond judiciously to threats
from a mere child. Mael, who was always first in Draga's
training classes, twitched with the desire to put Balor in his
place. "Just try to make me eat my words! Spawn of a foreign
sorceress, I'll gladly teach you the measure of your worth!"

Balor ground his teeth. It was not the first time that he had
heard his mother called a sorceress, an enchantress. It had
become a common, albeit covertly whispered, libel since the
Wise One had set it loose to run in the holding. Huldre
ignored it, reacting with the same aloof, disdainful tolerance
she showed everyone except the lord. She kept to herself.
She had no friends, nor did she seek any. Her only displays of
love and warmth were for Fomor—only for him—and yet
these days it seemed that even that small, open portion of her
heart had closed and grown cold. But she was no witch, no
sorceress, no evil enchantress. She was a woman. A strange
and elusive woman with an occasional precognitive lucky
guess; no more than that. And the chieftain had chosen her,
and to insult Huldre was to insult the wisdom of the lord. He
would force Mael's words back down his arrogant bully's
throat.

"Speak against my mother and you speak against the will of
the lord, for she is his woman and dwells among us at his
decree."

"Only because she's bewitched him!" Mael snapped, then
ducked, for he saw Balor's blow coming.

It was a sure, hard right, which would have caught Mael
squarely on the chin had he not parried it. As Balor stepped
back to steady himself, the heel of his left foot overreached
the edge of the inner rim of the embankment. As he lost his

balance he reached forward in a desperate effort to right himself. Despite this he fell, gasping in shock as he tumbled down into the interior of the ring.

He lay sprawled flat on his face and belly, inches deep in the stinking stew of mud, urine, and feces. The sudden intrusion of a human into the livestock's midst confused them. They buffeted one another, bellowing nervously, some of them clumsily rearing back and pawing at the flanks of others ahead of them, as though they wished to climb upon their backs.

Balor lay a few feet out from the edge of the ring wall. A sharp pressure on his back rent deep and cut him as a calf danced skittishly over him. For a moment he thought he would retch with pain and terror as he rolled desperately toward the wall and tried in vain to get to his feet. Gagging with revulsion, spitting slime and muck from his mouth, he was knocked flat once again by a heifer that seemed intent upon mashing him as flat as a hearth cake. She nearly succeeded before she moved on. Balor scrambled to his feet and flung himself against the wall of the ring, looking for a toehold. A fully grown cow backed into him, pinned him upright with her bony excrement-fouled flank.

He nearly swooned as she pressed the air out of him. Sickened, dizzy, he was unable to draw a breath as the cow pushed against him with all her weight. Certain that she was going to drive him straight through the wall, he could feel the stones cut his stomach and was only dimly aware of a fully penitent and terrified Mael shouting down to him.

"Get away from the wall! Grab a tail and pull yourself up! Up! Ride'm like horses! They'll squash you flat if you don't!"

But Balor could not breathe, let alone lift his arms. The cow had him pinioned, head forced back, neck burning where it met the base of his skull. Any moment it would crack, his jaw would break, and his head would shatter like a nutshell yielding to a mallet blow. It would be over then, and at least he would be spared the continued agony.

Then she moved. Suddenly. He breathed, and the hideous odor of the herd rushed into his lungs. It reeked with the promise of life renewed, and he sucked it in and stared ahead, relieved to find himself still among the living.

But for how long? The cattle were like captive fish leaping madly in a net. Desperate to be free, blind and mindless and on the very brink of panic, it would take no more than a crack of thunder to push them over the edge.

And then it came.

It was in this instant that Balor heard someone cry out: "All's lost! The gate . . . stand back . . . it falls before their weight!"

And then, like a serpent stinging out of the night, he felt a snapping, burning sensation against his cheek. He looked up to see that Gar and Mael and old Falcon stood above him upon the rim of the embankment. They had tossed down a length of rope. He grabbed for it and held on for his life as they jerked him up to safety.

No one spoke. He stood breathless, looking down into the ring, and saw that the youths, evidently at Falcon's insistence, had abandoned the cattle to their panic. There was no hope of holding them now. The massive timbers that supported the gate had sagged outward, yielding to the press of the herd. The opening across which the gate had been hung was narrow, slightly wider than the horn width of the largest of the cattle. Until Balor's untimely fall, the sight and scent of horsemen moving back and forth before it had been enough to keep the cattle confined. But now a bull calf screamed and hurled itself hard against the gate. It fell outward and allowed the frightened calf, rushing out into the storm, to knock it flat.

As Balor and the others watched, Fomor reined the big, black stallion hard into the gaping gateway in a valiant effort to keep the herd from following the calf. But the horse, like the cattle, was mad with fright. The stallion reared up, lost its footing, and fell backward, throwing Fomor to the ground, while seven head of cattle escaped through the aperture.

" 'Tis the end for us all," murmured Falcon. "There'll be no turning them back . . . not now."

Balor would never forget what happened next. Even the storm seemed to hold its breath. Fomor MacLir rose from the mud to stand before the ruined gateway, before the roily flood of hide and horns that threatened to carry him away to certain destruction. But he was not swept away. He kept his balance as, waving his arms, he attempted to turn the cattle back into the ring.

Draga, still mounted, forced his way forward through the

tide of cattle and extended his hand to his brother, shouting to be heard.

"Take my hand, Fomor! Mount up and save yourself. 'Tis finished for us here. Your son's ruined us. 'Tis as I warned—we have not enough horses to turn the herd back."

The words sparked an inner well of rage within the chieftain. It burst forth as a molten cry of anguish that rose to inhuman pitch before it swelled with pure resolve into a sound that rivaled that of the thunder.

"No! By the power of the Twelve Winds I will not have it!"

He fought his way forward, oblivious to the horns that ripped away his cloak and tattered his tunic. Muddied and bleeding, using his lowered head and massive body as a battering ram, with brute force he shouldered back a frenzied cow as she attempted to follow the others through the ruined gateway. When she balked and made to stand against him, he roared his anger and frustration. Terrified, she threw back her head and skittered sideways back into the ring, allowing Formor to wedge his body, arms and limbs spread-eagled, across the breach in the embankment.

"Are you mad, Brother!" Draga's statement was of a conclusion already reached.

"He'll be broken in half," whispered Gar, awestruck by Fomor's display of bravery.

But old Falcon's head went up. "Nay, Fomor MacLir will not be broken. In days gone by, there were those who wondered if he was not more than a man, strong enough to challenge the power of the Twelve Winds and bend them to his command."

As they watched, it was as though the elements chose to affirm the old man's words. As quickly as it had struck, the storm abandoned them, leaving the fens wet and steaming and suddenly silent with exhaustion.

Fomor continued to stand as a living gate, effectively penning the majority of the herd within the safety of the ring while Draga and the other mounted men, with quick-legged and agile-armed support from those afoot, roped and returned to the enclosure at least half of the beasts that had managed to escape.

In all, fewer than a dozen animals were lost to the bogs, and to everyone's relief, as the morning brightened, they saw that old Falcon was back at work beside his kinsmen, with his muddied, soggy grandson Rinn close at his side, apologizing for having wandered off in the wrong direction after being panicked by a bolt of lightning that had nearly struck him.

Stirred to tears of shame for having contributed to the stampede, Balor stared hot-eyed as the chieftain stood across the breach of the embankment while Draga and Dathen and Lomna Ruad labored to raise and resecure the fallen gate. No one questioned him now, and Balor trembled with pride as he watched his father.

Fomor MacLir was magnificent, his huge body splayed and unyielding, stronger than the timbers it replaced.

Never had there been such a man, thought Balor.

And from this moment on, never would there be a more obedient son.

3

Thus the herd was saved, and the old men of the holding were given new meat for the meal of their wonder tales.

The storm had been a messenger of the Twelve Winds, sent to test the lord. And when the testing was done and the lord found worthy, the clouds began to thin and tatter and yawn wide to expose vast stretches of clear, blue, untroubled sky. Across the fen and rolling moorland, a skylark sang its praises to the Wolf of the Western Tribes. Grasses, bent and pummeled and bruised by rain and hail, stood tall again and gave up the essence of fragrant thyme to the warm, gentle face of the sun, a gift for the chieftain, to sweeten this day of his valor. And the men of Fomor MacLir, many long critical of him, bowed their knees in fealty, convinced that his act of strength and bravery had been nothing less than miraculous. He had, as in days long gone by, bent the Twelve Winds to his power and restored the world to its proper balance.

That was what the storytellers said.

And it is indeed what happened.

Yet in years to come, when Balor was battle weary and far from the lands of his father, he would remember the day with bitterness. For a warrior knows that nothing is forever. Vanquish one storm, and there shall always be another just beyond the horizon... waiting in the misted, dark future, which no man may know... until it becomes the present and slips through his hands so quickly that he can neither hold nor control it.

They worked most of the day to resecure the gate and repair the ring. Balor was soundly cuffed by Fomor for his disobedience, and chastised, along with Mael, for his behavior, which had nearly brought the herd to ruin. They stood shamefaced, silent, like a pair of scolded pups. But they were both so anxious to prove themselves worthy of future trust that they were allowed to stay on to work with the other youths. This time Mael made no slurs against Balor's parentage, nor did Balor challenge the authority of those who set him to work appropriate for his age and size.

The work was exhausting and dirty. Inspired by Fomor's unparalleled strength and courage, they bent to the chieftain's will, eager to please him. Under Fomor's direction the men engineered drainage channels that would allow rainwater to run off from the foundations of the ring. Muck and storm debris were cleared from the fosse, where the run-off water would now be trapped, forming an encircling water barrier into which the cattle must plunge and swim if they would break free from the embankment again. Since the animals disdained swimming, the newly created moat would almost certainly discourage any future stampedes into the fens.

Soon the majority of the work was done, and all were satisfied that the cattle would remain secure within the ring until it was safe to herd them out to the quagmire the storm had made of the pasturelands. Meanwhile food would be brought out to the animals, and at dawn the next day construction would begin on a second ring around the first— another guarantee against the herd's instinctive drive to self-destruction during storms.

Women had brought food out to the workers early in the afternoon, but it was nearly dusk before they returned to the holding, hungry and exhausted.

*   *   *

The coals glowed in the fire pit of the chieftain's roundhouse as Mealla nurtured them into leaping flames, adding
reed stalks from the carefully stacked bundles that were kept
dry in the storeroom. A gruel of marrow broth, roughly
ground emmer wheat, and chunks of marsh roots was bub-
bling in the bell-shaped clay cauldron that perched above the
flames on a tripod of evenly spaced stones of equal height.

Huldre, using long tongs of antler, removed two flat cakes
of heat-hardened clay from the coals. Carefully she set them
upon the elongated level stones of the hearth to cool. A
fragrant steam, redolent with herbs and bog berries and
heavily salted fish, rose from thin cracks in the clay.

Hours before, she had taken two long, dried, smoke-cured
fillets from the storeroom, where they hung folded from racks
secured across the roof beams. These she had soaked in clear
water until they were soft and all traces of mold could be
easily wiped away. After drying each thoroughly and adding
the water to the gruel pot, she had rolled each fillet around a
breading of dried berries and meal seasoned with a sprinkling
of precious salt. Each fillet had then been totally enclosed in
a moisture-giving packet of clay. Covered with embers and
left to cook, the fillets simmered in their own juices while
absorbing the fragrance of the herbs and berries as well as the
clean, earthy essence of clay itself. When the clay was cooled,
it would be cracked open, and the fish inside would be ready
to eat.

Balor was exhausted and aching from the pain of uncounted
bruises, abrasions, and overtaxed muscles, but the aroma of
the steaming fish was almost as intoxicating as the hot,
mulled mead Mealla had handed to him. The liquid in the
chipped-rimmed beaker went down thick and hot, warming
and relaxing him as it diffused within his blood and belly. His
body and brain went happily numb with its sweetness.

The liquor was of fermented honey—a rich, dark brew that
tasted faintly of mold, a vague unpleasantness, which flavor-
ing herbs had not disguised. Balor licked his lips and knew
that the liquor had been too long within the mead jar. Only
yesterday Huldre had complained that the old vessel was
tainted, in need of replacement. There were no potters with
skill enough to duplicate such large, professionally turned jars
among the people of Bracken Fen. It had come from one of
the distant trading centers of the Beaker Folk. But Fomor

decreed that he was not about to send a trading party out from the holding. Balor had asked why, for it had seemed a splendid idea to him, but the lord's reasons were his own, and he had not chosen to share them. When the boys had pressed Mealla for further information, she had told them not to ask again, and Huldre, overhearing, had commented that sooner or later, whether Fomor liked it or not, his sons would discover their father's motives . . . not that they, anymore than she, would find them valid.

Now the lord sat silently upon a long, leather-strapped hardwood chest. A well-worn sealskin was thrown over it, but Balor knew that beneath the cover, the chest was beautiful, elaborately carved, and hinged with intricately worked copper tarnished by time to a rich green. The chest had not been opened since the warriors of the clan MacLir had wrested the holding of Bracken Fen from its native inhabitants and made it their own. Within Balor's mead-dulled mind, thoughts of those days sparked bright. How he wished that he had been a man then, a champion to fight beside his father and his kinsmen. How brave he would have been! How valorous! How obedient! How proud Fomor would have been of him!

His lids felt heavy. They closed. He tried to visualize the contents of the battle chest. Magic weapons forged of a magic metal. A great blade, gleaming. Retaliator. A name having to do with vengeance. Why, and against whom? He had asked his father, and the answer had been the same as with the trading center: no answer at all. Behind his lids a memory took shape. He recalled the adamant way in which Fomor had forbade his sons to open his battle chest. *Ever.* He had said that a curse blacker than death lay upon those who took up the weapons that lay within it. Its contents were forbidden to them above all things. The one time that he had ventured a peek, Mealla had caught him before he had managed to undo the leather strappings. It was the one time in his life that she had taken a stick to him and had cried woe to the boy who ever again saw fit to violate his father's strictest rule.

Across the room, seated upon the chest, Fomor exhaled a weary sigh. Balor opened his eyes and looked at his father. The chieftain's garments were in mud-caked, blood-darkened tatters; his wonderful cloak of wolf skins had been ruined. His massive forearms rested upon his thighs. He, too, had quaffed a beaker of heated mead, and its dark fire shone dully in his eyes as Huldre rose from the rush-strewn floor before the fire pit and came to him, carrying a wooden bowl of warmed water and a cloth of wadded wool.

She knelt before him, set the bowl down, and began to unlace the bindings of his leggings.

"They say it was like old times with you today." Her tone had an odd, hungry edge to it, yet it was soft, purring deep at the back of her throat.

He did not speak. His weariness put him beyond a wish for words. He sat still as her hands tended him, deftly, surely, cleansing him and bathing his wounds and bruises with such a light touch that he felt no pain at all, only pleasure.

Mealla rose from her crouch before the fire and stood before the chieftain, wiping her hands on her apron of deerskin. "All those who have doubted the wisdom of the lord, they will see. The years of hardship are behind us now. The storm has passed. It will be as Fomor has promised. The sun shines for us again. Now the fields will grow sweet again. There is enough seed left to set another crop, and we will know a good harvest this year. I know it . . . I can feel it in my bones!"

Huldre looked up at Mealla. Balor saw the expression of strained tolerance upon her face as she said, "I would not strip naked and prepare to dance around the harvest pole just yet, Mealla. The sun has come out for us today. But what about tomorrow? Would you ask the lord to guarantee tomorrow?"

Mealla's eyes went round and her face flamed red, but it was Fomor who spoke in anger.

"Be silent, woman!"

His tone would have withered anyone else upon the spot, but not Huldre. She shook back her thick, hip-length hair and ignored his command. "Do not listen to her, Fomor. As ever, she is but an echo of your own desires. But an echo is a thing of no substance . . . it affirms nothing. You must listen to me, my lord. I speak truth and substance to you. The storm has called up the wolf in you. Even Balor has felt it at his throat. Now is the time to move on, my lord, when there is not a single man, woman, or child who would not follow you. They would not question, they would not be afraid, knowing that the Wolf has risen once again to lead them."

Fomor's eyes never left her face. "And where should I lead them, woman?"

"Anywhere! But away from Bracken Fen! Away from the mud and muck and eternal rain, before it is too late, before—"

"It is not raining now!" interrupted Mealla in the way of one wishing to stop another in midspeech, before too much was said.

Balor did not notice. His eyes were on his father. The chieftain had risen and left his pallet to stand in the open doorway of the roundhouse. He stared expressionlessly out into the rapidly ebbing daylight.

"Why are so many youngsters gathered before the house of the healer?"

Balor suddenly went cold as he sat upon his bed of skins. Somehow he knew what the reply would be before Mealla spoke it.

"One of the boys was injured in a fall while trying to repair the roof of the council hall. Elathan has been there for hours, sitting vigil."

"Dianket!" Balor was on his feet, so light-headed that he almost dropped the beaker of mead.

"Yes," she replied, and there was pity for him in her eyes. "Your good friend, the healer's son. Sad it is that the boy's father died last year. Munremar's skill in the healing arts is limited, and the lad is sorely injured. I made no mention of it lest I blight your feelings of satisfaction about the saving of the herd; for it is said that if the boy lives, he will be a cripple for the remainder of his days."

Balor, trembling, was at the door and fully sober. Fomor barred his way.

"Easy, lad. There's nothing you can do for him, and you're exhausted. If the boy lives, you may sit with him tomorrow. What will be, will be."

"But it's my fault!" The words ripped from his throat. "It was I who was chosen to scale the roof, but I ran off into the fens instead!"

Fomor stepped aside and allowed his son to pass.

The house of the healer was small and musty. It sat at the end of a row of several similar circular huts at the far side of the compound, directly opposite the chieftain's roundhouse. A fire burned dully in a central fire pit, and an assortment of crocks and jars and baskets stood around the hearth. The

central roof pole was not nearly so high as that of the
chieftain's roundhouse. Where the rafters met the wall posts,
the ceiling was less than the height of an average clansman,
but then, the healer had been a small man who had claimed
to have small needs: a house that was easy to heat, with room
to dry his herbs and store the roots and necessary tools and
implements of his trade. A sound roof. A well-vented hearth.
A good and silent woman to tend his needs.

The woman had died eleven years ago, birthing the healer's only son, Dianket. Then, just one year past, the healer
himself had died, leaving the boy to occupy the house alone.
Dianket had attempted to continue his father's skills with
fine, deft hands, ever-questing eyes, and a cleverness for
healing that seemed to smell out the cause of sickness in
either man or beast. But he was, after all, only a lad and had
been the butt of many a jest for his efforts. Old Munremar,
the Wise One, had taken over the healer's tasks and had
looked after the boy these past months, prophesying that in
time Dianket would indeed be a healer of great worth to the
clan.

But Dianket had complained to his best friend, Balor, that
being tucked in a holding on the edge of nowhere, miles from
the trade routes of civilized men, he would learn nothing,
and what little knowledge he had would soon stagnate like
rainwater within a landlocked pool. He had confided to Balor
that when he was old enough, he would run away, and when
he had learned the secrets of the great healers of the world,
he would return to share his knowledge with his people.

. Now he lay broken and bloody upon a pallet strewn with
hides laid over a mattress of moldy bracken. His breathing
was a low, rhythmic pull of pain, which wheezed and bubbled
through smashed lips and broken jaw. His nose was also
broken, causing his cheekbones to swell up to meet his
battered brow, almost totally enveloping his eyes.

Most of the boys who had worked with Dianket before his
fall had gone back to their own roundhouses now that their
fathers had returned. A few of them still lingered just outside
the doorway, while Tethra and Indech, two lads of Balor's
age, stood inside, close to Elathan, behind old Munremar.
The Wise One sat upon Dianket's pallet. He held the injured
boy's right wrist in his gnarled hands, noting the pulse. His
youngest daughter, nine-year-old Morrigan, knelt at the head

of the pallet, soothing Dianket's brow as she applied some
sort of unguent with her fingertips.

She looked up at Balor out of eyes as lush and green as a
highland spring. Throughout the long, clouded days her skin
had retained the golden, tawny look of summer. She was
small and black-haired and as sharp-tongued as a raven. Balor
had always disliked her. She had a foreign look about her that
always made him uncomfortably aware of his own variant
appearance. Her mother had been a native of the fens, a
slave woman much cherished by Munremar, a member of the
tribe that had been vanquished and nearly obliterated when
the clan MacLir had secured the holding of Bracken Fen for
themselves. The mother had died of the wasting sickness
when the girl was five; indeed, all of the native folk had died
of it, as though they preferred death to captivity no matter
how mercifully they were treated by their captors. But
Morrigan carried on the look of them. She was a bold, dark
rose among her fair-haired half sisters. And Balor knew all too
well that she had thorns.

They pricked him now as her eyes met his, and she spoke
with a guileless candor that cut him more deeply than could
any blade. "Had you obeyed your elders, it would be you
lying here."

His face burned with shame as he felt the others look his
way. In the far shadows of the roundhouse, a delicate, gray-
eyed, golden-haired little girl sat upon a wooden bench, a
granite mortar upon her lap. Born in the same year as
Morrigan, the two girls could not have been less alike. Moon
to sun. Light to shadow. She held a stone pestle within her
hand and was grinding medicinal roots and herbs into a
powder. Balor noticed her now for the first time as she spoke
softly, shyly, but in his defense.

"It was not your fault, Balor. You must not blame yourself."

Dana, Draga's daughter and only surviving child, could be
depended upon to be kind, supportive of others even when
she knew full well that they deserved no support. Yet although Dana's soft, tender words had meant to soothe him,
they only made him more aware of how close Morrigan's
frankness had struck to the heart of truth. Dana's eyes were
red and swollen with tears, which she had no doubt shed
over Dianket's misfortune, as well as over the pain that that
misfortune must be causing Balor.

Slowly, hesitantly, he walked forward to stand beside the pallet. He looked down at Dianket and was so shaken by the sight of his friend that he could not speak.

Old Munremar measured his expression and said quietly, "The boy performed well and bravely—as well and bravely as you should have done."

Balor felt sick. "Will . . . will he live?"

"Aye, but no thanks to you!" snapped Morrigan.

"Hush, girl!" Munremar silenced her sharply. His eyes did not move from Balor's face. "Why did you not come to me when summoned?"

"I wanted to be with the men . . . to . . . to help my father, to stand with him if he needed me. But he didn't need me . . . not at all."

Munremar's small, dark eyes did not blink. They burned with unveiled animosity toward the boy. "Dianket served well in your stead. The roof was mended. The sacristy of the Twelve Winds was saved from ruin. But the cost of Dianket is on your head."

Balor's shame caused him to bow his head. "If I had been here, Dianket would not have fallen. I accept the blame, and I would take his injuries upon myself if I could . . . if *only* I could."

"Bravely spoken," said the old man, his words acidic with sarcasm. For a moment Balor tensed, expecting the Wise One's magic to be worked upon him so that he, and not Dianket, lay broken and unconscious upon the pallet. But the moment passed. Munremar worked no transformation. He spoke with unconcealed enmity toward the boy who stood before him. "Unfortunately we cannot call back the past, undo it, and reknit it to satisfy our sense of justice. We must live in the moment and, for the sake of the future, hope that we are wise enough to learn from our mistakes."

"I will learn, I swear it. I *will* learn!"

"His right leg's shattered, Balor," informed Elathan.

"Thigh and calf, ankle and knee," added Tethra.

"Aye," said Indech. "He fell from the high point of the roof. A rope snagged about his foot and pulled him away from the toe brace. He could not regain his footing. With the wind gusting the way it was, he fell like a stone. He's lucky to be alive!"

"Lucky?" Morrigan hissed the word as though it were an

obscenity. "Is that what you call it when at best he'll be a cripple for the rest of his life, even if he doesn't lose the leg to infection?"

"Oh, no, he will *not* lose his leg! He will *not* be a cripple!" Dana cried as though her heart would break. A cripple could never be named a man of the clan. A cripple would live his life forever as one apart, forbidden to sit at council with his peers, forbidden to partake of the joys of clan festivities lest the Fates, which had marked him, be offended by his presence and bring misfortune to the entire clan.

The realization of this truth struck Balor as cruelly as the cut of an ax. "I will tend him," he volunteered unflinchingly. "Day and night. For as long as it takes! Aye, you'll see. He'll be fine soon, truly."

Munremar's eyes spitted him with contempt. "You shall not expiate your sense of guilt so easily, Balor, firstborn of the lord."

"I can try!"

The old man shook his head. "With what skill? Your mastery of the art of disobedience has brought your friend to this. What has been done cannot be undone. It can only be dealt with. But not by you. I shall care for Dianket. The women of the clan shall help me, and the girls too, for they are blessed with gentle and sympathetic hands. When he is on the mend, since he lives alone, perhaps then you might come to stay with him, you and any of the lads who are of a mind to lighten the hours for him. He shall be long ahealing. But for now I have given him the mead of sleep and painlessness. He shall rest, as should you. This day has tested us all."

Balor quivered with frustration. "But I *want* to stay! I won't leave him here like this. I won't!"

The old man fixed him with a stern and reproving glare. "Do you *dare* to challenge my will yet again, Balor? Has this day taught you nothing? Will you never learn to accept the wisdom of your betters? You may be the firstborn son of the chieftain, but you had best learn that you are not yet lord of the clan!"

That night the people of the clan MacLir feasted. They drank the mead of abandon and built high the fires of

celebration. They forgot the misdeeds of the boy whose
disobedience had nearly brought them all to ruin. They
danced. They sang the songs of the Ancient Ones and enriched
them with new words to honor the deeds of their chieftain,
who had bent the power of the Twelve Winds to his command.

The children were given strong, specially sweetened mead
to grant them an early sleep from which they would not
awaken until well past dawn, lest they rouse their parents
from drunken slumber too soon and inadvertently rouse the
beast of mead sickness in them.

Balor drank greedily. He was eager for sleep—deep, dark
mindless sleep in which he might drown his feelings of
guilt over Dianket. He lay back upon his bed of skins and
closed his eyes. Behind his lids images of the fire-shot
holding danced as wildly as his kinsmen danced. Then they
ebbed, a tide of glowing, shimmering coals fading into blackness.

Words. Soft. Sibilant. In the deep, heavy darkness that
presaged the dawn, they roused Balor from his mead-drugged
sleep.

"Hear me, my lord. I have had a dream." It was Huldre's
voice.

Balor listened.

"I have seen a kingdom awaiting you . . . beyond the North
Wind. Beyond the Sea of Mist. In the spawning place of
legend and glory, born in the days when giants roamed the
world. All these many years it has been waiting for a lord
powerful enough to claim it. For you, Fomor MacLir."

The words bled away into a tremulous exhalation of resolve
as she stirred and sat upright, naked beside her lord.

"Are you listening, Fomor? You must go forth. You must
pursue the dream."

"Ahh, Huldre. Do you never tire of it?" Fomor's voice was
slow with sleepiness. Tolerant. He sighed. Shifted his weight
beneath the jumbled mounding of furs that covered him.
"Come back beneath the covers, woman. We'll pursue another sort of dream."

She drew back from him hissing, a sound that caused Balor
to open his eyes. Blinking sleep away, he stared into the
darkness and saw her. All white she was. As white as bleached
bone. As smooth and shining as polished ice. Aside from her

necklet of amber, her hair was her only garment. It lay upon her, a cloak the color of the moon.

He closed his eyes against the image of his mother. He did not want to see her. He wanted sleep, the oblivion that relieved him of all thoughts of Dianket. He closed his eyes, but could not sleep. Elathan was curled up beside him like a puppy, and not far off, on her own pallet, Mealla snored in gusty, sucking spurts, twitching against her dreams. Yet he lay awake.

Huldre's voice slurred on. "The land of which I speak is real, Fomor. It is beyond the waters of a dead sea, beneath the face of the cold sun, an island shining warm and sweet in the light of the misted moon. And there, guarded by a virgin, beside the Singing Stone of Destiny, dwells the beast—the monoceros, the creature that the traders from the south call unicorn."

Fomor sighed lovingly. "You've drunk too much mead, Huldre. Unicorns, singing stones, enchanted islands, ach, woman! I first heard those tales when still a suckling at my mother's paps. Enough of your childish nonsense. The day has been long. Can you not allow this weary man his rest?"

"How can you rest when you know that you shall awake again within this holding, with only cows and pigs to do you homage?"

"I am chieftain of this holding, woman. I am lord of this clan. I am content."

"In my dream I have seen you as lord of all the earth."

"Then go back to your dream. Leave me to my rest!"

Balor opened his eyes again. Coals in the central fire pit sparked now and again, giving off dancing stabs of light.

He snuggled deeper beneath his bed skins, pulling them high about his ears, covering the tip of his nose, and stared up through the thatching of the roof, where he could see bright, twinkling points of starlight between the tattered lacings of reed and grass.

His mother continued to speak softly—no more than a whisper, yet her words were prods, burning as hot as the coals within the fire pit.

"You, Fomor MacLir, whom the clansmen once again call the Wolf of the Western Tribes, you who have dared to stand against the Twelve Winds, here in Albion and upon the shores of the Far Island, Eireann, are you afraid to seek the Land of Promise?"

Fomor sat up growling, fingering back the wild tangles of his yellow hair. "I am afraid of no quest, woman! You of all people know the truth of that! But by the power of the Twelve Winds I am weary of your words!"

A pale, slender hand sought the broad sweep of his bare shoulder. "Are you not also weary of the life here? I tell you, Fomor MacLir, your kinsmen may well worship you tonight, but if the weather turns again, they shall whisper against you. They have not forgotten that they were warriors, not herdsmen and farmers. The blood of the People of the Ax flows within them. Think how it would be to take what should rightfully be theirs in this world."

"I *do* think of it, Huldre. That is why I am chieftain. I am no impetuous boy to commit my people to the unknown. Too many of my warriors died to secure this holding. I shall not set my clan to war and wandering to satisfy some mindless twitching of their spirit to conquer lands they do not need."

"If the weather—"

"If! If my balls wither away, I shall be a eunuch! Weep for me upon that day, not before! I tell you, Huldre, abide my judgment. There are reasons involved that you do not understand."

"I understand only that you could be master of the world. It was nearly so once. There were those then who compared you to the gods! It could be so again if you would dare to lead your people out upon the back of the Twelve Winds, if you would reach the Land of Promise. If only you could learn the secrets of the Standing Stone and take the gift of power that is promised to the man who captures the monoceros and dares to ride it!"

Even in the flickering darkness, Balor could see annoyance written on the ruddy, bearded face of his father. "I should never have taught you to speak the language of my kinsmen, Huldre. Indeed, often I wish that I had sold you into bondage along with your people."

"They were not my people. I was a slave to them and to their chieftain, as I am now a slave to you. But I have no regrets. My master was a vile man, as arrogant and cruel as his tribesmen. Often I wished upon my amulet that evil would befall them. But my amulet cannot defend you against their revenge. If we stay here, my lord, we shall be found and—"

He winced against her words. "Silence, woman! You offend me with memories that I would as soon forget. You and your cursed talisman of amber . . . black magic and a white-haired enchantress from the Northland, whose tongue babbles as constantly as a stream in full flood. Perhaps my clansmen are right . . . perhaps I am doubly cursed and should be rid of the both of you!"

She stared at him, unflinching. "Amber is a stone of rare magic, and the Eye of Donar is rarest of all. But in truth it is no rarer or more valuable to you than I."

Fomor snorted his disgust. "Stones would not nag me!"

She knelt back from him. Her fine long-fingered hands rested upon the sleek sweep of her thighs. Her breasts gleamed in the firelight, the nipples round and hard, brazen dark. Between them, on its strand of braided sinew, her single bead of amber, carved into the image of a hawk in flight, glowed like honey in sunlight. She fingered it. "This stone that I have brought with me from the land of my people, it speaks through me. It is your Destiny to hear the words, Fomor MacLir: He who learns the secrets of the Standing Stone, who dares to seek and capture the monoceros, that man shall own the earth and earn immortality. Why should you not be that man?"

"Because I am content. Because I do not believe in stones that keep secrets. I do not believe in enchanted beasts. Nor, I think, do you, Huldre. You are merely an ambitious woman who hopes that I shall either win the world for the sake of your greed or take you home again to your cold and distant Northland, where, no doubt, your kinsmen would make a slave of *me!*"

"Never! I am your woman. Forever. I have sworn it on the Eye of Donar."

He glared at her in the darkness. "And what arrogance makes you believe that if I were to follow this mad dream of yours and become master of the world that I would want you by my side?"

She smiled. She matched his stare with her eyes, which in the fire's glow seemed to take on the color of her amulet. Her tongue tip emerged to moisten her lips. She shook back her hair. Slowly, arching her back, her hands rose to cup her breasts. She lifted them, offering them to the lord. "You shall always want me, Fomor MacLir. Always. It is an enchantment that I have placed upon you."

Balor burrowed beneath the bed skins, pulling them up and over his head, not wanting to see or hear more of what must follow. He shoved his thumbs into his ears and closed his eyes. Tight. Tighter. A great expanse of gold appeared, spread out forever within the infinity of the boy's imagination. He allowed his thoughts to roam out upon it as far as they would go until slowly reality seeped away into the warm substance of a dream.

He was alone within it, on the golden plain, beneath the black sky. The colors of the northern lights whirled away above him. Ahead lay an island, rising tall out of a misted sea. He rode toward it, astride the back of a great white horse. Wild-eyed, exhaling steam from its nostrils, it shook its enormous head and pawed the earth until it bled. It quivered against the weight of the rider, sending the pure heat of power into the dreamer's clenched thighs.

Sound poured into the dream . . . a distant roaring? A moaning? A keening? Or was it a cry of acclamation? The dreamer could not tell.

He rode forth boldly toward the misted sea, his hand curled about the single, spiraling horn of gold that rose like a twisted lance from the apex of the animal's brow.

He was no longer a little boy. He was a man. He was Balor, son of Fomor, chieftain of the clan MacLir. He was a tall, powerful lord like his father. He rode the monoceros. He rode the unicorn. He was master of the world.

And he was not afraid.

4

For days the sun shone. For long, sweet, glorious days. Indeed, it *was* summer at last—the bright half of the year—when night was but a fleeting sigh of hours and winter was as easily forgotten as a long, dark dream.

Mealla had been right: There had been time enough to set

another planting. Now, many weeks later, the fields were green with promise. Protected within wattled fences or walls of stone from foraging cattle, the crops grew tall and nearly ready for harvest. Soon green would change to gold, and there would be four varieties of cereal ripe for the picking, including the tasty, starchy grain called barley, which had been introduced to Albion by the Beaker Folk, along with the equally tasty ale brewed from a mash distilled from its pulp.

To protect the ripening wheat from birds, hares, field mice, and bold, foraging marsh rats, traps were set, and boys of Balor's age were sent out by day with their bows and arrows and net snares. Encouraged to perfect their skills as hunters and archers, each lad's catch was brought home and displayed with pride for all to see. Even the smallest ravaging predators of the harvest, the rats and mice, were welcome—as food for the clan's dogs. Small seed-eating birds were packed in clay and roasted within the embers of the fire pit. When removed from their heat-hardened earthen packets, the feathers came away from the sweet, delicate, somewhat fibrous skin. The birds were then eaten, bones, beaks, and feet—crunchy morsels for snacks. Larger birds and hares were defeathered or skinned and stewed or spit roasted. The prime meat—breast or haunch—was awarded to the boy who had contributed the largest share to the family hearth fire.

Within the chieftain's roundhouse it was Balor who always won the prime portion. As firstborn his bow had been Fomor's when the chieftain had been a boy. Of ash, it was small and resilient, strung with twisted and oiled sinew that had been taken from the belly of a young doe. There were tiny, stylized carvings incised into the wood, of hare and ferret, wolf and fox, badger and bird—each in flight, pursued by the running figure of an archer. Each animal had an arrow carved through its heart to indicate a successful chase. It was a bow that had been copied for Elathan, but it had brought small luck to the younger boy, who had not the eye or feel for it.

Both boys were similarly equipped, carrying fine, long-shafted arrows, with heart-shaped, barbed heads of blue flint skillfully worked for them by Oblin the Stonecutter, and each wore an archer's wrist guard—a thick leather strap with a narrow, flat, elongated stone riveted to the leather with four copper studs—to protect the inner wrist from the sting of the bowstring. But it was Balor and not his brother who had mastered the bow practically before he was large enough to lift it and who was as good with it with his left hand as with his right. His arrows consistently struck meat fit for roasting. A day did not pass wherein he did not return home with several fat hares. Each night he enjoyed the hunter's portion.

As dusk softened the summer brightness of the fields, the boys of the clan were returning to the holding. Balor and Elathan lagged behind; dusk and the earliest hours of the morning were the times when the brothers made their easiest kills. Birds grew anxious to grab a last mouthful, and hares were often boldest in the soft, shadowing light of evening.

So they lingered awhile, setting the last of the traps and snares that would serve in their place throughout the night. Balor shot another hare, a fine, fat-thighed female, and Elathan netted two more linnets.

Then Balor froze, staring. At the far edge of the planted lands, a larger, red-hided, antlered buck had ventured out of the heath. It had found a poorly wattled section of fencing and was attempting to force its head through it so that it might eat the sweet, ripening wheat within.

Deer were rarely seen these days. Once plentiful, the years of bad weather had depleted their numbers as surely as they had depleted the numbers of the clan. Although every man, woman, and child within the holding would have welcomed the rich, gamey flavor of venison roasted with honey, mead, and sweet herbs, they were all grateful that there were few deer to be hunted: No other animal could so quickly and thoroughly devastate their crops.

The boys knew this. Elathan followed Balor's glance and exhaled with rueful excitement. "We'll have to alert the holding. Someone's got to take down that buck, and quickly!"

But Balor shook his head, and his eyes glowed with excitement. "If we were careful, we might be able to work our way downwind of it. . . ."

Elathan gaped at his brother. "You're not suggesting that *we* try to take it? I've only got a snare net, and you haven't the strength to kill the deer with such a small arrow."

Balor's palm tensed on the slender spine of his bow. "If I could get close enough . . ."

Elathan grew angry when he saw the look of pure intent in his brother's face. It was late. He was tired and hungry. The hunter's thong that he carried knotted across his chest and shoulder drooped with the weight of the birds he had caught in his snare, killed, and strung through their beaks. Also on the thong hung a large, unusually plump gray dove. Elathan was proud of that dove. They were difficult to net, wary and flighty, and every bit as tasty as Balor's hares.

As he stared off to where the buck was happily devouring tall, ripening strands of precious wheat, slow, deep resentment made him frown. If Balor could get downwind of the deer, he might just manage to make a successful kill. On any other day Elathan would have wished his brother luck. But not today . . . not when it was *his* dove that should occupy the place of honor upon the hearth! A dove might equal a hare, but a deer would be a man's kill, a cause for celebration within the entire holding. The antlered head of the deer would be hung above the lintel of the chieftain's doorway, and its hooves would be strung as a talisman for Balor to wear at his belt. Indeed, if Balor succeeded in taking that deer, Elathan might as well feed his dove to the dogs. Fomor would have no appreciation or appetite for it. He would be too drunk with pride in his firstborn. Elathan ground his teeth.

"Ho!" he cried at the top of his lungs, waving his arms and shouting until the deer, startled, bolted off, tail high, to vanish into the heath.

Balor was stunned. "Why did you do that?"

Guilt turned Elathan's momentary sense of accomplishment sour. "What matter? The deer's gone, isn't it?"

"Do you imagine that it will not return to graze all the long night under cover of darkness?"

Again Elathan shrugged. "We'll alert tonight's guards. They'll kill it."

"How can you be so sure?"

"Because."

Balor felt his anger rising. "Because? What sort of an idiot's answer is that?"

"Enough for you," he replied, and even as he spoke, he knew that Balor would cuff him. The blow was a hard, angry, open-palmed strike at his left shoulder, but it did not rouse his own anger. He knew that his brother's reaction was justified. He flushed, annoyed with himself for his selfishness.

"Come on along, Balor. It'll be dark soon. It's time we were home."

"Go on, then, if that's all you've the stomach for!"

Elathan blinked, taken aback, as Balor ripped off his hunter's thong, heavy with hares, and flung it at him.

"Here! I'm going after that deer!"

Elathan was suddenly nervous. He knew all too well the look on Balor's face, and it unsettled him: Balor had made up his mind, and there would be no turning him from his purpose now. Elathan cast an eye toward the darkening heath. It was wild, dangerous bog and moorland beyond the planted fields. Low scrub and scant stands of wind-bent trees rose to thickly forested, wolf-infested highlands.

"It's dangerous, Balor! It's forbidden to go off alone, and I'll not go with you . . . not with only a snare net."

"I'm not asking you to come. Get back to the holding. If I'm not there by dark, tell them where I've gone."

"Balor—"

"Go on! I sighted the deer, and I will claim the honor of killing it before it gorges itself upon our crops and robs us of our harvest."

"But it takes a man's strength to send a killing arrow into so large a quarry."

Balor grinned. The thought was heady with challenge. "We'll see about that," he replied, and then with a conspiratorial wink was off, calling back: "Don't worry. I'm sure the deer's close by. And I'll be back before dark . . . with venison for us all!"

Inexperience caused Balor to underestimate the ability of the deer to put distance between itself and the clan's wheat field. So the boy followed at a lope, paying no heed to either time or direction.

The far fields were on high ground, a good distance from the holding, and well upland of the cattle ring and pasturelands. Beyond, the country was wild—uncut, unplanted, unbrowsed, unexplored, and thoroughly unwelcoming. It was a maze of moor and bogland, forest and scrub, flat one moment, undulating and nearly vertical the next. It was the domain of beasts, not of men, yet Balor was so certain that he would soon sight and kill the deer that he did not hesitate to go on.

The buck had disappeared into a tall, fragrant, seemingly endless thicket of gorse. The flowers of the shrub were the deep, yellow-orange of flame, and as Balor forced his way through the increasingly tangled, shoulder-high growth, the blossoms, still warm from the heat of the day, smelled like hearth-roasted nuts.

The sun had set, yet Balor knew that at this time of year the sky would stay light awhile. There was plenty of time. He was certain of that, even though the snaggle-branched undergrowth now forced him to slow his pace considerably.

As Balor followed what seemed to be a clearly defined deer trail of broken twigs, he felt the reassuring weight of his quiver of arrows strapped snugly against his back and held his bow lightly in his hand, an arrow braced against his palm, ready to be nocked at a moment's notice. Soon he would be home with a fresh-killed deer slung across his back, and Fomor would be so proud of him that he would not think to reprimand him for going into forbidden country to win his prize.

But to his dismay he soon lost the trail. He stood still, suddenly disoriented, perspiring and panting, squinting and turning in all directions, trying to pick up the trail again in the now distressingly thin light. The flower-laden branches seemed leached of color. The air, only moments ago so fragrant and warm, now had an unpleasant, moist, acrid chill to it.

How had it grown so dark so suddenly? He strained his ears, hoping to pick up the sound of the deer crashing through the undergrowth ahead of him. But he heard nothing—nothing but the hammering of his heart and the pained draw of his breath.

He knew in that moment that he would never find the deer, let alone slay it. And he knew too, with a sudden, sinking, sick feeling, that if he did not hurry, he would not return to the holding before dark.

His mouth went dry.

Return? How? When he had turned in different directions to pick up the deer trail, he had lost all sense of direction. Which way had he come? Which way should he go?

Clad only in his lightweight sleeveless summer tunic, he shivered. He rubbed his right arm with his left palm to warm himself, then looked down, startled. In his excitement he had not noticed that the close-meshed branches had scratched his arms and legs above his leggings. Some scratches were deep enough to have drawn blood—enough to attract the attention of any predator that might happen to come close enough to smell it.

The thought was terrifying. Again he shivered. He could not remain here. He *must* quickly return home before Elathan alerted Fomor to his whereabouts. Again he felt sick with apprehension. Which would be more desirable? To remain here—lost, fodder for wild beasts—or to be dragged home by torchlight, reprimanded by his father? And what would Munremar, the Wise One, have to say about this latest display of disobedience?

This time he shivered with self-loathing. Taking a deep breath to calm himself, he licked his lips and turned his eyes up. The stars marked the way home. That was common Star Wisdom, which all young males learned as part of the clan's rites that culminated in their initiation into manhood. He did not know if girls also learned the Wisdom, but he knew that since Time Beyond Beginning, the People of the Ax had looked to the stars to mark the routes to distant lands of conquest; but he was a boy, not a man. Star Wisdom was still a mystery to him.

Close by, something moved in the undergrowth. Balor tensed, startled and terrified. Hungry wolves, waiting to pounce upon him? He lifted his bow, nocked an arrow, drew the bowstring, and stood at ready, his heart pounding, until a mouse scurried across his feet, then disappeared beneath a tangle of roots.

Balor's heart almost stopped with pure relief as his hands relaxed upon the bow.

"Some wolf!" He spoke the words aloud, chiding himself for his readiness to imagine the worst. But even as he allowed the bow to rest at his side, an owl called eerily into the darkness above him. Balor looked up. A shadow, broad-winged and silent, moved across the darkness, eclipsing the stars momentarily, then was gone.

Balor wondered if the mouse sensed the owl's presence as surely as the wolf must now sense his.

He was alone . . . a small, vulnerable boy with only a child's bow and lightweight arrows to ward off the predators of the night. The thought set prickles of dread running along his neck and shoulders. Tears of fear and frustration stung beneath his lids.

"By the power of the Twelve Winds, how am I to find my way home?" he cried out to the bitter blackness of the night.

And then, so suddenly that it was gone in less than a heartbeat, a huge, searing, white-hot track of fire branded itself against the heavens. A shooting star. A sign. An answer to his question.

Balor gaped. Never had he seen a star of such dimensions. He stared upward in wonder and disbelief, then understanding dawned, warming him with the strength of newfound resolve.

He was the chieftain's firstborn son, and the Twelve Winds had heard his cry. The power of the Twelve Winds had come to him as surely as it had come to Fomor MacLir when he had dared to stand against the storm.

Now he was no longer afraid. The Twelve Winds had written their answer to his question in fire across the heavens for him to see. They had pointed the way home.

Without hesitation, Balor followed.

The night deepened, and although he walked for what must have been hours, he saw no sign of the holding. He walked on, discomfited by the sensation of being watched. He paused. He listened. He turned around, squinting into the darkness with his heart hammering in his throat and sweat beading upon his brow as his eyes strained to see the shapes of predators lurking in the night. There was nothing, he told himself, except the monsters that stalked him within his own mind. He called out his father's name, just in case luck was with him and the chieftain was following close enough to hear him and be drawn forward by his cries. But there was no answer. There was only the silence of the night with all of its imagined terrors. With a gulp and a shiver of resolve, he walked on into it alone, hoping against hope that if he went far enough, time and the Twelve Winds would guide his footsteps home.

His eyes grew accustomed to the darkness; his spirit did not. It was a small, frightened thing shivering with panic deep within his belly. The sensation of being watched refused to leave him. He spoke aloud to himself, bold assurances against the conjured terrors of the night. He moved forward like a hunted creature, with his bow at ready, until at last the gorse wood thinned and the land opened wide before him, bending upward like the shoulder of a giant.

Balor paused. He felt suddenly sick with the realization that he was nowhere near the holding. The Twelve Winds had turned his footsteps into lands that were totally unfamiliar, to enormous, hostile hills that ranged off to he knew not where. He was lost. Totally, hopelessly lost. And exhausted. And hungry. And cold.

Aimlessly, still trying to ignore the feeling that he was being stalked, he followed a narrow, winding little stream, which led him into a land where massive outcroppings of stone rose up like gatherings of strange, silent beings. Here he paused, brought short by his own fatigue. He knelt and drank from the stream. The wind whistled around the rock formations until they seemed to be whispering to one another in a language he could not understand. Far off, wolves bayed and barked, the sound frenzied with the lust brought on by a successful kill. Balor shivered, wondering what poor creature had fallen to their slashing jaws and ripping teeth.

His stomach growled. He thought of the fat hares he had strung on his hunting thong earlier in the day. By now they had no doubt been eaten, along with Elathan's birds. It occurred to him that he might try to kill another hare. But he had not the skill to properly gut or skin the beast for cooking, and he had no idea how to make a fire without the aid of embers taken from a cooking pit.

He rose. By now his father had likely come out into the wild in search of him. If the deep, burning strain in his calves was any indication, he had been walking uphill for some time. He stood high above the gorse wood, yet when he looked down, he could see nothing but a sea of darkness—no torchlight flared. No one was coming after him. The clan had evidently abandoned him to a fate that he had brought upon himself.

He felt betrayed. Only hours ago, he had been so certain of his path, so positive that the shooting star must lead him home. But here he stood, lost, alone in the wilderness. The stars offered no further signs to guide him.

Far ahead on the moor a clustering stand of tall, round boulders formed a natural circle. They looked like a gathering of fat, gossiping women huddled together, frozen in time. It occurred to Balor that if he were to enter the circle, the rocks would perhaps hide him from predators.

He went forward, buoyed by his thoughts. Yes, the stones would shelter him. In the morning things would be better. He *would* find his way home again, or his people would find him, and he would never disobey clan law again. Never!

But suddenly the morning seemed as far away as the sheltering circle of the stones, for from out of the night a wolf appeared to stand between them and the boy.

No, surely it was more than just a wolf. It was the largest wolf that Balor had ever seen. It was as white as starlight. The boy blinked, half hoping that it would disappear and prove itself to be only one of his conjured terrors; but when he opened his eyes it was still there. Motionless. As long-limbed and high-shouldered as an elk. Its tail was down and tucked. Its great white head was outstretched. Its ears were up, sifting the night for sound as its dark nostrils expanded to draw in the scent of the boy, to smell his terror.

Balor stared. The wolf stared back at him out of eyes filled with star-fire, and the boy knew that once before he had seen this wolf; this white wolf, this beast that had snarled at him and had leapt at his throat out of the lightning on a storm-ravaged dawn. Slowly, barely knowing that he moved at all, Balor raised his bow and nocked an arrow. He stood, his young limbs splayed, then moving to gain the necessary balance as he took aim and drew the arrow taut. Yet he did not loose it. He stood transfixed. Connected to the wolf somehow. The same as the stars and the stones and the vast, taut rising of the land beneath his feet. He knew no fear. He knew only a strange, all-pervasive sense of oneness with the moment. There was magic in it. It was as though he and the wolf were locked together in the night, enmeshed within some dark and sweeping net that had snared them both and held them fast so that each might glimpse himself within the other's eyes.

It was what he saw within the eyes of the beast that terrified him—portents of power and darkness. He did not know when he loosed the arrow. It was reflex that sent it on its course. He only knew that suddenly, for one bright, terrible instant, it seemed that the night was falling in upon him, crushing him, driving the life from him as pain exploded within his right shoulder, so intense that he screamed and grabbed at it as he whirled around and dropped to his knees, gasping.

When he looked up, the wolf was gone. So was his pain, but not his terror. It was greater than before, compounded by confusion. Had his arrow struck the beast? What had caused the pain to flare within his own flesh, as though somehow his own arrow had turned to rend him instead of the wolf?

He looked for the beast as he scrambled to his feet and drew another arrow from the quiver upon his back. With trembling hands he nocked it, fear prickling at the base of his neck and making his skin crawl as he broke into a run and sped forward toward the sheltering circle of standing stones.

He had to turn sideways in order to wedge himself into the circle. The wolf could not enter here. The knowledge made him relax. Tears of pure relief stung his eyes as he felt his fear ebb within him. It was warmer here, out of the soft night wind. Grateful, and suddenly so exhausted that he could barely keep his eyes open, he slumped to the stony earth. He removed his quiver of arrows and leaned back against the lichen-crusted rocks. He lay his bow, with the arrow nocked and ready to be pulled taut, across his lap. Even if the wolf found a way to come at him, it would have an arrow in its throat before it knew what had struck. The thought was comforting. He promised himself to sleep lightly, and he did for a short while. Then the dreams came and took him down into darkness so deep that he seemed to be within a pit. He was immobile, unable to escape. While all the long night, a white wolf circled, its eyes full of death and star-fire.

He awoke in the first thin, blue light of dawn, startled and dismayed to discover that he had slept so deeply. Beyond the stone circle a cold, whistling wind moved across the moor, and although there was light enough to see by, he felt no desire to leave the protection of the circle. It was best to huddle warm and safe within the shelter of the stones until the white wolf and its foraging kin returned to their dens and the sun rose to warm the heath, pointing the way that must surely lead him home.

5

His nightmares were of dark, bloodied images of falling stars and ravaging wolves, of a strange land that rose and twisted and opened beneath his feet into wide, yawning chasms. He fell screaming into the black, cold maw of oblivion.

"Balor . . . Balor . . ."

"No!" he shrieked aloud and awoke with a start, shaking, terrified. He looked around quickly, then realized he had been dreaming. He felt foolish.

He arose, stiff and sore from yesterday's long uphill trek. The scratches on his arms and limbs had scabbed over, but when he moved, the scabs flexed and tore open. He winced against the hurt as he picked up his quiver of arrows, surprised to find that his right shoulder ached deep within the muscle and all along his clavicle. As he slung the quiver onto his back and secured it, he thought about the white wolf he had seen last night. He wondered if he had wounded it. Perhaps it had died. Strangely, the thought disturbed him almost as much as did the premise that the huge beast might still be lurking about somewhere near. With a sigh of determination not to be afraid, he peered out of the circle. He could see nothing. He walked out onto the sunlit moor, then paused and looked back. Strange. He could have sworn that last night the stones had been so close together that he had had to turn sideways in order to wedge himself through. But now he had just walked past them with room to spare on either side. It was as though the stones had moved; what had seemed a protective circle last night was an open-ended crescent now. Balor's brow came down. His memory must have been warped by weariness and hunger. He would have to be more careful in the future.

He saw now that all around the periphery of the stone circle, the earth was mottled with fresh bloodstains. So his arrow *had* found its mark. Odd that he could find no wolf prints where the beast had circled; but the ground was stony, not the sort of earth to hold a track. He knelt and lay his hands upon it, looking down, then back at the open-ended circle in which he had passed the night in safety. What had kept the wolf at bay? It could have taken him at any time.

But now a new day lay before him. The night and its terrors, both real and imagined, lay behind.

To his chagrin the land was as unfamiliar by daylight as it had been in the dark. Only one landmark sparked hope within him. A good distance off, a towering, gray-faced granite tor rose up against the horizon. It was so high that had there been clouds in the pure, brazen blue of the sky, the monolith would easily have pierced them.

Balor knew what he must do: If he could reach the tor's summit, there would be an unsurpassed view, and surely he would be able to locate the cleared pasturelands of his people and the location of the holding itself. He would be home long before nightfall.

With hope buoying his spirits, he went to the stream, drank deeply, splashed water on his face, and gently bathed his scratched limbs until the coolness of the water soothed them. Finding clumps of bracken fern growing along the stony bank, Balor unearthed several starchy roots and ate them. They were fibrous and bland, but edible. In no time at all his stomach was pacified into silence, and he felt stronger, ready to begin his trek to the craggy mountain.

It was well past noon when at last he stood trembling with exhaustion and exhilaration upon the summit. It had taken him what seemed forever to reach the base of the monolith, and then twice forever to scratch and gouge his way upward to the summit. It was much broader and flatter than he had imagined it would be. It was an island above the world, where wind-stunted trees offered little shade and shelter and strangely carved boulders indicated that others had been here before. He was too tired to explore his new surroundings. He stood looking out on a world of such vast beauty that he shivered with awe and amazement at the very sight of it.

Moor and gorse wood . . . forest and fen . . . pastureland and fenced fields . . . the holding itself, as tiny as a fortress built for ants . . . the ring enclosure, the cattle grazing close by as small as insect eggs strewn upon the green face of a leaf

...and beyond the holding, more hills...the bright, deep, moss-colored grass of the marshes...the silver of meandering streams and the broad, slate-gray channel of an estuary that opened out into the vast face of the sea.

The sea. Never before had he seen the sea. Nor had he imagined that any body of water could be so massive, so magnificent. It stretched out to the horizon without end, with the coastline of Albion a maze of soaring headlands and coves and wide, dark beaches running south and north until the mists of distance claimed them.

High above, the shrill shriek of a kestrel pierced the silence. Balor looked up and followed its flight as it winged outward, riding the thermals on motionless wings. Higher, farther, out across the sea, free against the blue vastness of the sky. The light of the sun glinted on the hawk's back and for a breath of time burned gold, an explosion of light and beauty...as though the amber amulet his mother wore had come to life and flew before him. It keened, summoned, beckoned. The boy's heart leaped. His spirit longed to fly up after it...away. Away from the storm-blighted fenlands of his people. Away across the world. As free and wild as the Twelve Winds.

He stood transfixed as the falcon shrieked and turned, banking so suddenly that it lost the sunlight and seemed to disappear.

The boy caught his breath and squinted, for beyond the infinite distances to which the little hawk had drawn his vision, he could make out the contours of another land, another coast. It was an island with high, soaring mountains—a sight that set the spark of recall flaring within his brain.

He remembered his mother's soft, sibilant, whispering words: *"The land of which I speak is real, Fomor, beyond the waters of the Sea of Mist...an island shining warm and sweet. And there, beside the Singing Stone of Destiny, dwells the monoceros, which the traders from the south call unicorn...and he who learns the secrets of the Stone, he who dares to seek and capture the monoceros, that man shall own the earth and earn the legacy of immortality...."*

"Balor!"

The call erased the daydream. The falcon vanished beyond the horizon. Balor looked down over the vertical face of the tor and saw Fomor MacLir standing below him with his terriers panting and wagging beside him.

"Father!" The word was an exclamation of joy.

Fomor scowled. Shielding his eyes from the glare of the late afternoon with his hand, he shouted upward: "By the power of the Twelve Winds, boy, I've been tracking you since yesterday's darkness. Have you not heard me calling out to you? And by what black magic have you found this place?"

"Last night I saw a shooting star," Balor replied, calling down. "I followed it, thinking it would lead me home. It led me here instead."

For a moment Fomor did not move. He stood immobile, staring upward.

"Did you hear me, Father?"

"Aye, I heard." There was a heavy, dark tone to his words. Then: "I'm coming up!"

He told the dogs to stay. They sat and whined, but did as they were told. Fomor walked a few paces to his right and then began to climb. To Balor's amazement he found handholds and footholds and climbed the crag as effortlessly as he might have ascended a ladder. When he hauled himself up onto the summit to stand beside his son, he was not even sweated.

Balor stared. "It took me forever to do that!"

"I knew the way. You did not."

"You've been here before?"

"Aye. Long ago."

Balor swallowed. His joy at being reunited with his father was suddenly shadowed by Fomor's stern, reproving glare. As on the night of the storm, his impetuosity had led to disobedience, and his disobedience had brought him to danger. He hung his head. "I'm sorry, Father. I saw a deer, and when Elathan spooked it, I thought that if I hurried, I could find it and flush it from the heath. I thought of how proud you'd be of me if I could kill it. I thought that I'd be home before dark. I thought—"

Fomor's eyes singed him to silence. "Enough! Elathan told me what you thought. But that's the trouble with you, lad. You do *not* think. You act without any concern for consequences. And always others must come after you to put your recklessness to right!"

The truth bruised Balor to the quick. His father was right, and he knew it. "I'm sorry," he whispered. "It won't happen again."

Fomor snarled, dissatisfied. "The very words you used the last time, when your folly nearly caused the herd to stampede to ruin—and nearly cost you your life!"

"I know, but this time I mean it. Truly. I swear it."

"So you say now, lad. So you say now...." He shook his head, then reached out and roughly ruffled his son's hair. "When I had not found you by yesterday's nightfall, I feared that the wolves would have you for supper. Why did you not answer my calls?"

"I didn't hear anyone call to me—except in my dreams."

Fomor's hands, palms down, fingers wide, remained resting gently upon Balor's head, as though he wished to reassure himself that his beloved firstborn was truly standing before him, alive and well. "The wind plays strange tricks in the wild, Balor. It is no place for an inexperienced boy to wander alone, especially after nightfall. Do you accept the wisdom of that now?"

"Yes. I heard the wolves and was afraid that they would eat me. So when the white wolf came out of the darkness, I wounded it with an arrow and took shelter within the circle of stones beyond the heath and—"

"A white wolf, eh?" Fomor frowned down at the boy. "And a circle of stones? I know of no such circle on the moor."

Balor would have pointed it out to his father, but even as his arm began to rise, it fell to his side. He stared down and across the moor. It was as Fomor had said. There were only scattered outcroppings of granite, and alongside the stream a line of tall, rounded boulders standing close in a row. He frowned and cocked his head, troubled by his confusion.

"But the circle was there. Last night it *was* there. It sheltered me."

"You were tired and hungry. Alone in the darkness, frightened and disoriented, you no doubt imagined that which you needed to see."

Fomor slung off the hunter's thong from across his broad back, along with his spear, his quiver of arrows, and his long, beautifully carved bow, and Balor saw that there were three fat-haunched hares strung on Fomor's thong. Hunger sparked within him as his father tossed his catch onto the ground at their feet.

"I took these earlier in the day," he said, drawing his skinning knife from the leather scabbard that was laced to his wide belt and casting a measuring glance toward the sun. "It's too late to start back to the holding now. We might as well spend the night here, where no wolves can reach us.

We'll roast these jacks now and have the cooking fire out before dark. Flames can be seen for miles around from this place."

Balor was so hungry that it did not occur to him to ask why Fomor MacLir should be concerned that their fire not be seen.

As they knelt together before the crackling fire pit, Fomor noted Balor's bow, which now lay beside his own. "Why did you not hunt for yourself when you grew hungry?"

"What good to hunt when I could neither make a fire nor prepare the meat? At home the women do these things. They are not a man's work."

Fomor drew back, balancing his weight upon the balls of his feet as he rested his forearms upon his thighs. "Well, we're not at home now, are we? Nor have we women to coddle us."

As Balor watched, Fomor rose, took up one of the hares, and held it high, dangling it by its rear feet.

"Observe the skinner's art, my boy," he said as, with his free hand, he untied a narrow roll of sinew thong, which hung from a loop at his belt. "Pay close attention, for you might as well learn the hunter's secrets now, to serve you in good stead when next you disobey your chieftain's command."

Balor flushed to his hairline. "There'll be no next time!"

Fomor eyed him with a strangely bemused cynicism. "Let us hope not, Balor, but if truth be known between us, you are the same pigheaded fool that I was at your age."

The admission stunned the boy almost as much as it pleased him.

Fomor went to one of the tallest of the nearby trees and, with the sinew thong, bound the hare upside down by its hind feet to a sturdy branch. He gestured Balor forward.

"Watch how it is done, for I will not show you twice."

Deftly, with his copper splaying knife, he cut around the skin of the hare's rear feet. Then, with carefully positioned fingers and the knife held in his teeth, he took a firm grip on the skin and jerked it downward. It peeled back from the flesh of the animal, and when the skin reached the forepaws and head, Fomor pulled it down until it hung loose, then severed the head and the forepaws and, along with the attached skin, tossed them over the edge of the crag to the terriers. Next he gutted the hare and threw the entrails, except the heart and liver, to the dogs. The heart and liver were stuffed back into the body cavity.

With Balor at his heels he went back to the fire, knelt once again, and spitted the hare on a skewer, which he then held out across the flames.

"This one's mine. You skin and ready your own for roasting."

Although Balor's knees went weak with disappointment and his stomach made a lurch and a growl, he was determined to impress his father with his obedience. Even though inexperience slowed the work, he kept at it until it was done. He spitted his hare and crouched beside his father, holding the meat over the flames until it began to singe and drip. The fragrance was more than he could bear. He could wait no longer. He withdrew the spit from the flames and would have ravenously begun to gnaw at the meat had Fomor not snatched it from his hands.

" 'Tis underdone," he said. "The meat of a hare is much the same as swine flesh. It must be thoroughly cooked if it is to be eaten safely."

"The dogs eat it raw and know no ill effects!"

Fomor's ruddy blond brow arched with cool speculation. "Are you a dog, then, Balor? An undisciplined cur that would continue to run wild and untrained? Or are you the firstborn son of the MacLir, who would learn the Wisdom of the Wild, which has been passed down among our people from father to son since Time Beyond Beginning?"

Although he salivated with desire for the meat, Balor waved the spit away. Would he never learn to do as he was told? "As you have advised, it is underdone," he said, ashamed of himself.

Fomor did not withdraw the haunch. "Take it. Cook it until the juices turn clear and the haunch joint turns loosely in the flesh."

Balor accepted the spit and put it back over the flames. At last, when the chieftain nodded his approval, Balor took the spit from the fire. Although he was dizzy from lack of nourishment, he did not fall upon the meat to gnaw and rip it from the bones as he would have liked to do. He forced himself to eat it slowly, almost delicately. This time he would be obedient!

Fomor observed his son from the corner of his eye. He had already consumed the first hare and had set to roasting the last. He watched Balor in stoic silence for as long as he could before he broke into laughter.

"By the power of the Twelve Winds, boy! You'll put me to shame with such a display of control! It isn't human! I'd have wolfed down the carcass whole had I been as hungry as you!" He lifted the nearly cooked third hare from the fire and with a wink said: "This one's all yours, laddie! You've earned it!"

Balor grinned at his father over the rapidly disappearing haunch. "I *do* want to learn, Father. Someday I want to be a man like you and find my way by day or dark and start a fire when there are no hearth embers to be had and catch and kill and skin an animal for cooking whenever I am hungry. And someday be a chieftain, a lord who knows so much that no man in all the world would dare to challenge my wisdom! Oh, Father, there is so much that I *need* to learn! There is so much that I do not know!"

Love and empathy and a warm, almost lyric sadness surfaced in Fomor MacLir's deep-green eyes. "If you can admit to that, my son, then perhaps you have already learned the greatest and most important lesson of them all."

Father and son sat together, their hunger satisfied. As their cooking fire died they watched the sun set beyond the peaks of the distant island. The world flamed crimson, then cooled to pink, soft gold, mauve, and gray—subtle, ever-deepening colors that played upon the face of the earth until at last they merged into the thin, cold blue of evening. A wind rose from out of the distant highlands and gusted across the summit of the tor as it swept westward toward the sea.

Balor stared off across the miles, across the sea, to the distant island. Its mountains bulked up like storm clouds against the sky. Tall, rough-edged mountains, with summits peaked and rounded, naked and proud in the cold sweep of the sea wind.

"Is that the enchanted isle of which Huldre dreams?" he asked.

The chieftain shook his head disparagingly. "Mark me, boy, the isle of which she dreams is naught but a fabric spun of a Northwoman's overly fanciful imagination. It does not exist, except in her head. But *that* island"—he pointed off—"is real enough. A great, savage, mountain-ringed, bowl-bellied land whose cursed shores I had hoped never to see again."

"Why? Have you been there?"

"Aye. Long ago, in the days when our clansmen were sea raiders. It is the isle of Eireann, lad. Home to many a warring clan . . . as it was home to the clan MacLir once, long ago, in the Days of Glory."

A twinge of excitement ran up Balor's back, tickling deliciously. He sat very still, as rigid and expectant as an arrow ready to fly from a bow. "I wish I had been with you in those days! I wish I could have sailed in your raiding ships when you and the other clansmen were warriors. I would have killed many men and carried away their treasures. I would have been brave and made you proud of me. I know I would!" He paused and gulped a breath. "Tell me of how it was in those days, Father! Tell me why we are no longer warriors and why we have no ships and—"

The chieftain waved him to silence. "Take a breath, boy, before you pass out from lack of wind!" His brow furrowed, and a look of sadness invaded his eyes. "We are no longer warriors because it is no longer practical for us to go raiding. We have no ships because they were burned at my command."

Balor was stunned. "You burned our ships? Why?"

"For good reason, boy." Fomor's expression hardened into a scowl of bitterness as he stared off across the sea. "Ach, a man has only to look at that cursed island and somehow his thoughts are turned to war. Perhaps, in its way, Eireann does carry an enchantment, but not in the way of Huldre's foolish dreams. There are no magic beasts, no horned horses, no enchanted creatures whose capture shall guarantee immortality to a man. But mark me, Balor, there *are* beasts dwelling there—for every man who steps upon its cursed shore is transformed into one . . . not by magic, not by sorcery, but by the black lust of his own greed for gold and power."

Fomor saw the look of wonder and excitement upon his son's face and growled. "Aye, Balor. Gold. Great, gleaming, fist-filling globs of it. Nuggets the size of a man's fist, more numerous and shining than the stars in the sky. Gold, lying for all men to see at the bottom of that island's rivers and streams. Gold, waiting in mountains, in veins as thick as a warrior's thigh. And there's copper too! And tin! Oh, yes, all of the elements of madness are there, ripe for the taking."

Balor cocked his head, not understanding. "Then why did you burn our ships? Why did you settle us in the fens of Albion? If there's gold to be had on the shores of Eireann, why didn't you take it?"

"But I did take it, my boy! I did take it. And the curse of that taking has followed me to this very day. In blood and in death, that is how I have paid for the gold and the power that I won upon that island. So do not speak to me of gold, laddie. Do not ever speak to me of gold."

The warning within the chieftain's eyes was black and as sharp as any blade.

Balor swallowed a thousand questions and, suddenly chilled by the night wind, shivered as Fomor unrolled the traveling cloak of finely softened elk skin, which he had brought with him. He slung the garment on, pulling it up around him like a tent as he gestured to his son to come closer.

"I'd forgotten how cold the nights can be up here. We'll need to keep this close about us if we're to get a decent night's sleep," he said.

As Balor gratefully nestled close, Fomor enfolded him in the cloak and slung a huge arm protectively about his shoulders. The boy basked in the moment, forgetting all thoughts of gold and distant islands. He had never been alone with his father before. He snuggled up against Fomor's lean, powerful side, drawing in the scent of his maleness, of warm skin and oiled leather, of hide garments tanned to the suppleness and fragrance of newly furled leaves. He looked up adoringly at his sire, at the broad brow, the bold, narrow span of nose, at the green eyes staring off through dense lashes as tawny as his beard and the long, wrist-thick, sinew-wrapped braids which fell forward over his heavily muscled shoulders. Balor sucked in a little breath of adulation, wondering if there would ever be a day when he too would be such a magnificent man.

Fomor felt the tremor of Balor's breath and looked down, his eyes warm with paternal concern. "You shiver, lad. Gather the elk skin closer. It, and the warmth of my body, will soon warm you."

The boy did as he was told, yet asked: "Why don't you

want to keep the fire burning? There's enough wood to keep it high all night."

"A fire might draw wolves, my boy."

"No wolf could climb the tor!"

"Not the four-legged variety."

"Is there any other kind?" Balor was incredulous, visualizing eight-legged wolves as agile as spiders.

Fomor saw his reaction and smiled, but when he replied, there was a bleak, tense guardedness to his tone. "Aye, boy. There are two-legged wolves. Foreign wolves who stalk the earth in the guise of men. Sharp-eyed with long, unforgiving memories and strong warrior's hands that could climb this tor as easily as I."

Balor blinked, incredulous. "Are they men or spirits?"

"They are of flesh and blood, as you and I." Disturbed by the turn the conversation had taken, he rose, suddenly restless. "Go to sleep now. It grows late, and I am weary of words." He left the cloak to Balor as he went to stand at the very edge of the tor, moodily staring across the darkening world.

The boy remained huddled in the cloak before the fire pit, waiting for Fomor to return. But the lord remained where he was, immobile, arms folded across his chest, his face set and hard.

Balor stared at his father until stars pricked the night with tiny lights that pulsed like a heartbeat. Sleep veiled his eyes, and vague, insubstantial dreams moved across his mind.

Then, slowly, the dreams took on the substance of a vast, black sky, with stars marching like bands of nomads against the face of infinity. Balor saw the sun and the moon, and he saw his father standing between them with his hunting bow held high, an arrow pulled back, straining the bowstring. Fomor released it. The arrow flew in a great, high, sweeping arc. But then the arrow became a shooting star, which flamed across the darkness, leaving a white-hot pathway along which Balor ran for his life! Pursued by wolves, snarling, hungry wolves led by a huge, white beast with blood and star-fire in its eyes! The great pale wolf leaped at him, and the others followed, scrambling upon his shoulders, ready to consume him.

"No!" he screamed.

The sound of his own cry woke him. He looked around,

startled to discover that it was past dawn. His father bent over him, one large, heavy hand upon his shoulder.

"It's time we went from this place, boy."

Balor arose, grateful to be free of the nightmare. Stiff-backed and with aching limbs, he stretched, rubbed sleep from his eyes, then took up his bow and followed his father.

As they stood at the edge of the tor, ready to descend, Balor looked across the new day toward the sea. How beautiful was the world, how vast, how beckoning. Fog shrouded the horizon, obscuring the far island. There were tiny, flickering lights where he knew the holding must be. And far off toward the south, along the headlands of a distant promontory that jutted far out into the sea, there were . . . ships . . . ?

Balor blinked and strained to make certain that he saw correctly. Yes! They were so small that he might easily have failed to note them. But they were real enough, floating on the sea, tacking slowly downcoast and southward against the wind. From the height and distance of the tor, they seemed no larger than torn fragments of red leaves eddying upon the surface of a stream. But they were ships, with sails the color of blood. And at the center of each wide, red span of sail, Balor could just make out a single, huge, black running wheel emblazoned like a dark vortex whirling in a sorcerer's eye.

He pointed off. "Look, Father! Sailing ships! Do you see them? Do they move toward another holding, so close to our own? Surely the lights on the far promontory seem no more than a few days' trek from our own fields!"

Fomor's face was as gray as old ashes. "Aye, I have seen them. I have been watching them since first light. And the ships . . . aye, I have seen those ships in my dreams for over half a lifetime." He shook his head as though to clear it of a bad memory. Then wearily, but with great resolve, he put his hands upon his son's shoulders. "Mark this moment, Balor. By the power of the Twelve Winds, you have received a great gift. The shooting star that led you to this place was a sign, my son—a sign such as I was given when, many years ago, I too saw such a star and followed it to this very place . . . and looked down on Bracken Fen for the first time and knew that I must lead my clansmen there, deep into the hills and marshlands, to dwell in peace . . . forever in peace, if the Twelve Winds would allow it. And now, through you, once

more the star has brought me here, where I might find a
message written in the dawn. Had you not followed that star,
Balor, we would have had no warning—none at all—until it
was too late."

"Warning? Of what?"

"Of the wolves, my son. Of mad, vengeful, man-eating
wolves! They run beneath the colors of the red and black, led
by a warlord known as Nemed MacAgnomain, a man who has
sworn to take my head and nourish the earth with the blood
of my kindred."

6

Balor's world changed that day. But like the tide, the
change came slowly, inexorably. The boy could no more have
stopped it or altered its course than he could have caused the
sun or the moon to stand still in the heavens.

They came down from the tor in good time and started
homeward across the moor. Hours passed. The miles slipped
away. The dogs showed signs of tiring. They were content to
keep close to their master's heel as Balor strained to keep
pace with Fomor, frustrated by his silence. The lord had been
in a black mood since sunrise, grimly preoccupied with other
thoughts, striding forward so aggressively that the boy had to
jog in order to keep up with him. Since yesterday, in some
strange, indefinable way, the chieftain seemed older. Since
they had come down from the tor, he had withdrawn, brooding
in a world of his own—a lonely, desolate place bastioned by
walls built high of thoughts that he refused to share with his
son. Balor, remembering the closeness they had shared the
night before, found the lord's aloofness to be as painfully
intolerable as his pace.

He tugged at Fomor's tunic. "Please, Father, I can't keep
up! There are blisters as big as crow's eggs on my heels. And
we haven't eaten since last night. Let's stop awhile. Please!"

The chieftain paused, eyeing his son as though the boy's
request had reached him through a deep, dark, unpleasant
dream. He nodded. "Yes. Of course we'll rest. But only

briefly. I want to be safely across the bogs and back at the
holding before dark. Tonight I must call an assembly of the
clansmen, and Munremar will need time to sanctify the
council hall."

The words struck fire to Balor's heart. Except for meetings
convened prior to festivals and sacred feasts, assemblies were
only called to discuss matters of the gravest concern to the
entire clan.

The chieftain saw the apprehension in his son's eyes.
"There may be wolves at our back. They may be sniffing out
the fenlands as we speak. I must warn the others as soon as
possible so that a proper decision may be made as to how best
to deal with them. So, as soon as you've caught your breath,
we must go on. We'll eat when we reach the holding. If you
cannot keep up with me, I will carry you like a babe."

Balor's face flamed with resentment. "I'm no infant in need
of carrying! I'll keep up."

"Good."

Sullenly, Balor once again fell into step beside the lord,
determined to keep pace with him, ignoring the pain of his
blisters, the emptiness in his belly, and the burning ache in
his back and limbs.

"You might at least tell me who these 'wolves' are. And
how do you know that Nemed Mac . . . Mac—whatever you
said his name was—is there, where the ships were off the
coast?"

Fomor did not break his stride as he replied caustically, "I
don't. Nemed MacAgnomain should by rights be dead, but
death does not come easily to a man made strong by hate.
Before we settled in Bracken Fen, I had heard that Nemed
had won his freedom and married an Achaean queen. The
ships belonging to the Achaean royal houses can be identified
by their red sails. And the symbol of Nemed's father's house
was the black running wheel. The ships were in the harbor of
the newly established settlement of Beaker Folk, although I
never thought to see the Folk come so far north. Yet I should
have known that the day must come, for there are no more
avaricious merchants in the world than they. They'll have
their traders out scouring the moors and marshes for new
sources of income. And if Nemed is alive—and somehow I
am certain that he is—he will have his spies among them.

Soon enough they will discover Bracken Fen and learn the identity of its chieftain."

"And then?"

Now the lord paused and sighed and looked down at his son out of weary eyes. "Then they shall seek us out and kill us, boy. Every man, woman, and child of us."

A tremor of incredulity went through the boy. "But why?"

Fomor's green eyes narrowed. Yet as the boy stared into them, he was stunned by what he saw: pain and power, bitterness and remorse, and bold, dangerous riptides of pure, black hatred. Then—and the sight of it made him gasp—he saw something else, something unthinkable. Something so repugnant that it sickened him with disgust. He saw fear.

"You make it sound as though you brought us into the fens to hide...as though you were afraid to face this Nemed Mac... Mac...whatever his name is! But you couldn't be. Not *you*! Not Fomor MacLir! Not the Wolf of the Western Tribes!"

For a moment the chieftain did not move, did not even breathe. The sadness in his eyes was so deep that Balor nearly drowned in it. Then, slowly, Fomor drew a breath, held it a moment, and exhaled it along with his reply. "But you are right, Balor. That is exactly why I brought my clansmen into the fens. To hide. To live as far from the madness of the world of men as was possible. To dwell in peaceful anonymity, to be forgotten by all who might still remember the name and deeds of the Wolf of the Western Tribes."

Balor gaped. He felt betrayed. "I don't believe you!"

"It is true, my son. But my reasons are not what you might think. I am not afraid to face Nemed MacAgnomain. I am afraid to face myself... to face what I must become if Nemed and I ever meet again."

Balor blinked against the tears that had suddenly stung beneath his lids. "I don't understand."

"No. Of course you do not." Fomor's tone was soft with compassion. "And if the power of the Twelve Winds is still with me, if I am able to convince the council to vote with me tonight, you never shall."

They returned to the holding at dusk, a soft, mauve, windless hour, full of night's lengthening shadows, fragrant with the lingering scent of summer sunlight on ripening fields. Balor took no note of it. Nor did he heed the well-deserved reprimands that he received from his kinsmen. He cared only that the long, aching agony of the day was over and that he could rest at last.

But there was to be no rest for Fomor. Offering no explanation to his kinsmen, he called for an assembly as he walked through the great gateway in the palisade. The people who had assembled to greet him stood in stunned silence, watching as he stalked off to the bathhouse, where he would cleanse himself before taking his place before the altar of the Twelve Winds. A soft, questioning murmur swept the crowd as Mealla came forward to hurry Balor through the throng. She shoved him along the plank walkway that led to the chieftain's roundhouse, cautioning him to silence as the crowd pushed close and called them both rude names when Mealla refused to satisfy their curiosity.

"What has happened?" asked old Falcon, and a dozen voices rose to echo him.

"What sort of trouble has the whelp brought upon us this time?" It was Mael's question.

Anger flared within Balor at the sound of the youth's open derision and hostility. He paused and turned around, trying to see his pug-nosed antagonist amidst the throng, but he was too small. Bodies pressed all around. Mealla's strong hands dug into his shoulders and spurred him forward again, impatiently. "Come along, Balor. You must have your rest!"

Rest . . . aye, and when he was rested, he would make Mael eat his words and choke on them.

Never had the walk from the compound to the roundhouse seemed so long. Little Dana came to the front of the crowd to slip a friendly arm through his, skipping along beside him, her golden hair entwined with field flowers, her smile more welcome than she would ever know as she proclaimed her joy in his safe return. Then Morrigan appeared ahead, standing with Elathan at the open entrance to the roundhouse. She was clad in the knee-length, loose-fitting boyish tunic that she preferred to more feminine garb. Her wild dark hair was braided like a boy's, and her black-lashed, forest-green eyes spitted him as sharply as skewers.

"We've been taking odds on the chances of your return.

Indech and Tethra and all the other lads were certain that the wolves had finished you. But I knew you'd come home. What wolf with any taste would want to eat you?"

As tired as he was, he snarled a rebuke at her, but she laughed it away.

"Father says you're getting to be like a bone lodged in the throat of the clan," Morrigan said seriously. "If I were you, Balor, I'd be more careful in the future . . . lest someday they decide to spit you out!"

Mealla gave the girl a withering glance, elbowed her aside, and shoved Balor forward into the house. Elathan and the dogs followed, but Morrigan, Dana, and the others were ordered away as Mealla closed the weather baffle.

The darkness of impending nightfall had already claimed the interior of the roundhouse as Balor crossed it and sprawled facedown, exhausted, upon his pile of bed skins. The big female terrier, Sure Snout, sighed down close beside him. The tallow lamps had not yet been lighted, and the only illumination within the room came from the fire pit in a warm, shimmering, ruddy glow.

Huldre stood near the fire. Tall and very still. She stared at him as though she could not have enough of the sight of him.

Balor closed his eyes. His weariness put him beyond caring. He lay spread-eagled upon his belly, frustrated because he was too young to join the men at the gathering, hurt because Fomor had not made him privy to his secrets, and although he might wish to deny it, glad that he had been sent home. His body craved rest. Every muscle ached. His blisters throbbed. Hunger was an aching presence begging for satisfaction.

Huldre knelt beside him, offering a haunch of cold hare. She poked his shoulder with it, rousing him from his torpor as she shooed the dog away.

He eyed the meat over one shoulder and sighed with shivering relief as he took it. He was so tired that he did not even attempt to sit up or ponder the reasons for her uncharacteristic solicitude. He rolled onto his side and lay like a baby in the womb, gnawing hungrily, trying not to meet his mother's stare.

But as always, when those pale, wide-set eyes sought his, he found it impossible to look away. It was a power that Huldre had over him. Sometimes in the night he would awaken and know that she was staring at him. He would feel her vision walking upon his skin, trespassing into his flesh and spirit as though she could accompany him at will into the substance of his thoughts and dreams.

And yet now he had no wish to look away, for what he saw both troubled and perplexed him. The flickering firelight set deep purple shadows beneath her eyes. There were dark hollows beneath her cheekbones. She seemed weary, gaunt, paler than usual, and somehow vulnerable, like a frail child who has gone for many nights without sleep. Had it been concern for him that had caused her to lie awake in the night? No! Huldre did not worry about her children like other mothers did. Of that Balor was certain. It was her pregnancy that distressed her. Although it had progressed nearly to term, it was not going well. She was still as ill and tired as she had been during the weeks when the child had first set down the roots of its life within her. Even the special medicinal mead that Mealla had prepared for her seemed to do her little good.

"Listen to me, Balor," she said, and her words were like marsh mists moving sinuously in the dawn. Cold, without texture or substance, yet real. Of the same dimension that spawned her foreign tales of magic and enchantment. "He who is the Thunderer...he who rules the stars and looks down on the world through hawk and eagle eyes...he, Donar, who walks with the white wolf and the lightning bolt ever at his side, has saved you and marked you as his own. The god has worked his will through you. And now, Balor, you must heed what I say, lest you offend his favor."

"No!" Mealla had come close, her brow furrowed with worry as she puffed herself up like a broody hen, hands upon her hips. "Do not listen to her, Balor. Huldre, come away from the boy. You are distraught. You must rest, sister of my hearth, lest the child you carry be stillborn like the last."

"Child..." The word ran out of her like blood seeping from a wound. One pale hand lay protective upon her belly, the other strayed from her amulet to rest upon her son's shoulder. "It *is* Donar who has saved you. He shall save us all through you!"

He shivered. Her eyes still held him. How blue they were, pale, nearly transparent. Clear, crystal pools in which a tiny dark speck hung, at the very center, like a raven suspended upon a cold wind. For an instant, before he put the notion aside as foolish, he thought he had glimpsed her soul. But no, it could not be. No soul in all the world could be so black, so full of fear . . . so desperately lonely, and so full of inconsolable love for him.

Love from Huldre? No. "I do not care about Donar, I do not seek the favor of your foreign god! Leave me to my rest!"

He had spoken through a mouthful of meat and would have turned his back upon her and taken another mouthful had she not snatched the haunch away from him and held him fast with her free hand. "Stupid boy! You have been doubly blessed! The gods of two peoples are yours. To reject any of them offends the Fates and invites disaster! Tell me, Balor, son of Fomor, grandson of Manannan, who prefers to nurture ignorance of your mother's people, do you honestly believe that it was only a deer that led you into the wild country?"

Her sudden vehemence startled him. "What else but a deer?"

"Elathan told me that its hide was as red as blood, but I say that it was as red as Donar's beard, with antlers as snag-forked as the lightning that Donar hurls across the sky. Indeed, Balor, I tell you that it *was* Donar. In the form of a deer he led you into the wild country so that, because of your disobedience, malcontents might at last openly rebel against my lord, dissenters who threaten to break the order of his sovereignty and impel him to prove the righteousness of his rule by force . . . a force that may well lead him back to the way of life to which he was born—as a warrior of the Twelve Winds!"

He stared at her, stunned. Had the clansmen in fact gathered to speak against his father in Fomor's absence? He had no chance to form the question, for Mealla answered it, openly distraught.

"You must stop such talk, Huldre! You must not speak of foreign gods and magic. If not for your own sake, then for the boy's. Munremar speaks against you both and has demanded that Balor be brought before the council. His continued disobedience to clan law has angered the Wise One."

A look of pure contempt moved upon Huldre's face. "I do not fear Munremar."

"You had *better* fear him!" Her attention turned to Balor now. "And you! What am I to do with you? You are the lord's firstborn. And you have taken grievous advantage of that fact. First you defied the Wise One's command by following your father when you had been forbidden to do so—and disaster nearly befell us because of it! But Munremar forgave you then, as he has forgiven you always for all your law-breakings and challenges of authority. But this latest act of disobedience . . . Ach, Balor, when Fomor put himself at risk for you, when he broke from the searching party and did not return, dark, ugly things were said about you and the mother who bore you. By Munremar. By Draga. And by those who have grown increasingly loyal to your father's brother during these long years of darkness and endless rain."

Defensiveness sparked within the boy. "I care not what Munremar thinks! Nor about Draga and his band. I am Fomor's son . . . the chieftain's firstborn. That is what matters."

Mealla snorted a rude rebuke and jabbed her arms skyward as she rolled her eyes. "May the Twelve Winds grant me patience! By the Fates, Balor, don't you understand that even a chieftain's firstborn can stretch his luck too far? When your father put himself at risk for you, so also did he put the clan at risk. Had he not returned, the chieftainship would have been open to dispute. Draga would no doubt have tried to claim it for himself so that he could lead us all off to war and wandering again. The older men, those who are loyal to your father, those who fought at his right hand in the Days of Glory and understand his reasons for leading his people to a settled, peaceful life, they would have risen as one to fight against Draga's rule. The blood of brothers would have been spilled by brothers. The unity of the clan would have been shattered forever. And all because of you!"

Balor felt sick. "I didn't mean—"

He had no chance to finish his sentence, for at that moment a voice called into the roundhouse. It was Lomna Ruad. Mealla bade him enter.

A little older than the lord, Lomna Ruad was a tall, broadly built, brown-bearded man. He stooped as he folded back the weather baffle and peered in. He had evidently come from the council hall, for his face was painted in ceremonial patterns, which the men donned for assemblies.

"The firstborn of the lord is to come with me."

Mealla stood between the man and Balor, her stance

defensive. "What do you want with him? The chieftain sent him here to get some sleep!"

"Sleep?" The question rolled like thunder upon Lomna Ruad's tongue. "Woman, he'll be sleeping permanently if he doesn't come with me, and quickly! Munremar's after the boy's hide, but the lord has convinced him to allow Balor to speak in his own defense before a judgment's brought against him."

"A judgment!" exclaimed Elathan, aghast upon his perch atop Fomor's battle chest.

Weak-kneed, Balor rose. The room seemed to be spinning. Everything seemed suddenly bright. Then Huldre put her hands upon his shoulders, and as her touch summoned his glance upward to meet her, everything slipped back into its normal and proper perspective.

"The lord is your sire, Balor. He will allow no harm to come to you. Remember that. As surely as you must remember that the deer that led you off into forbidden country was Donar, guardian of all the world. He was with you then; he is with you now. Do not be afraid. You will be within the sacristy of the Twelve Winds because you are their son . . . as surely as they are Donar's children."

"You! Son of the lord! Come forward!"

Munremar's imperious roar was clearly a command, but try as he might, Balor could not obey. Within the firelit vastness of the council hall, he stood paralyzed and wide-eyed with fear beside Lomna Ruad at the entrance to the great room as the assembled clansmen turned to stare at him. They were seated cross-legged on piled furs and skins on the floor. Gold glinted at their ears and throats, upon their arms and in their hair. Their faces and bodies were painted. Hostility and curiosity glowed darkly in their eyes.

Balor winced against their scrutiny. He turned his eyes away from them and stared around him at the great hall. Never before had he been inside, and never, even in his wildest imaginings, had he visualized anything that came close to the reality. Awestruck, he gaped at the impossible heights of the vaulted ceiling. Shadowed in the firelight, it seemed to hang threateningly above him, like the open mouth of some predatory beast ready to devour him.

He shivered and forced his glance away, but there was no comfort to be found. Everything seemed menacing, shimmering in the light of the twelve sacred tallow lamps, each set into one of the twelve posts that supported the roof, each burning with a smoky and unnatural flame. Blue. Green. Purple. Gray. Abnormally intense oranges, scarlets, incandescent yellows, and a white so pure that it burned the eyes. There must be magic within those fires, just as there must be magic within the twelve posts, for each was as thick as a warrior's thigh and ornately carved and pointed. Serpents and sea monsters, strange birds and beasts, climbing vines and disembodied eyes and hands, creatures conjured up out of some primordial nightmare. In the pulsing illumination of the lamps, they seemed alive. They breathed. They leered. They writhed. They leaped. They beckoned.

Just as Munremar now beckoned from across the vastness of the room. "Balor! Come forward!"

He stared across the hall to where the Wise One stood in his ceremonial finery at the right hand of the chieftain, in front of the covered altar of the Twelve Winds. No doubt the shrine had been shrouded to prevent it from being profaned by the eyes of one not yet consecrated to its power. Yet even if the covering had fallen away, Balor's eyes would not have been drawn to the altar, nor would they have rested upon the Wise One. He looked upon his father and stood transfixed.

Fomor was seated upon the ceremonial chair of the lord of the clan. He had donned the massive golden collar and wrist guards that proclaimed his rank. Naked to the waist save for the collar and a broad, copper-studded leather belt worn over one shoulder, he wore a knee-length skirt of fringed leather and another massive belt from which hung, by two golden hooks, his twin ceremonial daggers. In his left hand he held an exquisitely worked, double-headed killing ax of stone set into an intricately carved haft of antler. Upon his head—its animal eyes replaced by stones of blood-red, highly polished carnelian—the head of an enormous wolf snarled at the assembly with its teeth bared and its lower jaw cut away. It was an impressive and superbly savage crown, and the stern, painted face that appraised Balor from beneath it seemed a double image of its raw magnificence.

The boy caught his breath. All fear ran out of him as he again experienced the wonder and pride that came to him when he looked upon his sire. Yet there was no assurance, no comfort, no warmth within the chieftain's eyes.

"Balor!" Munremar's command was a slap of sound. "Come forward!"

The boy was shaken to the core, but he did as he was told, too frightened to do otherwise.

Munremar glared down at him with eyes round with rage. "You! Bend your knee before your lord! Would you bring the wrath of the Twelve Winds upon us as penalty for your bad manners?"

Balor felt nauseated. He knelt and bowed his head, then waited for Fomor to tell him to rise, but the lord did not speak. Moments passed. Long, throbbing moments. He was still bone weary from his trek home from the tor. His knee began to ache. His thigh began to burn and twitch. Slowly, fearfully, without lifting his head, his eyes strained to meet those of his father so that Fomor might understand the extent of his weariness, but the chieftain deliberately looked away, and suddenly it dawned on Balor that his willingness to obey was being tested. He resolved to endure the discomfort. He swayed a little but remained as he was while numbness crept up the limb that held the bulk of his weight. At last he heard a murmuring of approval from the clansmen behind him.

"Enough!" Munremar begrudgingly bade him rise. His tone could not have been more hostile. He had set a snare for the boy and quite obviously felt cheated. "It seems that your father is right. You *have* learned from your errors of the past few days. Before the altar of the Twelve Winds I'll admit that I never thought to see the day when you'd take an order without questioning it! Rise up now, boy, before you fall down."

The murmuring of the clansmen intensified. Balor rose obediently, rubbing the stiffness from his thigh before it spasmed into a cramp. This time when he sought his father's eyes, he saw approval there. Relief flooded him, then vanished as quickly as it had come. Fomor's lids half closed, and Balor saw a warning deep within the green of the chieftain's eyes: *Beware. Be on your guard.*

The words stirred within him, a gift from his father.

One look at Munremar told him why the gift had been given. He knew that the old man had never liked him, but he had never realized the scope of that dislike until now.

Munremar's eyes centered on him as cruelly as if he were a sacrificial animal about to be disemboweled so that magical portents might be divined from its death throes. So Mealla had been right to fear for his safety; a punishment was in store for him, and if Munremar had his way, it would be as unpleasant as possible. Not even the chieftain could sway the Wise One's decree if the clansmen voted to support it. It was the way of the clan MacLir since Time Beyond Beginning.

Balor found it difficult to breathe. He tried to calm himself, remembering that Huldre had promised that Fomor would allow no harm to come to him. Surely there was no way that all of the clansmen would vote with Munremar against their lord? The chieftain had too many allies, too many old friends. Besides, what had he, a mere boy, done that was so terrible? Then he remembered Mealla's words: *"When the lord put himself at risk for you, so also was the clan put at risk. Had he not returned, the chieftainship would have been open to dispute. The blood of brothers would have been spilled by brothers. The unity of the clan would have been shattered forever. And all because of you...."*

He shivered, appalled by the realization that, in fact, he could have committed no greater crime. And all because, once again, he had been a disobedient fool.

Munremar came down from the altar and bent so close to him that the boy could smell his fetid breath and feel the warmth emanating from his thin, aged skin.

"Look at me, Balor, son of Fomor, grandson of Manannan."

Balor looked. The Wise One's hair and beard and flowing mustache swirled like smoke around his shriveled face. His brows were ragged puffs upon his furrowed forehead. The fringed, ceremonial skins that he wore were painted with the whorling patterns of flame. Indeed, to Balor he seemed ready to explode into a pillar of fire. Inadvertently the boy stepped back, afraid that he would be burned.

Munremar snatched him forward. "Do not back away from me, boy! You shall tell us now of your reason—if there *be* a reason—for going into the wild country alone, for yet again defying the command of your chieftain and the laws of your clan!"

"I..."

"Speak out!" The Wise One's long, twisted right index

finger emerged from his clenched, gnarled fist to poke at Balor's shoulder, deliberately bruising him. "Explain yourself!"

"I . . ."

Again the white, lump-jointed finger shot out to stab him. "What you did is forbidden. You knew that. Say nay and I shall name you liar!"

"I . . ." Balor's tongue seemed stuck to the roof of his mouth. His mind went blank, yet still the old man pressed him cruelly, his finger jabbing like a blade until the chieftain rose and stepped forward to stay the offending hand.

"Tread more easily, Wise One, lest your clansmen be given cause to wonder if your title is misplaced. The accused is but a lad and will be treated accordingly."

"Lad . . ." Munremar hissed, a coagulation of pure loathing. It was an ugly sound coming from a man. "There are many other lads within this holding, my lord, all with an itch to prove their worth with a bow or sling or dagger or snare net. But not one would have knowingly dared to break clan law. You have sworn to us all that even though he is your firstborn, you would grant him no special privilege."

"Nor will I. Yet I will not see him unfairly abused."

"Unfairly?" Munremar shrieked a protest. "He knew the law, my lord. And yet in order to pursue a deer that he could not possibly have killed with his child's weapon, he wantonly broke that law and, as a result, caused others to risk their lives so that he might be brought home. Men might have died because of him! *You* might have died because of him! And it is not the first time that his thoughtless impetuosity has brought us to near ruin!"

"No. It is not. But this time he may well have led us to salvation."

The clansmen whispered among themselves and exchanged looks.

Fomor's face showed no emotion as he continued. "I have called you to gather here in solemn, sacred silence within the sacristy of the Twelve Winds. You have bathed, and painted the totem signs of your families on your bodies. Do you truly believe that I would have summoned you only to punish one young lad? Have you come to believe that I, the chosen lord of the clan MacLir, am not capable of deciding upon the proper disciplinary action to be taken against my own son?"

The question was dangerously provocative. No one spoke.

Balor felt the silence pressing down upon him until the vast, shadowed, firelit room seemed suddenly small and airless. He turned and looked out across the assembly. Amidst the throng he saw Draga and his supporters, Donn, Gar, and Nia. Also Lomna Ruad, Broen, Bahur, Echur, Dathen, and old Falcon and Oblin. Supposedly familiar faces, they appraised him, like the beasts on the roof posts—painted, emotionless, shining darkly.

"It is our right to affirm or deny any punishment you may choose for him," said Munremar. "This is the law of the clan."

"I am the lord of the clan, Munremar. I do not need you to remind me of its laws."

The old man's face twitched with anger and frustration. "I am the Wise One! I am the guardian of the knowledge of the clan MacLir! I am the nurturer of our people's faith and wisdom! It was I who stood at the right hand of your father in the Days of Glory, and when he was slain it was I who saved your life and when you were but a boy-king taught you to be a man . . . a lord . . . to draw strength from the laws and traditions of your ancestors!"

A sigh went out of the chieftain, the sort of sigh that a son makes when he seeks patience with a parent who refuses to acknowledge the fact that its child has long since become a man. "Aye . . . and aye again. But I am no longer a boy-king, Munremar, mentor of my youth. I am chieftain of the clan MacLir and arbiter of any justice that you, as Wise One, may prescribe." There was still patience in his voice, but it had a hardness to it now, a sharp, taut edge that was clearly a rebuke despite the respectful tone in which he couched his words. "In my absence, Munremar, you have overstepped your authority. You have assumed my role. You have spoken to my clansmen as though it were your right to determine punishment for one who has not even been allowed to speak in his own defense. This is hardly the behavior of one who professes to be a guardian of his people's traditions and laws . . . hardly the behavior of a Wise One."

The old priest recoiled, stung by truth as well as by humiliation. Never before had Fomor chastised him in front of witnesses. Never. But never before had he pressed the lord so far. Yet it *had* to be done. For the good of the clan. Yes. He must make Fomor understand. "My lord," he said, bowing his head with utmost deference as he spoke, "my actions were *re*actions to your absence...an absence brought about by the continued lawbreaking of your firstborn son. You were gone so long. We feared you were lost to us when Draga and the others returned to the holding without you. The boy...he is trouble, my lord...always and invariably...he is trouble." He paused and sucked in a breath, holding it as though he needed all of it to sustain him. Slowly he exhaled and raised his head to meet the eyes of the chieftain. "My lord, this *must* be decided. Nothing may take precedence over it. I do not stand alone. There is not a clansman here who does not share my fears. The night of the great storm...did the boy not openly defy me to go out to the holding ring even though you had commanded him to stay at home? Aye. He did. And is not the youth Dianket now a cripple because of your firstborn's defiance? Aye. He is. And when Balor challenged the authority of the boy Mael, did we not nearly lose the herd because his actions caused it to stampede? Aye. We did. And nearly saw you trampled to death but for the grace of the Twelve Winds. They served you...but for how long, my lord...for how long...?"

Again he paused. His mouth had gone dry. He gulped and tried to work up moisture within it, to no avail. For the good of the clan, he thought as he framed his next supposition. But at the back of his mind memories jabbed. A small, pale-haired, pale-eyed boy, outguessing him at his own conjurings. Today the sick old woman at the stonecutter's hearth shall die. Tomorrow the sun shall shine all day long. At noon the piebald ox would go lame. Little things. Lucky guesses. Everyone had lucky guesses now and again. But the boy had more than his share. Like his mother. And both had robbed him of the lord's affection. He who had been like a father to the chieftain, who had saved his life and ruled as regent by his side in the Days of Glory, was unable to exert much authority at all these days. He was but a shadow of his former self, a shadow that was destined to grow paler and paler as the boy's power to subvert the lord's admiration eventually displaced him entirely. The thought caused him to shiver with loathing and jealousy. No. He could not allow this to happen. For the good of the clan. Yes. Of course. Always the Wise One must think of the good of the clan.

"My lord," he continued judiciously, and resolve put the juices back in his mouth so that the words flowed smoothly once again, like oil running out on the surface of a sun-warmed stream. "I do not speak easily... nor without regret... but as Wise One, I *must* speak. The boy's continued disobedience... it is indicative of only one thing. It is not as though he were your only son. You have another. Elathan is a sound and prudent boy. An asset to the clan. But Balor... if this firstborn brings bad luck, what good shall any punishment be? How can we suffer him to live among us?"

No words in all of the world could have been more frightening to Balor. Bad luck was inherited. Everyone knew that. Like the color of one's eyes, there was no way to change it. Such a person was a blight on all who came in contact with him, and there was only one way to be rid of him—a bringer of bad luck had to be buried alive in a bog, staked down with the seven woods of magic so that he could not rise again. It was dangerous to kill him first. Like all evil, a person born with bad luck was deathless. It was essential that he be buried alive so that his soul would be trapped within his body, held captive within the bog forever.

"No!" he cried. "It isn't true! I've learned my lesson! I will never be disobedient again! I swear it! Please, you must believe me!"

Fomor's hand closed upon his shoulder. "Be silent, Balor. No son of mine begs. No grandson of Manannan is a bringer of bad luck. And no son of the Wolf will ever be buried alive in a bog, lest those who would carry out that act face me first in battle!"

Draga hooted with laughter. "It would be worth the risk... if we could see you once again take up the weapons of a warrior!" Draga's unexpectedly good-natured shout broke the tension of the moment, and the other men chuckled gratefully—infuriating Munremar even further.

Fomor eyed his brother speculatively, then smiled. "I've always said that luck made it possible for me to set my weapons aside, my brother. And I tell you now, as I have been trying to tell you since you first came into the hall, that it was luck that lured Balor into forbidden country."

"Luck? From that one?" Munremar's question was a sour curdling of disbelief.

"No one may ignore the call of the Twelve Winds. It was they who summoned Balor from the holding. If you insist upon punishing him, I must warn you that you will bring down the wrath of the power that has granted good fortune to the clan MacLir through him."

No one was more stunned than Balor. As Fomor seated himself once again in the chieftain's chair and summoned the boy to come and face him, he did as he was told in a frightened and confused daze. He looked into his father's eyes and again saw the warning...as bold and intense as high noon upon a summer's day.

"You must tell them, Balor. They must hear it from your lips. Leave nothing out. Tell them of how it was, from the first moment until the last. Tell them about the deer that left no tracks...the falling star that called you to follow...the stones that moved to shelter you on the moor...from the white wolf that took your arrow but left no trail by which it might be followed...tell them about the tor, and the ships we sighted on the distant shore in the first dawning of this day. Tell them, my boy. Of the ships that we sighted far off upon the sea...ships tacking beneath red and black sails that carried them southward, against the wind. Tell them. Do not be afraid."

He was not afraid. He was terrified. And yet he dared not disobey. Dry-mouthed, he began slowly, unsure, but soon the tale was told, and he stood blinking out at the assembly like one just roused from a dream. Later he would be told that he had put magic into his words, and that he had named the deer as Donar, red god of thunder, father of the Twelve Winds. They were Huldre's words, as though she had somehow stood invisibly beside him, her thoughts entering his mind so that they might issue from his lips. The thought made him cold.

And when Balor had finished his story with a description of the red and black sails, the assembly whispered in unison: "Nemed MacAgnomain."

The name ran through the room like a rat running loose in a field, until Draga cornered it and sent it into hiding.

"Ships with red sails, off a settlement of sort...but what makes you so certain that Nemed MacAgnomain is involved? His is not the only house to carry red and black as its colors. And at such a distance, how can you be certain that you saw the running wheel?" He challenged Fomor directly, emotionally. "And look at you, taking the boy's story so seriously! He's embellished it, no doubt, to keep himself out of trouble. I tell you that his deer was only a common buck of flesh and blood, and only his own ignorance kept him from picking up its trail. There was no white wolf. There were no standing stones. And he climbed the tor not because a star led him there, but because any fool knows enough to seek a high place from which to regain his bearings."

"But how can we be certain?" It was Oblin, the stonecutter, a lean, middle-aged man with thinning yellow hair faded by age. "I say that the lord Fomor is right. We dare not punish the lad lest we offend the forces that determine our Destiny."

"The stones on the moor . . ." Dathen spoke thoughtfully, turning the ends of his blond mustache meditatively between big, blunt fingertips. "It was said by the people of the fens that the stones on the moor are enchanted. That they know and protect those who have been chosen by the gods. That could account for them moving from a line to a circle."

Balor stared, incredulous. He had never heard such a tale before. Indeed, he had never even heard of the stones upon the moor until he had seen them for himself.

"Long ago, on a far plain," intoned Lomna Ruad, "I was with Fomor when he sighted a falling star. A rare and wondrous thing it was, a huge, bright finger of white fire. It traced a pathway to the tor. The lord went alone to scale the heights—to see the moor and fenlands and the holding of Bracken Fen for the first time. That star changed our lives. It was an omen then. It could be an omen now."

"But of what?" asked the ever-pragmatic Draga. "*If* the ships that were sighted from the tor are Nemed MacAgnomain's, and *if* he is still alive and nurturing his vow of vengeance, then we are all in mortal danger, my friends. And I, for one, see no good luck in that!"

"Then you have the vision of a newborn babe sucking blindly at its mother's breast!" Fomor exhaled a wordless curse of annoyance. "Can you not see it, Draga? We shall never know whether it was a god or a deer, a sign or a star, but it does not matter. What *does* matter is that, by his actions, Balor has made us aware of an old and perhaps too-long-forgotten threat. You who have been so restless these past long years of peace should, of all people, be pleased. Our days of a settled life may well be over, Brother.

If we do not face this threat immediately, we may soon awaken to find raiders at our throats."

Balor realized that the raiders who had last descended upon this holding were the very clansmen who now sat gathered within this room. It was an unsettling thought and, oddly, a deeply exhilarating one.

Draga stood. His red hair was loose to his broad, unclad shoulders. It was a wild, coarse mane of a darker hue than his brazen multi-braided beard and mustache. He was sweating, and his hairy, darkly painted torso and face glistened in the light of the tallow lamps. "It's come, then," he said, trembling so with excitement that he had to fight for control. "I always knew it must. By the Twelve Winds, if we only had more horses!" His beard split with a broad, white grin as he looked at Balor and shook his head. For the first time since the death of Draga's twin sons, affection for Balor shone in his eyes. "By all that I hold sacred, Nephew, I'll vow that Munremar and I have both misjudged you! From now on I shall call you Balor the Lucky! Thanks to you, we'll be opening the battle chests at last. We'll be taking out our killing blades and axes and weapons of forbidden power that have not seen the bright dawn of a warrior's day in all too many years. We'll be—"

Fomor interrupted him coolly. "We'll be acting like impetuous boys if we do not stop now to think about the situation."

"Think?" Draga sputtered. The word clearly appalled him. "There is no 'situation,' Brother. The time for action has come!"

"Aye," agreed the lord. "But not the sort of action you may imagine."

7

Exonerated. Exhausted. Relieved. They sent Balor from the council hall. Oh, how he wished that he were a man! Oh, how he wished that Fomor had not commanded him to go immediately home to rest. He had wanted to stay. Now they would uncover the altar of the Twelve Winds. Now they would drink the sacred mead of contemplation and chant the holy incantations known only to those consecrated to the power of the Twelve Winds.

It was fully dark, a moonless, cloudless night against which the stars shone like snowflakes swirling across the black cape of forever. Balor walked toward home along the plank walkway. All around him the holding was hushed, sleeping. Assemblies lasted all night. Those not in attendance usually retired early.

A sharp, brittle snap, like that of a dry branch breaking, startled him. Although none of the dogs barked, he wheeled in time to see a shadow fall along the wall of the council house. It was small and dark and hairy. It fell like a stone and exhaled a muffled wheeze of pain as it landed hard. It sat sprawled a moment, a shapeless lump, neither man nor beast. Then it rose, crouching down on all fours as it peered furtively about. Balor caught a quick, fleeting glimpse of a hideously wrinkled, unnaturally white face beneath a mass of wild black hair. Then the thing vanished, straight up the side of the council hall . . . and into it, as though it had simply walked through the wall.

Balor stood stunned, blinking, scowling into the darkness as he wondered if his weariness had robbed him of his sanity. But the shadow, whatever it had been, had been real enough. There was no way that he could go home now. He had to investigate!

His stomach tightened as he retraced his steps, then left the raised walkway to pursue the shadow to the spot where it had fallen. He knelt and touched the ground with questing fingers. Yes. It *had* been disturbed, and even his poorly trained fingers could detect footprints. They led directly to the wall of the council house. He followed, then paused and gasped. Something was moving above him on the wall of the council house. Even in the darkness he saw it—a slight variation of tone and texture. Darkness on darkness. A thin, long, wormlike thing moving up against the wattling of the wall. With no thought to his own safety, Balor reached for it. It spasmed violently upward in his hand, straining to be free of him. Yet he held fast, sensing that somehow this alien creature, whatever it was, intended to work some evil upon the gathering within.

Then he felt the fool. He stared at the thing in his hand

and knew what it was. It was half a rope ladder, which someone—or something—had let down through a breach high in the wall.

Again it strained against his hand, but he would not release it. He reached out and fumbled for its companion strand in the darkness, pulling down hard, reaching out with his right foot until he felt the first narrow hardwood rung. He trusted his weight to it and, with his heart in his throat, began to climb.

Halfway up, his left foot encountered a broken rung. His innate sense of balance kept him from falling, and he knew now that the sound that had alerted him to the shadow's fall had been the snap of that rung breaking. He paused in the darkness, grateful that he had not suffered the same fate. A brief, unpleasant memory of Dianket as he had appeared in Munremar's roundhouse after the fall from the apex of this same roof turned him cold. He wondered what sort of a creature could fall from even half of that great height and not be broken. Suddenly the apparition appeared above him—a small, white, hideous face that glowed like a ghostly moon amid tangles of wild black hair. It peered down at him from out of the wall itself, hissing viciously in words barely loud enough for him to hear.

"You persistent idiot! Are you going to cling to that ladder all the long night? If you do, I swear that I will cut the ropes. Then you'll be dead, and no one will know my secret."

He should have known. It was Morrigan. No one else, not even an evil spirit, could be so predictably nasty. She scooted back from him on bent knees as he climbed into the breach, amazed to find a rush-strewn floor instead of a drop straight down into the interior of the council hall. He was further amazed to find that he could not see into the hall at all, for the breach in the wall was actually an entrance into a small room secreted behind the altar. Together they pulled up the ladder, and then in silence she took a large square of what looked like a wattled shield and placed it into the breach. They were immediately closed off from the night, sealed in warm, close, confining darkness.

"No one can see us from the outside now," she whispered. "Or from the inside, either, unless we wish them to."

He heard her move in the darkness, then a light flickered, soft, barely a light at all, but enough to illuminate their

surroundings. It was a cramped cave of a room, filled with
crocks and bags and beakers. There was a familiar acrid scent
about the place. He sniffed, trying to place it.

"It's the smell of the smokes from the great hall below us,"
she said. "We are directly above the altar. Speak softly or
they'll think the Twelve Winds are addressing them."

She saw his confusion and gestured him forward. "Come
here. Lie flat. When I tell you, look."

He did as he was told, obeying not Morrigan, but his own
curiosity. She extinguished the light again, and he felt her
move to lie close beside him. She reached out in the darkness
and moved a small section of wattled wall aside, revealing a
narrow slot through which he could look over the great hall.

"When I extinguish the light in here, I can look out on the
assembly and watch my father without anyone seeing me. He
tells me what to do by secret gestures."

He turned his head and, despite the blackness of the room,
was shocked to see her face glowing white beside his, floating
on the darkness like a ghastly, incandescent moon. Black lines
radiated outward from her brows and downward from her
nostrils to her chin. Her lips shone green. Her eyes were
outlined in red.

She saw his look of horror and grinned loftily. "It is called
luminescence. Munremar mixes the colors with special sub-
stances made from the ground bodies of rare insects and from
powders made of even rarer stones."

She paused. Her smile faded. Her eyes, half-closed, glowed
softly in the darkness with a warmth that had nothing to do
with the shining paint that surrounded them. She sighed and
moved closer to him. "I would tell you *all* of my secrets,
Balor . . . all of them . . . whatever you would wish to know. . . ."

Her tone put him on edge. There had been something so
soft about it. So open and vulnerable and trusting. Not at all
like the bold, brazen girl whom he so thoroughly disliked.
"What would you know that I could possibly care about?" he
snapped, hating himself, and her, in this moment because he
heard the trembling in his voice and knew just how thoroughly
her masquerade had shaken him.

"I know all of the secrets of my father's magic."

"Not likely! He's the greatest magician in all the world! All
the clan knows *that*! He'd never share his magic with a girl!
And especially not with you!"

"What's wrong with me?" she queried, and the question came out hard and strong even though it was whispered and the darkness hid the hurt down-curling of her mouth.

"Everything!" he replied, and was glad when she closed the viewing window and slid away from him. In a moment she had relighted the lamp and seated herself beside him, although not as close as before. She did not look at him as she plucked idly at the shaggy, time-worn curls of her black bearskin garment.

"You disappoint me, Balor. I thought we were two of a kind, you and I, always questioning, always questioning. But the look on your face when you first saw me! You're just like the rest of them . . . as gullible as a toddler!"

He glowered at her, flushing red because he did not like the sound of truth. "You startled me, that's all. I knew all the time that you weren't . . . whatever it is you're supposed to look like. I saw you fall and came to help."

"Bah! Don't look so embarrassed. Most people wouldn't have been brave enough to follow a spirit. Besides, my father has worked very hard to make certain that no one would ever discover that I help him to make the magic that is attributed to the Twelve Winds."

The words were more than he could swallow. "I don't believe you. Munremar would—"

She put her right index finger to his lips, silencing him. "It's true. Look around. There's magic all around you."

He looked but he saw nothing—only a tiny cell filled with ordinary things. She shook her head as though admonishing an ignorant child.

"The lamps within the great hall . . . I saw you gaping at them when Lomna Ruad brought you before the gathering. The elements that burn blue and green and white are all in this room, simple things ready to be drawn up out of my crocks and bags and beakers. If someday someone should catch me replenishing the lamps, my father will cry out, 'Vanish spirit!' and off I shall go. No one would dare to follow if Munremar forbids it. So my secret is quite safe—or was— until the ladder broke and you saw me fall."

He shook his head, not wanting to believe her.

She pursed her lips. "If you doubt me, hand me the little leather bag with the falcon's feather strung to its cord."

The bags were neatly lined up on the floor. He found the

one she sought and handed it to her, fascinated in spite of himself as she untied the cord and with strong blunt-nailed fingers removed a pinch of dark, glossy powder from the bag. "When my father stands before the assembly and calls upon the power of the Twelve Winds, this is what he secretly throws into the altar fire so that it may seem as though the Twelve Winds have granted him a sign." Brushing the floor rushes aside, she took her little tallow lamp from its shelf and set it before her upon the floor. Her fingers flicked outward, releasing a spray of powder. As it fell downward toward the flame, golden sparks flared and cascaded like stars.

Balor stared, wide-eyed with enchantment and delight. "It is wonderful."

"Yes, and considered magic by those who do not understand what they are seeing. Father is quite careful that no one ever sees him throw the powder. If they did, they would soon understand. Anyone can do it. It's all in knowing which powders to use. They all burn differently, you see. Gold. Orange. Silver. Each color is from a different powder or mix of powders, and the finer the granules, the more explosive the flame. The rising heat from the wick is enough to ignite most of them. This one is ground from a certain rough, dark stone. It is rare, as are most of the metals from which the powders are made. Indeed, we are nearly out of most of them now. But if need be, even finely grained flour can make a fiery display." She took up another tiny pinch from the bag and flicked it outward over the flame. Golden sparks flared instantly. "It is beautiful, isn't it?"

As the golden sparks cascaded and faded, it seemed to Balor that some inner brightness within him faded with them. "You mean that it's *all* trickery—all of it?"

Her eyes seemed suddenly sad. "All that the Wise One ever works... all that I have ever seen..."

Balor had never seen sadness upon her face before. Unexpectedly, it touched him. Behind the grotesque painted-spirit disguise she seemed a different girl, as vulnerable and trusting as the fair and delicate Dana. "Why have you told me your secrets, Morrigan?"

She looked at him as though he had slapped her. All softness vanished from her face. "Oh, but you *are* a thick-headed boy! I have told you *nothing!* And if you should ever choose to reveal otherwise, then I will be forced to reveal to my father, and to your father, and to all of the clansmen, how once again you chose to disobey the chieftain so that you might selfishly pursue your own whims!"

"It's you who lured me here! I've done nothing wrong!"

"Nevertheless, you were told to go home. You came here instead. You have learned things forbidden to all but the Wise One and his assistant. Oh, yes, they will bury you alive in a bog this time! My father will see to it!"

They sat together, face to face, two young animals set to spar. Then the tension was broken by the drone of voices in the hall below them. He moved to leave.

"Stay awhile, Balor," Morrigan said, distracting him. Her voice was soft, imploring. "I'm not angry. Really I'm not."

"I don't want to stay. Not with you."

He made to rise, but her small hand closed around his. "Please, Balor. I won't tell on you. Truly I won't. I know that you want to stay . . . to hear what the men are saying. They have already passed the sacred cup and drunk the mead of contemplation. They'll debate before they set to ritual again. You can leave then. There will be plenty of time. Please, stay. I won't tell on you. I'd *never* tell on you."

He glared at her. "If they had wanted me to hear their discussion, they would not have sent me from the hall."

She shrugged. "What matter? You're here now. Besides, they'll never know. . . ."

There was a fever among the clansmen. It burned bright in Draga's eyes. "Long ago, when I was little more than a boy and we were as wolves raiding at will across the land, it was the report that Nemed MacAgnomain was alive and well and traveling with an army of Achaean warriors that first sent us fleeing into the fens. And now, once again, a rumor about him must stir us to action. Fomor is right. If the ships he sighted from the tor do come from a new trading settlement of Beaker Folk and if Nemed MacAgnomain still lives, he will have his spies there. They will be searching for our where-abouts, for there is no way that Nemed would have forgotten his vow to see us all dead as payment for the price his own people paid for our vengeance and glory."

"Glory..." Fomor exhaled the word thoughtfully, as though he were unsure of its meaning. "Was it truly that...?"

"How can you even ask?" snapped the redbeard impatiently. "It was you who led us to it! It was you who refused to kill Nemed, but chose instead to have a slave's collar fastened to his neck so that he might suffer ultimate humiliation as you took his woman and set your kinsmen to slay his father and clansmen and savor his sisters before his eyes. You made him weep and beg to die before you sold him and his sisters into bondage to foreign traders. And yes, Fomor—it *was* glorious! A terrible and righteous glory! For no man in all the world could have been more deserving of the fate that you served up to Nemed MacAgnomain on that day when you avenged our parents' murder and won the loyalty of the clansmen of MacLir forever!" He shivered with pride in his memories. "Ach, Brother, you could not have known that he would survive... or that he would return to haunt us like a specter risen from the black, bottomless belly of the Otherworld. But I for one am glad, for I would see you once again be the man you were in those days of long ago."

In the darkness Balor's heart was pounding so heavily from Draga's revelations that he was certain that Morrigan could hear it. His breath came in short, quick stabs, and he was light-headed with excitement, with images of battles and bloodshed, of his father as he had always wanted him to be—a warlord, not a herdsman. A Son of the Ax, not of the plow. A merciless destroyer of enemies, a sacker of villages, the Wolf against whose name and power all men trembled.

One of the younger clansmen spoke out. "We who have come to be consecrated to manhood here in the fens have but sketchy knowledge of the clan's history. We know that we are of a warrior race. But the lord has forbidden many of the tales to be told. Nemed's name has been proscribed until this day, yet it seems that he is a mortal threat to us. If this is so, my lord, why have we not taken up our arms, sought him out, and killed him long ago?"

Draga was so intoxicated with the moment that he replied in Fomor's place. "It has been the will of the chieftain that we forget our warrior past so we might forge a new and lasting future for our people in peace. But now it seems that if we are to have a future at all, we must lay the past to rest. And it *was* a glorious past. Nemed MacAgnomain . . . the name has gone unspoken for far too long."

"Speak of it, then," commanded Fomor with grim resolve. "The time has come to pass down the lore to our younger men."

Draga went on, thoroughly drunk upon his memories. "Nemed's father was Partholon, one of the most powerful chieftains of the far island, Eireann. He and our father, Manannan MacLir, had been enemies for many years. Of all the chieftains of the far island, only Partholon refused to pay tribute to Manannan's raiding ships. Over the years many on both sides died in endless skirmishes and battles. One day, when they had failed to raise an army to stand against Manannan, Partholon, with Nemed at his right hand, staged a raid on Manannan's secret place of holy pilgrimage. It lay far to the west of Eireann, upon distant Tory Isle. . . .

"Never shall I forget that place. Treeless. Desolate. With great, monster cliffs rising like pillars straight up out of the deeps. It is said that there are no cliffs in all the world like those of Tory Isle. I still see them in my dreams, as they were upon that day when I journeyed there with Manannan and Munremar, my mother and Fomor and my five other elder brothers. Young men they were—fine and bold and full of taunting laughter and good sport. I was eight that summer, and Fomor just thirteen. They lowered us over the cliffs to gather seabird eggs, and our mother cried in fear for our lives, but we were very proud and told her that we were not afraid. The ropes were as strong and trustworthy as our brothers' hands. And we were Manannan's sons, a warlord's spawn, and so would show no fear, although from clifftop to sea it seemed a thousand miles, and surely if a boy fell from the heights, he would be an old man and gray before at last he plummeted to certain death on the rocks below. Yet our brothers held us safe, and we gathered in the seabird eggs from nests along the wild scarps and listened to the voices of the Twelve Winds as they blew all around us. We were glad to be Manannan's sons and in this holy place where only he and his priest and his immediate kin were allowed to set foot.

"That night we feasted on boiled eggs and fish roasted in pits of sand lined with moist, sweet sea grass, and Manannan recounted the age-old story of our race, of the People of the Ax, and of how, always, since Time Beyond Beginning, we

were warriors moving across the world with the Twelve
Winds at our backs. Munremar blessed us all when the meal
was done. By starlight we journeyed to the sacred shrine at
the neck of the isle and looked westward across the Great Sea
and wondered if there were lands beyond it that might
someday fall to the power of the People of the Ax through the
sons of the clan MacLir.

"There was magic in the night. We lit the fire of sacrifice
and made our offerings of food brought forth from our meal.
The wind took the flames and sent them high, then turned
and whirled them round and blew smoke and ashes into our
faces. Munremar was troubled. It was a dark omen. He
stayed that night to meditate beside the sacred flame, to
drink the mead of contemplation so that he might more fully
be able to define the omen. We left him there. The night was
too beautiful for us to find shadows lurking within it. We
escorted my mother back to our encampment. Tired she was,
and great with child, and full of hope and dreams of the
riches that we would all win someday when Manannan had
secured the overlordship of Eireann. Gold. Tin. Copper. And
power. Yes. Power to unite the clans. To bring peace to all.
And then, together, to build the long ships with the great
green sails, with which the sons of Manannan would someday
dare to explore the far horizons beyond the Great Sea. Who
knew what riches lay there for the taking? Only those who
dared to seek them.

"We slept deeply that night. Unarmed. Unprotected by
our clansmen who had remained behind within our stronghold upon the western shore of Eireann. Tory Isle was
hallowed ground, sacred to the Twelve Winds. No lord of
honor would attack another while he sought sanctuary there.
But Partholon knew not the meaning of honor. Nor was he of
our race. He knew no fear of the gods of the Twelve Winds.
With weapons purchased from his kinsmen in distant Achaea,
he came against us. I do not remember how many warriors
were in his band. Many, I can tell you that. Dark men and
fair, from all the star-crossed lands that have ever sent their
power-hungry sons against the people of the Western Isles,
all sailing beneath the red and black sails that mark the colors
of his clan. With him was his youngest son. A boy of Fomor's
age. Nemed. Black-eyed, half-breed spawn of a witch of
Eireann whose clan was called MacAgnomain. It was her

people who had made Partholon a chieftain upon the far island. And in the dawn they came, beneath the sign of the great black running wheel, emblem of eternal life and power emblazoned on their shields and sails.

"They came, and Manannan rose from his bed and stood to them, informing them that his kin had brought no weapons onto this sacred isle lest it be defiled. He asked only to be granted a warrior's right . . . to face Partholon man to man, equally matched, bare-handed or with any weapon that Partholon would choose to place within his hand, for he could fight with any. But Partholon laughed, and as his men held me and my brothers fast, without warning he took Manannan's head with one killing swipe of his blade . . . a blade the likes of which we of the clan MacLir had never seen . . . no dagger this, but a magic shaft forged of god's blood and star-fire in the far and distant land of Achaea. A sword. Aye. They called it that and said that they would win the world with it! But not before they cut down my brothers one by one with similar weapons . . . and when she would not beg for mercy for herself, with his own hand Partholon cleft our pregnant mother in two so that the unborn child was exposed to her as she died. Then Fomor and I were dragged out into the dawn, with Partholon carrying Manannan's head upon a spike, brandishing it for all to see before he threw it from the cliffs into the sea, where it became fodder for fishes . . . dishonored . . . deprived of immortality."

Draga's voice broke. He took a breath and held it a moment, steadying himself before going on. "It was because we were boys that they did not kill us at once. They mocked us. They humiliated us. They mutilated our mother's body before our eyes and laughed when Fomor went mad with rage. They beat him then, and pushed us both before them to the edge of the great cliffs. They let us see the death that awaited us. They let us stand, close at the edge, and feel the abyss. Then they laughed and told us to call upon the Twelve Winds to save us, for we were the sons of the great Manannan, lord of the clan MacLir, and it was only fitting that, as 'Sons of the Sea,' we should be consigned to its care.

"They threw us over. And to this day the terror rises as bitter as vomit in my mouth when I think of it. We fell. Forever it seemed. Twice I hit the cliff face and tried to grab at it, but it was no use. They were raining arrows after us, and I could hear them hooting with delight as we plummeted to what surely should have been our deaths. I took an arrow in the back and another through the shoulder. I felt neither, for the third time I bounced off the cliff, I lost consciousness. I do not remember hitting the sea. I remember only the sensation of drowning. Of terrible, deep cold. Of cramping limbs and lungs near to bursting. It was Fomor who pulled me from the depths, though he had taken an arrow through the thigh and was so bruised and battered from the beating and the fall that to this day I know that he survived only because the Twelve Winds *were* with us both.

"The surge of the combers saved us from the rocks. If we had gone into the water a moment later or a moment sooner, we would have been broken. But the water took us and carried us safely into a cove deep beneath the overhang of the cliff. Partholon and his men were certain that we had died. We lay huddled and hurt upon the shore, listening to the sounds of their revelry for hours. All the long day it lasted. And all the still-longer night. When at last we watched their ships sail away, taking our own vessel with them like a captive beast, the fever of illness had taken us both. We'd have died if Munremar hadn't found us. He'd hidden himself well and seen it all. It was his Wisdom that healed our bodies even as he nurtured the hatred within our souls.

"It was days before our kinsmen came out to the island to see if Manannan was alive or dead. Our fortress upon Eireann had been raided. Many had died. The attackers had been driven off, but they had sworn to return with reinforcements. Now that Manannan was dead, they vowed that his clansmen would soon pay tribute to his murderer. Without their great and legendary lord of the far island to lead them, they would have no heart to fight. His sons were dead. And his woman. Best to swear allegiance to a new lord.

"But they misjudged the Sons of the Sea. Under Munremar's guidance, the clan abandoned its stronghold and took its ships northward along the hostile, westernmost coast of Eireann, into the track of the gales and mists that rise out of the Great Sea. Here we dwelled, hidden away, growing strong again—forging alliances with the western clans whose hatred of Partholon was nearly as great as our own. For four long years Munremar, the Wise One, ruled as regent while Fomor, eldest surviving son of Manannan, grew to manhood, swearing righteous vengeance against those who had slain his father and mother and all too many of his kinsmen. Despite his youth, soon it was clear to all that the soul of Manannan had risen from the sea to speak a chieftain's wisdom through Fomor's mouth. The power of the lord of the far island was alive in his body. Four years after the dawn that had seen the two of us thrown from the cliffs of Tory Isle, when evidence from spies told us that Partholon was convinced that he had broken and scattered the remnants of the clan MacLir forever, Fomor arose from the 'dead' to smite our enemies.

"In the dead of winter, with the black wrath of the power of the Twelve Winds at our back, we took our ships out of hiding and set out for Partholon's stronghold upon the eastern shore of Eireann. With the tribesmen of the western coast as our allies, we smote Partholon. With his own hands Fomor stole the great, magical blade of Achaean power and named it Retaliator as he struck off Partholon's head. While Nemed was forced to watch, the head of Partholon was thrown into the sea, and in the name of the Twelve Winds we claimed our righteous justice in glory and in blood!" Draga was trembling against the emotion his telling of the tale had caused to rise in him.

Fomor sat immobile, his features set into a scowl of bitterness. "And yet... after that... we continued to live as raiders."

Draga exhaled with amazement. "Of course! What other life *was* there for the People of the Ax! Had we not sworn upon the honor of the clan MacLir to fulfill our parents' dream... to take and hold all of the riches of Eireann for our own... to build a great fleet of ships... to sail out across the Great Sea in search of uncharted lands and spoils and riches beyond our wildest dreams!"

A murmuring rose in the hall as Draga's words stirred his listeners to restlessness. Balor could feel it within himself. Warm. Tingling. As though he had quaffed a draft of mead too quickly.

Fomor surveyed the gathering and nodded, reminding sarcastically: "Ah, yes... the Days of Glory. How easily you forget, Draga, and all of you, that Partholon was only one of Eireann's many warring chieftains, lord of only one of many southern and eastern clans... none of whom submitted to their role as the vanquished in our dreams of glory. They fought against us and fought well. Soon the tribesmen of the western shore began to work secretly against us, satisfying their own ambitions at the cost of ours. And I, Wolf of the Western Tribes, in my attempt to be lord over all, knew that only one false move would bring the entire pack down on my back, to devour me so that greedier wolves might take my place. Oh, yes, Draga, those *were* glorious days. But then, you were not the Wolf, were you?" Fomor stood down from his chair and walked through the gathering to face his brother. "Tell me, how many would-be Wolves did I have to slay to keep the pack at bay? How many of our number were lost while attempting to unify the clans of Eireann so that we might more profitably lust for its gold? But then, you were very young—barely twelve when we took revenge upon Partholon, as I remember—and did not do any fighting. Glory is always more desirable when viewed from afar, through eyes fogged by time and the misconceptions of youth. The blood that your kinsmen shed in those days, perhaps it does not seem as red to your eyes now as it was then."

Draga flushed angrily. "I know only that eleven years ago, when the Wolf was still the Wolf, we took freely from a world that dared not stand against us." Draga turned his back on the chieftain and addressed the clansmen. "Until, on a trading venture, a merchant from the south spoke of an ex-slave from Eireann who had married his mistress, a wealthy Achaean queen. He had become a lord, this slave had, a prince among the peoples of the wine-dark seas, the commander of a warrior band and merchant fleet as rich and powerfully armed as any in the world. He had one ambition, had this ex-slave, one ambition that overrode any other in the world . . ." He turned to face his brother. "To seek out and destroy the man who was known as the Wolf of the Western Tribes. The ex-slave's name was Nemed MacAgnomain."

Excitement thrummed in the room. Balor watched, waited breathlessly.

The redbeard did not balk. He turned back to the gathering. "Yes, we had lost countless men in battle. But there had also been sickness in our camp that claimed many lives. And we had made many an enemy among those of the western shore who refused allegiance to the Wolf. We knew that we would be few to Nemed's numbers, and if he had taken up with the Achaeans, then his weapons would be of the new metal—the magic metal, the great, hard, golden shafts of pure power against which our axes and spears and even our copper blades would be useless. So we did the only reasonable thing: We turned our ships northward and headed for lands where Nemed would not think to search for us... bleak, weather-blighted lands far from the trading centers of the world of commerce. We held a council and decided that the time had come for us to dwell in peace. So we burned our ships and took ourselves inland, far to the north, across wild and desolate and unsettled land until we sighted the holding here in Bracken Fen and fell upon it and claimed it as our own. Here, as Fomor promised, we have lived in peace, if not in plenty, until this day when once again the specter of Nemed MacAgnomain has risen to haunt us."

"Aye," agreed the chieftain, returning to his chair. "And that, Brother, brings us to the predicament of which I spoke earlier."

"Predicament!" Draga exploded. "There *is* no predicament! The course of action is clear enough to me! Our women have not had new baubles or fancies in an age! Our mead jars are cracked and tainted. We have not tasted good, fresh barley ale in so long that I have almost forgotten its flavor. And why? Because we are so afraid of Nemed MacAgnomain that we dare not venture out of the fens. But now, thanks to Balor the Lucky, the time has come for us to face that fear and Nemed before he destroys us! The time has come to open our battle chests, to bring out our raiment and weapons! We can take our few horses and go out as warriors to this new trading center of the Beaker Folk. If Nemed is there, we will kill him. If his spies are about, we will find them and slit their throats. And if anyone in the settlement tries to stop us, we will sack the place and burn it to the ground!"

To a man the clansmen rose to their feet, clamoring approval of Draga's words, shouting acclamations of their faith in their lord to become once again the Wolf of the Western Tribes. Even old Falcon was up, hopping from one foot to another, brandishing his fists. Balor was so excited that tears of happiness stung his eyes. Beside him Morrigan reached out and lay a warm, moist palm across his wrist.

"Wait," she whispered. "Watch. The lord rises. He shall speak true wisdom."

But what Balor heard did not please him—a cold, contemptuous rejection of Draga's emotional suggestions. Caustically

Fomor MacLir reminded them that although some of them might be bored by the peaceful life at Bracken Fen, a rich harvest was waiting to be brought in. He spoke of their pregnant wives and their newborn children. He spoke of the elderly, healthy now for the first time in several years. He spoke of the herd, with its new calves and sleek young bulls and fertile, fat heifers. He spoke of the young boys of the clan MacLir who had managed to grow to manhood, unmaimed and untested by battle. He spoke of the young girls who had blossomed into womanhood, never having known the grief of mourning for a lover or a father crippled or slain in war.

A hush fell over the room.

"Why then, my friends," he queried softly, "are you so ready to rush off to battle and death? Surely there are more acceptable cures for boredom. And there is a much better way to discover if, in fact, Nemed MacAgnomain is alive to threaten us."

Draga spoke. "We could pick up our tails, run, and hide again. But he'd only come after us. Sooner or later, if he lives, we are going to have to fight him." At last he sat down, mumbling nastily to himself.

"Perhaps." Quietly Fomor began to outline the plan that he had evidently been devising ever since he had come down from the tor.

"Knowing and appreciating your appetite for action, I must apologize for my plan's blandness, but as long as you name me lord, I will not lead you impulsively into battle. Our objective is to determine if Nemed MacAgnomain is alive. I have decided to travel to the new settlement with a hand-picked group of men. We will dress in our poorest, shabbiest garments. We will take oxen and carts, not horses. We will go into the trading center to barter cattle and items of little worth for such paltry things as beakers and beer and, to please our womenfolk, a few buttons and beads. We will stay long enough to discover what we need to know. There will be minimal gaming, minimal drinking, and minimal wenching, lest we inadvertently draw attention to ourselves and accidentally expose our identity."

"And what happens if Nemed is alive? What happens if he's actually there?" asked Lomna Ruad. His brother had been one of Manannan MacLir's trusted champions. He had died long ago, when Partholon's men had attacked the stronghold of the clan on the coast of Eireann.

Draga brightened. "We'll have to fight him then."

"Gladly," said Lomna Ruad, grinning without humor. "We'll be well armed. He won't be expecting us. We'll have our best fighters with us and—"

"It is not my intention to fight him. It is my intention to dupe him. You forget, old friend, that Nemed is a rich Achaean now. He'll not travel alone. Nor will he be without allies in any encampment. Our arms can be no match for his. No, the advantage will be all on one side, and if he has lived this long, you may be certain that he has infected others with his hatred of the clan MacLir. Even if I were to face and kill Nemed, his men would have our heads, and soon enough they would find our holding and destroy everyone and everything that we have worked to build and to secure."

"Then we shall bide our time until one of us finds him alone," Draga said. "We'll kill him then, and no one shall ever know who took his life!"

Fomor eyed his brother darkly. "And if we are found out, there shall be war."

"I, for one, am willing to take that risk!" protested the redbeard.

"Yes, of course. *You* would take the risk, and *I*, as chieftain, would bear the responsibility. No, we shall do this my way."

"And how would you dupe him?" Munremar was openly curious.

"Many years have passed since Nemed and I last met. No doubt time has marked us both since those dark days. I do not think that I would know his face, nor he mine. But I would know his eyes... never, even in the face of a battle-maddened warrior, have I seen such eyes. Black they were—a raven's eyes. Full of death, as though he grew strong upon it."

Munremar's brows came together across the bridge of his nose. "And such a man has sworn to kill you. To kill us all."

"Aye, and so I shall give to him the gift of our deaths," Fomor said, a wry twist to his face.

No one spoke. They were too stunned.

Fomor smiled. Then he laughed heartily. "It is the simplest thing in all the world! While we are at the settlement we shall let it be known through casual conversation that long ago every man, woman, and child of the clan MacLir was wiped out by a plague. It is a common enough occurrence. No one would have reason to doubt it. If Nemed lives, sooner or later he will hear our lies. And then, my friends, the people of MacAgnomain and the people of MacLir can live in peace, free from the hatred that binds them to the past."

"As long as he lives I cannot be free of that hatred!" spat Draga. "As long as he lives I will remember how they slew our father and mother and brothers and threw us into the sea to what should have been certain death! Indeed, Brother, I will not be at peace until, in the name of righteousness, Nemed MacAgnomain knows death at the hands of the clan MacLir and the Twelve Winds sing the sweet song of vengeance worked in our name!"

Fomor measured Draga as a parent might observe a beloved but misguided child. "Is vengeance truly so sweet? It was I who stole away Huldre, Nemed's woman. It was I who took off his father's head and gave the order that his kinsmen either be slain or enslaved. I have wrought enough vengeance upon Nemed MacAgnomain in this life. Perhaps we shall meet and do battle in the next; I do not know. But for now I would be content to know that he is no longer a threat to me. I have no wish to fight him."

Balor felt sick with disappointment. When Draga spoke out, he echoed the boy's thoughts.

"Is this the wisdom of the Wolf who once led us to glory? You would rob us of honor by using such a trick!"

Balor's eyes were burning, and a hot, gagging sob of shame escaped his lips. He choked it back as suddenly the tiny room seemed to be suffocating him.

"Where are you going?" Morrigan asked. "They've only just begun to debate."

He ignored her words as, in the darkness, he moved to find the coiled ladder and open the breach in the wall. The fresh, clean air of night cooled his face as he quietly lowered the ladder.

Morrigan whispered accusingly: "You're like the rest. You think glory can be achieved only through great, wanton displays of blood and death. But the lord knows there is a time for all things. Did you not listen? We are outmanned and out-armed. Our time for battle is over. It took courage for him to bring such a decision before the council. It will take all of the cunning of the Wolf for him to convince them of its rightness. I think that he is the wisest and the bravest man that I may ever know."

Balor was grateful for the darkness—he did not want Morrigan to see his tears. "He is not brave. He is not wise. He is not cunning." He wept and hated himself for his weakness. "He is everything that I hate! He is a coward!"

With that he climbed out and downward into the night. Morrigan leaned out of the breach, shaking her head as she whispered in acidic condemnation, "And you, Balor, son of Fomor, grandson of Manannan, are a fool!"

Balor was roused from sleep by the sound of chanting coming from the council hall. He did not remember coming home. He did not remember anything except his father's words: *"I have no wish to fight him."* He squeezed his eyes shut, trying to conjure images of his father as the Wolf, images to erase a young boy's shame. At last one came, and he saw his father as he had readied himself to battle the great storm. But then, unbidden, he heard the words that the lord had spoken to Huldre—Nemed's woman—*"The wolf in me has died. I shall not be a warrior again."*

Although Balor had not wanted to believe him, it was true. Balor stared at the chieftain's locked battle chest. Bitterness soured his mouth as he ground his teeth and vowed with a resolve that set him to trembling: "Someday," he whispered to the power of the Twelve Winds, "someday I will avenge Manannan's death. Someday when I am a man full grown, I shall open the chest, take up the great sword, and with the power of the Twelve Winds to serve me, the Retaliator will sing the song of battle once again. I will lead my people to glory, and I will not be afraid."

8

Fomor was to have his way. The "trading" party was assembled in less than a day, and the scrawniest cows were culled from the herd to be driven to the settlement for trading. The group left the holding while birds awoke to herald the rising of the sun. It was a dawn with the hint of autumn chill to it. As the party moved forward into the awakening day, their breath congealed and hovered before their faces.

Balor, with the big terrier Sure Snout trotting faithfully beside him, walked behind the huge, heavily laden, four-wheeled oxcart. He had not wanted to come, but since there was an element of danger involved, the two lads who would serve as fetch-and-carry boys for the women who would cook for the band had been chosen by lot. No volunteers had been accepted, nor had any lad in good health been allowed to demur. The bag that held the Stones of Choosing was passed around by Munremar, and each boy closed his eyes, reached in, and drew out a single pebble. All the pebbles save two were black. Tethra withdrew a white stone and hooted with pleasure, for he would have volunteered had such an option been possible. When Balor's turn came, he too withdrew a white stone, but it was Draga who laughed aloud, proclaiming with a joviality that had an undertone of nastiness: "It seems that once again the Fates have called you forth, Nephew! Truly, you *are* the lucky one!"

But Balor did not feel lucky. Oh, yes, there was pleasure knowing that he was setting out from the fens to the far shore of the Western Sea, across lands that he had never seen before, to the settlement of the Beaker Folk with all of its wonders and enticements. But he was clad in rags, with mud smeared in his hair and on his body. He was not going forth proudly, traveling steadfastly and boldly as the firstborn son of the Wolf of the Western Tribes. No. He was traveling in stealth and deceit, because the Wolf, whom he had so adored only days ago, was now clearly no wolf at all. He was only a coward who feared an enemy who, for all anyone knew, was dead and turned to dust or ashes long ago.

Balor's right hand closed around the little hawk-shaped amulet that Huldre had forced upon him. She had placed it about his neck as he had prepared to leave the holding. They had been alone in the chieftain's roundhouse.

"You must wear this, my son," she had said. "It is the Eye of Donar. Like the true hawk, in whose guise the god is often seen, the amber hawk sees all things. Let no one set eyes upon it lest its power be turned against you. Its magic is for you alone."

She placed her hands on his shoulders and studied him, her pale eyes mirroring the face so much like her own, so unlike the rest of the clan. "Although you do not wish it, you *must* go, Balor. Draga is right, you know. The Fates *have* chosen you. I have known it from the day of your birth. You must begin to learn of the world beyond the fens, Balor. As firstborn son of the Wolf, it will be yours someday."

"I do not believe that the Wolf is still a wolf," he told her. "I do not believe that he shall ever be a wolf again."

Her pale brows arched toward her hairline. Something rose and darkened within her clear blue eyes; like a gathering of semitransparent fish, it schooled, then broke, causing the blue to shimmer like rain patterns upon the surface of a storm-shadowed pool.

Distracted, he had spoken a truth he had not intended to share with anyone. "I am no longer proud to call him Father."

She drew in a little breath, took her son's hands. "If Nemed lives, the Wolf will rise again. You must believe that. It must be so."

"And if Nemed is dead?"

"A man must be what he has been born to be, Balor. The Wolf *must* live as a wolf. If he continues to walk inside an alien skin, he will suffocate."

The memory disturbed him. As he walked along behind the oxcart, his hand tightened about the amulet. How warm it was, as though a living spirit had breathed life into it. Could he feel his own pulse beating through the substance of the stone, or was it the heartbeat of the amulet itself? He released the talisman, and it fell under his tunic, as hot as a heart torn from a living beast.

He stopped. What if the amulet truly did have magic powers? Truly *was* the Eye of Donar? Surely then, it could see into his heart and might even have the power to grant a wish to him.

Morrigan would scoff at such an idea, but she was only a nine-year-old girl, even though she was the Wise One's daughter. Why should he believe her? At Munremar's request she was along on the expedition so that she might purchase certain items much needed in his work as a healer; his age made the journey too much of an undertaking, and so

Fomor had allowed the girl to travel as his representative. Her knowledge of the old man's medicines was extraordinary for one her age. But in the soft blue light of morning she was nowhere to be seen.

He trembled as, hesitantly, then boldly, he stuck his hand down through the lacings of his tunic and allowed his fingers to close fiercely around the small, hawk-shaped talisman. He closed his eyes so tightly that his lids ached and multicolored stars flared to life beneath them. Only the god, Donar the Hawk, Donar the Thunderer, Donar the Guardian of All the World, would know his wish.

"Let Nemed be alive! Let the Wolf rise to do battle with him! Let the clansmen of MacLir once again know pride in a life of glory!"

The stars beneath his lids suddenly flamed into a burning flare of heat and light, which seemed to fuse his lids together. He saw the sun and the moon shining against a vast black plain, with Fomor standing between them, his bow held high, an arrow pulled taut. And then the arrow flew in a great, soaring arc. But it was not an arrow. It was a shooting star. And Fomor was not Fomor. He was a pale-haired stranger with the proportions of a god, and a white wolf ran at his side with star-fire in its eyes.

"Donar!"

With a start, he opened his eyes. He had cried the name aloud. As the world came back into focus he felt foolish; his vision had been no vision at all. He had been daydreaming. Yes—he was very tired, and it was very early. The rationalization was reassuring, yet oddly disappointing. Blaheen, one of the two middle-aged cook-women, stared back at him from the front of the cart where she sat at the reins with Tethra beside her.

"What was that you said, boy?"

"Me? I . . . er . . . nothing . . ."

"Dozing on your feet, were you? Well, you're welcome to ride up here with us, if you like. But if you've a mind to walk, watch where you be stepping. We're not out of the boglands yet."

From the first the cook-women worked him and hazel-eyed, sandy-haired Tethra hard, but the boys did not mind. It was the first time in Balor's life that he had traveled any distance, and it was in the company of men, with each member of the group having work and responsibilities. He found it a heady feeling to be treated as an adult, more satisfying than food or mead or sleep. Why was it, he wondered, that being but a boy sat so uncomfortably on his shoulders?

The days were long, spent walking ever southward, driving the cattle ahead of them. Draga was there, with Gar and Nia. Dathen, with a handful of others who had once been battle champions, kept close to Fomor. Prudent, trustworthy Lomna Ruad had remained behind, in charge of the holding, but old Falcon was along, supervising the cattle, and he had Mael and his grandson Rinn with him. Oblin was there too. At night he slept in the cart with his wife, Enda, but not until late, for he usually gambled with the others or joined with them in games of wit. They traveled each day until the sun was nearly down, and then they set up encampments beneath the sky, keeping warm not only by their night fires, but by their comradery and unity of purpose.

For reasons Balor could not understand, there seemed to be some wonderful intoxicant in everything he saw or smelled, touched or tasted. Not even Morrigan's presence could dull the days for him. Colors and landscapes had never seemed to be in sharper focus. Gruel had never tasted so good. The touch of the tracings that guided the oxen, the feel of his own pale hair as he twisted it into a braid each morning, the sensation of good, gritty earth against his fingers as he used it to scour out the cooking pots after the meal at day's end, all set his senses tingling. He hopped from one task to another eagerly, as energetic as a water ouzel bobbing in a pool.

"And who lit the fire under you, laddie?" queried Enda. Horse-jawed and snaggle-toothed, she wore a little leather cap on her head. Tied tightly beneath her chin, its purpose was to bind up the first signs of wattle and to hide her balding head. Balor had always liked her.

She and her friend Blaheen had been chosen with great care. Not only were they excellent cooks, but more important, they would encourage no would-be suitors who might prove to be a source of trouble at the Beaker Folk settlement. If Enda was aging and plain, Blaheen was the antithesis of the very concept of femininity. She was the target of much humor

at the holding because her name meant Little Flower, yet she
was as tall and muscular as a man, with a sunburned face as
meaty as a hog's. She had warts on her chin from which
brittle white whiskers sprouted. When she threw back her
head to laugh, which was often, her earlobes wiggled and her
teeth showed like mushrooms sprouting out of green moss.
But she was a robust and good-natured soul with a sense of
humor and zest for life that made her welcome everywhere.
She had outlived two husbands and doted on children, her
own or anyone else's.

For reasons that totally eluded Balor, she even liked Morrigan
and openly fussed over the girl, savoring her company, while
with the boys she was a sterner taskmistress than Enda,
driving Balor and Tethra from dawn to dusk. Yet it was
Blaheen who personally saw to it that they received more
than their share from the gruel pot and roasting spits, and
who made certain there was room for them beneath the
oxcart so that they might sleep sheltered. She treated them
with equal harshness or concern, granting Balor no special
consideration because he was the chieftain's son. The boy was
grateful for this.

He felt shame and betrayal at the very sight of the
chieftain, and prayed that Donar and the Twelve Winds
would cause the Wolf to rise again from the skin of the
coward. Until that day, if it ever came, Balor had made up his
mind to prove to his clansmen that although he was Fomor's
son, he was not a coward. Nor would he ever wilt from any
task assigned to him, as he felt his father had shirked his
duties as lord of the clan MacLir by refusing to flush out the
clan's mortal enemy and kill him.

The days passed quickly. When night would fall, after Balor
and Tethra had seen to the oxen and gobbled their fill of
whatever was reserved in the pot or on the spits for them,
they would finish their chores and then crawl under the
oxcart, doing their best to drive the ever-present Morrigan
away. She would pout and hold her ground, and they would
ignore her as they lay awake with Sure Snout curled close
beside Balor, the boys watching the men as they lounged
around the campfire. Now and again there would be im-
promptu wrestling matches, or two men would match their

skill with staves. The boys watched with delight while others wagered and took odds as to who would be the winner. Draga was always the winner at wrestling except once, when Dathen took him down and pinned him fast.

On the third night Fomor was coerced by the others to put his "little brother" in his place. The lord had chosen to keep to himself, retiring early, allowing his clansmen to enjoy their sport without him. But now Draga and the others would not hear nay from him. At last he rose and cast off his cloak and tunic. A cheer went up as he shook himself like a hunting hound coming up out of water. He was ready for all comers and obviously enjoying the challenge.

Balor could barely breathe. Fomor and Draga had not engaged in mock combat for over a year. Dathen tossed a stave to the chieftain. It was a long, time-smoothed length of hardwood half the span of a fighting man's wrist and half his height. Fomor tested its weight and found it to his liking. He and Draga circled close in the firelit darkness, and everyone saw the redbeard's wide, white grin as he spoke softly to his brother, taunting him.

"This is like old times, Brother. It's been too long since I've seen you act the warrior."

"Aye . . . perhaps it has at that. I think I will enjoy giving you a trouncing once again."

The circling continued. Then stopped. Then commenced again, in reverse.

"Beware, Fomor. The Wolf is older, and this cub has grown since last we sparred."

"True," the lord agreed, his glittering eyes never leaving Draga's face. "But the Wolf still has his teeth. And the cub . . . has he grown in brawn or brain? Knowing the cub as I do, I doubt it is the latter. So be wary, Brother. The Wolf outweighs you in both weight and wit."

Laughter went up in the camp as the men responded with pleasure to the usual insulting banter that went on between opponents before—and after—the first blows were struck.

Balor rose from beneath the oxcart to stand stock-still, one hand on the forward wheel of the cart. He stared at the circling twosome with such intensity that he forgot to blink until his eyes began to burn and tear. Was this what he had prayed for? Was his sire shedding his coward skin and becoming the Wolf again, as Huldre had prophesied?

Slowly now, the circling grew more measured, and then suddenly, with a cry ripped from his belly, Draga leaped high, and the match was on in earnest. His stave hissed out and would have broken Fomor's neck had it struck him, but the blow was parried expertly, and Draga stepped back, laughing and nodding appreciation of his opponent's move.

"Well done!" cried Dathen.

"Aye, and so!" agreed Draga. "The Wolf has not forgotten how to fight. How is it, Brother? Does your blood not run hot with the memory?"

But no answer was offered as the fierce dance of power continued. They leaped. They whirled. The great, hardwood staves clashed and strained as the weight of the two giants went against them. In the light of the cooking fires, against the blackness of the night, the brothers gleamed gold with sweat and their long, loose hair seemed aflame.

It was over quickly. A few more moves, and then suddenly, with an expulsion of air, as if from a bull being dropped to its knees, Draga was flat on his back with Fomor standing over him. The chieftain held his stave like a spear, pointing it at the redbeard's throat. One thrust and Draga would have been mortally wounded.

"I concede," said the downed man, grinning broadly. "The match is yours."

A smiling Fomor extended his free hand to Draga and laughed heartily as he pulled the stave back. "Well fought, Brother. Well fought, indeed!"

Draga took his brother's hand and allowed himself to be jerked upward to his feet. He was slippery with sweat, wheezing and straining to even out his breathing. He pounded his brother on the back, well pleased. It had been a good, clean bout, and Draga was exhilarated from having seen the chieftain with a weapon in his hand. He looked at Fomor, his eyes aglow, and said, "Had I been Nemed, you'd have broken me in half. It could have been. It could yet be! By the power of the Twelve Winds, Brother, if he's alive, face him, kill him. Put an ending to it!"

Silence fell. Balor's hand sought the amulet in the darkness.

Now, he thought. *Now! By the power of the Twelve Winds . . . in the name of Donar, guardian of all the world . . . let the Wolf rise now!*

But the Wolf did not rise. Fomor MacLir's face then

hardened until no emotion showed. He looked at Draga as if at a stranger. "You have learned to fight like a wolf, little Brother. It is a pity that you have yet to learn to think like one. I hope that I have not made a mistake by thinking that you might be an asset to this party." He hurled his stave away with disgust and stalked out of the circle of firelight and into the darkness.

Balor did not watch the gaming after that. When his work was done, he took up his cloak and, with Sure Snout trailing close behind like an ever-present shadow, sought solitude at the periphery of the encampment. When the fires began to burn low, Blaheen would ferret him out and drive him back beneath the shelter of the cart to sleep. By then it would be late and Tethra and Morrigan would be asleep. Thankful that he would not have to talk, Balor would lie awake watching the stars walk across the sky in the slow, inexorable procession that marked the passing of time until eventually he would fall asleep.

Then, one morning, there was a different sound to the world, a different scent. He stuck his head out from beneath the cart to see that fog lay heavy upon the land. Somewhere, high above in the gray belly of the mists, gulls circled and cried, and far off something enormous slurred and hissed like the wheezing breath of a giant.

Balor scooted out from beneath the cart. He took in a breath. The air was thick and cold and tasted of salt.

Tethra had already risen. He stood beside Blaheen and Morrigan, sniffing like a curious young hound. "There's something different about this fog."

Blaheen snorted and looked at Tethra as though she could not believe that anyone could be so ignorant. "Why, 'tis the sea, boy! 'Tis the wide, dark sea!"

The lord had led them far to the south before he had turned them westward. Now they would travel north, along the coast, so that they might approach the holding from the south. It was a part of Fomor's plan, so no stranger might know the true direction from which they had come.

For the first time since they had left the holding, they began to see other people. Tiny fishing hamlets dotted the cliff tops and coves, and here and there an isolated farmstead sat upon the headlands. Although the travelers avoided all unnecessary contact, when strangers would come upon them, Fomor would greet them.

Balor would cringe in these situations, for the lord of the clan MacLir did not go forward as a chieftain. He sidled like a simpering cur, affecting the speech of the baseborn and the manner of an imbecile who imagines himself to be clever, and using the name he had chosen for the duration of the journey.

"Good day to ye," he would say to them. "I's Scallatha, head o' this here band. Come here from the south, we has, looking to barter our cows. Heard there's a trading center northwards o' these parts that has need o' beef."

The reply was always the same. "Aye. Up to Point of Ale is where you'd be headed then. There's Beaker Folk there." They would titter then, not always politely. "And bathhouses!"

Fomor would finger his lips and mimic with the laugh of an idiot. "Bathhouses, ye say? Well, as ye can no doubt see, me an' me kin here, we're not much for baths. But we do know what to do with a beaker o' ale, eh?"

The clansmen would agree to a man, boisterously echoing Fomor and evidently enjoying the game that he had set them to. But Balor felt sick with shame. The chieftain had chosen the name Scallatha with great care. It meant filthy or muddy. And Fomor had seen to it that his kinsmen were certainly those and more: They had not been allowed to wash since they had left the holding. They wore their hair and beards uncombed and unplaited. They reeked, and their garments had begun to attract flies. As a final insult, the helmet Fomor had chosen to proclaim his rank was the most disreputable headgear that Balor had ever seen—horned, with earflaps of frayed leather and a chin strap of cow tails. One horn, fractured and discolored, turned up and slightly forward; the other was snag-tipped and twisted downward so that now and again, when the fancy took him, he would whistle into it and giggle like an amused child.

Balor was not amused—nor was Draga, if the boy could judge from the scowl on his uncle's face—but everyone else seemed quite pleased with Fomor's charade. No one in all of the world would ever guess that this motley band of travelers were members of the clan MacLir or that the filthy, simpering idiot who led them was, in fact, the Wolf of the Western Tribes.

They first sighted Point of Ale, the trading center of the Beaker Folk, at noon, beneath a breaking cloud cover, with seabirds reeling overhead and a rainbow shimmering across the sky.

Enda drew up the oxen and pointed. "Look! 'Tis a good omen, that!"

They all came to pause, while Falcon and Mael and Rinn trotted around the cattle to bring them to a halt. Since they had set out before dawn, the beasts were weary and therefore easily collected into a small, milling group. They stood passively, heads bent to crop at the brittle grasses and tender wildflowers of the headlands.

The settlement was still a fair distance away, rising on a low, wide peninsula, which eased itself outward into the sea. Balor stared, spellbound, for never had he seen so many buildings in one place. There were stockades and houses, lean-tos and little fenced gardens. Yet his eyes were drawn past the complex of the trading center and downward to the calm, blue bay, sheltered from the wind by the curl of the land.

What lay upon the sleek skin of that bay took Balor's breath away. Ships, boats, vessels of every size and description moved in and out of the bay or lay upon the water like seabirds at rest. The boy's heart was filled with awe at the sight of them.

Which were like his father's ships had been?

A tremor went through him, deep and hot, and for a moment he imagined that he saw the ships catch fire and burn. His father's ships. Manannan's ships. *His* ships. Yes! They *would* have been his had his father not ordered them burned. In time, as firstborn of the MacLir, he would have *made* them his! His father had destroyed his very birthright on that day, the privilege of sailing as a raider, his magic sword pointing toward a red horizon, toward yet undiscovered enemies-to-be—

"Balor..."

A hand touched his shoulder. He wheeled, startled. Fomor had come to stand beside him.

"I want to talk to you, Balor."

The boy stared up at him, dressed in rags, with unkempt hair, and a battle-helmet in his hand that made an obscene joke of the word *warrior*. Something turned and twisted in his gut, something ugly and black and foul with hatred and frustration. "Why should I want to talk to you? I do not even want to look at you! You are not my father!"

He fled then. He ran until his heart was beating in his ears and he thought that he would be sick. He ran until he tripped and fell, and only then, when he lay sprawled and stunned in the deep, prickling grasses of the headlands, did he realize that he was bawling like a babe.

He was given no time to regret his outburst. Blaheen's yodeling called him back to work, even as Sure Snout came bounding after him.

The traveling band was setting up camp on the cliffs within sight of the settlement when Balor reluctantly returned to the wagon. He was just in time to see a small group of mounted representatives from the trading center gallop imperiously into the gathering of clansmen.

There were six of them astride large, fine horses with elaborate trappings that glinted in the sun. Two of the men set Balor to gaping, for he had never seen such dark and swarthy people in his life. They had round, sharp-featured faces, with short, neatly cut beards, but no mustaches. Their hair, like their oiled beards, shining in the sun, was raven black and as curly as combed sheep's wool. All were impressively armed with copper-headed spears, sheathed knives at their belts, and strange, intriguingly short bows slung across their backs. One of the fairer men—the leader of the group, Balor knew by the arrogant way in which he sat his horse—had an ax rammed through his belt by its haft. Tethra nudged Balor and whispered in awe, "Look at that ax, would you! Have you ever seen the like?" Balor had not. The head of the ax was not of stone; it was of copper, and it lay against the man's side like the shining, silken head of a golden serpent. From the way it gleamed in the sunlight, Balor surmised that its bite would be deadly.

The man who wore it brought his horse to a stop with a brutal yank on his reins. He was big and tanned from the sun, with protruding, watery blue eyes, flowing mustaches, and long, weather-bleached brown braids. Beneath his well-made garments his muscular body tended toward fat. Life was evidently good in the settlement of the Beaker Folk.

Fomor approached him, sidling close with the obsequious deference of a dog not certain if it is about to be beaten. "Good day to ye," he said. "An' who might ye be, an' what might ye want o' this poor an' simple company?"

The man appraised him with open contempt. When he spoke, his voice was thickened by an accent that Balor would in later years come to associate with certain tribes from Land Beyond the Sea. "I be—I mean I *am* Horsa, factor of Point of Ale. What is your business here?"

"Why, I's Scallatha, head o' this good an' peaceful band," Fomor replied, bowing like a maid, not like a man. "We's come up to Point o' Ale to trade our beef for beer an' pleasures an' what small items of barter that the likes o' us poor souls can afford."

The factor's eyes narrowed in well-practiced speculation as he raised himself to look out across the gathering to where the herd grazed and lowed. He scowled. "There's more horn and hide upon those hooves than meat, man."

"We's come a long way," said Fomor.

"Well, the luck of whatever gods you pray to must be with you, for we have a large party of Stone Worshipers here on some sort of pilgrimage up the coast. They are not picky about what they eat. A queer lot, studying and measuring the stars. Not much for trading or manly pleasures. But they do eat. And this time of year the center's its busiest. We can use all the extra meat we can get, scrawny as it is. But don't expect to turn much of a profit from it."

Fomor moaned and extended his hands upward, palms out, fingers splayed. "But 'tis prime stock!" he wailed, as though he were a child just deprived of his mother, father, and all of his kin. "We's come so far. Surely ye'll not cheat us o' the fruits o' our labors?"

"Cheat?" The factor snorted. "It is I who shall be cheated, you filthy cur! We'd get more meat from a pound of seawater than we'll get from your cows!"

*   *   *

The sun was still high when the first of the tradesmen came out to eye the herd, and it was not yet dusk when all but a few of the animals had been sold and herded off by their new owners to the slaughtering pens, which stood on the periphery of the settlement. Not one of the clansmen, including Fomor, had expected such a quick and successful sale. The factor had evidently not exaggerated the settlement's need for fresh meat. No doubt many of the cows would be on roasting spits before nightfall.

The boys stood by and watched, with Morrigan close by in her tomboy's clothes and ragged braids, as enthralled as they by the sight of so many strange-looking people within the encampment. Horsa himself returned with his men to make certain he would not be cheated of the factor's share of the profits.

Order was maintained and tallies were taken as little clots of people of varying sizes and colors gathered to squabble with Fomor and the clansmen. Now and again loud storms of disagreement in strange languages brought individuals nearly to blows. And then, as though an invisible signal had been given, the bartering was done and Horsa and his men were driving cattle and clamoring, quarreling humanity back to the settlement, cursing and cajoling as they went.

Although the boys did not understand much of what they had just witnessed, they were amazed to see that the camp was now full of baskets and beakers, and Fomor MacLir was happily festooned from chest to nose with necklace upon necklace of small shells. He stood with his arms held high, turning slowly so that all might see and appreciate the necklaces.

"Look at all that we've reaped," piped Blaheen, beaming as the children came to stand beside her at the wagon. "And we've not even brought out the trade stuffs from the wagon. Don't stand there gawking, boys! And you, Morrigan, get yourself ready. We'll be going out to the settlement now. It is a fair sight for one who's had little more than marsh frogs to barter with over these past long years!"

Tethra was staring off toward Fomor as the lord began to chat with Draga and Dathen. The two men seemed captivated by the shell necklaces, and more than pleased as Fomor began to remove them and hand them out. "What'd anybody want *them* for?" asked the boy.

Blaheen stopped examining a small, beautifully decorated beaker to stare at him. "Them necklaces is made of cowries. 'Tis a foreign word, cowrie. It means little pigs because some folks thinks that's what they looks like. Valuable as gold, is cowries. Use'm as money, boys."

Balor and Tethra exchanged looks. Then Balor broke the silence, shrugging yet again. "What's money?" he asked.

She nearly dropped the beaker. "By the Twelve Winds! We *have* been in the fens too long!"

They went out from the encampment at dusk, after lots had been drawn—Dathen was chosen to stay behind with the dogs and the few remaining head of cattle to guard their belongings. Tomorrow he would take his turn at pleasure while the others would choose lots to stay behind. As the sun set beyond the western rim of the world, the calm, deep waters of the bay turned as dark and as smooth as slate in the soft light of the dying day.

Fomor had given each man, woman, and boy an equal share of the cowrie-shell necklaces. And then, as he gathered his people around him, he gave them a warning: "Remember, if there is any trouble from any of you, I shall personally see to it that the offender is skinned as close to the bone as a well-cut fillet. Horsa has welcomed us into the trading center, but he has also assured me that the Laws of Honor are strictly enforced: Thieves will be publicly blinded. Manslayers will be impaled. Any man who sets upon a woman by force shall be castrated. And anyone who deliberately does damage to another's wares shall suffer the loss of a hand. So be wise. Be wary. And at all times remember the purpose of our journey. You are to listen for word of Nemed MacAgnomain, and if you should hear anyone mention the name of the clan MacLir, you are to assure them that, as far as you know, it has ceased to exist. Now let us drink together to bind us to our purpose." His head nodded toward Enda, a signal that she was to fetch the mead horn. She scurried off to the wagon, where the big, now nearly empty crock of mead from the holding stood in the shade of a wheel. A horn of a bull fashioned into a drinking vessel hung from the rim of the jar by a hook, which had been inserted into the horn for that purpose. Enda filled the horn to brimming from the crock. As she hurried back to the circle, dark liquid flecked with dregs from the bottom of the jar sloshed over her fingers and ran down her forearm.

Balor winced at the lord's toast as he took the horn and raised it high.

"We shall now reaffirm that to which we have all agreed before the sacred altar of the Twelve Winds. To assure the life of the clan, let us now drink to its 'death' and to the hope that we shall discover that Nemed MacAgnomain is also dead, so we may return to Bracken Fen to live in peace."

He drank. The horn went round the circle as each in turn drank from it. Draga scowled into the cup as he tipped it back, swallowed, then backhanded his mouth as though he wished to keep his gorge from rising. Balor shared his uncle's feelings, and when the horn came to him, he stood staring into it as though it contained poison. All watched him until Blaheen, who stood beside him, jabbed him and whispered down imperatively out of the corner of her mouth: "What's the matter with you, boy? Drink! All must drink!"

The warning in her whisper was unmistakable. He was grateful, for he had momentarily forgotten that Fomor had drawn them into a circle. This had not been done without purpose. The circle was the symbol of life everlasting, of things bound one to another from birth through death and then through birth again. To refuse to drink to a vow sworn within a circle was to put oneself outside of that circle and beyond the brotherhood of the clan forever. And this, despite his feelings toward his father's strategy, was something that Balor would never do.

And so he drank—even though it sickened him to do so.

The peninsula upon which the settlement had been built came up out of the sea like a huge, broad-backed whale. Where the back of the whale dipped and narrowed toward its tail, it met the coast, forming a natural windbreak, a harbor as welcoming as any seaman could desire.

Even a landsman could see the potential of the location, and as the travelers approached it, the lord explained to the younger men that the settlement was no doubt a stopover for those en route to or from the far island or the Great Glen, which was the major trade route running along the rift that cleft the northern backbone of the island of Albion.

"The world turns on trade," he said. "Vast tides of men moving back and forth across the land and seas . . . all of them hungry . . . all of them itching to satisfy appetites for items unavailable in their native lands."

As they walked the well-worn trail that ran along the cliffs and then downward to the long, curving shore where it intersected with the main path leading up to the settlement itself, they saw that they were not the only traders to have made encampments on the periphery of the trading center.

"Only the gods know how far some of them have come," commented Fomor. "Magan, Tarshish, Ophir, Thule . . . aye, you'll find them all here. And you'll find much to distract within the settlement. Though I would have you take your pleasures freely, do not forget our purpose here."

Balor was in no mood to listen, or to keep close company with anyone. He shouted at Morrigan when she sought to keep stride with him, and his sullen behavior soon sent Tethra walking on ahead. As they came out onto the beach, Balor fell back from the others, gawking openly at the fishmongers. If possible, they were even dirtier than Fomor's band. In the deepening dusk they lounged beneath squalid little makeshift shelters while their women hunkered over smoky fires of driftwood and dried seagrass, roasting tiny skewered fish and boisterously hawking them to anyone who passed by. The fish smelled delicious, so enticing that Balor found himself drawn by the crook of a hag's finger. She eyed his cowrie necklaces with obvious greed and gestured to him that one string of shells would win him a fish. He was about to complete the trade when old Falcon came up behind him and put an end to the deal.

"Give her three cowries for the fish, boy. Not a shell more!"

The woman eyed the old man as though she wished to skewer and roast him. She shouted at him in a foreign tongue to which he responded with a negative shaking of his head. He gave Balor a little shove as indication that they should walk away, and as they began to do so, the woman suddenly shrieked as though she had been mortally wounded. She held up three fingers with a moan of acquiescence.

Balor unstrung three shells, retied the necklace, gave the woman her cowries, and took the fish, startled as she began to wail.

"Pay her no mind," advised Falcon, guiding him away. "You must learn to haggle with these people, boy. They're experienced traders and will take advantage of a callow youth. If you learn nothing else this journey, learn this: Believe yourself strong and clever, and others will believe it of you . . . and when they believe it, you will know that it is true! So walk with a strut and a swagger, lad, as if you knew where you were going and what you would have when you got there! But be not so bold that others will itch to knock you down. Stick close to old Falcon here. I'll see to it that you stay on your feet if you've a mind to learn the way of it!"

They walked together in silence while Balor ate his fish. Then, bending to remove his shoes, the youth yielded to the desire to feel the sea against his skin. The beach was stony and it hurt his feet, but the water was as clear as the amber of Huldre's amulet and as cold and colorless as her eyes. It soothed him as he waded into it and allowed the gentle ebb and flow of the surf to wash about his ankles.

The fish had made him thirsty. He bent, scooping up a palmful of the sea, then brought it up to his face, where he tasted its brew and licked his lips.

"'Tis salty," he said, smiling, "and sweeter than mead."

Old Falcon stood by the water's edge, watching the boy out of rheumy eyes. "Spoken like a true son of the clan MacLir," he said. "Sons of the Sea. Aye, that name fit us like a good, tight skin once—in the days when we were sea raiders."

The words caused the boy to rise and look off down the beach, past where small boats lay at rest, to where the first of the quays jutted out into the sea and larger vessels lay at anchor. "Which of those ships are like Manannan's?"

The old man squinted against distance and time. "None. Ours were large, though. Sleek keeled. Double prowed. Broad beamed. Long beaked too, with wolves' heads carved into the prows. There was room for thirty oarsmen in most— some were even larger. Great, proud green-sailed ships they were, with Manannan's own vessel, *Wave Sweeper*, greatest of all, built to strike fear into all who looked upon them. There were those of us who wept when the lord set torch to them. But he was right to do it. Aye, he was, although it took a wiser and a braver man than I to see it. But come away now. The days of the MacLir are gone forever. We's men of Scallatha now! And there's good ale waiting for us up there in the settlement, and a thousand sights and experiences to intrigue and educate a lad who has never been out of the fens!"

Old Falcon was right. Although he assured Balor that as trading centers went, Point of Ale was relatively small, to Balor it was overwhelming.

Halfway up from the beach they lost the scent of the sea and were awash in a tide of aromas. From the far side of the settlement, the wind carried the stink of the stock pens and slaughter yards to mix with the smell of hides curing on tanning frames and of wool set to dry or to soak in dye vats. There was the smell of food too; of fish and meat, boiling and frying and roasting, and of bread being baked. There was the pure, rank smell of humanity, washed and unwashed, scented and reeking. And mixed into it all there was an all-pervasive stench that was totally unfamiliar and offensive.

Old Falcon's big, flappy nostrils flared. He grinned like a happy fool. "Do you smell that, boy? Ach! There's no smell like that in the world! 'Tis barley beer abrewing, and no one can brew it better than the Beaker Folk."

Balor wrinkled up his nose. "Yuch!"

"Yuch indeed! They've taken a monopoly on nearly all of the major trading centers from the Western Isles to their homeland along the great river that they call Rhine. And not because they're famed for the fine crocks and beakers that their women make, or for their reputation as great tinkerers in copper, which they are . . . but what average man can afford copper? And there's the crux of it! Everyone can afford a beaker o' barley beer! These days a trader can't seal a deal without a cup o' ale to toast it, not if he wants to be taken seriously." Falcon pointed toward the main stockade. "There's the vats that they brew it in. And look back down to the bay. You can see those big crocks lined up along the quays. They're full of ale, I'll bet, ready to be shipped to all of the known ports in the world!" He paused to fill himself with the scent of it. "Ach! Ecstasy! Have you ever smelled anything to equal it, boy?"

Balor sniffed, then nodded, shrugging to show that he was unimpressed. "It smells like piss to me. You'll not get me to drink it!"

The old man gasped as though the boy had spoken a blasphemy. He cuffed the lad sharply. "Watch your mouth, lad. Around here, an opinion like that might well cost you your head!"

9

If he had been given a month to explore the trading center, Balor would still have felt lost. There was no plan to the place. Everything rose helter-skelter. A main stockade was built around a cluster of older structures, and the factor's quarters were there, facing the sea and taking advantage of the view that would alert the settlement to all comers—friendly or otherwise. There were fortifications and well-kept walkways, but beyond that point all was confusion.

There were roundhouses and longhouses, open spaces and palisaded enclosures; there were shops and stalls and eating establishments, little more than tented areas or open spaces in which benches were set up around braziers. There were potters' sheds, where beakers and vessels of all shapes and sizes were made and displayed, there were grain shops and bakeries and hostels, which were little more than thatched roofs beneath which weary travelers might take shelter for the cost of only a few cowries. There were gaming pits in which animals were set to fight while men gathered to make wagers. Nearby, a healer who specialized in the ills of smaller beasts treated wounds and mange and feather blight and, rumor had it, sold those beasts he could not heal to the neighboring vendor, who specialized in meat pasties.

There were sellers of shoes and sellers of clothing. There were women who would wash a man's hair and pick the nits from it with copper tweezers for the turn of an extra cowrie. There were bathhouses and gambling houses and houses where, old Falcon said, women could be bought, but for only a span of time; there were wide, roped-off areas in which wrestling and sparring matches were held. Not far away a hunchbacked woman sold caged fowl. A ragged, cruel-eyed child hobbled close in her wake, ready to dispatch the bird on the spot with a dull-edged stone ax so that the buyer could take his purchase to be scalded, defeathered, and roasted by a blind old hag nearby, who performed this service for a reasonable fee.

Balor stayed close to Falcon, enthralled by the sights, the sounds, the scents. As darkness fell, torchlight illuminated streets and alleyways paved with plank and wattling. Balor and Falcon paused to watch a coppersmith pour molten metal into molds where it would cool for later refining. Balor stared at the stacked ingots of the metal, and then in awe, reached out to touch several examples of smith's art on display. Daggers. Arm bands. And an ax that set his heart to racing with pure wanting, for it was a bold and deadly and beautiful ax, such as he had seen at Horsa's waist. But before he could inquire as to how many cowries it cost, Falcon read his mind. With an elbow jab that was clearly meant to silence him, the old man scolded him.

"What's the matter with you, lad? Wasting my good time here! What would herdsmen such as the likes of us do with such wasteful things as these? These are rich man's trinkets. Come away now. There is nothing here to interest a common man."

Reluctantly, Balor obeyed.

Ale shops were at nearly every turn, and at nearly every one old Falcon sampled at least one brimming beaker of beer. Although the boy refused to taste the sour brew, he did not mind waiting for the old man. He used the time to ogle the endless variety of objects offered for sale in the neighboring stalls and shops. He traded nearly half of his cowrie shells for a long coil of exquisitely cured and curled sinew, which he would use to restring his bow when he returned to the holding. Then he bought a bowl of hot, spiced milk in which oysters had been cooked and left to lie, slippery sweet within their shells. He drank the broth and sucked the shells clean of meat, then wandered to a stall where baubles were displayed. He would have liked to linger, but a burly, hawk-eyed man with a pocked face and a ring in his nose warned him off.

He found old Falcon not far away, chatting with Oblin the Stonecutter in front of the large stall of a flint merchant. It was an enormous, leather-canopied booth, with great bags and baskets of varying types of flint stacked high and trays set out on the ground to display various samples of blanks, which men could buy and then have finished according to their needs. Falcon and Balor watched as Oblin traded shells for some small flints he would use as arrowheads, and then began to haggle with the flint merchant over a larger, beautifully proportioned piece, which Balor saw at once would make an axhead to envy.

He listened, fascinated as the two men argued.

"Now look at this," Oblin was saying as he held up the roughly chiseled blank. "This is a fair piece. But you're asking far too much for it. See here—this shadow running crosswise through the rock?—it'll split clean through and shatter as soon as the stone's worked. There's not a flint knapper alive who could cut more than a child's axhead out of this, and not a very sound one at that."

"Come back tomorrow by the light of noon, and I'll have made you a man's ax out of it. But you'll pay an honest man's price."

"I do my own knapping, thank you. I'll give you half of what you're asking. And even at that you'll have skinned me in the deal!"

The flint merchant was not buying any of Oblin's argument. "What do you take me for, eh? That's porphyry you're handling, man! It's damned near as rare as greenstone from the Land of the North Wind. It was brought here all the way from the mines south of the great plain where the Stone Worshipers have built the greatest of their temples. They're buying up all the good flint they can get, those people are. Good, fine-grained porphyry's hard to come by these days. Flawed or not, it's worth every cowrie I'm asking for it."

"I'll give you twenty less and not a cowrie more."

"I'm a merchant, man, not a fool!"

"That's worth debating, friend. For what you're asking, I could buy a copper ax. And right up the way and around the corner!" He turned to go, gesturing to Falcon and Balor to follow.

"Wait! All right. Damned smiths will put me out of business yet! I'll come down ten cowries on the deal. But not a shell more, or I'll be selling it to you at cost!"

Oblin paused, grumbled to himself, and weighed the flint in question with a frown and a fractious flicker of the eye. He sighed. He cursed. He grumbled. "All right. Done, then. But you've had the better of me and should be ashamed!" He paid the man and took his wedge of flint, shaking his head as though he could not understand his own stupidity.

When they had walked away from the stall and were beyond earshot of the merchant, Oblin gave a little hoot and a whistle.

"By the Twelve Winds, there'll be an ax fit for a chieftain out of this! I've never seen a finer cut of porphyry!"

Balor frowned. "I thought you said that it was flawed!"

Oblin winked. "The only flaw was in the merchant's eye, my boy. And I hope you paid close attention to how I put it there. I am well pleased with myself. Come now. I'll buy you both a beer to toast in celebration!"

Oblin and Falcon were off to the nearest ale stall, with Balor in their wake, protesting that he did not want any beer. Oblin gave him the price of a cup of mead and sent him off, but he was soon distracted by something bright, deep within a wool-canopied enclosure.

He entered the stall, which was set back from the others on the street. It was filled with cloth and clothing such as Balor had never seen or even imagined. Bolts of soft, pliable, wondrously colored fabric—nothing like the crude, gap-warped, rough stuff spun by the women of Bracken Fen—cascaded from display racks hung high from the rafters of the canopied roof.

With infinite appreciation Balor wandered among the fabrics, oblivious to the looks of abhorrence from several customers whose nostrils spasmed as he passed . . . until he came to the item that had first caught his eye.

It was a cloak, of a wool so fine and thick that he was certain that in all of the world there could be no finer example of the weaver's art. It had been dyed to a red as rich and as dark as blood. Emblazoned in the center of the back, a huge black running wheel, the symbol of the Circle of Life, had been woven into the cloth. Balor reached out and touched it. The wool was at once warm and cool against his hands. He knew that he had to have this cloak, even if it took the last cowrie that he owned in order to possess it.

"Hey, there! You! Get away from that!"

He turned, startled to see an angry-faced man coming toward him, parting his way through the hanging racks of fabric like a great, meaty-faced bear emerging from a forest.

Balor saw no reason to back away from him. He remem-

bered the advice given to him by old Falcon, and also by
Oblin, and stood his ground haughtily. "This cloak is not of
totally inferior quality. I would have it."

The man was of the same race as Horsa, one of the Beaker
Folk. Red-faced and somewhat squint-eyed, he measured
Balor from beneath beetling yellow brows tipped with gray.
"You would, eh? Can you not see that this is a man's cloak?
It's too big and too good for a flea like you. It is already
promised to another—a lord, a prince from far lands whose
family is one of the chief investors in this trading center. It
was loomed as a gift to him, in honor of his visit here from his
distant country of Achaea. Now get out of my stall before you
smell up my goods and drive my customers away!"

No one, not even Munremar, had ever spoken to him with
such contempt. He took a breath to calm himself, then
remembered that it was only a part of the game of barter. "I
would also be a customer," he said, trying to be as sure of
himself as old Falcon or Oblin would be, were they here
beside him. "I would have this cloak, Merchant! Or another
like it! I am not without cowries, as any man with half an eye
can plainly see." He spoke with authority; he was, after all,
the firstborn son of a chieftain.

But the weaver was not impressed. His expression changed
from contempt to open hostility. "Why you insolent little
turd! Go buy yourself a bath with your cowries! You haven't
enough shells around your neck to buy a single thread of my
fabrics! Go find the dog from whose mangy back you've fallen
before I squash you flat and use your insect guts and blood as
a dye in my vats!"

Someone laughed.

Balor's temper flamed as red as the cloak. Never had he
been so angry. There was no controlling it as it surged
forward, sweeping him away with it.

He did not will the words to form. They roared out of his
mouth, and he heard them distantly, as though someone else
spoke them. "Do you know whom you dare to call a dog, you
pig-faced son of a—"

He was not aware that he had been struck from behind
until he awoke out of darkness, dangling like a doll from one
of Draga's big fists. He heard the redbeard speaking out of a
pulsing haze and terrible, painful roaring in his ears.

"Miserable excuse for a boy, isn't he? Sorry if he's troubled

you. Never have been able to teach him manners. Not worth
what I paid for 'm, I can tell you!"

And then the weaver's voice, coming through the roaring
and the haze, nasty and sour. "If you paid anything for him,
you paid too much. He's not worth his weight in cow manure!
Now get out of here, for that is what you smell like!"

Draga did not speak to his nephew. He set him down upon
his feet and with a brutal poke and a shove that almost sent
him sprawling, prodded him forward until they put two
streets and an alley between them and the weaver's stall.
With one hand curled sharply into the boy's shoulder, Draga
paused at an ale stand, and only when two brimming beakers
were served to him, did he release the boy, turn him around,
and with a sharp, swift kick, send him trotting toward one of
several empty benches at the far side of a deserted drinking
area.

Draga followed and seated himself and, with a nod of his
head, indicated that Balor was to do the same. When the boy
hesitated, the redbeard growled.

"Sit down or I shall knock you down."

Balor did as he was told.

Draga handed one of the beakers to him. "Drink."

"The smell of it makes me sick."

The redbeard's face twitched with contained anger as he
shoved the beaker hard against Balor's chest, sloshing beer
onto his tunic. "Take this and drink every last drop of it. And
do not stop drinking it until I say 'hold.' If you wretch up
your belly into the beaker, then you'll drink that too. For
once, Balor, you are going to do as you are told, or before this
night's done, you'll have given me cause to inform my
brother that his firstborn son was trampled to death by a bull
in the stockyards."

As his fingers strayed to the lump at the base of his neck,
the boy eyed his uncle warily. "And you'd be the bull?"

"With pleasure, I can assure you."

Their eyes met and held, and Balor knew that he had
better drink.

Draga watched him until the beaker was nearly drained
and the boy's eyes were bulging from the strain of his
obedience.

"All right," said the redbeard. "Enough, enough. I'd not have you puking on me."

Balor lowered the beaker and as he looked at his uncle was surprised to find that there seemed to be three of him.

Draga scrutinized him with a scowl. "Good. You're drunk. That'll slow you down some. Now tell me, what did the weaver say to make you lose your temper?"

"He called me a turd... and a flea... and then he told me to run off to the dog from whose mangy back I'd fallen." The words came thickly, as though they wished to stick to his tongue and run back down his throat.

Draga's scowl deepened, and he lowered his voice so that it was barely audible. "And so you nearly named the dog as Wolf for the sake of your pride?"

"I was angry. I didn't think."

"I'll tell you now, Nephew, it was a lucky thing for all of us that I happened by in time to shut your mouth for you! I may not approve of my brother's plan, but I have vowed on the Twelve Winds to do nothing to interfere with it. As have you."

The truth was sobering. The world was slowly coming back into focus as the numbness began to ease in his face. The bruise at the back of Balor's neck was beginning to ache and throb. He put his hand to it and with gentle fingers explored the extent of the injury. There was a swelling knot at the base of his skull. It was bleeding.

Draga downed his ale in several loud gulps, then shook his head as he fingered foam from his mustache. "I'm sorry I had to clout you so hard."

"I know," said the boy, suddenly tired and feeling sick from the ale. He looked directly into his uncle's eyes. "I was angry because I was ashamed by the way I am forced to look and act and smell for this game of ours. I am even embarrassed to claim Fomor as my father. Uncle, how do you learn to bear the shame?"

The question took the redbeard off guard. A strong, broad hand reached out to lie open upon the boy's thigh in a sign of friendship from one who for too long had not been a friend. "I think, perhaps, we are not unalike, you and I. You know how I feel about this charade, Nephew. I have made no secret of my feelings. But it *is* the lord's game, and as long as the council votes to support him, we must play it his way."

They sat for a time in silence. Then a party of laughing, rowdy young men came to occupy the benches nearest to their own. Balor's head had begun to ache mercilessly, and seeing this, the redbeard made him sit still while he examined the injury. He exhaled a low whistle and clucked his tongue.

"I did serve you properly, didn't I, laddie? I'll have to remember to remove my ring next time I clout relatives. Come along, Balor the Lucky. I know of a place where we can get something to ease the hurt of this. We'll have you feeling quite out of this world in no time at all!"

They walked together along the streets, which were no longer quite so crowded. Here and there Balor noted that stalls and shops had closed for the night. Tarpaulins had been dropped to seal them off, or vendors had simply put out their lights and lay curled up asleep in the darkness beside their wares.

In a particularly narrow, dead-end alleyway, they paused before a stall from which hung a long, narrow banner indicating to passersby what was offered for barter within. The fraying cloth was a deep, unpleasant purple in the darkness of the unlighted street, and an exotic-looking, swelling seedpod on a long stem had been appliquéd onto the fabric, with petals folded back as though at rest.

"Ah, here's the place," proclaimed Draga. "That's the pod of peace on the banner. One sip of the nectar that is made from the oil of its ground seeds, and you'll know no pain at all, Nephew! That I can guarantee!"

They entered the stall. The only light was given off by a single tallow lamp set at the back of the room. Unlike other stalls, this one was walled all around with heavy fabric, and there were rush mats upon the floor. Baskets and sacks were lined up neatly along one side, beakers and crocks along another. Dried herbs hung from the rafters along with dead, dessicated birds and bats and other things that Balor did not wish to identify. He winced at the sight of them and was nauseated, for the room, although it appeared clean and orderly, was redolent of strange, heavy scents—alien and rank and strongly medicinal. His head began to throb even as he fought to keep his gorge from rising.

There were several pallets in a row toward the back of the stall. Two were occupied by men who lay quite unconscious. One had a face swathed in bloody bandages, and the other, even in the dimly lighted room, had the gray-green pallor of a new corpse. Balor was certain the man was dead until he snorted, rolled onto his side, and began to snore and slobber in his sleep.

Something warm and silken wrapped itself around one of Balor's legs and vibrated softly. Startled, Balor kicked at it, and with a sound such as he had never heard, it screeched and ran off into the shadows, leaped into a huge basket, and turned to stare at him out of the darkness. Its eyes glowed yellow, the vertical pupils the merest slashes of black. It hissed, and then made its strange sound again. *Meeooowsh*. Its impossibly long tail flicked.

"What in the name of the Twelve Winds is it?" he asked, gripping Draga's forearm in terror.

The redbeard laughed. "Have you never seen a cat before, Balor?"

Balor gulped. He had not. There were no cats within the fens, and he was glad of that.

Someone was coming toward them out of the darkness, a man carrying a lamp, holding it before him so that the light flowed forward and he remained in darkness. "Does no one in this settlement ever sleep? Who's there? Are you ill or wounded?" The voice had the clipped, precise tone of one who speaks well in a language not his own.

"I've a boy here who is a little of both. He could use a sip from the nectar of the poppy."

The man made an exhalation of annoyance through his teeth as he set the lamp down upon a small, low table to his left. Balor could see him now. He was middle-aged, fair-skinned, dark-eyed, clean-shaven, and as bald as an egg. His jaw had the bluish shadowing common to those who razored their beards. He wore a long robe of what looked like linen, well loomed and belted with a simple woven sash. He eyed them sagely. "The poppy is it? Always it is the poppy, and always they know where to come in search of it! I am a healer, not a dispenser of dreams. But come here, boy, let me see the injury and look into your eyes to see if there is dilation."

Balor would not have moved, but Draga shoved him forward, and suddenly he was in the healer's grasp, being manipulated by strong hands with probing fingers as merciless as the talons of a hunting bird. He cried out and tried to pull away, but the healer held him fast and did not let him go until he had surveyed the wound and looked deeply into his eyes, moving a finger before them as he did so.

"*Hmmph*," he said at last, releasing the boy. "You'll be all right. The poppy will do for you. But the wound is deep. It should be salved and stitched."

And so it was, although as Draga had promised, once he had drunk from a vial of poppy juice, there was no pain at all. He sat still for the stitching, even smiled through it, imagining that he saw things that were not there. The cat, as black as the shadows of the room, watched him and smiled. Balor smiled back like a ninny and then laughed because he found the prick of the healer's needle to tickle unbearably. He spasmed against it, giggling. The healer told him to be still. He was. As still as a rock, and suddenly, as heavy. He watched, fascinated, as the cat seemed to flow down from the basket and melt into a lake of shadows upon the floor between a pair of man-sized jars. With a start, he thought he saw a face peering out at him from between the jars, floating above the lake of shadow. White. Wide-eyed. As watchful and wary as an owl in the night. It was Morrigan's face. A bolt of pure shock rent him. He blinked, and in the blinking the face was gone and the cat was back, curled in the shadows where the face had been, purring loudly as it licked its paws.

"He has not partaken of the poppy before, I see," said the healer. "Keep him close to you for the next few hours, until he is himself again."

He did not know exactly when he regained his senses. He knew only that he was wide awake again and things were back in perspective. He was lying on his side, wrapped in his cloak, at the periphery of a large gathering of men. He heard them talking—low, night's-end sort of talk, words slow with sleepiness, laughter deep and somewhat dulled, like occasional sparks popping in a fire that has nearly gone out.

Time had passed. How much he could not have said... several hours perhaps. The sky above him was grayed by a thinning veneer of clouds through which the stars shone like

distant campfires. From the way they stood in the heavens,
he knew that dawn would be a while in coming.

He knew even before he was able to rouse himself to look
around, that Draga had brought him out of the main settlement and nearer the stockyards. He could smell them, and
now and again a cow mooed or a horse nickered softly. There
was the distant, soothing sound of the sea too, and the
whispering slur of wind in tall grass. But it was the sound of
the men's voices that had drawn him out of the black, heavy
mindlessness induced by the poppy. That, and something
else . . . an awareness of someone very close to him, touching
him, fingering his amulet, which had fallen free of his tunic as
he had slept.

He sat bolt upright, grabbing the talisman and stuffing it
defensively back into his tunic, staring angrily at the trespasser—
the cruel-eyed child whom he had seen earlier in the evening
following in the wake of the hunchbacked woman who had
been selling caged birds.

"What're you doing?" he demanded.

The cruel eyes were as wide as a serpent's. "Your uncle's
paid me to keep an eye on you while you slept. He's off there
with the others, gambling. That's a rare amulet you wear. I've
never seen a clearer bit of amber, nor one cut quite like that.
Odd to see the like on one from so poor a band—and on
someone from the south. It'd bring a fortune if you were of a
mind to barter it. I could show you where it'd fetch the best
profit for you, for a small cut of the take, of course."

"It's not for sale!" Balor stared, startled as an amazing
realization dawned. This child was no child at all. He was at
least sixteen, a man, and a dwarf. And there was something
about him that sent a shiver of pure warning running cold in
Balor's gut.

The dwarf measured him out of eyes that cut him to the
bone. They were as gray as the dark hollows beneath them
and as sharp as the thin, dry lips that parted to reveal an
adult's set of large, crooked teeth. "Sorry," he said. "I didn't
mean to make you angry."

"Where is my uncle?" Balor asked, rising, wanting to be
away from the deformed man.

"At his gaming, and not being exactly lucky. If I were you,
I'd not disturb him just now . . . unless you can make that
charm of yours work its magic."

Balor hefted his cloak and checked to make certain that the unpleasant stranger had not relieved him of either his cowrie necklaces or the coil of sinew he had looped to his belt. "What I can or cannot do is not your concern. Leave me now. I want no part of you."

Perhaps it was the magic of the amulet. He would never know. He could only be certain that Fomor and the other clan members were nowhere to be seen, and from the moment he came to stand at Draga's back, the redbeard began to win, and kept on winning at everything he set his hand to. He tried his skill at archery contests, at ax hurling, and at the particularly tricky art of hurling a stone out of a sling at a target. Bored with this and growing more drunk by the hour, he set to gambling again at the more conventional games of pitch and toss and soon had won a good pair of new sandals from a shoemaker and a copper earring from a begrudging smith. Drawn back to the more martial games, he soon came away from a lengthy, hotly contested round of spear tossing against a horse trader with a fine gray pony. The horse dealer nearly collapsed with apoplexy and swore that he would double the stakes if Draga would only give him one more toss. But by then the redbeard had tired of the game. It was growing late, and he told Balor that he was looking forward to eventually bringing the pony home to Bracken Fen as a gift for his daughter, Dana, to demonstrate to her the riches to be had in the world beyond the fens.

Besides, something else had caught his eye and thoroughly distracted him: A hawker of two women, collared and leashed like tethered hounds, had arrived to display his wares. Each was covered from head to ankle in a hooded cloak, not only to ward off the chill of the night and the sea air, but to create an aura of mystery and curiosity. He led them into the area where the men had gathered for their gaming, proclaiming the quality of pleasure he offered to those willing to pay.

Someone guffawed and chided: "Come on now, man! You've been dragging that same twosome about the settlement since noon. Don't you ever let the poor girls sleep? Look at them! How can they dance beneath a man if they're too tired to move?"

The hawker grinned, displaying gaps in his gray teeth, and

protested: "My girls sleep in the morning hours while most of you are busy at your trades. But from noon till dawn . . . those are the hours in which I must work *my* trade, selling time upon these good and serviceable 'dancers.' Is there a fair and decent man among you who would deprive a man of his living? Are there not some among you willing to toss a workingman a few cowries so that he may at least display his wares for you?"

Shells were tossed—not many, but enough for the man to gather them up and, smiling and nodding, put them greedily into a little pouch at his belt. He jerked the tethered women forward then, leading them to stand in the pulsing glow of a large, nearly depleted bonfire.

Balor and Draga had been set to leave for the clan's encampment when the hawker had arrived. They might well have been out of earshot had the pony not faltered. Tender-mouthed from abuse, the animal had balked at its halter, and Draga, a lover of horses, had paused to readjust the halter rope and soothe the nervous beast with soft words and gentle strokings.

The hawker had evidently caught sight of the glint of copper at Draga's ear and taken note of the strands of cowries he flaunted about his neck. "You there, Redbeard. Would you squander the last fleeting hours of the night with only a boy and a pony for company? Why not greet the dawn astride a spotted mare with coloring to match your own . . . or ride a black from the far and distant harbor of Punt, to the south of Thebes, where the grasses burn and men risk their lives to deal in ivory?"

Good-natured snickering went up from the gathering. Balor heard someone say with a laugh, "Beware, Redbeard! I've heard that the 'spotted mare' bit off a man's nose earlier in the day, and the black may well give a double return on your investment—pleasure *and* the pox! But then, with your luck, who's to say that you're not immune to the pox and can break the 'spotted mare' so she'll give us all a better ride?"

The hawker cried out a protest, but it was laughed down until someone called for him either to display the women or return their cowries. He poked the women viciously with his riding quirt until they dropped their cloaks and stood naked in the firelight.

Balor had never seen women thus displayed, nor had he

ever seen a fully black human before. This one was darker
than anyone he had seen within the settlement. In the poor
light of the fire, but for the oil upon her skin, her slave collar,
and the thread-thin bands of copper at her throat and ankles,
she might well have been invisible. She stood with her
close-cropped head bowed, bent-legged and drooping on her
feet like a weary grazing animal. Balor could not help but feel
pity for her as the hawker poked her again so that she would
stand erect and display herself to his advantage.

The sounds that went up from the men were mixed as the
hawker named the price he would have for the black girl's
time. They were, nearly to a man, a tired lot. Only two of the
younger men actively haggled over the girl. Unable to agree
as to which of them was to take his turn upon her first, they
laughingly rose together and led her off into the shadows to
share their time with her.

The second woman remained for viewing. As the hawker
had claimed, her coloring matched Draga's. She was as white
as chalk and as wild looking as a wind-riled lake. Her hair hid
her body to mid-thigh, as brazen red and full of fire as her
eyes. Only when the hawker gave a brutal yank upon her
collar did she lift the cape of flame away from her shoulders
so that all might see that another of her master's claims was
true. There was not an inch of her that was not sprinkled with
freckles. Truly she was a spotted woman, and the men
laughed and made rude comments as they pointed at the
unmistakable triangle of red above her thighs and below her
white belly.

Balor flushed, wondering what it must be like to be as
powerless as the spotted girl, forced to do the will of others,
even when it meant total degradation. He turned away, not
wanting to be a part of it.

But Draga stood rooted, staring at the spotted woman with
a look on his face that Balor recognized; he had seen it in the
darkness of the roundhouse when Huldre rose to stand naked
before the lord, lifting and offering her breasts to him,
moving her body in a way that always made Balor—who was
thought to be asleep—blush and bury himself beneath the
bedskins. Now, as Draga looked hungrily at the spotted
woman, his breathing came fast and shallow.

"Take the pony back to the encampment, Nephew. See to
it that it is tethered out of the damp and given a warm mash

made from grain taken from the gruel sack. I'll be along when I'm finished here." He walked out of the shadows and through the gathering as though in a daze, ignoring the comments of those who made room for him to pass. He had eyes only for the spotted woman.

The hawker narrowed a shrewd and speculative eye at him. "Not so fast, friend. This one doesn't go cheap. She gives a wild ride, and it'll take all of the cowries you've got, plus that copper earring if you want to try to break her!"

The others hooted and taunted and warned Draga that he was being thoroughly fleeced. But Draga did not hear them, or he chose to pay them no heed. He stopped in front of the girl and did not take his eyes off her as he removed the copper from his ear and the cowries from his neck, handing them to the hawker even as he snatched the girl's tether and led her off into the darkness beyond the gathering.

Balor turned away. With a sigh of resignation he began to lead the faltering pony slowly toward home, wondering what madness drove an otherwise rational man to give away money simply so that he might lie upon a woman.

10

In the dark, the stars veiled by cloud cover, Balor was uncertain which pathway would lead back to the encampment of his clansmen. As he led the pony off, he noticed that the dwarf was watching him. He quickened his pace and cut across a wide hummock of tall, brittle, salt-rimed grasses, then ducked behind a wind-stunted copse of trees. As he expected, the dwarf trotted past him in his odd, rolling, limb-stunted gait. Balor could hear the strained suck of the little man's breath as he limped off into the darkness. Goose-flesh pricked cold at the base of Balor's neck, rousing pain in the recently stitched lump at the base of his skull.

He stood gentling the pony so that it would not stamp or whinny to betray him, not understanding why he had taken such an aversion to the dwarf, who had done nothing more than to show a perfectly understandable interest in Huldre's amulet.

There was something genuinely disturbing about the misshapen little gnome, something that had nothing to do with his deformity... a subtle insinuation of danger and threat. Balor had seen cruelty in his eyes and had reacted with revulsion at the very touch of his hands. He made up his mind to keep out of this one's way.

Only when he was certain that the dwarf had left him far behind did he take what he thought must be a shortcut across the grasses, walking surely and steadfastly until he realized that this was not the route he and old Falcon had taken up from the beach. He was walking along the cliffs, with the sea far below him. He could hear the surf and could see the glowing orange lights of the settlement out on the peninsula to his left.

That was when he stopped. *Left?* They should be to his right if he were headed south. And then, suddenly, a voice shouted "Hold!" and a man emerged out of the darkness to block his way.

It was an encounter that was to change his life, although he did not know it then, nor would he realize it for several years, for there was nothing outwardly extraordinary about the man at all. He was a skinny fellow whose pale coloring and clothing caused him to shine in the darkness, even though there was no moon.

The pony shied back, rearing and fighting to win its head, half jerking the lead from Balor's hand. It took all of his strength plus the assistance of the stranger to calm the animal.

"I'm sorry," said the man. "I didn't mean to startle you— only to warn you off the trail. It ends dead up ahead. Where the track used to run down to the cove, there's been an earth slide. The cliff plummets straight down into the sea. A man can make his way up easily enough by daylight, but in the dark, not knowing of the danger, you'd not have seen the drop."

The pony tossed its head. Balor held the halter close so that the horse's cheek was against his shoulder and he could feel its breath. He thanked the man and would have turned away, but the stranger stayed him by reaching out to lay a hand gently upon his shoulder.

"Why did you come this way, boy? There's nothing down the way save an encampment of my fellow travelers. What business would you have with them?"

"Not knowing who they might be, I would have no business with them at all. I'm on my way back to my people's encampment on the cliffs above the beach to the south of the trading center. I must have taken a wrong turn somewhere beyond the cattle yards."

"Perhaps not," said the stranger in an oddly speculative tone.

Despite the darkness, Balor could feel the man's eyes upon him, measuring, summing. The pony stamped restlessly, and Balor felt suddenly anxious to be away. "I must go," he said, turning abruptly, relieved when he felt the stranger's hand fall away.

"The way is dangerous in the dark, boy. Why not wait with me until first light? I've a fire made not far from here. Besides, your pony's left rear hoof should be tended to as soon as possible. He'll come up lame if it isn't seen to."

The invitation had been made in a friendly enough fashion, yet somehow Balor felt uneasy. Why would the stranger say the pony was lame when it obviously was not? What if the man were a thief? A slaver? Balor was alone and totally vulnerable on this dark and wild stretch of cliff. Only the Twelve Winds knew what the stranger had in mind for an unwary boy and a valuable pony once he managed to lure them to his encampment.

"I must be away," said Balor, turning and beginning to retrace his steps, the pony trotting close behind, its gait sure and sound. He paused just long enough to bring the pony up beside him, then flung himself up onto the pony's back, gouged his heels hard into its belly, and with a shout, urged the animal forward into a run.

But the boy was no horseman. The animal broke into a gallop, raced ahead, and then without warning came to a complete stop. Balor went flying, then landed in a daze flat on his back, with the world spinning around him. Stunned, he sat up to see the pony standing close, head bent, nickering softly as the stranger knelt beside it. The animal stood passively, its left rear limb raised as the stranger deftly probed its hoof, looking at Balor as he clucked his tongue with admonition.

"Didn't I warn you that he'd come up lame? There's a small stone here. By riding him you've worked it up into the hoof. It'll have to be cut loose if he's to suffer no further damage from it. What's the matter with you, eh? Did you imagine me to be a thief with plans to steal your pony and leave you dead along the cliffs?"

"I did. And who's to say that you aren't and that you won't?"

"No one in all of this world, boy. But if such were the case, you'd already be dead and tossed down into the sea, and your pony would be safely grazing by my campfire . . . and better off for the bargain." He rose then, took up the pony's lead, and began to walk off into the night. The pony hobbled trustingly behind him. "My campfire's just up the way," the stranger said without looking back. "It's the other side of the little rise of land just ahead. I'll see to your pony's hoof by its light. You can follow or not. It's up to you."

Balor felt frustrated by uncertainty. "How do I know that I can trust you?"

The stranger did not slow his pace. "You don't. But that's the way of life, boy. We never know what awaits us around the next bend in the road. Only one thing's certain: Whatever it is, it shall be our Destiny. So there's no need to run away or to be afraid. Sooner or later it will have us in the end."

Balor followed. He was not certain it was a good idea, but he had no choice.

If Balor knew his uncle, the pony, injured or not, had better be at the encampment when the redbeard returned from his time with the spotted woman . . . or else Balor might as well not bother returning himself. The prospect was sobering.

He followed the skinny stranger over the rise, relieved to discover that the man was, in fact, alone by a small fire. The fire, so well made that it was nearly smokeless, glowed within a natural depression in the earth, and atop the far hill, a tall, narrow stone stood silhouetted against the night.

The pony had been tethered to a fallen tree, and the stranger sat before the fire, tending the animal's hoof with utmost concentration. Somehow, although he did not look up, the man sensed Balor's presence across distance and darkness and called out a welcome to him.

"Come closer, lad. As you can see, I am quite alone. You will come to no harm, and I could use an extra pair of hands to steady the pony as I try to repair the damage that ignorance has done to him."

So Balor went forward, albeit cautiously, until he stood beside the stranger and did his bidding. The pony's hoof was freed of the stone, packed with some sort of healing balm, and wrapped in a swath of good, clean cloth, which the man ripped from the strip of linen he carried in his traveling sack.

"You can lead him home in an hour or so. By then it will be light enough for you to see your way."

Balor felt embarrassed for his earlier suspicions and said so as he thanked the man and sought to pay him with his few remaining cowries for his ministrations to the pony.

"Nonsense, lad! I'd take no recompense for a deed done for the sake of kindness."

In the firelight Balor saw the man clearly for the first time. He was old, upwards of forty if the boy were to judge from the many lines about his eyes. His nose was a great, hump-bridged span above a long, weather-cured mouth that curled upward at the ends like a half-bent bow. He was a broad-shouldered, skinny fellow, with yellow hair faded nearly white, cut bluntly to just below his ears and then brushed sideways across the top of his head to disguise encroaching baldness. He wore a simple, short-sleeved summer tunic of undyed wool, scrupulously bleached and devoid of decoration. His arms and limbs were long and sinewy, but from the tension of the muscle beneath the tanned skin, Balor knew that he would be deceptively strong, quick, and resilient.

A soft, chill wind had risen to blow inland from the sea. As Balor knelt close to the fire to warm himself, he looked across the glowing fire pit at the stranger and asked him his name.

"I am called Star Gazer," he replied. "Although it is not my name. It is my profession; I gaze at stars and seek to understand them."

"It seems an odd sort of profession. Your companions, the ones you say are encamped up the way, are they also star gazers?"

"Oh, yes. Night after night—cloud cover allowing, of course."

Seated upon the fallen tree, he leaned forward, arms resting upon his thighs, hands hanging down. His eyes found Balor and held thoughtfully. "After we completed the raising of the stone and made all the necessary alignments, I wanted to be apart from men for a while. That is why I am here alone. Besides, I think I knew that you would come."

Balor frowned. "I took a wrong turn. No one could have known where it would lead me, or even that I would take it."

"I knew."

The boy's lips worked over his teeth. The conversation was carrying him into depths that made him uncomfortable. Best to change the subject. "You said you raised a stone? Which stone, and why?"

"The tall stone on the hill behind you. It was first raised by the followers of my faith over a millennium ago. Word came back to us that it had fallen during one of last year's winter storms. We have traveled here to raise it again and to make certain that it is perfectly aligned—"

Insight flared as Balor interrupted. "You are one of the Stone Worshipers! In the trading center people say that your followers have raised temples along all of the coasts of the world and that you are completing a great stone circle far to the south, on a plain that is a magic place: They say that you use sorcery to raise the stones, because no man could lift them!"

The man looked annoyed. "What ignorant, superstitious rot! We do not worship stones, boy, so don't call us Stone Worshipers. We *do* raise them, but to mark the rising and the falling of the stars, the movements of the sun and moon. We are the People of the Stone, mathematicians and students of the stars. We do not deal in either magic or sorcery."

Balor was disappointed. Magic was more interesting than mathematics. "I'm afraid I've never been one to pay much attention to my lessons of Star Wisdom."

The stranger smiled, amused. "I assumed as much when it became evident that you could not tell north from south. I hope that your inattention reflects the inability of your teacher to make the lessons interesting, and not the dullness of your own brain."

Balor flushed with embarrassment and was glad for the darkness. He saw that Star Gazer's eyes still fixed upon him, steady, nearly unblinking. He wished the man would stop staring at him. Perhaps if he said something intelligent, Star Gazer would turn to other more comfortable subjects of conversation. "I *have* learned that man can look only to the earth and the heavens for constancy. This is what my people counsel. When I am older I shall naturally take more of an interest in these things. Star Wisdom is not for children, after all." There.

"And your people should be told that Star Wisdom, when not taught by idiots, proves but one truth: that there is no constancy at all in the earth or in the heavens—not as men perceive it. Man, beasts, the earth, the seas, the stars, sun, and moon... all are caught up in an ever-ebbing, ever-flowing tide of eternal change, of birth and rebirth. I ask you, boy, if the earth is constant, why are there places in the world where it rises and roars to make a shambles and a mockery of the lives and endeavors of those who dwell upon it? And if the heavens were constant, how then would you explain a falling star?"

Balor tensed, appalled by totally new and unacceptable concepts. "The earth cannot move! And falling stars are signs from the gods written in the heavens for men to see. Everyone knows that!"

"Do they? Well, boy, the earth *does* move. And *yes* the stars *are* signs, but they are not for the ignorant or for the superstitious. If they are to be understood, the understanding must come from mathematicians and students of the sky who observe and record the infinite pattern of Creation."

Balor bristled. "Well, I am no scholar, but not long ago I saw a star fall huge and white across the sky. I was lost, so I followed it. It led me to a circle of standing stones, and the next day my father found me. Everyone said that the star had been a sign. And it was, for things have not been the same for my people since."

Star Gazer was sitting so motionlessly that, but for the wind in his hair, he might have been carved of stone or wood. With a shudder he closed his eyes and drew a breath, nodding in affirmation of an obviously unsettling thought. "After all of these years... nearly a lifetime... yes, I should have known. I too saw that bright and wondrous star. It *was* a sign...." His eyes opened, and though they fixed on the boy, they seemed to see beyond him. "It is foretold by the People of the Stone that someday the sun shall grow dark... the earth shall sink into the sea. When the bright stars fall from the sky, wolves shall rise and the world of this age shall crumble. Then shall the Mighty One come to his kingdom. Then shall all men live in darkness. . . ."

Balor watched breathlessly as the stranger rose and slowly, like a sleepwalker, moved to the crest of the hill atop which the tall stone stood, dark and featureless against the night. Balor did not know why he followed the stranger, for surely he was tired and troubled by the man's words and would have preferred to sit alone by the fire. The towering stone at their backs, they stood for a long while in silence, facing the coast, where they could see the lights of the settlement, an occasional glimmer of a flickering campfire, and the lights of ships moving far out to sea.

"The days of men are fleeting," said Star Gazer. "Today word came to me that one of the great warlords of all time has died—not in battle, in fulfillment of a destiny he had chosen for himself, but ignominiously, of the plague. He and all of his kinsmen with him—like so many grains of sand washed away by the tide. How meaningless it all seems. And yet, somehow, there *is* a pattern to it."

Balor trembled. So Fomor had accomplished his mission. As far as the world was concerned, the clan MacLir and the Wolf of the Western Tribes were dead.

The man put his hand upon the boy's shoulder as he spoke to him, gently, as a father might. "Mark me, my young friend, the world is not turned by men. Even the greatest and most powerful of them are vulnerable before the forces of Creation. Some day the earth shall be no more and no men shall be left alive save those who have dared to imagine that it is the destiny of mankind to walk the pathways of the wandering stars."

Balor looked up. The words made no sense to him. He was tired. His head had begun to ache again. "You speak in riddles, Star Gazer."

"All life is a riddle, boy. Somehow, before it is too late, we must puzzle it out."

"Not me. I'm tired. It's nearly dawn. I should be going now."

"Wait." It was a plea. Star Gazer turned away from the sea and knelt before the boy. "When a man sees a falling star, he has borne witness to his future and his past, and has been linked with the forces of his own creation. Those People of the Stone who have seen such stars—who have dared to follow them—have been called by the infinite to seek the salvation of mankind within the great truth from which most men turn away in terror."

Balor shook his head. "I truly don't understand you. I must go, before my people begin to wonder what's happened to me."

Star Gazer rose. His hands went up to the heavens. "Is it so difficult to understand? The stars are reflections of our world. We are a part of their cycle. Our periods of light and darkness, of drought and storm . . . there is a pattern to it, and we are slowly beginning to comprehend it. Perhaps we never shall completely, for so much is forgotten as each age ends and another begins. Yet our faith has survived since Time Beyond Beginning, since men first saw the seasons change, since the world was cold and ice moved upon the earth and clouds hid the heavens from us. Men, searching for ways to survive, forgot the past, not realizing that there could be no future without it." His hands had come to rest gently upon the boy's head, touching him with no more pressure than the wind. "The darkness is coming. The signs foretell it. Join with us, boy. You are one who has seen Destiny's star. Stay with me. I shall teach you. You shall be a priest of the Stone, chosen by the stars, a man of peace."

It was the word peace that tore the moment. Somewhere, far out on the peninsula, someone blew into a horn, announcing the birth of a new day. The presence of the tall, dark stone so close to his back sent prickles of revulsion running up Balor's spine. It was a symbol of peace, not of power, and he wanted no part of it.

"I must go," he said.

Star Gazer's eyes narrowed as he withdrew his hands and nodded. "As you will, boy."

They walked back to the fire, and Star Gazer stood silent beside the fading little lake of light as Balor took up the pony's lead, thanked him for his hospitality, and then started on his way.

"Be wary, boy."

Balor paused and looked back. "There's light enough to see the trail clearly now. I'll be fine."

"I hope so, Star Seer. The world grows dark despite the dawn. The Mighty One is rising. Soon there shall be wolves loose upon the land. When you tire of running with them, remember that those who have seen Destiny's star are always welcome among the People of the Stone."

11

The pony was limping again when at last Balor came in sight of the encampment. The sun was well up, and Blaheen had been watching for him. He was not yet within hailing distance when she came stalking out to him, red-faced and puffing.

"By the Twelve Winds, boy! Where have you been? Draga was back hours ago, furious when he couldn't find you. He wanted to trade this pony for a woman—a spotted woman, he said. Why any sane man would want such a creature, I can't imagine. And now you've brought the pony in lame! Ach! Perhaps it's too late to worry about it. He waited for you until nigh on exploding with frustration. Then he was off again, in a rage to win her at any cost. Dathen tried to calm him, but Draga knocked him flat. Dathen has gone off to find Fomor. He stayed the night at the settlement, and from what I've heard, he's put out the rumor of our 'deaths.' If Nemed MacAgnomain lives, word is bound to get back to him of the demise of the clan MacLir. If Draga doesn't ruin everything first! He's drunk and impetuous and of a mind to fight. There'll be trouble, I can tell you! He's bound to betray our identity if he isn't stopped in time."

Although he had not slept or eaten in hours, Balor left the pony in Blaheen's capable hands and ran back to the settlement. With his head pounding, he jogged along the cliffs, down the trail to the beach, past the fishmongers' stalls, skirting the now-bustling harbor, where not even the presence of large, splendidly built, newly docked ships with great red and black sails furled upon their decks caught his eye.

By the time he reached the center itself, his skin was afire with overexertion and his heart was beating frantically at the back of his throat. He stopped for a moment, pulling in deep gulps of air, then went on. He knew that he might be able to calm Draga by explaining about the pony and apologizing for his ineptitude—and, even more important, assuring him that, given just a little more time, the animal could be used in trade.

He guessed that Draga would be at the gaming area on the far side of the center, within sight and scent of the stockyards. He was correct. Draga was there, at the center of a large, rowdy crowd, and on a drunken, fevered roll of good fortune.

But he was not engaged in any simple inconspicuous games of pitch and toss. In his frustration he had evidently forgotten—or had deliberately chosen to ignore—Fomor's warning to maintain a low profile. Draga had stripped nearly naked and, with Gar and Nia to hold his garments and winnings as they drunkenly goaded him on, had set himself to take on all comers who might fancy that they could best him at any of the martial arts.

As Balor elbowed his way through the throng, he heard and felt the excitement of those who had gathered to stare at the spectacle Draga was making of himself. He had evidently already won the girl, for she stood, head bowed, tethered to Gar's belt. Balor came up beside him and tugged at his sleeve. The hazel-eyed young man looked down at him and grinned stupidly as he informed him that Draga was in the process of becoming a wealthy man.

"He's bested all comers at spear toss, ax hurling, and now he's about to show them all a thing or two about wrestling. Look, see the man who's just stepped out to challenge him? He's the local champion."

Balor looked ahead to the center of a large clearing, where Draga was bent forward in a match of close-quarter grappling with a huge, meaty man whose flesh lay in rolls about his belly and dimpled the backs of his enormous thighs. They were head to head, arms reaching, gripping, limbs splayed, bodies tensed as each sought the leverage that would throw the other off-balance. The challenger held the advantage of weight, but Draga was taller, younger, and clearly more agile. The hours of drinking may have dulled his judgment, but coupled with the presence of the spotted woman, they had put an edge to his fighting spirit.

With deft footwork he caught the fat man off his guard and brought him down. A tremor of shock went through the crowd. The fat man crashed down like a boulder, and although he desperately attempted to twist away from the pounce of the redbeard, Draga was on him in seconds, roaring in triumph as he straddled him, pinned him flat, and held him down until the dwarf sprang forward into the makeshift arena to shout out the count. Draga's arm shot up in victory, and the crowd roared with approval.

Draga leaped to his feet and began to strut, obviously enjoying himself. This was what he loved best in all of the world: the testing and proving of his physical strength and skills.

At that very moment clouds swept across the face of the sun and the world went suddenly gray and bleak. As the wind rose, an exquisitely dressed man came forward through the crowd. "You! Do not look so smug! I shall take you on and bring you to your knees!"

There were many others at his back, bodyguards from the look of them—heavily armed and wearing conical helmets made of a dark, burnished metal that Balor had not seen before. Each guard carried a long, deadly looking spear with a tapering head made of the same metal as his helmet. At each man's belt there was a dagger and, sheathed in red leather, an impossibly elongated weapon that was nearly the length of a man's arm and not much wider than the shaft of an oar. They carried bows slung over their shoulders, and in beautifully worked quivers their arrows were held at ready, each feathered in either red or black. Balor had never seen such an impressive group of men. But it was the man whom they served who took his attention.

He was also armed, albeit lightly. He carried neither bow nor spear, nor did he wear a helmet. Horsa stood close at his side, clad in his best, puffed up like a posturing gander, apparently both proud and nervous to be in his presence. The personage wore a sleeveless tunic of white linen sashed in red wool, and next to Horsa's garment of bold green with blue stripes, it seemed all the more beautiful in its simplicity. There was a jeweled dagger at his waist, and from a heavy golden chain a massive weapon such as his guardsmen carried fell to below one knee, hidden inside a red sheath emblazoned with a single black running wheel and studded with gold along the seams and edges.

Balor stared. The design on the sheath was familiar; he had seen it on the magnificent red cloak in the weaver's stall . . . the very cloak that now hung down the back of the newcomer.

A tremor went through Balor. So *this* was the lord of whom the weaver had spoken with such reverence, the prince from a far land whose family was one of the chief investors in the trading center. No wonder Horsa looked nervous. If his mentor approved of what he saw, Horsa would be rewarded. If he disapproved, the management of Point of Ale would probably be given to a new factor and only the Twelve Winds knew what would happen to Horsa.

Balor measured the newcomer, resenting him because of the cloak, and thought that he had cold, dark eyes as forbidding as the black clouds that presaged the approach of the North Wind. There were spiraling circlets of gold around his forearms, a ring of gold at one ear, and the cloak was fastened by two circular gold brooches. He was older than Draga, probably over thirty, closer to Fomor's age. Although he was not tall, he was powerfully proportioned, yet graceful and lean. He wore his thick, curly black hair cut short in the fashion of men from the south, and his beard and mustache were meticulously trimmed and oiled. He might have been considered handsome but for a long, white scar, which ran from above his left temple to his lip. His hair had gone gray where the scar ran into the scalp, and the features of the left side of his face were pulled slightly upward into a perpetual sneer.

He eyed Draga. "I have been long at the sea and could use a good workout." Before the statement was finished he had removed his earring and was sliding his arm ornaments down off his arms.

The fat man whom Draga had bested was wheezing as he labored to his feet. "The redbeard's tired," he said, shaking his head and sending sweat flying. "He'll be no match for you, my lord."

"Tired? I am just now beginning to warm up!" proclaimed Draga, rubbing his upper arms and dancing upon his feet like a horse held at close rein when it wishes to run.

The man observed him, then smiled obliquely at the fat man. "I never thought to see you bested, Creugas. Where was it that I last saw you fight, eh? Ebla? The Aegean? In the fighting rings of kings? But you've gone to lard since then."

Creugas bowed his head, accepting the insult.

The prince's face remained expressionless, yet somehow it seemed that he smiled as he turned back to Draga. "How about it, Redbeard? You do not look tired to me. Shall we have a match, or do you only test yourself against fat old men?"

Draga lowered his head, openly measuring the prince. Then, impudently, he sniffed the air. "You smell as soft and sweet as a scented woman. Are you certain that you can fight like a man?"

It was the usual sort of banter that men always engaged in before tests of strength. The crowd responded with laughter. Only the newcomer and his guardsmen were not amused.

Now the newcomer sniffed the air, scowling. When he spoke, however, the words flowed slowly, smoothly, as though they brought pleasure to his tongue. "You smell like a hog, Redbeard—a hog that should be spitted for his arrogance. I intend to fight you to the death; then I will have my bath. I shall need it, after strangling a swine."

Draga was not the sort to walk away from such a challenge. Beneath the gray and misted sun, with the sea wind rising and the crowd pressing close, with wagers flying and time passing in an agony of tension, the two men fought.

It was as the wrestler had said: Draga soon began to show signs of weariness. He was like a great red bear grappling with sunlight, unable to get a hold on it so he might wrestle it to the ground, where he would surely tear it to pieces.

Across the fighting circle, in a gathering of their own, Balor could see Fomor and Dathen watching. Had they been there all along? How could they have stood by and not stopped Draga from accepting this challenge to the death? How, in fact, had Gar and Nia refrained from discouraging the redbeard? Balor glared up at them. They were a pair of fools. They would never stand against Draga. He was a god to them.

But the god was clearly mortal now, and Balor felt a stab of guilt. He too had stood by, watching, waiting for others to act.

The boy did not think that he had ever seen a match last so long. The two men circled. They danced. They mocked. They struck out. They fell and grappled and then came up

again and again until, in a sudden, unexpected rush of pure
power, Draga crashed forward into the stranger, knocked him
off his feet, and took him down in a killing headlock that
would have ended the match had the opponent not gouged
Draga in the eye and bitten off half his ear. The redbeard
drew back, startled, bleeding profusely, giving his opponent
time to slide free of his grasp.

"Why, you treacherous little weasel! You bite like a woman!"

"There are no holds or moves barred in a death match,
bumpkin!" He rose and licked Draga's blood from his mouth
as though he savored it. "What's the matter, Redbeard?
Losing your stomach for the game so soon?"

Draga answered with a curse and a snarl, and the match
was on again.

Now they made contact more often in a brutal test of skill
and daring until each man shone wet with sweat and blood
and those close to them could hear skin slipping against skin
as the holds were made and broken. It seemed an age before
someone called for a pause and indicated that ale had been
brought out for the antagonists. Both men were grateful for
it, and Draga drank his share deeply, gargling and sloshing a
portion of it over his face to cool himself as he proclaimed
that, although he had begun the match drunk, he was sober
now and this new portion of ale would serve to rouse his
senses so that he might more fully enjoy the victory.

"You'll finish this match dead, Redbeard," assured the
challenger.

Draga made an obscene gesture, and with that the match
was on again.

The wrestler Creugas had come to stand near Gar and Nia,
close to Balor. He rubbed his neck and spoke softly: "Pity
about your friend. He's a good fighter, but he can't win at
this. That black-eyed killer out there won his freedom in the
fighting rings of the Aegean years ago. He's a champion
against men and beasts. That scar is from the horn of a bull
whose neck he broke with his bare hands. He fights well; he
fights to win; he fights dirty. There isn't a trick he hasn't
mastered. It's made a prince of him—he's married to an aging
queen who likes the stench of power in her bed. They prefer
their heroes ruthless in that part of the world, and this one
tops them all."

"The redbeard will beat him," said Gar, and cowries were shown and wagered to back up his words.

The wrestler shrugged. "Your loss either way, friend. If he loses, you'll have lost a companion. If he wins, he'll lose his head. You see the prince's guardsmen? They're as ruthless as he is, and loyal to a fault. His Achaean queen has sworn them to avenge him in blood if he ever comes to harm. So if I were you, I'd be away from here or hope for the death of your friend."

Achaean. Achaea. Where had he heard that before? Where?

A light rain had begun to fall out of the lowering clouds as Draga dropped to his knees, clutching his chest, and stared ahead with his eyes bulging as he gasped for breath.

"Ah, here's an interesting turn," observed the wrestler. "I'd wager that you friend's been poisoned . . . by the guards I'd say. Yes. They've run a risk by interfering, for the prince won't like this bit of treachery if he smells it out. He's enjoying himself too much, looking forward to a proper kill. You can see it in his eyes. No man in all the world has eyes like that. Raven's eyes. Full of death."

Balor was too stunned to react.

Now he remembered. Suddenly it all fit. *Achaea.* The red cloak with the black running wheel. The black raven's eyes, which Fomor MacLir had seen so long ago on the cliffs of Tory Isle and the far island of Eireann. Eyes he would never forget. The eyes of a man he had sold into slavery. The eyes of a man who had wed a queen in the land of Achaea. The eyes of a man who had become a lord, a prince among merchants.

The eyes of Nemed MacAgnomain.

He was circling Draga now, crouched like a bird of prey, alert and suspicious, ready to pounce. "What's this? What's the matter with you?"

Draga could not speak. He keeled over onto his side, rolled up into a ball, and lay in a spasming heap.

The predator kicked him brutally, once, twice. "Get up, you flea-bitten lout! What kind of a trick is this?"

Draga did not respond, did not even move except for an occasional spasm and a thin, gasping moan. Balor was certain that he was dying. He made to run to Draga, but strong hands gripped his shoulders and held him in place.

"Bring no attention to yourself, lad."

Balor struggled to wriggle free, but Dathen's hands held him painfully. Gar and Nia looked at Dathen curiously, but it was to the boy whom he spoke, bending close to whisper: "The lord has a plan. Trust him. It is Nemed himself, boy. Speak out of turn and we're all dead men."

The healer from the stall of the poppy had been summoned and quickly came forward from where he had been standing not far from Fomor's men. He knelt over Draga. The misting rain pearled upon his bald head as he looked up at Nemed.

"This man is dying. It's his heart from the look of it. The match is over."

Nemed MacAgnomain's face congested with rage. "The match is not over! Not until one of us has slain the other. This is a trick, a scam, a bumpkin's way of saving his worthless hide! Well, he'll not make a fool of me! I will not have it!" He wheeled and pointed at one of his guardsmen. "You! Bring me my sword!"

The guard sprinted forward. He paused and half bowed before his master. He held one of the long, sheathed weapons that Balor had seen earlier. With a snarl of impatience Nemed unsheathed it and, as the crowd gasped, slashed the air with as sleek and as dangerous a length of metal as any of them had ever seen. Before anyone could voice a protest, he held the blade poised over Draga's head. Dathen pulled Balor back and clapped his hands across the boy's mouth to prevent him from screaming.

"Get up and fight me, you filthy, sniveling wretch, or I will end this match right here and now and set the younger boys to playing kick ball with your head!"

Balor stared in horror, desperately wishing that Draga would move, but the redbeard lay gasping, fighting for every breath as Nemed tensed and readied himself to swipe down with the blade.

"Stop!"

The cry stayed the execution. Nemed stared into the crowd as a man stepped forward, his face hidden by the cowl of his filthy cloak, a horned helmet atop his head, and a long, wooden stave within his hands.

"Pardon me interference . . . but I would not have ye kill me poor brother while he cannot rise to fight back with ye. It does not seem right or honorable. No. It does not."

Nemed stared a moment. Then, fully contemptuous, he

smiled viciously as he made ready to fulfill his threat against Draga, but as the blade poised and hung ready to slash, without warning Fomor's stave came whirling out with such force that it struck the weapon from Nemed's hand and nearly broke his arm. The great, shining shaft of metal went flying as he cried out in pain. He turned, pale and fully startled, to gape at the dark-robed, towering horned figure who had dared to stand against his will.

"It is a rare man who will strike off another's head when he cannot stand to defend himself." Fomor's tone was deep and dangerous.

He knows, thought Balor, and trembled with an elation so intense that he went weak. *He knows and now he will kill Nemed. In memory of Manannan MacLir, the Wolf of the Western Tribes will rise to strike vengeance!*

But no one moved except the guardsmen. Even as Fomor's stave had swung to strike, they had stepped forward out of the crowd with deadly purpose, spears at ready, some with blades unsheathed, others with arrows nocked. It seemed that for every man gathered about the makeshift arena, there were two guardsmen who wore the colors of Nemed MacAgnomain and the royal house of Achaea.

Slowly Dathen's hands relaxed and slid away from Balor's mouth to rest tensely on his arms. In a second they could lift the boy, and Balor finally understood that Dathen had been sent here by Fomor to guard him—to whisk him away to safety if need be.

Fomor had seen the armed men move to the ready, yet he continued to stand over Draga, with the stave held steady. Moments passed . . . long, pulsing like heartbeat, and rain began to fall steadily. The dwarf emerged carefully from the crowd to move forward to where Nemed's sword had fallen. He picked it up and, half expecting to be slain upon the spot, brought it to Nemed, bowing before him until his forehead touched the ground. Then rising cautiously, he proffered the blade.

"Here, my lord," he said in a deep voice, which made a mockery of his size. "Show these people what this brand of glory can do. I doubt if there are many herein this wild and barbarian climes who have ever seen a weapon of bronze."

Nemed snatched the sword from him, and for a moment it was obvious that he contemplated halving the dwarf with it.

But then, with an expression of open repugnance, he kicked the dwarf away and slowly, with murderous intent, advanced on Fomor, with both hands curled around the haft of the weapon and the long sweep of the deadly blade angled out from his chest.

Balor screamed in horror as, with one brutal, sudden lunge, Nemed attacked, laughing. Fomor parried the blow and, with the skill of a man trained in hand-to-hand combat, whirled away from the force of the blade. The metal came down on the hardwood stave and shattered it. The crowd gasped; some of them cried out with delight at what they had seen. The metal had sung out a high, resonant vibration of triumph as it rent the wood.

To Balor's shock and relief it was the spotted woman who screamed in rage. "A coward's sport! Give him a sword if you would fight him, or let him be, for he has done you no wrong by seeking to defend his brother. Would the great and noble prince openly cut down unarmed men?"

The Achaean was in a killing mood, but the woman's words had found their mark. "So be it," he said magnanimously. "Someone hand the big pig a sword, and I shall give you all a demonstration of how easily a swine may be slaughtered."

A guard came forward and thrust a sword at Fomor. It was not so fine a weapon as the one Nemed held. The chieftain stood immobile, staring down at it for a long while, then ran his hand down the flat of the blade. Balor saw that its haft was simply worked but heavy. Fomor's long, strong fingers braced it expertly. A thrill went through the boy as, without conscious thought, his right hand sought Huldre's amulet. The amulet was magic. Donar and the Twelve Winds were answering his plea. Scallatha, the man of mud and prince of the marshes, was about to cast off his rags and transform himself into Fomor, son of Manannan, Lord of the Far Island, and then, as the guardsmen fled in shock and terror, the clansmen of MacLir would rise up to become the awesome warriors they had once been.

Balor stared at his father as he stood over the sword, head bowed as though at prayer.

The amulet seemed to burn into Balor's flesh as his hand curled around it. *Now!* he thought. *Let the Wolf rise now!*

Fomor stood erect. Within the cowl his head went up, shadowed, his face unseen. His limbs went wide. His arms outstretched, then rose until the sword was held high, as though he would call down the power of Donar's lightning through its tip.

There was not a man there who did not hear Nemed MacAgnomain draw in a little breath of what had to be fear as he witnessed the metamorphosis of his adversary.

Slowly the guardsmen began to close a watchful circle about their master.

It was then that Fomor's hands flexed and tightened about the haft of the sword. Balor could see the broad, rain-pearled knuckles whiten as the towering figure within the cloak tensed and drew itself up to strike.

Now! Now! thought Balor.

But Fomor cried out, a deep, heartrending exhalation of agony, and only an innocent, ignorant boy would not have known that it was the cry of a caged animal, the outpouring of rage from a man who wants to kill but knows that if he does, not only shall he be struck down, but all of his loved ones with him. Fomor saw what Balor could not see—guardsmen in Nemed's colors at the boy's back and close to Dathen's side, and that Horsa had pointed out Scallatha's clansmen to a grim-faced master-of-arms in a red tunic with a bold black running wheel at his breast.

So he stood, and as Balor stared in disbelief and utter shame, Fomor began to whimper and snivel like a babe, as his hands fumbled, all clumsiness and ineptitude, at the haft of the blade. As members of the gathering began to laugh, he dropped the weapon with a shriek and winced back from it as though it might rise of its own to sting him.

"Oh! 'Tis a magic thing! A foreign thing! It hates me! Oh! Get it away! Away!" With a gasp and a wail that bordered upon the effeminate, he prostrated himself on the now muddy earth at Nemed's feet and began to work his body like a worm. "Oh, mighty and magnificent one, kill me now, for I am not worthy to fight you."

Nemed was so taken aback by the unexpected display that he stood appalled, his weapon hanging limp from his hand.

The guards relaxed and appraised the twitching, whimpering form of Fomor with disgust. It was raining heavily now. Horsa came forward, apologizing, as one of the guards, a man who evidently walked high in Nemed's favor, came to MacAgnomain's side and commented with revulsion: "Leave them both to wallow. To kill such wretches with your blade would be to dishonor it."

Nemed scowled, ill at ease with the whole situation. He was wet with rain. A sudden chill caused him to cast a jaundiced glance at the sky. "Perhaps you are right. So be it, then. I am growing hungry and would sit to Horsa's table after I've enjoyed a good, hot bath! Grant these curs their lives—a gift from me. I feel generous today after the good news that greeted me when I arrived."

"News, my lord?" Horsa asked, coming forward with Nemed's cloak and making a show of putting it around him.

"Haven't you heard it, then? It's all over your trading center. An old wolf has died—an enemy whom I've been hunting for many a long year is no more. But we'll talk about my good fortune later. I'd forgotten how miserable the weather can be on this northerly stretch of coast. After nearly a lifetime spent in the Aegean, I find that the climate hereabout isn't fit for even such pigs as these who wallow in it!" With that he kicked Fomor brutally, once, twice, and again. Then, weary of the sport, he slung a friendly arm about Horsa's shoulder and, with his guards at his back, turned away and began a conversation of such a light and careless tone that anyone would have thought that his near encounter with death had actually refreshed him.

As he walked away, Balor stared after him. He was shaking, unaware of the rain that cooled the hot tears that fell from his eyes. He stood alone, for the crowd had followed in Nemed's wake, and Dathen and the others had rushed to Draga and Fomor.

Balor saw only his father. The chieftain was helped to his feet. The ridiculous helmet had fallen when he had prostrated himself in the mud, and he had not picked it up. His face was gray, and his eyes were the eyes of one who has gone beyond weariness, beyond sadness. One hand was pressing at his side, where Nemed's kicks had sorely bruised, perhaps even broken, his ribs. The other hand rose and, as he met Balor's gaze, extended toward his son.

The boy fought against a wave of emotion that threatened to overwhelm him. As he walked forward, he violently jerked the amulet from around his neck. The braided sinew cord burned as it broke against his flesh, cutting deep. He did not feel the pain. He walked past Fomor, rejecting his hand, refusing even to look at him as he went to see if he could be of help to Draga. As he looked down at his dying uncle, he hurled the talisman into the mud at his feet.

Star Gazer had been right. The world had gone dark despite the dawn and wolves. The colors of the house of Nemed MacAgnomain had been loosed upon the land. But if a Mighty One were rising, he would not rise here, where Scallatha the coward lived and ruled in the skin of one who had once been called the Wolf.

From this day on, Balor vowed, he would make his own luck! And someday, even if it must cost him his life, he would find a way to kill Nemed MacAgnomain and win back the glory of the clan MacLir. In the name of Manannan MacLir, in memory of the Western Tribes, he, Balor, would do this! And he would be unafraid.

BOOK II

12

Luck is a fabric spun of many skeins, and men are individual threads worked into the whole by the hand of Destiny.

The dwarf, Coman, stood alone in the rain as the gathering dispersed. How gray the world was, he thought, looking at the mud at his feet. How miserable and disproportionate for one such as he. Yes, he had managed to pilfer a few cowries and trinkets from unwary spectators at the death match and had even dared to insinuate himself into the attention of the newly arrived mentor of the trading center, hoping for some small reward. But instinct had warned him that the time was not right. He had best wait until the man was fed and rested, for to walk in the shadow of such a man, hoping to glean crumbs from his favor, would be risky at best.

The dark prince was like the great, sleek sharks that the dwarf had occasionally seen swimming in the clear waters beyond the shallow coves. There were always tiny fish swimming close to the sharks, ever ready to snap up leavings from the predators' feasts. But often the hunter would turn around and eat the tiny fish. Coman felt no remorse for the careless fish; he admired the sharks and wished that he were like them.

He took a little breath of longing and stood watching as a party of men carried away the fallen, redbearded giant. He wondered if the man would die, then dismissed the thought— he did not care. Best to go back into the settlement, to get out of the rain.

As he turned to go, something hard pierced the ball of his foot. He cursed; he danced about, gripping and squeezing the injury, and then in disbelief forgot all about the pain as he stared down at the muddy ground.

There . . . could he be seeing correctly? Yes! The shape was unmistakable. A tiny hawk, the amulet he would have stolen last night had the boy who owned it not awakened in time to snatch it back from him. And now it seemed that the careless, pale-eyed lad had left it for him to find, as though the Fates had intended him to have it all along!

"Oh, Coman, luck has come your way at last!" he proclaimed as he bent and plucked the talisman from the mud, wiping it clean with his sodden, ragged shirt of wool until, even in the slate-gray light of the summer rain clouds, it shone with a deep, clear color that only the finest amber could possess.

"I'm rich!" He squealed, and sobbed with joy, then laughed and tittered to himself as he danced a little jig of pure delight... until a sobering realization made him pause and mutter to himself.

"You can't sell it. No one would believe that you could have come honestly by such a treasure. No, they'll name you thief and cut off your hands."

Frustration made him shiver, and for a moment he stood perplexed, resentful. But then, slowly, a new insight dawned, and he wondered if the amulet had not already begun to impart its luck to him, for he had never possessed much in the way of insight before now.

He lifted the talisman, stared at it, and was suddenly very calm and happy. He did not have to sell it. Indeed, no one need ever know that he possessed it. It was the possession itself that was the supreme gift. With such a talisman a man could make his own luck, and even a dwarf such as he could dare to swim with sharks and profit from their predations.

A surge of pure power ran through Coman's misshapen body. He felt there was something different in this talisman. It had true power. With care he could turn the tide of Fate with it... he could carve his own niche in the world... he might even dare to seek a place of honor in the court of the dark lord Nemed MacAgnomain, far from the bleak headlands of Albion, in the warm, rich land of Achaea, which lay in the southern sea that men called Aegean, where sharks swam with impunity... allowing small fish to grow sleek and fat if they had luck on their side.

They fled from the trading center, running like dogs, the dying Draga in the wagon as they traveled southward for a full day before turning east and then north toward home.

To his amazement, Balor learned from Dathen that the redbeard had not been poisoned by Nemed's guardsmen; he had been drugged by Fomor and was expected to recover within a matter of days.

"Do you not remember the words of Creugas the wrestler?" Dathen asked, responding to the boy's gaping incredulity. "'Twas a no-win situation for your uncle. Indeed, your father saw the danger and took the only option available to him, although, by the power of the Twelve Winds, it was a hero's gamble!"

Balor sneered, his mind reeling. "Playing a hysterical fool is hardly the act of a hero."

Dathen's blond brows arched to his hairline. "If the match had gone on much longer, Draga, blow bag that he is, was bound to have bragged about his true identity. Had that happened, we'd all have been slain on the spot as reward for his drunken blustering. On the other hand we'd have been spitted just as quickly by the Achaean's guardsmen if Draga had won the match. And if he'd lost . . . well now, boy, you wouldn't expect your father to stand by and watch his brother die without lifting a hand to save him, would you?"

"Save him how? By groveling in the mud like a worm? If Nemed had advanced instead of retreated, both of them would have been cut down like dogs!"

"Aye, so the lord knew all too well. Yet by risking his life and Draga's, the rest of us would have been allowed to walk away unharmed, and the blood of Manannan MacLir would still live on in you and in your brother."

"In shame!" Balor protested. "The blood of my grandfather still cries out for vengeance! Why didn't my father stand and fight Nemed like a true warrior? 'Twas what a man of honor would have done!"

Dathen appraised him sagely. "And risked the lives of his kinsmen? Nemed outnumbered us at least three to one, with weapons of bronze . . . it is he who would have won the day. Clearly and without doubt."

"There is only one thing that I have come to see clearly and without doubt, Dathen, and that is that my father would rather grovel at the feet of his enemy like a simpering cur than risk his life by daring to face him in combat like a man!"

Dathen exhaled in impatience, and his long blond mustache shivered like brittle strands of tree moss blowing in a strong wind. "May we all be preserved from the blustering bravado of badger-brained boys! Stand and fight! Bristles up, and battle to the death against all odds! And then what?

There's no glory in the grave, boy. Only darkness. Only death."

"Better death than dishonor!"

Dathen measured him with open reproof. "Someday, Balor, if you live long enough, you may learn and understand the true meaning of the word *honor*. Then, and only then, will you be worthy to walk in your father's shadow. Until that day know this: A wise wolf chooses his own time to fight. And he fights not only for his own needs, but for the good of the pack. One cannot exist without the other. A lord cannot be a lord unless the clan agrees to name him sovereign, and a clan cannot long exist without a lord to forge it into a united force dedicated to the survival of all. Survival! *That* is the key. For if all are slain, Balor, who then shall be left to speak of honor?"

The reprimand was not welcome or heeded. Indeed, Balor blamed Dathen for the terrible dreams that haunted him in the nights that followed: dreams of a white wolf and its pack running wild across the land, ravaging, consuming one another until the earth ran red with their blood and ravens circled and descended to feast upon their flesh while within a battle chest a sword lay gleaming, breathing as though it were alive, until an arrow flamed across the dream, as white-hot as a shooting star, as deafening as a crack of thunder while a lightning bolt struck Fomor's battle chest and cleft it in two. The sword lay bared, roaring at him from out of the darkness.

"In the name of Manannan MacLir, in the memory of the blood of your kinsmen whose lives cry out for vengeance, come! I am Retaliator! Take me! I am for you!"

He would grasp the sword, and it would sigh like a woman in a man's arms until suddenly it would sear him to the bone, and he would fling it away as the cruel-eyed dwarf appeared out of the darkness to laugh at him. Balor would look down and see the bloodied body of a wolf at his feet and the sword melting away into the earth, transposing itself into a towering dark stone as Star Gazer materialized to stand before it, beckoning to him, calling out his name even as the stone fell to crush him. And all the while, high above, the blindingly bright and dispassionate Eye of Donar stared down at him, and somewhere beyond the dream a white wolf howled, a child cried, and a woman mourned.

Mercifully, within a week, the dream left him. Draga began to recover. For days he had lain limp and as useless as an infant, and the spotted woman, whose name was Uaine, sat with him constantly and stroked his brow.

The days continued to slip away, as Draga recovered his strength. Uaine managed to distract him into a satisfaction that kept him "recuperating" with her inside the wagon long after it had become quite obvious that he had fully recovered from his ordeal at the trading center. Indeed, even after they had returned to the holding, Draga stayed with her inside his roundhouse for long hours at a time, even in daylight.

"I shall have my amulet now," said Huldre, extending her hands to Balor.

They were alone within the chieftain's roundhouse. If Balor lived to be as old as the spirits that were said to haunt the marshes and the distant moors, he would never forget her reaction when he told her that he had thrown it away.

For a long time she stood still. Then, out of a corpse-white face, she whispered, "He will find it. The Fates will guide it to his hands. He will remember. He will know it as mine." Her hands flew to her bare throat, and she whispered his name as though it were a death rattle. "Nemed MacAgnomain . . ."

Balor felt sick. "He'll never find it. *Never*. It's buried in the mud by now, ground deep by the weight of a thousand careless feet. Anyway, there must be thousands of such bits of amber for sale in the trinket shops of Point of Ale."

Yet even as he spoke, the words of the dwarf rose to name him liar: *I've never seen a clearer bit of amber, nor one quite like that. . . . A man could own no greater charm in all the world. . . .*

As so often happened between them, she seemed to know his thoughts and replied to them as though he had spoken them aloud. "There is no talisman like it in all the world. It *is* the Eye of Donar, given by the god himself to our ancestors when the earth was new."

"I saw no sign of Donar within the settlement of the Beaker Folk, although it may please you to know that I *did* call upon him. He did not answer me, so I do not believe in his magic. I have sworn to make my own luck, Huldre, for I have come to think that those who wait upon the Fates are fools!"

A strange look crossed her face. It was as though a wind mysteriously stirred and trembled beneath her skin. Her eyes grew wide, cloud-filled, focused inward. "Time will name the fools among us, Balor. If Nemed finds the amulet, he will know it as mine. It will speak to him of the hooded giant who stood against him at the trading center and the redbeard whose warrior skills far exceeded those of any simple herdsman. He will realize that the Wolf of the Western Tribes still lives and has again duped him. You have thrown away our luck, Balor. Even now the amulet is leading him to us. We will have no defense against him without the Eye of Donar to protect us."

"What's this I hear, woman?" The question hurtled into the room like a stone hurled by a giant as Fomor stood gaping, incredulous, at the entrance to the roundhouse. "Did I overhear you say that you gave the boy your amulet? Knowing that we journeyed forth to seek out Nemed's forces? Knowing that we would all be in mortal danger if his eyes should fall upon it?"

"I gave it to the boy as a talisman to ward away danger, because I knew that you would have refused it! He was warned to keep it from all eyes."

"And what action of Balor's has ever given you reason to believe that he would obey you?"

Her eyes moved to Balor, measuring without condemnation. "His action confirms my warning. We must leave this place. We must unite with the Western Tribes and stand against Nemed MacAgnomain, to destroy him. Only then will you know the peace that you would claim as your own."

His great, golden head swung on his neck, and his eyes were as bleak as the moors at dusk. "With the blood of how many of my men? With the bones of how many of my kinsmen to lay as cornerstones at a new holding? No, Huldre. The vow that I swore upon the altar of the Twelve Winds shall not be broken. This Wolf runs no more."

Balor trembled with bitterness. The words that issued from his lips were as venomous as an adder's bite. "This 'Wolf,'" he snarled contemptuously at his father, "is no wolf at all!"

Fomor's blow came without warning. One moment Balor was on his feet, the next he lay stunned, blinking in shock, his lip split in two places, the taste of his own blood hot and salty within his mouth.

Never before had his father struck him. And yet as he stared up at Fomor, Balor was glad that the lord had hit him! In his anger Fomor MacLir seemed every inch the wolf that his son so desperately wanted him to be . . . righteous in his rage, magnificent in his wrath, absolute in his power. But then suddenly Balor remembered how his father had groveled in the mud at Nemed's feet. The tears that stung his eyes had nothing to do with the pain of the blow that had felled him.

The weeks that followed were golden weeks, busy, occupied with the business of life—of harvesting, of culling the herd, of storing up precious supplies against the coming dark half of the year. Balor did his best to keep out of his father's way. He took up residence with Dianket, grateful for his old friend's hospitality and eagerness to hear about the wondrous sights of Point of Ale and tales of far lands that Balor had heard from Huldre.

Within the span of a moon's turning, Draga was fully his old self again. To no one's surprise Uaine, the spotted woman, was pregnant, and because the redbeard had no desire to cause animosity between his two women, Eala too was ripe with the first signs of life and boastfully bearing the illness that presaged it. Draga was strutting proudly, eager to spend time with the youths of the clan upon the training field. He took pleasure in Balor's company, and together they gave little Dana lessons on the pony he had won for her at Point of Ale. Under the girl's meticulous care and currying, the little horse turned out not to be gray, but as white as the fabled monoceros of Huldre's stories of enchantment. Dana, having heard the tale from Balor, named the pony that and took delight in placing garlands of flowers and fragrant leaves upon its neck as she galloped the pony around and around the central compound while the other girls trailed close behind and Morrigan held out obstacles for the gentle little animal to hurdle.

That year the autumn seemed to last forever, a season sweeter than summer because the nights were cool, the harvest work done, and the fragrance of late-blooming blossoms lingered in the air. When the first snow finally came, Huldre continued to prophesy doom, but all signs seemed to portend the opposite. After so many years of suffering miscarriages and stillbirths, she was delivered of a healthy, hardy daughter, whose seemingly endless cries were so welcome to both parents that the child had been named Bevin, Melodious Lady.

No longer did the clan MacLir dwell under the comforting assumption that they were alone and forgotten at the end of the world. Although the trading center of the Beaker Folk was many days' journey to the south, it was still too near for security. At the lord's decree the clansmen had begun to redesign and strengthen the holding's fortifications. Timber had been cut and brought down from the forests to bolster and enlarge the palisade. Great, encircling earthen mounds were being raised around it, later to be connected into a huge protective ring. Even a single man approaching the holding would easily be seen once it was completed. Command posts were situated at strategic locations along the ring to repel attackers; if any should ever manage to breach it, they would find themselves confounded by three massive, labyrinthine inner ramparts, with several gates placed in such a way that the actual entrance to the holding was impossible to detect until one stood before it, totally vulnerable beneath the high, mounded encircling arm of an inner wall.

Now, after five years of constant work, although the ringed fort was far from completion, the clansmen continued to labor with a sense of purpose and pride in their efforts as watchmen kept lookout from stations throughout the fens, ready to set a signal fire at any encroachment by strangers. As in days long gone by, the men and boys of the clan MacLir were encouraged to look to their skills in the martial arts.

And in this, especially since he had entered his Year of Trial at the beginning of the bright half of the year, fifteen-year-old Balor enjoyed an ever-deepening fellowship with his uncle Draga. Of all the redbeard's students, with the possible exception of Mael, Balor proved to be the best and the brightest, filled with a pure and burning desire to learn. No longer did he balk at the more difficult lessons, which demanded hours of study and deductive reasoning. Instead he listened. He watched. He learned.

And in the nights, when the youths gathered around the storyteller's fire or joined with Munremar in the darkness beyond the holding to learn of Star Wisdom, Balor would sit in silence, looking up at the heavens, remembering Star Gazer. How wrong the man had been to say that no man knew his Destiny, save to understand that the fate of all mankind was linked to the stars.

Each time he saw a shooting star tracing its death in brilliance across the sky, he would remember the old man's words of wisdom and the great star that had led him to the tor... to the trading center... to the enemy. And although Fomor MacLir and such philosophers as Star Gazer might be content to dwell in peace, he, Balor, grandson of Manannan, firstborn of the Wolf, was not.

Each day as he worked with the youths of the clan at the tasks assigned to him, or sweated and strained to hone his body into the proportions of the man he knew must soon walk within his skin, he reaffirmed the vow he had made in the rain at the trading center at Point of Ale.

Someday, somehow, he would take up the great sword Retaliator and take the life of the man who had slain his grandfather and turned the Wolf of the Western Tribes into a passive dog satisfied to cower within the fens, locked within a prison of his own making.

There was blood on the snow. Balor saw it and drew rein. In the thin, cold light of the early spring morning he slid from his horse's fur-blanketed back and knelt, reaching down to touch the red stains in the snow.

"Wolves... this is the third calf kill they've made in as many days."

"They grow bold," said Elathan, scowling down from the back of his own mount, then casting a speculative glance at the sky as he blew on his hands to warm them. "Let's get back to the holding, Brother. Our watch was over at dawn, and there's no sense hunting farther for the calf. The wolves won't have left enough of her to feed the ravens. There's nothing to gain here but frostbite. By the power of the Twelve Winds, it's cold for this time of year!"

Balor rose, his breath congealing in the frigid air as he frowned. His eyes followed the bloodied, telltale tracks of the wolves as he flung himself up onto his horse's back and turned it in the direction the beasts and his dog Sure Snout had taken. "No death should be left unresolved," he said.

Elathan cursed. "Be reasonable, Balor. There's a spring storm lowering on us. There's nothing to be gained by us continuing on, not with Sure Snout so near to term with her pups. Call her back or you're likely to lose her too. She's no match for wolves in her condition."

Balor knew the truth when he heard it. He eyed Elathan's dog as it stood patiently tethered by a thong secured around his brother's wrist. It was a good and soundly proportioned animal, but not half as stouthearted and sure of scent as his own dog. He whistled Sure Snout back and watched as she emerged from beneath a thornbush, panting and droop-bellied. A pang of guilt stung Balor. He should not have brought her. Next time, even though she was certain to howl and protest, he would tie her to the centerpost of Dianket's roundhouse when he rode out from the holding.

Elathan observed the big terrier and laughed. "That'll be a sorry lot of pups she'll soon be sprouting. No doubt the elkhound's sired them. That big brute of Draga's is almost as pant-tongued over your terrier as you are over the redbeard's daughter!"

Balor glared. Had Elathan been closer, he would have whipped out at him with the ends of his reins, but his brother had anticipated his reaction and, laughing, had kneed his mount back and away.

"Don't look so flustered, Balor! Everyone knows you're tongue-tied over her. But then, there's not a man in the holding who isn't looking hungry for Dana these days. But you're too young to have a chance with her! Best forget her if you know what's good for you."

The anger that flared within Balor came so quickly, so unexpectedly, he was glad that his brother had maneuvered himself out of the range of his blows, for surely he would have given Elathan an unjustifiable trouncing. As his anger ebbed, he watched his brother's mount carry him off across the frosted pasturelands, down toward the bogs where by necessity Elathan forced the animal to slow its pace as they approached the holding.

Balor sat still. He heard nothing. Felt nothing. Saw nothing... except the soft, pale, gray-eyed face of a golden-haired young girl. Dana's face. He realized that Elathan had trespassed into a deep, all-too-vulnerable inner portion of himself, which until this moment he had not known was there at all.

13

Draga awoke yet did not rise, for when he tried to move, pain ran through every quadrant of his body, stabbing him in his back, high at his broad shoulders, as deep as a spear piercing his spine.

He did not cry out. He lay very still. In a few moments the fiery flood would ebb away, and then, slowly, he would attempt to move again, flexing each muscle so cautiously that the pain would not be able to catch him unaware before he managed to sit up and summon the women to give him his morning rub. He would be able to groan then, as their sure, hard strokings brought the blood into his muscles, relaxing them, warming them, driving the pain away. The women would assume that his groans were sighs of pleasure, for he was far too young and virile to be stiff-jointed from overwork or—the thought that followed terrified him—to be showing the first signs of bone blight.

No! He would not have it! Bone blight was an old man's curse! And he was young! Young! He had not lived to see as many as thirty summers. And yet as he lay unmoving under his sleeping skins, he knew all too well that not only the old were stricken. In the past, when winter had reigned over the marshes, bone blight had eaten freely of the people of Bracken Fen. The young had been crippled by it as well as the old. Their ghosts walked behind his eyes: Weakened, bent, their fingers swollen and twisted like burls of misshapen trees, their eyes sunken and haunted by constant pain, they had soon withered into hideous, desiccated, gray-haired remnants of their former selves. When at last they had died, only the sight of their weeping parents or children offered any clue to the fact that they had died young.

By the gods! The thought was intolerable! He would not accept such a fate! Surely it could not be his portion! He would have risen boldly to deny it, but the pain kept him down as he tensed in righteous indignation.

And yet the unwelcome truth stood behind his denial, and he nearly wept. He was in his prime, the very shank of his manhood. There was not one lad now enduring a Year of Trial whom he could not easily devastate on the training field. Yet unlike the older men—thanks to his brother—he had yet to prove himself in actual battle. And thanks again to his brother, he had yet to win true glory to his name. If he were to die tomorrow, Munremar would have few words to say when standing above the barrow.

"Here lies Draga, son of Manannan, brother of the Wolf, second always in all things.... Draga, who faced Nemed MacAgnomain and was beaten by him, Draga, who might have been a warrior...."

Might have been.

The words ran round and round within his head, squealing like rats tossed into a fire. Memories of his humiliation at the hands of Nemed flooded him, surged like a tide of gall. He could have killed Nemed but for the poisoned ale. And but for Fomor he could have roused the men of the clan MacLir into the fighting force that they had once been. With him to lead them they would have canceled the Achaean's threat once and for all, in the way of men, with honor, in blood.

If only he had been more forceful in organizing the men against Fomor before they had set out for Point of Ale! Things had been bad for the clan then. Many of the younger men had sided with him secretly against the lord, and even some of the older warriors had begun to listen to his dissatisfaction. Old Munremar had come close to speaking for him in the council. If only he had dared to openly challenge the chieftainship of his brother then and there, before the sacristy of the Twelve Winds, he might well be lord now.

He trembled. That thought had not stirred within him for many years ... not since the weather had benevolently smiled upon the fens; not since he had brought Uaine, the spotted woman, into his house; not since the birth of his children had eased the pain caused by the earlier deaths of his twin infant sons. No. Life had been good in Bracken Fen these past five years, since Fomor had rallied the clan into a life of peaceful purpose beneath the fair, mild skies of Albion, far from the dangers and turmoils of the world of men.

Although the blood of Manannan MacLir remained unavenged, even Draga had been content. Until now. Contentment congealed into dissatisfaction as the pain gnawed deep within his bones. Slowly, wiping the sweat from his brow with his fingertips, he looked out across the fire-lit interior of his roundhouse—at Uaine as she sat before the hearth pit nursing their newborn son while their tiny daughter played and babbled beside her... at Eala, loyal, lovely, kneeling over the gruel pot with Lorcan, a little scabby-kneed, red-haired replica of Draga standing close to her skirts, pestering her with endless questions... at Dana, dreamily combing her long, golden hair.

The sight of the girl made him frown. She was fourteen. A woman grown. The realization stabbed him as sharply as the pain. He winced against it, startled. The years *had* flown away! Perhaps he was not so young after all? A sick feeling churned in his gut as, for the first time in his life, Draga realized that mortality was not a condition peculiar to other men. If he were ever going to win glory so that he might leave a legacy of pride to his family when he was gone, he would have to do it soon.

But how? Who would side with him now after five long years of peace and plenty under Fomor's rule? What cared the people of Bracken Fen for glory? Men were not moved to action during times of peace; they became passive, loath to embark upon any endeavor that might deprive them of their comforts.

Uaine knelt back from the gruel pot. She looked at him out of speculative eyes. "You've slept long, my lord. It's well past dawn. The youths have already begun to assemble on the training field."

"We've set your garments to warm by the fire," added Eala. "It's snowing. And this the month of the Planting Moon! The lord's sons have just returned from the pastures. They say that wolves have taken another calf! I hope these are not omens for the return of the black and foul winters of the past."

Dana frowned. "Snow is not unusual in the spring. It will

soon melt, and we will have sun and warm soil in time for the planting. Don't you agree, my father?"

Slowly, doing his best to ignore his pain, Draga rose and crossed the room to stand before the doorway. As he brushed the weather baffle aside, snowflakes blew softly against his skin. Squinting his eyes, he looked out across the compound to where the youths were gathering. He saw Balor's pale, pollen-yellow hair amidst the others, and as insight and inspiration rose within him, Draga smiled.

"Who is to say how the Fates may turn?" he said thoughtfully. "Bring me my garments, Eala. The hour grows late. The future's waiting for me out there in the snow."

Today their training involved axes. Short-handled, viciously honed, stone-headed axes designed to hack bone and flesh. They worked despite the snowfall, with Draga teaching them about the fine points of the weapon for which their ancestors, the People of the Ax, had been named. The redbeard was in a strange mood, somehow distracted and yet unusually intense and impatient.

"Look at the lot of you! You've grown as soft as milk-fed lambs! And to think that you are the descendants of men who came out of the kingdom of the Golden Plains to conquer most of Land Beyond the Sea and then, not satisfied with that, moved westward to claim Albion and Eireann as their own! With only stone axes and horses trained to battle, they held half the world hostage! Bah! Not one of that noble breed would step forward to claim you as kindred!"

He made them stand in a line for his inspection, and they tried not to shiver against the cold. He stalked by, arrogant, mean, and stiff, so aggressive that there was not a youth present who was not intimidated.

"Of course, you are sons of your fathers, and your fathers are servants of the lord. It is he who's encouraged the softness in you. It comes with the peaceful life that he has proclaimed for us all. Not that I speak against him, mind you . . . but look at the snow and mark the season, my fine, baby-bellied young men! It is the month of the Planting Moon! Is there one among you who does not remember the starving years, the years of wanting, of sickness, when the sun abandoned us to die in the muck of the bogs like drowning pigs? Aye, I see the answer in your faces. You *do* remember. And I say to you now, though the lord says nay, the starving years could come again. And then what? Will you stay here to die or march forth as warriors to win better land for your people through glorious battle?"

Draga came to a pause, stopping in front of Balor, his blue eyes narrow and intent upon his nephew's face. The young man stared back, questioning, weighing the sedition in the redbeard's words.

"The lord has called us to be trained so that we may *defend* the holding in the event of an attack," Balor reminded.

The redbeard measured Balor. His face was expressionless. "Aye, and so, Nephew. But to defend or to attack, a man must know one thing well. He must know how to kill. And as Sons of the Ax who have been forbidden to go raiding, who know nothing of the deadly new weapons now used by our enemies, you must learn how to kill with *this*!" Without warning he wheeled and hurled his own battle-ax, haft over blade, sending it in a deadly trajectory flying across the compound to land with a whack in the lintel of the doorway to the chieftain's roundhouse, where it struck with such force that the axhead cracked clean through to the shaft hole. The handle fell to the ground as Mealla burst outside, back-arming the weather baffle aside to stand, hands on hips, glaring up to measure the damage done to her house, then turning to shout at the redbeard.

"Have you lost the use of your eyes or your brain, eh? The house of the lord is no fit target for your weapon, Draga! And if you don't know that, you are no fit instructor!"

He bowed and offered what seemed to be a sincere apology. "I meant no offense to *you*, good Mealla."

Balor caught the emphasis and looked at Draga, wondering if he had imagined it.

Mealla harrumphed and nodded, apparently mollified. "Well, see that it doesn't happen again. You've proper targets to aim at there in the compound! And if I were you, I'd take that axhead from the lintel of my doorway and mend the gouge as best I could before the lord returns from the far pasture. He'll not be pleased to know that his brother's eyes are failing him!"

"My eyes are fine, woman of the lord. And make no

mistake, from this day forth, when I take aim, I shall not miss my target."

By midmorning the skies had cleared, and young and old gathered at a safe distance to watch the boys as they learned the axman's stance and balance, then the hurling of the weapon into wooden targets. Of all of the youths, Mael, nineteen and considered a man now for almost four years, was truly the most gifted, but Draga easily remained the uncontested champion.

Balor, who had done well with his weapon with both his right hand and left, basked with pride at his uncle's effusive praise and looked forward to the evening's contests of skill, which they would all soon enjoy during the feast following the rising of the Planting Moon.

But by late afternoon the snow returned. The world went white and silent. The people of Bracken Fen, reading dark omens into the springtime storm, sought shelter indoors, while within Dianket's tiny house Balor drew his bedskins close to the fire pit and sought much needed rest.

It was quiet; that rare, fine, breathless quiet that only comes when clouds have settled to the earth and the snow falls soft, straight to the ground, unstirred by the wind. Within the little house Balor slept. There was no noise to disturb him—only the soothing sounds of the occasional settling of coals within the fire pit, Dianket's soft, lyrical voice as he hummed a tune, and the rhythmic scrape and pull of his flint stylus as he worked to carve a tiny toy horse from a piece of antler—a gift for some child within the holding, Balor had assumed, for Dianket made a practice of turning his talents and free time to the children's pleasure.

But Balor was to be denied his rest. Without a knock or an invitation Morrigan entered the house and called an enthusiastic greeting as she settled herself onto the rush-strewn floor, cross-legged next to the fire pit, opposite Balor.

"Wake up, you!" she demanded in her usual gruff, offhanded manner as she deposited a trencher of piled oatcakes onto one of the wide, flat stones that formed the curbing of the hearth. "I just baked these. Eat them while they're still warm, the both of you!" Her words were a command. She blew aggressively into her small, weather-whitened hands, then shook herself, sending snowflakes flying from the thick cape of her long black hair. "Go ahead! Eat! What's the matter with the two of you? What are you gaping at?"

The two young men continued to stare at her. They were not surprised to see her, for lately the youngest daughter of Munremar had been finding all sorts of excuses to visit the house of the healer's son. But today there was something decidedly different about her. For one thing, never before had either of them ever seen her with her hair combed loose; she always wore it like a boy, carelessly plaited into braids, bound with thin bands of sinew and devoid of any sort of adornment. And although she wore her usual heavy, mannish, shapeless winter tunic over a pair of trews laced snugly from ankle to knee above her plain leather boots, today she had chosen to belt the tunic with a bright-green sash of fibers woven of nettle plants; a variation that hinted contours distinctly, indeed profoundly, female beneath it. Even her face seemed different. She did not color her cheeks or lips with berry juice as did the other girls of her age. Or did she? Surely a quick jog across the compound would not have put such an attractive glow to her face, even if it was snowing.

"Why are you staring?" she asked again.

"You don't look like yourself," responded Balor, propping himself onto an elbow, observing her openly, with a candor that more than hinted of scorn. "You almost look like a girl."

She bristled, but the flame of a blush was unmistakable, as was the slight twitching of a pleased smile. "Bah! It's me, same as ever. I just didn't bother to do up my hair, that's all. The cakes were hot, and I thought you might want to share them, so I just came as I was. Besides, my half sisters were at their usual female prattling. I couldn't bear to listen to them for another moment! What superstitious ninnies they are! All doom and gloom and pestering my father to throw the Bones of Divination just because we're having a little late spring snowstorm."

Dianket observed her thoughtfully, as though he were a calm, wise sage studying a brazen child whose behavior obviously troubled him. He was a slender, gentle-eyed youth. And yet he seemed a man, for his strong face reflected the five long years of pain that had shaped his life since his fall from the roof of the council hall. Due to his handicap Dianket would never be recognized as a man in the eyes of the tribe.

For him there was no Year of Trial, no competing for a wife, no siring children. He did not sit upon the floor, as did Balor and Morrigan. He sat upon a wooden bench with his crippled limb extended, as stiff and inflexible as the hardwood crutch he had designed to help himself move about. The thigh and calf had never healed properly. During inclement weather the leg ached mercilessly; he had long resigned himself that it would be so until the day he died. There was no use complaining, lest it frustrate others as it had once frustrated him. Pain was a reality that he had learned to live with. He did his best to ignore it as he leaned out, helped himself to a cake, and tossed one across the fire pit to Balor.

The chieftain's son had drawn himself up into a seated position. He caught the round, flat little cake and held it at arm's length, observing it with all of the repugnance with which he might have held a cowpat fresh from the pastures. "By the Fates, you don't expect me to eat this?"

"I do," affirmed Dianket, eyeing him with annoyance, knowing that he was deliberately baiting Morrigan. The girl was renowned for the high quality of her hearth cakes; she ground the flour thrice fine, used the best mead for sweetening, and had achieved a high degree of skill at the griddle stones so that each cake came away from its frying light and tender and crisped to perfection. But Balor and Morrigan had engaged in nasty little word games ever since they had been children. Now that they were nearly adults, they had difficulty speaking civilly to one another. One of them would hurl a barb; the other would feel obliged to hurl it back, twice as sharp. Yet now, as Dianket looked at the girl, she made no attempt to respond to Balor's insult. Indeed, she watched him with a wide-eyed look of hopeful eagerness, obviously wanting his approval. The expression of adoration upon her face was so alien to her usually volatile, quarrelsome nature that she confirmed a suspicion Dianket had held for years: Morrigan was in love with Balor.

But the object of her affections was oblivious to her condition as he brought the little hearth cake to his nose for a wary sniff. Sure Snout, lying close by his side, lifted her head, eyed the cake, and whined softly in appreciation of its fragrance, obviously asking her master to share it with her. Balor looked down and fondled her ears with his free hand.

"Yes, I know you'd like a bite, old friend. But there's a question, you see—is it fit to feed to a dog?"

This was too much for Morrigan. Her face congested with righteous indignation, and only Dianket noticed the tears of hurt that she managed to blink from her eyes as she glared defiantly at Balor. "You insufferable, insolent ingrate! If there's any question to be asked, it's this—which one of you *is* the dog?"

Balor laughed, amused by her retort, satisfied by the sight of her anger. He enjoyed riling her. Indeed, these last few weeks he had found her to be a particularly unsettling intrusion into his life. A change had come over her, one that perplexed him almost as much as it annoyed him. Often when on the training field with Draga and the other youths who had entered their Year of Trial, he would see her standing with the other women and girls; a rare thing for a wild, disagreeable tomboy who, if given a choice, was always with the boys, bending a bow, or knapping a flint, or riding a pony to a lather. But there she would be, her eyes on him, her face transfixed. She had taken to following him about, offering bits of gossip or gifts from her cooking fire, or samples of herbs or roots for Dianket to add to his growing collection of healing aids. Yet, even when she spoke to Dianket, she looked at Balor, stared at him until, unnerved, he would shout at her and deliberately rouse the fire of anger in her. Somehow she was more tolerable to him this way, in her old guise.

Now as he looked at her across the warm, glowing coals of the hearth pit, he was gratified to see that he had once again succeeded in igniting her wrath. Her eyes met his unflinchingly, in a clear contest of will. With a snap of his fingers he sent the hearth cake flying into the fire pit, where it landed upon the coals and began to steam and shrivel. Sure Snout whimpered against his folly, but he paid no heed to her.

He lay back upon his sleeping skins, flung an arm across his eyes, and said with annoyance: "Go home, Morrigan. It isn't suitable for a female of your age to be wandering about the holding at whim, or to—"

Her eyes flashed as she interrupted with open hostility. "I'd wager that if I were Dana, you'd not want to send me away!"

The accusation took him by surprise. He thought of Elathan's teasing. Were his feelings for Draga's daughter so obvious to everyone, when he had only just begun to admit them to himself? Slowly he drew back his arm and glared at Morrigan with pure loathing. How dare she trespass into his most secret thoughts? "If you were Dana, you wouldn't have to be reminded of your place, Morrigan. And yes, come to think of it, if you were Dana, you *would* be welcome, for she's as kind and easy on a man's spirit as you are a burr and a bruise to it!"

She rose, her face red and her fists clenched. "And who told you that you are a man, eh? You've yet to prove your worth, Balor, and I, frankly, doubt that you ever shall!"

"Hold now and easy, the both of you," soothed Dianket, ill at ease with the role of arbitrator. His next words were spoken gently; he had no wish to further injure the girl's pride. "Tongues *are* beginning to wag, Morrigan. We aren't children anymore. Balor is right. It is not suitable for a young female to—"

"What does my gender have to do with it! Just because I've come of age, must I also become a different person? Must I begin to simper, bat my lashes, and fuss about my clothes as I tend to my cooking and pot making? By the Twelve Winds, if given half a chance, I'd prove to you that I am capable of more than that! I can ride as well as any man and shoot an arrow with just as keen an eye!"

Dianket's brow worked with speculation. "No one would dispute that, Morrigan, but you are now a woman and someday shall carry the future of the clan within you. There is no task that is more important than that. You are not expected to excel at—"

She cut him off with a snap and a snarl. "I will choose which tasks to set my hand to, and I will excel at any I choose."

"Then go home," suggested Balor icily, putting his arm back across his eyes again. "Sit with your sisters. Set your hand to learning to behave like a proper female. Excel at that. If, in fact, you are a girl at all."

"Oh!" The word was a shriek as she stamped her foot. "By the gods my mother swore by! By the name of the father whose seed set life to me! If I'd been born a man, I'd put shame to the both of you!" With that she whirled and stalked from the house, but not before she had kicked the trencher of hearth cakes into the fire.

The moments passed in silence. Then Dianket spoke softly. "You mustn't want Draga's daughter."

The words roused Balor from the edge of sleep. "Who said that I did?"

"No one has to say it. It's all over you." Dianket turned the toy horse within his fingers meditatively. An expression of pure longing moved across his eyes and would have exposed his own love for Dana had Balor been looking at him. He added with a levity he did not feel: "Dana shall be for the best and the bravest. Draga will see to that."

Balor did not respond. The thought of Dana being given to another made him twitch as though ants crawled beneath his skin. Until recently Dana had been just another girl; then clan law proclaimed her a woman, and half the eligible males within the holding were ready to come to blows over her. Indeed, it was as though she had been transformed overnight. Perhaps the change was within him as well; he could not say. He only knew that the quiet, kind little girl was gone, and in her place was a tall, graceful young woman as golden as a summer sunrise, as tender and ethereal as mist rising over the marshes. He could no longer speak a simple sentence to her without stammering, nor could he keep the image of her beauty from invading his thoughts with a pervasive constancy that seemed to make everything else unimportant. When Draga spoke of the girl's many suitors, it seemed to Balor that his blood would boil in his ears until he would go deaf with frustration, for although Balor was a year older than Dana, despite his size and strength, he had yet to complete his Year of Trial. By clan law he was still a lad who had yet to prove his manhood and was therefore ineligible to sue for a woman. Not that he wanted one. And this was what most confounded him. Surely he did not want a woman at this stage of his life.

Yet he found himself saying belligerently to Dianket, "Who's to say that I'm not the best and the bravest! And who's to say that Dana wouldn't prefer me to the others?"

Dianket shook his head. He would never fully be able to resign himself to Balor's natural arrogance. "You know as well as I, Balor, that by law Dana cannot choose you, not until you have completed your Year of Trial and have endured the Rite of Passage that initiates you into the clan as a man of rank and obligation."

"It is a stupid law!"

"Although it may not serve you, Balor, it is not stupid. It assures that a man must remain a bachelor if he cannot protect or provide for a woman or the children she may bear him. It is steeped in time and tradition and serves the welfare of all concerned."

Truth stabbed deep. Balor sat up, glowering. "I'm as tall and as strong as nearly any man within this holding. Draga says that I'm the most promising student at arms he's ever had. In time I'll best them all! You'll see! They'll all see!"

"Aye. But promises cannot turn time, Balor. Dana's a year past coming to full womanhood. She could have named a man last spring, but she refused to make a choice. As a virgin, that is her right. Some women wait years... but not the pretty ones, for a virgin's right is canceled if dissension erupts among those who would have her. To keep the peace the chieftain may be forced to invoke clan law in the matter. Mark me, before the Marrying Moon rises in November the lord will force Dana to name a man. If she refuses, Draga will do the naming for her. Forget her, Balor. She is not for you. Besides, I thought you told me that you wanted never to marry?"

Confusion swarmed in Balor's head like angry wasps. "I don't! But—"

Dianket smiled sadly. "I know. When you look at Dana, even though the clan says you are not a man, you cannot help but want her."

Balor was too concerned with his own thoughts to notice the longing within Dianket's tone. He thought of Mael, his chief antagonist. Cocky, pugnacious, as smug and self-assured as a strutting gull gulping down mud beetles along the marsh strand, Mael openly courted Dana and stood high in Draga's favor among the girl's suitors. If the chieftain were to force Dana to make a choice, she would probably name Mael, if only because she knew that her father liked him. Everyone knew that Dana adored her sire and would go to any lengths to please him. By playing upon Draga's affection, Mael was virtually assured of winning Dana.

"It isn't right!" Balor said savagely. "I know I'm young, but

I'd make her a better husband than Mael! It's an unfair law that would keep me from proving it!"

Dianket sat very still, measuring his friend, disturbed by what he saw. "Nevertheless it *is* the law, and your father would be wise to invoke it if it will ensure peace among his clansmen."

"Peace! I care not for his cursed peace!" Balor rose, restless beyond bearing, then knelt, balancing his weight on the balls of his feet as he rested his forearms across his thighs and stared into the fire pit. As he glared at the coals they seemed to glare back at him. An idea struck him. He spoke it aloud as he looked up at Dianket, his spirits lifting. "You know, if I were to go to Draga, if I were to ask him to put the others off just until I'm able to act as a suitor... Everyone knows that Dana's in no hurry to name a man. And Draga and I have been close these past years... aye... very close...."

"It is forbidden, Balor. You cannot speak to Dana's sire as a suitor until you are officially recognized as a man. To do so, you would be deliberately breaking the law. That is something that I'd not risk doing again if I were you, old friend... not with your past record. And I'd not willingly put myself in Draga's debt these days. The payment he may ask might be more than you are willing to pay. There's something dark eating at his soul."

Balor scowled. "Aye! And rightly so! It is called dissatisfaction with the life we lead here—a dissatisfaction that we share, Draga and I! If you had been with us at Point of Ale, Dianket, you would understand."

"I understand only that the law is the law, Balor. It is the fiber that binds the strength and the unity of the clan. That cannot be changed."

"No?"

Dianket was scorched by the heat of the resolve that burned in Balor's eyes. He had seen it there before, a fathomless thing, turbulent and full of pain. Dianket wished that he could console and understand Balor. They had always been closer than brothers. But Balor had changed since his return from Point of Ale five years ago. He had hardened, as though his spirit had been honed and reshaped, like a rough-edged flint that has come away from a knapper's hand, its purpose redefined. Yet whatever that new purpose was, Balor had not revealed it to Dianket. Although they lived

together and shared may of their innermost thoughts, Balor
was often like a troubled, secretive, restless stranger. So now
Dianket spoke soothingly, not wanting to strike an unknown
bruise. "You've had a long day, Balor. Why not rest awhile?
We can talk about this later."

The wine of weariness ran in Balor's veins. He acknowledged it as he lay back upon his sleeping skins again and
closed his eyes. "What use is it to sleep? I'll only dream of
Dana." He sighed and mused darkly. "You're right. I'm
thinking like a fool. I don't want a woman. But by the Fates, I
think females must be a curse upon the world, born to
befuddle men. Don't ever fall in love, Dianket. It's a sorry
and confusing state."

"Yes," said the healer's son softly. "I know."

The coal in the fire pit settled. Dianket made no move to
rouse them. Balor slept. Sure Snout yawned. Outside, snow
turned to sleet, scudding across the thatching of the roof and
beating a thin, steady rhythm.

Dianket turned the little carving of the horse over and over
between his long, slender fingers, observing it as though it
were the work of a stranger. Not much larger than his thumb,
it seemed to prance within his grasp, its mane flying, the tiny,
spiraling horn upon its brow a stab of defiance, a challenge to
the natural order of things—for the carving was not of a horse
at all . . . it was of the fabled monoceros. It was not to have
been a gift for a child, it was much too fine for that. It had
taken him days to carve it. It was to have been for one who
loved its legend best of all, a gift for one whose gentleness
and beauty had brought the sweet pain of love to his heart, a
gift for the fair Dana.

Now, as he looked across the fire pit at Balor, he saw the
strong, undeniably handsome youth that his friend had become and, for the first time, forced himself to admit to the
extent of his own foolishness. Could he actually have imagined that Dana might share his feelings?

Before the weather had turned so cold again, only days
ago, they had stood together to watch a butterfly emerge
from a chrysalis that was attached to a crevice within the
timbered wall of the palisade. Dana had caught her breath
with appreciation and delight as the butterfly emerged from

its cocoon—wrinkled and twisted, a bedraggled, exhausted thing, which soon unfurled like a wonderful bit of multicolored cloth until it stood bold and brilliant, wings spread, antennae flexing, ready to respond to the instinct that sent it riding high on the back of the wind.

Sadness had touched the girl in that moment. "The cycle is complete for it now, Dianket. Soon it shall die."

They had stood so close that their arms had touched. He had seen tears lake between her eyelids, and although her nearness disoriented him, he had sought to soothe her. "No, Dana. It shall be fulfilled. It shall seek a mate. Through their children it shall be reborn again and again and forever."

The words had not comforted her. A haunted, hunted look had crossed her face. "But *it* will die. Oh, Dianket, I wish I could keep it safe, alive. I wish none of us ever had to grow up. I wish . . ." She had paused, and her eyes lingered on his face, gently, so openly that he had blinked, startled, for what he had seen within them had surely been a trick of the light or purely wishful thinking upon his part. It had been love. Radiant. Intense. Love. For *him*.

But then she had blushed and looked away, distracted as Balor and several other young men had passed on their way to the training field. Bold-eyed, they had all looked at Dana appreciatively, but Balor had inadvertently fallen out of step with the others, mooning back at Dana, lovestruck. To the uproarious delight of his companions, Mael, who often accompanied the younger men to their training so that he might assist Draga with their instruction, tripped Balor with his stave and bellowed with delight as the youth had gone sprawling. But Mael's catcalls had rapidly deteriorated into resentful mumblings as Dana, without a moment's hesitation, had flown to Balor's side. In that moment Dianket had known that what he had read into her eyes had been the wishes of a fool. It had not been love. It had been pity.

Pity for one who, by clan law, would never be named a man. Pity for one who, crippled and deformed of limb, would never be allowed to paint his face and body with woad or madder to proclaim the totem signs of his ancestors. Pity for one who would never be allowed to take a wife, or sit at council, or share in any of the responsibilities of decision making. Pity for one who would not even be allowed to offer sacrifice to the Twelve Winds lest his ill-healed limb offend the gods and invalidate the offerings and intentions of his clansmen. A healer he might be, for this had been his father's craft, and Munremar, taking pity on him, had granted him a special dispensation to practice it for the good of all. And perhaps someday some aging widow would take pity upon his needs and come to share his hearth with him. But Dana would be for another.

Slowly his eyes focused forward out of memory and held upon his sleeping friend. Bitterness scalded him. It was Balor who had crippled him! It was Balor who had robbed him of any chance of winning Dana for himself. He was glad that the Fates had seen to it that Balor would also be deprived of the girl.

But no! He rebuked himself. He was not being fair. No one could have been a better or more loyal friend than Balor. While those who had once called him comrade ignored him, or worse, sought to coddle him as an invalid, Balor had gotten it into his head that patience and resolve might yet make Dianket whole again. During the past years Balor had helped him splint and bind his leg so the two of them could ride out into the countryside. Sometimes Elathan or Tethra and Indech would go along, but usually it was just the two of them, and he suspected that many times Balor disdained other activities with his friends so that he might be with Dianket instead.

Balor would take him where streams ran fresh and cool, where fish came up greedy, eager to swim into their nets. Sharing his ever-expanding knowledge of the ways of the men of the clan MacLir, Balor taught Dianket to make flies of horsehair, to carve fishhooks of antler, and to weave fiber nets of such exquisite construction that they were nearly invisible. Balor taught him how to hunt with a bow too, and gave him a weapon—one that Balor himself had made for Dianket, under Dathen's tutelage—a bow of compound construction, hardwood and sapwood for superior resilience, its ends tipped with ferrules of polished bone, the handgrip wound with row upon row of fibrous thread to provide an extra-firm grip as well as to absorb the sweat from an archer's palm.

"I have no need of such a fine weapon, Balor," he had protested, overwhelmed by the gift.

"Nonsense," the chieftain's son had retorted. "You'll be

well and strong again someday. You'll need a man's skills. And a man's weapons."

Balor had taught him to use a blade, an ax, and a cudgel, and often at night or during long, dark winter days, using the crossbeams of the healer's little roundhouse for targets, the two of them would lie on their backs, happily drunk on mead, shooting at knotholes and vermin until they grew sleepy and fell into a mindless state of pure contentment. Dianket would dream wonderful dreams in which he was whole again and all the world praised him for his excellence in the manly arts. But always when he awoke, the cripple awoke with him, and life was as it had been since the day the great storm had robbed him of a man's future.

Yes. The storm, Dianket told himself. *It* had robbed him. Not Balor. It had called to the beast of pride from his soul, and he had made no attempt to leash it. He had rejected the use of safety ropes; he had wanted to prove that he was braver than Balor; he had wanted to win the adulation of Dana, for—yes!—even then he had loved her. He had won her pity instead, and if she expressed her love for him now, he must be mature enough to admit that it was the same sort of love that she would show to any broken, battered thing.

Far beyond the holding wolves howled—a cold, lonely sound that touched Dianket to his heart. A wave of remorse went through him as he looked down at the tiny carving of the horned horse in his hand, and suddenly the sight of it was painful to him.

The time had come to be done with dreams and live in the real world. As he told Morrigan, none of them was a child anymore. If he were ever to be a truly successful healer, he had best learn to heal himself. He must *be* a man, despite the fact that the clan would never accept him as one. This moment then would be his Rite of Passage. In silence and without complaint, he would endure it, for if he were ever going to live in peace—with his clansmen or with himself—he, like Balor, must give up his dreams of Dana.

With a flick of his thumbnail he sent the carving of the little horned horse spinning into the fire pit. It settled into the now-gray embers, leaving no imprint at all, except in the heart of the young man who rose from the hearth bench and, limping, turned away.

14

Falcon entered Dianket's tiny house, knelt, and prodded
Balor. Sure Snout, recognizing the old man, did not bark at
him, but lay still, sniffing at his garments. The chieftain had
returned from the far pastures, Falcon said, and all the holding
was in a stir, for although the bulk of the herd was safe within
the holding ring, the chieftain had discovered that yet another
of his wandering cows had been brought down by wolves. He
had had enough of these increasingly bold predations and had
declared that a hunting band was to go out from the holding at
first light in pursuit of the wolves. Balor and the other youths in
their Year of Trial were to accompany them.

Excitement warmed Balor against the chill of the room as
old Falcon left him to prepare. He ignited the tallow lamp
closest to him, donned his clothes, gathered his weapons,
strapped on his wrist guards, and filled a goat-bladder flask
with watered mead. A brief moment of reflection caused him
to lament his earlier confrontation with Morrigan; her cakes
would have been a welcome addition to a traveling larder
consisting of a sack of blanched grains and a few strips of
dried meat rimed green with winter mold.

Dianket sat up and bundled his sleeping skins about his
shoulders. "I wish I were going with you."

Balor paused a moment and nodded. "So do I. You shall on
the next hunt, mark me, we'll ride together then. But
meanwhile I'll fetch you home some pelts for a new robe, and
a wolf's head for each of us to tack to the lintel of your door,
so all who pass by will know that two hunters dwell beneath
this roof!"

Dianket looked at Balor, silent a moment, wondering if he
actually believed what he was saying. Yes. He probably did.
To the chieftain's son the Fates were like a bow, meant to be
bent to the will of man. Thoughtfully he counseled: "I've
heard the old men say that wolves are a lot like men, Balor.
They're wary, protective of their own, and dangerous when

pursued into their own territory. If you're fortunate enough to track them down and corner them, be careful, old friend. You'll need the luck of the Twelve Winds on your side."

Adrenaline was already flooding into his veins as Balor made for the door. Although he was no longer a boy, there was still a rough edge to him, a wild, thoughtless impetuosity that was destined to be tempered in blood before it would be cooled and refined into the hard resilience of manhood. He glanced back over his shoulder. "Get the tanning frame ready for the pelts I will bring you, and prepare the stakes for hanging the wolves' heads over our door. And stop worrying about me, Dianket! I've told you before, I make my own luck!"

The hunting band assembled by torchlight while the people of Bracken Fen gathered to hear Munremar's blessings and assurances that all signs portended well for the hunt. As dawn touched the sky with pink and marsh birds cried far out upon the snowy fens, the clan spoke their good-byes and watched the hunters ride out from the holding. Huldre, with pale-haired little Bevin walking beside her, followed them until, at Fomor's decree, she turned back.

Dathen, not realizing that Balor was within earshot, said to himself, "Gives me the creeps, the sight of that one does, like a marsh mist following in our wake. By the Twelve Winds, she's always been a strange one, but since we returned from Point of Ale there's been something downright spooky about her . . . like she's seen into the future, knows what it has in store for us all, and has gone mad from the sight of it. . . ."

The words disturbed Balor. He recognized the truth in them. Huldre had, indeed, always been strange, but the loss of her hawk-shaped amulet of amber had unsettled her so much that not even the birth of little Bevin had cheered her for any length of time. Even though he found her to be an embarrassment to him, she *was* his mother, and he felt a son's loyalty as well as an occasional stab of guilt for having been the one responsible for casting off her talisman. So he said to Dathen, and tried to sound offhanded about it: "Pay her no mind. She's odd, I'll grant, but in many ways she's like the rest of her gender. By the Fates, Dathen, since when do you pay heed to the superstitious babblings of women?"

Dathen ruminated a moment, then said, "I'll tell you, lad.

There's been talk of late circulating about the holding that it is your mother who has brought the snow to blight the fields so that they will not be ready to accept the seeds of life at the rising of the Planting Moon. And although Munremar has portended well for this hunt, your mother came to the council hall door, keening for us all as though we were already dead men. 'Twas a bad thing. A very bad thing. The lord was forced to chastise her publicly, but before she would return to her hearth she swore that Munremar was a false prophet and that if we did not leave Bracken Fen to resume the old ways of war and wandering, we were all destined to die."

Balor was shocked, angered, yet he said calmly, "Come now, Dathen! Those are hardly the words of a seeress. We're all destined to die sooner or later. And Huldre's been trying to persuade the chieftain to leave this holding ever since I can remember. She's been a warrior's woman. To her this settled life we lead *is* death. Frankly, there are those within this holding, including myself, who do not find much reason to disagree with her."

Dathen's eyes narrowed. "The lord leads us wisely, Balor. I would have thought that by now you would have begun to see that. But perhaps you are too much like your mother. And you spend altogether too much time listening to your uncle. That is not wise, boy. Draga is too restless for his own good these days. I do not know what prods him, but mark me, if he does not watch himself, there will be trouble over it. Big trouble."

It was the second time in only a matter of hours that Balor had been warned to avoid too close a relationship with Draga. But it was too late for such warnings; the bond had been made in the mud of the fighting arena at Point of Ale when Draga had dared to stand alone and fight to the death against Nemed MacAgnomain.

So it was that Balor bridled against Dathen for having spoken against the redbeard. "I'll choose my own friends, thank you," he said as, with a snap of his reins, he urged his horse forward and sought to ride beside his uncle.

Draga, clad in winter furs, with his elkhound running close to the massive, shaggy hooves of his big red stallion, headed his own contingent as the chieftain, well to the right and out of earshot, led the band across the bogs toward the far pastures and highlands beyond. Balor was quick to note it was a gathering of Draga's old, loyal friends and those who openly sought to court the redbeard's daughter as a wife. They were so rapt in their conversation that they took no note of the chieftain's son as he brought his sorrel to a trot beside them.

"I tell you, Draga, you're right! It makes no sense! We could all do with a bit of excitement, but there are too many men along to allow for a decent hunt. Surely by now the wolves have broken for the distant hills. They'll have seen us and scented us and felt the weight of our horses vibrating out to them through the earth. They're perceptive buggers, wolves are. A man can't expect to round them up like they were cows. What could the lord be thinking of?" Nia's voice was wheedling, impatient.

"You forget, old friend," reminded Draga, "that Fomor was once known as the Wolf, and not just because he was as strong and stalwart as one of them, but because he was a 'perceptive bugger' in his day." His use of the past tense had not been accidental. "It is my guess that he has decided that a wolf hunt would be just the thing to distract us from the bleak turn in the weather. A little excitement and spice of danger will brighten the monotony of our days and keep us content when we return to the holding to resume the endless building of fortifications designed to keep away an enemy that he knows will never come." He had spoken slowly. Now, suddenly, he snapped sharply, wanting them to be pricked by his restiveness. "By the Twelve Winds, sometimes I think that it would be a relief to know that an enemy *was* coming after us... that our labors on the fortifications have not been for naught... that the youths I train in the fighting arts will someday use the skills that once brought power and glory to their ancestors in battle, not in mere games and festivals and contests of strength and daring." He paused, and his eyes glittered. "By the Fates, imagine how it would be if we were to ride out from this place... to seek out the holdings of other clans, to forge alliances with them or to break them for their wealth and women and weapons of bronze... to ride proud against any who would stand against us, with the heads of our enemies hanging from trophy ropes about the necks of our horses!"

The words struck hard at all who heard them. They stared at Draga as he smiled as a fox smiles when it has worked successfully to rouse its prey from hiding—tensely, patiently, watchfully.

"Mark me now," he continued with a benign deference that

reeked of insincerity, "I do not speak against my brother. Has he not given to us the gift of a peaceful, productive life for which we should be grateful? Is it not, after all, better to hunt wolves than to hunt men? Is it not better to live in quiet boredom, hiding from our enemies, content with our cows and our crops, rather than to risk questing for what was once rightfully ours in the days when we dared to call ourselves warriors?"

The silence that followed was as heavy with portent as the silence that presages a crack of lightning.

The riders were still too intent upon Draga to note that Balor, cloaked and cowled against the weather, was riding at the outer edge of their group.

Nia, riding at the redbeard's right hand, leaned close to Draga and informed him conspiratorially, "I'll tell you this: Since the weather's turned on us, there's been talk within the holding—low and careful talk—about whether our luck has turned against us once again. Old Munremar says that a proper blood sacrifice has not been made since we first took Bracken Fen. Even the chieftain's second woman, as mad as she is, has dared to speak a warning to us all."

"Aye," agreed Draga readily. "And is there one of you who does not fear that the witch may at last have spoken truly?"

Balor winced against the reference to his mother and might have spoken had not the redbeard continued on with a bold, purposeful intensity that allowed no interruption.

"It is said that there are those of her race who are often blessed with the power to see into the future. Fomor himself told me that when he led the clan MacLir against the forces of Nemed and Partholon upon the far island, that Huldre—she was Nemed's woman then—knew beforehand that the warriors of Manannan MacLir would come to seek vengeance in his name. And yet now, when she warns us against approaching danger, the lord ignores her."

He shook his head ruefully, and his blue eyes burned. "By the Twelve Winds, if I were lord, I would not entrench myself in this godforsaken marsh and moorland, nor would I allow my people to be vulnerable to the whims of the weather, nor would I lead my men to harry wolves when our avowed enemies still live to threaten us! I would not rest while the one who has dishonored my murdered father, Manannan MacLir, lives in splendor, enjoying the fruits of a world, which by right should be ours!" He paused and trembled as his mouth tightened with grim resignation. "But I am not lord. And although I too am a son of Manannan MacLir, by consensus of the council the Wolf, such as he is, still rules."

Again silence settled, heavy and ominous, broken only as the hooves of the horses came down onto the hard-crusted snow and the leather trappings creaked and rubbed. Balor could hear the flat, grating sound as the horses jerked their heads out, straining to take the bone bits between their teeth. He curled his fingers tightly about his reins and recalled the warnings about Draga so recently given to him by both Dianket and Dathen. But the redbeard's words had set fire to his emotions. Draga could hardly be blamed for his frustrations and dissatisfactions. Indeed, Balor had shared them for years. And so it was that he spoke out boldly.

"Perhaps the time has come for the clan MacLir to name a new Wolf to lead us."

All eyes were on him in an instant. No one spoke. They reined in their horses and glared at him with a hostility that cut him to the bone and made him aware that his intrusion into their company and conversation was unwelcome.

Draga's eyes scorched him. "You speak unwisely, Balor. Take back your words."

Balor, surprised by his uncle's reaction, looked around to meet the resentful stares of the others. He flushed. "Why should I? Is there a man here who does not know that it is my uncle, and not my father, who should be lord?"

Draga paled. For a moment it seemed that a smile twitched on the broad span of his mouth, then it was gone. His eyes narrowed, sought a sum of Balor and then, finding it, widened with a satisfaction that was not evident in his voice as he said: "It seems that some things in life do not change, Nephew. Your tongue still needs trimming, and your ears obviously mislead you. You have misunderstood the tack of our conversation."

"It seemed clear enough to me," Balor insisted.

The redbeard's brows came together. "Be wary, Balor. As a boy born to the fens and marshes, you should remember that water often seems clearest when it lies over quicksand."

Anger stirred within Balor. "I am no boy," he replied. "And

I know well where I ride... and with whom I would place my loyalty."

There was no mistaking the black look of jealousy on Mael's wide, snub-nosed face as he glared at Balor. "You're a piss-piddling pup and would be well-advised to ride with others of your own age instead of eavesdropping on men whose loyalty to Draga is beyond question!"

Balor's temper flared. He had still not forgiven Mael for tripping him in the compound to make a fool of him before Dana. The bruises on his elbows and knees were new enough to ache as he straightened purposefully upon the back of his sorrel and glared at Mael with hard and unforgiving eyes. "Loyalty? I'd not talk about that if I were you, Mael. I see many of my uncle's old friends here.... But you and your ilk... I wonder if you will still ride with Draga if you should lose the contest for Dana."

The words hit a nerve, and had Mael not been separated from Balor by several other riders, he would have flown at him. As it was, Gar and Echur had to hold him down as he shouted: "Why, you son of a white-haired witch, how dare you speak so to me? As though you had the right to question the loyalty of any man! You, who would turn upon your own father!"

"I do not turn against him. It is he who has turned on me. I am a grandson of Manannan MacLir, heir to the customs and traditions of the People of the Ax. It is in my blood—even if it is not in yours—to side with strength against weakness."

Mael strained against those who held him. With a downward snap of his head, he spat contemptuously on the ground. "Strength? Aye. Draga has that. But I can think of a better word for a son who would call for a king-making at his own father's expense!"

Balor could feel the eyes of the others fixed upon him; their stares had intensified. Something snagged far at the back of his brain—a memory roused, yet not fully awakened; it begged for transcription, yet at the same time eluded it. Something about how a man claimed the chieftainship of another... but what?

It was Echur who spoke. "Ease your temper, Mael. It is obvious that he does not understand what he has said. Balor, we who now ride with Draga are dissatisfied and *would* provoke the lord to turn back to the old ways of the warrior, yes. But there is not a man here would call for a king-making nor, surely, is there a one of us who would seek to be lord in his place. For by the customs and traditions of the People of the Ax, before a new chieftain may claim sovereignty over the clan, the old chieftain must die . . . by the hand of the man who would displace him."

Balor felt suddenly sick, disoriented.

Echur observed him and nodded. "There! Do you see? Look at his face. I told you he didn't know. If he had, he'd never have spoken out as he did. After all, what sort of youth would wantonly seek to bring about the death of his own kin?"

"What sort indeed?" queried Draga, as though the question required an echo, but not an answer. He urged his horse around, and as the others reined their own mounts aside, he brought the big red stallion close to Balor so that he might put an avuncular arm about the youth's broad shoulders. "Come now, lad. Don't brood on it."

Balor looked at his uncle, earnestly wanting him to see the truth of his next statement. "I didn't know. . . . Truly I didn't."

"Of course you didn't. The clan MacLir hasn't seen a king-making since Manannan himself was named lord. And that was so long ago that few are left alive who were witness to it."

Mael snarled with open disgust and resentment at the sight of uncle and nephew, close and conciliatory. "We didn't ride out into the cold dawn to coo over our relatives! There are wolves to hunt out there!" With a brutal yank on his reins, he wheeled his horse around and was off at a gallop after the main body of the hunting band.

The others followed. Draga watched them for a moment, then gave Balor's back a rough and friendly slap. "There now! Did you not hear Mael? Wolves await us, my boy! And although it's late in the season, all signs point to them still running in pack. If we're fortunate, perhaps you and I can track down the leader. Now *there* shall be a beast worth skinning! As wise and wary and strong as the North Wind. So come along, Balor the Lucky, ride with your aging uncle Draga!"

"Aging? You? Impossible!"

The redbeard laughed, but somehow there was no merri-

ment in the sound. "Come along, Nephew. Time's not to be
squandered. Ride with me and I'll show you how to bring
down a wolf. Aye, with the two of us working together, it
shouldn't prove too difficult. No, I doubt if it shall prove
difficult at all!"

Huldre stood alone on the platform high atop the palisade.
With one hand resting on the topmost edge of the palisade
and the other shielding her eyes from the glare of the dawn,
she could see for miles. And everywhere she looked the land
was red, aflame in the dawn. The hunting band was silhouetted against a sky and landscape of fire. Men . . . horses . . .
dogs . . . they were black figures in motion within a cauldron
of light and heat; as though they were not men and beasts at
all, but charred, grotesquely animate fragments of bone
settling into red-hot coals. Any moment they would be
consumed, gone forever into the Otherworld, and there
would be only the heat and the flame and the bold, burning
eye of the sun.

And she would be alone. Or dead, beside them.

Her pale eyes teared, scalded by the light as, deep within
her, something caught fire and burned. It was fear, her
constant companion. She gasped against it. Closing her eyes,
she put back her head. The dawn wind was rising all around
her, combing back the long, moon-colored strands of her hair.
It was a soft wind, as warm as Fomor's breath against her
throat. Yet it did not warm her. She trembled, chilled, as the
fear that had risen to sear her vision turned her cold with
dread.

Something was wrong.

Something dark and hideous lurked beyond the burning
dawn; an eye, a huge, black raven's eye, watching, unblinking, all-seeing, seeking her out across the miles. The Eye of
Donar. *His* eye now. The eye of Nemed MacAgnomain.

Absently, her fingers moved to seek out her amulet, that
smooth carving of magic that interpreted her visions and
soothed her fears so that she might deal with them. But the
amulet was gone, and with it Donar's power of protection, as
well as her ability to define her premonitions. Again she
shivered as, behind her closed lids, fear throbbed and burned,

clotted her thoughts, drove away all hope of rationality as it welled within her like blood rising within a wound.

The Eye of Donar is *Nemed*'s now. With it he watches. With it he waits. With it he shall come for us. Soon now. He *shall* come.

"Mother..." Elathan had come up the slatted ladder of peeled logs to stand beside her. He put a hand gently on her elbow. "Father and Balor will come to no harm. Let's go home now. Bevin is crying for want of your comfort."

Huldre opened her eyes and stared blank-faced at her younger son. She was disoriented. These days it was often difficult for her to tell today from yesterday, or to keep the past from blotting out the present. The color of the dawn had faded, cooling the world, causing her vision of blood and fire to ebb. Yet she did not see her son. Her mind was filled with sound, with boiling clouds, with vast, appalling distances of memory across which a young girl ran, pursued by baying hounds and a laughing, black-haired man with raven's eyes and a slave collar in his hands. She heard the blaring of horns and saw slavers waiting in their great, long ships while her people, oblivious to danger, drove their herds of reindeer ahead of them. The young girl with moon-colored hair clutched the Eye of Donar and cried out a hysterical warning.

"We must leave this place! We are in danger here! Why does no one listen? Can't you see? It is not I who warns you, it is the god who speaks through me!"

Elathan frowned with concern. She seemed to be looking through him. Her face was so pale that he was certain that she was going to faint. He tightened his grip on her arm to steady her. "Mother... are you all right?"

She blinked, startled. Who was this tall, broadly built young man? Why did he call her his mother? Her heart quickened. She looked into the face of the youth and saw not Elathan, but Fomor MacLir as he had been long ago, on the day he had brought his people to settle within the fens, to live in peace, swearing that Nemed would never find them.

"No!" she cried, wrenching her arm away. "We must run free before the Twelve Winds. We must live as wild and wise as the wolves who howl in the night. We must not settle. We must not ever settle. Those who dwell long in one place soon grow soft. Behind walls men fatten upon complacency; they grow as nasty and treacherous as badgers too long confined within their dens by winter snows. I tell you, Nemed shall find us, and no walls shall keep him from taking final vengeance on us."

"Nemed thinks us dead, Mother. After all of these years, surely he has forgotten us."

Mother. Again he called her that. This time, slowly, she recognized him. Fear was a cold wind howling deep within the misted recesses of her soul; her fingers plucked at her throat as a dying man's hands pluck at the air. "He shall never forget us, Elathan," she hissed. "At night I lie awake and can feel him breathing across the miles. Perhaps he has already found the amulet. He shall know it as mine and realize that he has been tricked. Then he shall come for us. Soon now. Yes. He *shall* come."

"Let him then. We are not afraid. The lord has made our holding strong. You may be certain of that."

"Without the Eye of Donar to grant clarity to my Sight, I am certain of nothing."

Her last words had been soft mewings, like the sound of an animal exhausted by hours of straining against the pitiless grasp of a trap. Elathan looked away, relieved to have been distracted by the sight of old Munremar passing below them on the plank walkway that led to the council hall. Elathan was shocked by the depth of the hatred for Huldre that burned in the old man's eyes. Fear stirred in his gut like a clutch of worms squirming beneath an overturned rock. Elathan would not choose to have Munremar as an enemy—his powers were great. His anger was terrible to behold, and although Elathan had never seen the old man do anything more sinister than threaten, he had seen Munremar work his magic at clan feasts and seen him send sacrificial beasts to the Otherworld with his sacred dagger.

It was said that in days gone by the Wise One had slain human captives as sacrifice to the Twelve Winds, until Fomor had put an end to the practice when they had settled in the fens. Elathan cringed against a sudden image of the old man bent over his victims, opening their throats from ear to ear with one sure stroke of his blade, watching, satisfied as the red heat of life spurted out into the muck of the bog graves into which the victims were then tossed, still alive, still conscious, as earth was shoveled over them and groundwater oozed up to drown them even as they suffocated and bled to death.

The youth gulped and put a hand to his own throat, as though to stay the imaginary blade, then felt foolish. No one had gone to such a fate in years. Still, the worms of fear continued to churn in his belly as Munremar walked away, for he knew of his mother's earlier confrontation with the Wise One. It was the talk of the holding—a brazen and wanton breach of clan discipline. No one spoke to Munremar the way she had dared to speak. No one challenged him, unless it was the chieftain, and then only in an assembly. Yet, Elathan thought with some small measure of relief, his mother was the chieftain's woman. As such, there was not much that Munremar could do to her unless Fomor and the council approved—and that was something that was not likely to happen. Fomor was fiercely protective of his second woman. She was the mother of his children. There was still the heat of passion between them, real and deep. Munremar would have to be careful if he even sought to ill-wish her, lest he bring down upon himself the wrath of the chieftain.

Elathan's eyes moved back to his mother. "Come away now, Mother. You should stay out of the Wise One's sight until his anger toward you is gone. Until Father comes back."

His voice seemed to be coming from far away. Slowly Huldre's mind was coming back into focus; she looked at Elathan and spoke his name, reconfirming that he was her son and not Fomor.

Elathan's frown deepened. Why did she speak his name like that? By the Twelve Winds, perhaps the gossips were right. Perhaps she truly was mad. But no! He would not believe it. "Come now, Mother. Bevin has need of you."

"Bevin?" She sighed the word, then nodded and smiled. "Ahh, yes. Bevin. My daughter."

"Of course she's your daughter! Who else's daughter would be crying for you?"

Her pale, slender brows, like stalks of sun-silvered corn etched across the snowy expanse of her forehead, twitched with irony. "I have miscarried five daughters, Elathan. Sometimes it is difficult for me to realize that the Fates have at last allowed me the joy of mothering a girl-child. Yet it does not matter. Soon the joy shall be no more, for we shall all die if we do not leave this place."

He did not wish to be impatient with her, yet he knew that he sounded very much like his father when he snapped: "By the power of the Twelve Winds, woman, you've been dishing up that warning since I was a suckling! Will you never tire of it?"

"I have seen blood in the dawn, Elathan. Blood and fire."

"The blood of wolves! The fire of hunting encampments! Be reasonable, Mother. Was there ever a woman born who did not fear the worst when her men were off on a hunt?"

"And was there ever a man born who would listen to reason when he heard it?"

He laughed then and with rough fondness gave her a hug as though he were the parent and she the child. "When you speak reason, Mother, then we shall listen."

She shrugged off his embrace. Her arms rose and folded across her breasts, rumpling the soft skins of her tunic as her hands crossed and lay softly against her throat. "The day shall come, Elathan, when you shall remember that you have mocked me. You shall all remember. But then it shall be too late."

The wild heath stretched out toward the distant highlands. The chieftain drew rein and raised his arm, signaling those in his company to gather before him while Draga and his contingent continued to ride well behind, engrossed in conversations not intended for their lord.

Tracks in the snow had led Fomor here—neat, concise little fox tracks set down in last night's fresh powder. It was as though a covenant had been made between the two species; where the wolf walked, so also walked the fox, following in the footsteps of his larger cousin, waiting patiently to feast upon his leavings.

The location of the kill would have been easy enough to spot even if the dogs had not scented it, for ravens had swooped down to feast upon what was left of the cow's carcass, and as the dogs went after them, barking aggressively, the birds flew up, cawing a raucous protest.

Fomor eyed the dogs as they rooted and snorted in the bloodied snow. They nosed through the scattered rubble of bones and bits of hide and fragments of flesh, snapping and growling at one another as they instinctively competed for scraps. Impatiently the chieftain commanded that the dogs be restrained as he surveyed the faces of the assembled hunting band. They seemed as intense as their dogs, as eager for the hunt and the kill that would follow it. The winter had been long for them. Too long. The months of cold and darkness had made them restless and quick-tempered. Fomor was actually thankful that the leader of the wolf pack had presented him with a reason to lead his men out of the holding for much-needed diversion.

Shifting his weight on the fur-blanketed back of his stallion, he saw that where the fox tracks left off, wolf tracks could be seen leading up-country into the heath, and no doubt into the highlands beyond. Experience had taught him that wolves, like men, usually sought high ground for their habitation, from which they could observe the approach of potential enemies.

As his brow furrowed with thoughtful observation, Fomor nodded to himself, satisfied. The number and varying sizes of the paw prints confirmed his suspicions: This was no mere individual family group consisting of a male, a female, and the usual pair or triad of yearlings hunting together to provide for themselves as well as for the cubs that would be secreted within the family den. No. This was still a winter pack, and a large one; the unseasonably cold springtime weather had kept them grouped together. It had made them bold and dangerous and reckless.

The leader of the pack had made a fatal error—the animal had unwisely chosen to bring down the calf in fresh powder at the end of yesterday's storm. As the skies had cleared during the night, the temperature had plummeted and the tracks of the wolves had frozen solid. Fomor knew that they would lead the men of the clan MacLir into the pack's territory, and although most of the wolves would escape, many would end up as pelts, which would warm the people of Bracken Fen against the cold nights of next year's winter. Traps would be set for those animals who managed to elude the hunters' spears and arrows. The men of the hunting band would also use their dogs to sniff out those places where the wolves buried and cached portions of their kills. These would be poisoned, and in the weeks to come many a wolf that might otherwise have lived to prey upon the herds of the men of MacLir would die. In the night, when the mate of such a beast would bay in loneliness to the moon and stars, the men of the hunting band would listen and say to their people: "The wolf sings a lament... one that we have written for him."

A rush of empathy stirred within the chieftain. He, who had once killed four male wolves with his bare hands in a fighting pit of the Beaker Folk, felt no animosity toward the beasts. He sought to kill them because they had trespassed into what, by right and will, he had claimed as his own territory. He would prefer to leave them at peace, for they reminded him of days long gone by when he and his father, Manannan MacLir, had sought shelter within a ravine upwind of a den of wolves. They had gone there to observe, and as the days had passed, the boy Fomor, with his father to teach him, had learned of loyalty and bravery and filial love... from wolves, not from men.

He drew a breath and reluctantly let the memory ebb away as another rose briefly to replace it... a memory of a night not so long ago, when he and Balor had sheltered together upon the tor beneath the broad, star-bejeweled sky of Albion. With the boy warm and close and trusting within the fold of his father's arm, time had seemed to stand still, benevolent, soft, and full of promise.

Now, as his eyes sought Balor among the approaching contingent of Draga's followers, he saw a stranger there. The boy was gone as surely as his own youth, and as he was stung by the cold, contemptuous hostility within Balor's eyes, he wondered if they would ever be close again.

Surely and steadily the dogs led them after their prey, following not only the paw prints in the snow, but the scent of the beasts that had laid them. The dog pack fanned out in excited pursuit of the wolves, who had evidently broken into smaller groups, each making off in different directions to confuse and mislead their trackers. Fomor informed the hunting band that they should encourage their dogs to follow only the tracks that led upland across the heath, but before he could explain his reasons, Draga, in surly challenge, offered his opinion that it would be better to divide the hunting band, to set each man and a partner on individual tracks so that each wolf might be followed and slain. So cocksure was he that the chieftain, after a moment's hesitation— his green eyes not failing to note that the redbeard was surrounded by a growing band of loyal supporters—agreed, but not before he said: "Of course, if we find ourselves being led round in circles, then we'll agree to do this my way."

"Of course!" assented Draga, nodding with a deference that he obviously did not feel, intoxicated upon the moment as he took leadership of the hunting band with Balor and Mael close at his side, commanding the others to each choose a partner and, with their dogs, be off after a particular set of tracks.

But soon the paw prints of the wolves became difficult to follow as they made their way along stream courses and beneath low tangles of brush, running in wide circles, then backtracking. After an hour's time most of the hunters found themselves led back to where Fomor patiently awaited them.

Fomor saw the resentment in his brother's eyes and the flush of shame on his face and looked away. The older members of the party had chosen to remain behind with Fomor as Draga had led the others off. They had hunted with the chieftain and had fought beside him in days gone by; they trusted his judgment in all things. Visualizing the bounty in pelts and wolves' heads that would, thanks to Fomor's wisdom, soon be theirs, they tested the weight of their weapons and snare nets as those who had chosen to ride with Draga now eyed the redbeard with unspoken criticism. He had roused them against their chieftain's judgment, and now that judgment had been proved sound. The Wolf *was* still the Wolf for all of Draga's doubts, and although their desire to win his daughter kept them from openly rebuking him, they exchanged telling glances and Draga knew that in the future he would find it much more difficult to rouse them against Fomor.

Sensing their critical scrutiny, Draga's face congested with belligerence. He did not know what annoyed him more: the fact that they had obviously lost confidence in him, or the fact that he had been proven wrong. Angry with them and with himself, he reached for the bladder flask that hung from a thong about his horse's neck. The long ride in the cold dampness of the morning had roused the all too familiar pain that browsed perpetually within the marrow of his bones. He had hoped that movement would ease it. It had not. His back and shoulders ached cruelly, and when he flexed his fingers, fire seared his joints. He lifted the flask and drank deeply of the mead within it, a brew that he had liberally laced with anesthetizing oil of willow before he had left the holding. Soon the pain would be dulled, but not his feelings of antipathy toward his brother. Once again Fomor had managed to outshine him in the eyes of his clansmen. He glared at the chieftain, and when he spoke, backhanding mead from his mouth and beard, his words issued as growls, as low and vicious as the snarls of a cornered wolf.

"If you ask me, it's all a waste of time. There'll always be predators making off with a few head now and again. Our herd of cattle has grown large; we can't hope to protect them all. So I say, why not leave the wolves to the wild and dare to do a man's work—drive our cattle south when the calving's done. They're prime, fat stock. They'd fetch a fortune at Point of Ale. After all of these years I doubt if there'd be much risk in the venture. Who'd remember us, eh? And even if someone did, well, now we'd be armed and ready for them this time—not like it was before . . . not—"

"Be silent, Brother! This is not a council, nor has anyone asked for your opinion. You've already led us round one circle today, so keep your suggestions to yourself lest once again you prove yourself the fool!" The chieftain measured Draga with a scalding, yet not totally unsympathetic eye. "We've been all through this before. Yes, five years have passed since last we left the holding to journey to Point of Ale, but we are still bronze poor, and I say to you now, as I said then, that our livestock *is* our fortune. It grants us independence from the world beyond the fens. From it we gain all that we need, and that small portion that it does not grant to us is given freely from the earth when the harvest of our labors in the fields is reaped. What more could any fortune in all of the world buy for us, Draga? By the Fates, man, will you never understand the value of the life I have won for us here? Will you never be content?"

"Never!" hissed the redbeard.

There was not a man within the hunting band who did not suck in his breath, startled by Draga's open defiance of his brother.

Fomor's brow lowered as his green eyes darkened and filled with riptides of anger. His mouth spasmed as he fought to control his temper. "Beware, little Brother. Someday you will go too far with me. . . ."

15

Morrigan sat in the darkness with her lean young limbs curled beneath her. Her arms extended downward, pale stalks showing through the wild black fall of her hair, supporting her weight on small, tense hands as her fingers flexed catlike and her eyes stared wide and unblinking into the night. She was as alert as an animal drawn suddenly out of sleep, ready to spring against unseen danger.

It was very late. Munremar's roundhouse was full of the sound of sleeping women. They purred like cats. Content they were, Morrigan's half sisters, as plain and plump as geese fattened and ready for the pot.

They might as well be dead, she thought impatiently, for all of the enthusiasm and sensitivity they showed toward life. They were passive creatures, satisfied to live and grow old within their father's house, currying his favor, seeing to his needs and coming and going to his beck and call, never complaining, for surely no other man would spoil them so.

Cows. Dull-witted ewes. The girl nearly spoke the words aloud, yet choked them back in time lest the old man know that she was wide awake and watching him. He had risen from his pallet and had donned his cloak. Now, in careful silence, he was moving through the darkness, across the room, toward the door, bandy-legged and as frail as an old heron, leaning on his staff much more heavily than he would have done had he known that he was being observed.

The girl's half sisters did not hear him. They slept on undisturbed, openmouthed, with their stringy yellow hair skeining out across their sleeping skins as they sucked air in and snorted it out, serene and mindless in their dreams. Morrigan watched them with contempt and wondered how those who so adamantly professed to love the Wise One could be so insensitive to the stirrings of his soul. When one loved another, there was that unspoken sixth sense between them, a knowing, a cadence of thought and heartbeat. Morrigan had sensed his restlessness. It had summoned her from her dreams as surely as if he had called her name.

Ever since the hunting band had left the holding three days ago, her nights were filled with dreams of Balor—troubled dreams, in which he was in some ill-defined danger—and then, in the deep silence that came after midnight, when the stars began their long plunge toward dawn, the old man would rise and she would find herself suddenly awake, watching him as he went out into the darkness. At first she assumed that he had simply gone out to relieve himself, but he stayed away much too long for that, not returning until the approach of morning. When he returned she would sense his weariness as he sought out his pallet, crawling beneath his sleeping skins as though wounded. Shivering, sleep eluded him, yet each morning he would rise, his face gaunt with worry and fatigue, stretch, and yawn as he informed his daughters of how well he had slept.

Sensing his need for secrecy, Morrigan had not told him that she knew of his nocturnal wanderings. But tonight her concern equaled her curiosity. She was determined to follow him. Somehow she sensed that doing so was important to them both.

Slowly, quietly, she rose and drew on her cloak of undyed, roughly woven wool. Barefooted, she went after her father into the darkness. Beyond the doorway the world was filled with mist. Munremar had vanished into it without a trace, and she followed him as through smoke to the council hall.

Unaware that Morrigan followed, he went to stand droop-shouldered before the lamp that was always kept burning upon the altar of the Twelve Winds. The small, tender flame that drew life from the oil within the sacred lamp of gold cast a frail and trembling light upon the old man.

"Spirits of power from worlds beyond, invisible forces that bind Creation from Time Beyond Beginning until Time Yet to Be, once again I come before you. I beg you, I must have a sign from you. . . ."

The words were barely audible. Morrigan drew back, close against the doorway. She stood very still, unexpectedly rent to the heart by the sight of her father. Never before had she heard him beg for anything, and never had he seemed so old, so frail, as trembling as the flame before which he stood and as vulnerable to the winds of fate.

"A sign . . ." the old man implored, yet his words were as dry and devoid of hope as autumn leaves whispering lifelessly upon the ground. "Have I not been loyal? Have I not served you well? Yet I am only a man . . . a magician . . . and if I have been forced to resort to trickery in order to represent your will, it has not been because I have wanted it so, but because you have been absent from this altar. But now I *must* have a sign. . . a *true* sign. I must be able to stand before my people and foretell what has happened during the hunt. If I cannot, the white witch from the Northland shall have succeeded in shaming me."

The girl remembered how the chieftain's woman had stood before him only days ago, naming him a false prophet and portending her own omens of doom for them all. But Huldre always promised doom. Everyone knew that she was mad, that the lord pitied her as much as he desired her, and that her ravings were without substance. But Morrigan also knew what her father knew—that if the Northwoman's prognostications proved correct, the validity of Munremar's power would be open to question and his authority as Wise One seriously undermined. She also knew that his power was based in sorcery, in the most ancient art of showmanship, in sleight of hand. It could be worked only by those who could understand the fears and desires and inherent gullibility of their fellow man.

He had told her uncounted times that there was no power save the power of bold and clever men who used their wisdom to manipulate others so that their own will might be served. So it seemed a betrayal somehow, to see him here, begging a boon of forces in which he had sworn he did not believe. And so it was that his next words took her by surprise.

"The girl's mother would have known. Aye, sweet Anu, who bore Morrigan to me. She was a true priestess—she had the Sight, the Inner Eye, in the way of the Ancient Ones. She would have known." Suddenly his breathing quickened, and he began to speak to the Twelve Winds as though they sat fully visible upon the altar before him and as fully deserving of his reprimand. "Do you remember what she said? That you would have no power here, and in the end it would be the gods of the moor and marsh, of the Standing Stones and stars that would drive us from this place. Is it true then? After all of these years am I to be forced to admit that there are greater powers in this world than even the clan MacLir may dare to dream of?"

Morrigan could scarcely breathe. The past was heavy in the room. She remembered little about her mother. A small white face. Pale eyes. Black hair as thick and silken as the down on a raven's breast. A soft woman, a silent woman, as fragrant as wild thyme. Munremar rarely spoke of her. And never had he told Morrigan that she had been a high priestess of the Ancient Ones or that she had claimed to possess the Power.

The old man drew in a loud sigh and angrily threw aside his staff and prostrated himself upon the immaculately swept floor. For a long while he did not speak. Silence congealed within the room, weighting the darkness. Then, surely, Morrigan heard a sound she had never thought to hear. Nor did she wish to hear it. Munremar was weeping.

She turned away. The night air was cool as she leaned back against the thatching of the wall. She closed her eyes. She could not bear to hear him weep. Not Munremar, not the Wise One, not he who had always been so strong, so mighty in her eyes.

Then with a clarity of thought and will that startled her, she knew what she must do. She opened her eyes and stared out into the night. If her father needed a sign from the gods, might she not act in their stead? If she were careful and quick and quiet, he would never know that it was she and not the spirits who had given him a sign.

She trembled with excitement at the thought. He, who was old and filled with doubt, *could* be made to believe that for the first time in his life the spirits had actually chosen to commune with him—not through trickery, but through a power that he had always claimed to possess and had never truly owned. He had trained her well. She too was a master of magic. And if, as Munremar had always counseled, magic was made credible by the faith of those who believed in it, then how much more powerful that magic would seem to the eyes of those who beheld it if the magician believed in it himself!

Yes! The girl suddenly knew that within her hands was the ability to grant her father a sense of power that would be greater than anything he had ever known before. Surely he, who had been her nurturer and teacher, deserved no less from her.

Once again she closed her eyes, drawing in a deep breath to strengthen her resolve.

Munremar would have his sign from the Twelve Winds!

So it was that Morrigan found herself within the secret

little room high above the altar of the Twelve Winds. In the darkness she sought a bag of "magic" powder. She pursed her lips in annoyance; nothing was where it belonged—she had been in the process of restocking and organizing and taking inventory of her supplies, as she always did at winter's end.

Ah, well, she thought, it was not important which powder flared into the altar's lamp, so long as Munremar have a sign. Any sign. *Something* that he had not engineered, something to inspire him to faith in his own powers as a seer. So she reached blindly for whatever bag of powder was nearest to her and scooted forward in the darkness to lie prone as she slid aside the vertical hatch directly over the altar.

It was the simplest and most effective of all of the tricks he had taught her: the slow release of powders, falling invisibly from the heights until, ignited by the heat of the sacred flame upon the altar, they flashed red or green, blue or gold, silver or incandescent white.

"A sign..." Munremar's words bled up to her out of the darkness. She saw him below her, an old man savaged by self-doubt as he lay splayed in the lamplight on the floor before the altar. Something tightened within her heart and throat, and she knew that she loved him with all of that portion of her heart that was not reserved for Balor.

Without a moment's hesitation she worked her hand into the bag and pulled out a generous fingering of powder. Its fine texture allowed it to fall slowly, like a cloud of moistureless mist, and she instantly recognized which powder she had randomly chosen: It was a mixture of two rare silvery, crystal-line minerals. One was ground from a hard stone, the other from a soft; both had been treated with a colorless, yellowish acid, which transformed them into a highly explosive compound. The moment it came in contact with the heat of the flame within the lamp it flared red, popped, and crackled as each tiny grain of powder burst into thousands of remnant particles of itself. It stank. It gave off a hot, acidic stench that lingered in the air and rose, glowing like a miasma, to permeate the floorboards and thatching of the walls of the secret room.

But Morrigan was not there to smell it. She was gone.

Never had she made better time in leaving and securing the secret room, descending the ladder, and racing across the compound to her father's house. When he burst into the room only a few minutes later, as she had known he would do, she was curled up in her sleeping place, feigning sleep, covered from head to toe with her sleeping skins lest he note that she was still wearing her cloak.

He was aflame as he called out her name. She sat up, her sleeping skins up around her neck, pretending to be groggy as she asked him what he wanted. Her half sisters roused themselves resentfully, complaining about being awakened when it was not yet dawn. Even though the room was unlighted, Morrigan could see her father's rapt face clearly. The eyes were enormous. The pupils floated round, surrounded by white, like dark berries on balls of snow. But there was nothing cold about them. They burned.

"Have you been there all along, girl? Sleeping?"

"Of course." The lie came easily. "Where else should I have been?"

"I thought . . . for a moment . . ." He paused, then took a great gulp of breath and went to the waist-high mead jar, which stood just at the entryway to the roundhouse's little storeroom. Taking up the wooden dipper from the crock, he sloshed it deep into the brew within, then lifted it to his lips and drank so greedily that he choked. The dark liquid ran into his beard as he sputtered, wiped it away, and drank again.

"What is it, Father?" asked the plumper of the half sisters, stifling a yawn. "You seem upset."

"Upset? I am inspired! By the power of the Twelve Winds, this night, in the lamp, the spirits of our ancestors have spoken to me out of the sacred flame!"

The girl yawned again, bored. "They always speak to you." She lay back, snuggling close to her sister beneath the bedskins. "'Tis late, Father. Let us sleep."

The old man roared and let the dipper fall into the crock as he slapped his thighs. "Go ahead, go back to sleep, chew the cud of your unimaginative dreams. I would not expect you to understand."

Morrigan smiled, content, as her half sisters turned their sleepy backs on him. By her will and action her father had been transformed. The defeated old man she had followed to the council hall was gone. The Wise One had returned to life, posturing with restored arrogance. Her smile deepened. It pleased her to see the change in him and to know that she was responsible for it. "Tell me, Father, what do you mean?" She put the question to him so innocently that only a true prophet could have seen the guile behind it.

He seated himself beside her. "I have had a sign from the Twelve Winds... a true sign. The flame was red, daughter of Anu." His voice was the voice of a man restored to his prime—confident and full of significance, like distant thunder on the moors, with the white-hot spice of lightning to give it depth and meaning. Beneath his white brows his lids narrowed as, between them, his eyes gleamed as hard as polished stones. If there was vision within them, it was focused inward, the hungry, ambitious glow of one who spins his thoughts into a webbing to support the substance of his own desires. "It *was* a sign. At last. Yes. The Power *is* mine, and I shall use it well."

Morrigan stared at him. She, who had elected to be the instrument of the Fates, could see the power rising in him. Yes, he was right, it *was* his at last, as she had wanted it to be. Yet as he rose to his feet, suddenly distracted, chewing his lower lip, chafing his hands, pacing as though his bones were restless and would burst through his skin if he did not allow them to walk about within it, she felt cold.

"What have you seen in the red flame, Father?" she asked, already knowing the answer.

"What I have known that I must see for many a long year. It was the color of blood, *their* blood—the blood of the white witch, who has dared to test the power of her Vision against mine... the blood of her pale-eyed whelp whose lawlessness has all too often undercut my authority, who has made others think me inadequate by claiming that the stones upon the moor were transformed by magic so that they might shelter him, who dared to claim that the omens of the gods were written for him in the sky with a brand of star-fire, while I, Munremar, saw nothing!"

She knew his words for what they were—not the outpourings of Vision, but of jealousy. Was this, then, how her gift was to be used? For a moment she thought that she would drop the sleeping skins and show him that she still wore the cloak she had donned before following him to the council hall; she would speak the truth to him and in the telling of it reduce him back into what he had been only an hour ago—a

frail, frightened old man. But no. She loved him too much for
that, so she said softly: "You speak of the past, Father. And
you speak against the woman and the firstborn son of our
lord. Beware, lest what you have envisioned in the flame
portend the red wrath of the chieftain, without whose confidence you shall not be allowed to speak at all."

"It is Fomor MacLir who should beware! The tide has been
turning against him for a long time now. Soon it will sweep
him away, and then the council of elders will decide in
whom they shall rest their confidence. In the meantime,
Morrigan, look not with longing after the firstborn spawn
of the white-haired witch. I have seen his blood in the fire
this night!"

It was the fourth day out from the holding, and the band
had divided into small groups of hunters. Balor went with his
uncle, avoiding his father's men. The hunting band had not
spent a single hour in any action more exciting than setting
snares, digging pit traps, poisoning buried caches that the
wolves had secreted along their runs, and nocking arrows for
the killing of small game. They had not seen a single wolf,
and now not only were the trails going cold, but the hunters
were beginning to weary of the pursuit.

"Somehow I thought it would be different," said Balor to
Draga.

The redbeard looked at him with raised eyebrows. "And
how so? Did you fancy that it would be all danger and death
and facing down fanged-toothed beasts single-handed, with
nothing between you and their slavering jaws but your bow
or blade?"

"Yes . . . something like that."

Draga snorted through his nostrils in obvious amusement.
It was high noon. They had paused and tethered their horses
within a sparse copse of thin-trunked trees at the edge of a
broad expanse of moor. Beyond it the land stretched out as
green as algae on a summer pond, tilting ever upward toward
the highlands and the tor, which soared against the horizon.
They had eaten a repast of whatever remained in their
traveling larders; Balor had little appetite. The sight of the
tor had robbed him of hunger as surely as it had piqued his
memory of the night he had shared with Fomor upon its

summit. Nostalgia stirred achingly within him as he sat with
Draga, staring off across the miles while Mael and the others
lay napping in the shade of the trees.

"Hunting wolves is tedious, boring work. If you believe
otherwise, then you've been taking the storytellers too seriously, my boy," said Draga, picking his teeth with a twig.
"You should know by now that in order to embellish history,
part and parcel of their craft is learning to stretch truth to just
the point of breaking it . . . but not quite beyond."

Balor's eyes moved to his uncle. "Are you saying that my
father did not kill those four wolves bare-handed in the
fighting pit of the Beaker Folk as legend says?"

"Oh, no, laddie! He killed them all right. Alone and
bare-handed. Just as surely as he took the head of Partholon
and stole the magic Achaean sword Retaliator and led the
clan to glory with it. But that was long ago. The head of
Partholon has been picked to bone by fishes at the bottom of
the sea. The sword lies locked away within his battle chest.
And the warrior's soul of my brother has flown away on the
back of the Twelve Winds, never to return, I'm afraid." He
paused, allowed the words to settle, saw the way they roused
restlessness within the youth, then smiled, satisfied. Since
their return from Point of Ale Balor had been loyal, a
steadfast friend and obvious admirer. Given time and proper
handling, Draga had no doubt that the impetuous, hotheaded
youth could be provoked into challenging his father. Let the
king-making, when it came, be on Balor's head. Then Draga
would be lord, and he would suffer no guilt in the knowledge
that his ascendancy had been at the cost of his brother's life.
A man had a right to claim glory in his lifetime. Indeed, he
had an obligation to his heirs to do so. And life was short. So
brutally, irrevocably short.

"I would have him as he was years ago . . . when he had the
warrior's soul . . . when all men called him Wolf."

Draga's eyes were hard and his face set as he said bleakly,
"We are none of us as we were, boy."

"No," replied Balor, "we are not. And I am no boy, Uncle."

The redbeard appraised him, squinting a little as he realized that Balor was right. How long had the lad been so
broad of shoulder, so keen-eyed, so sure of himself? Although
he had yet to complete his Year of Trial, Balor would soon be
a man to reckon with. The realization further disturbed

Draga, made him again aware of the passing years. He was suddenly resentful of his nephew. Balor possessed that which he could no longer claim as his: youth and unblemished vigor and the full potential of manhood. Jealousy rose at the back of his throat, as thick and bitter as bile. He spat it out.

"Come on away now," he said, rising, slapping the debris away from his backside. "We've lingered here long enough."

The others were rousing, sitting up, yawning, and stretching, as were the dogs who dozed beside them.

Balor would never be able to understand exactly what happened next. He only knew that as he got to his feet the sight of a hawk winging high above the distant tor set dizziness racing through his brain. He stood motionless a moment, watching, yet somehow seeing nothing save the turbulent churning of time racing back... back... reflecting images of yesterday out to him from the black pool of the past. The moor... the falling star... the tor... a great green-sailed ship... and a white wolf howling out of a summer night to send a young boy cowering in terror....

"The wolves will be there." He pointed off toward the tor, not knowing that he spoke at all.

Mael snorted in mockery. "Leash him up, friends. He's on the scent even before the dogs have sniffed it out!"

They all laughed, but it was Draga who gave him a cuff and a shove. "What ails you, lad? No four-legged beast could climb that rock! Come now. Stop dawdling. Blanket your horse and let's be off!"

Balor shivered, suddenly cold despite the warmth of the sun. It was all very clear to him, as clear as his mother's eyes. He knew it for what it was, and although he had no wish to acknowledge it, he heard himself say, "I tell you, there are wolves there." He drew a breath. The haze of Vision ebbed. He felt light-headed and foolish. He told himself that he had simply risen to his feet too quickly; things had flown out of the normal perspective. He shrugged apologetically, trying to reason it out as he explained, as much to himself as to the others: "The tor stands on high ground. From its base there's a view out over all of the moor and westward to the sea. It's where I would go to make my lair... if I were a wolf."

There was laughter again. The horses were led out and blanketed. The dogs put their noses to the scent and led the trackers far across the moor, away from the tor, and as time passed, Balor was relieved to have been proved wrong.

The slow work continued. The skin of the land was thin and bony where it lay exposed between broad swatches of new grass. There were little lakes of meltwater here and there, and the dogs went wading out across them in broad circles, whining and grinning, pant-tongued, as dogs will do when they are nervous, with their tails straight down and rigid with concern. The scent was eluding them. The cunning wolves had run through water when they could, thus leaving no scent at all. The band followed tracks that were evident, but they led nowhere, proving that the wolves had backtracked and circled, a manner that won their trackers' respect as well as their anger and frustration. Soon the riders were forced to dismount, leading their horses as they bent to the earth in search of even the subtlest trace of wolf sign, but from all they could read from the land, the wolves had disappeared. They whistled for the dogs; they came, ears back, tails tucked, eyes full of "what do we do now?"

The men decided they had gone far enough. They had set enough snares to suit them and had not discovered a single cache since yesterday's noon, a sure indication that the wolves had led their pursuers away from their usual hunting trails. Fomor declared it time to begin the long trek back to the holding, checking their snares and traps as they went, killing any beast that had fallen prey to their baited nets and pits. The men divided into groups, and Balor followed Draga and his men.

No longer taking time to track or set new snares, they made good time. Before dusk they came upon the first snare net, which had done its work. Laid with all of the skill that had been handed down to the men from their ancestors, it had been camouflaged and rigged in such a way that no scent of man or dog remained upon it. Buried under a thin layer of pebbly soil beneath a tall, wind-bent birch to which it was secured by strong fiber ties, when a wolf stepped on the snare, the weight of the animal would spring the trap, enmeshing its victim and whisking it high into the air where it hung helpless, like a piece of fruit waiting to be picked.

It was a docile and bewildered wolf the trackers came

upon. Thinking it dead, they began to prod it with their short, flint-headed killing spears until it flailed and growled, snapping and slavering, mad with fear and rage. It was Draga who set the first wounding to it. As leader and elder within this hunting unit, it was his right and privilege. He stepped close to the net, daring to poke the twisting bag of living fur and flesh and snapping teeth with his finger, as though he would make a covenant with it.

For a moment the yellow eyes turned back, round and huge with terror and frenzy, then Draga stepped back and, so that the pelt might not be spoiled, thrust his spear deep and hard into the animal's exposed side—low, angled so it went downward into the belly. The wolf screamed and spasmed as the weapon was withdrawn, jerked back hard and straight through muscle and bone, loosing blood and pulling a portion of intestine with it. Draga did not intend an immediate kill. He would allow the others their turn at the bloodletting before the prey became a corpse and robbed them of their sense of power over it. All stepped forward in turn, driving their barbed spearheads deep, twisting them before withdrawing so that they might find pleasure in the sight of gore extruding from the wound.

Only Balor stood back, sickened, seeing no sport in this, wanting no part in it. His spear remained unbloodied until Mael, noticing his reticence, accused him of possessing a stomach as squeamish as a woman's in her first months of pregnancy. *Baby-bellied*. That was what Mael called him, eyeing him with contempt and open derisiveness. It was only then that Balor put his spear into the wolf. By then it was dead. They had cut it down. It lay limp and lifeless within the strong bonds of the fiber-roped net, a large female. His spear went into the soft flesh, and when he drew it out, Draga knelt and set himself to the task of gutting and skinning.

The others stood close, watching, pleased when the redbeard discovered that the animal had been in the last stages of pregnancy. When he drew the still-living cubs from her mutilated womb, discarding two that had been killed by the hunters' spears, he declared that these would be given in honor of the spirits of the moor, to the Twelve Winds whose power had apparently blessed the hunt. Bloodied, blind, but still breathing, the tiny animals were hung from the birch tree by thongs of sinew noosed about their necks. It did not take them long to stop twitching, although death itself came slowly, while Draga spoke a reverent chant to the Twelve Winds.

Balor stood with the others, not sharing their obvious satisfaction in the moment. He felt ill at ease, wondering how such an act could please men, let alone satisfy the spirits of the earth. Not that the killing itself had disturbed him, for he had killed before, but never a trussed and captive thing, and always he had killed quickly, as he had been taught by his father. It was only common sense, after all, for when pain and terror ran in the blood, the muscle fiber tensed and grew bitter; such animals were always unpalatable, tough and fit only for heavily seasoned stews. Not that they intended to eat this wolf. No. They would consume only its heart and liver, the blood meats that would give them the life-force of their victim, thus ensuring that its spirit would live on within those who had taken its life. This was a tradition among hunters of his clan. Balor knew it well, and so when the time came, he accepted his portion out of respect for the ways of his people, as well as out of respect for the wolf. Yet as he thought of the way in which the beast had died, the raw slivers of blood meat, usually so coveted for their sweetness, went down hard. He gagged on them as Mael watched him, noting his pallor with openly malevolent enjoyment as he pointed out to the others that, for all of Balor's size and swagger, he was still far from being a man.

Balor's temper flared. He forced himself to swallow and hold the meat down. "It does not take much of a man to slay a wolf in a sack!" he retorted.

Draga silenced the two of them. He had evidently taken Balor's comment as a slur against his own manhood. He eyed the youth with resentment. "When we come upon the next beast that has taken our bait, perhaps we shall set you to the kill, eh, Balor? It's your Year of Trial, after all. Yes. The next beast is yours. Then you shall see, Nephew, that it takes a man to kill a wolf."

"I'll stab no beast while it's helpless in a net," he said. "Nor shall I stand at the edge of a pit trap and shoot arrows down at it!"

Mael snorted a laugh of pure mockery. "You'll loose it from the net and run it down, I suppose? Or leap into the pit and wring its neck, bare-handed?"

The others laughed.

Balor glared at them. "Long ago, on a far shore, my father was thrown into a pit with four male wolves. He slew them all, bare-handed. I am his son. I would not be afraid to do the same!" he declared.

"We all know that you do not lack for bravery, Balor," said Mael. "It is brains that you lack...and good judgment. But then, as you have said, you are the son of the Wolf... born to him in the year that he lost his teeth. And they do say that sons are reflections of their fathers."

Balor flew at him before he could say another word. Hard and fast, Balor took him off-balance and came down upon him as they both went to the ground. He had a knee in Mael's groin and a fist in his eye before Draga could pull Balor off him.

The redbeard cursed them both for being hotheaded fools. "By the Fates, we were sent out to skin wolves, not each other! I'll not return to the holding with less than a decent show of pelts because you two young whelps can't control your tempers! You can settle your differences when we return to the holding—on the training field, with Munremar and the elders to judge your combat—as custom, as well as clan law, decrees. But for now we still have enough light to see us on our way. I'll kill and skin another wolf before dark and will suffer neither of you to stand in my way!"

It was a moment before Mael was able to sit up, stunned, hurt, and dizzy from Balor's blows. Still another moment passed before, propping himself onto an elbow and gripping his groin with his free hand as he moaned against his pain, he hissed out Balor's name. "You... son of a white-haired witch and whelp of a Wolf who has forgotten the meaning of a warrior's honor... I'll not forget this... by the Twelve Winds, from now on you'd best watch your back."

Balor eyed him coolly. "That would be your style: wolves in sacks and men in the back."

Mael flinched and glared at him through slitted, hate-filled eyes. "I'll have your head for that!" he promised.

"Perhaps I shall have yours instead," replied Balor, and knew for the first time the cold, bleak feeling that came with the knowledge that he had made a blood enemy.

*   *   *

They had dug the pit deep and overlayed it with branches. It lay hidden where the bracken grew high and the duff lay thick beneath a stand of trees near a narrow, snow-fed stream. They reached it at dark and, by the light of makeshift torches, stared down at the huge wolf that glared up at them in silence from the darkness of its captivity.

It was Mael who suggested that Balor leap into the pit and slay the animal with his bare hands, as he had boasted he could do. Balor, eyeing the size and color of the beast, felt his mouth go dry and his palms begin to sweat.

The wolf was white, a nightmare image risen from the past. No conjured figment of a boy's imagined terrors, but real, scarred high upon the shoulder where Balor's arrow had struck it so long ago. Broad of back and massive of jaw, as torchlight swam gold within its yellow eyes, reflecting the silhouettes of the trackers, its lips trembled, not with fear, but with threat as they drew back to reveal its teeth, set into black gums like daggers shining deadly sharp, honed for slashing and killing by years of gnawing bones and ripping flesh. A low growl came out of the beast, deep and sepulchral with threat, a challenge to those who would soon torment and kill it.

Balor stepped back, and Mael, seeing his sudden pallor even in the glow of the torchlight, laughed nastily.

"What's the matter, Balor? You look sick."

Balor was given no opportunity to reply, for Draga commanded both of them to be still as he stood staring down into the pit, rapt, his breathing shallow. "This kill is mine," he said.

"No," said Balor, not knowing why, or even that he spoke at all as the redbeard commanded him to stand back. Draga peeled back his cloak and handed it to Mael, then removed his weapons: his bow, the short-handled ax at his belt. A strained, white-lipped grin of tension had split his beard as his brow expanded outward toward his temples, where blue veins had risen to visibly pulse. He began to breathe deeply. In and out and in and out, again and again, as Balor had seen him do when he had fought with Creugas in the arena at Point of Ale.

The wolf's growl deepened, then rose, resonating like the wind when it sang in the lines that secured the thatching of the clan's roundhouses during winter storms.

Draga growled back, then laughed. "With these bare hands I shall break your neck, wolf, and wring the life from you so that the clan MacLir shall know that not only the firstborn of Manannan has courage enough to face such as you within a pit!"

It was as though the wolf understood. Its ears lay flat. It lowered its head and licked its snout and began to back off, tail tucked, to the far wall of the pit where, when the man leaped down upon it, it would have ground enough for one desperate spring, straight for the hunter's throat and the jugular vein within it.

And that is exactly what it did as Draga, with a bellowing scream, arms spread out like wings, hurled himself down into the pit.

The floor of the pit was a quagmire, a slippery ooze of mud where water had seeped upward to seek the level of the nearby stream. Draga, anticipating firm ground, came down wrong, wrenching the bulk of his great, powerful body sideways to avoid full impact of the wolf's spring. As the animal came up from its crouch as though propelled from a sling, Draga landed with most of his weight on one foot, gasping in shock not only against the full weight of the wolf, but in surprise when the ground went out from under him and his right ankle twisted back in an excruciating rip of pure pain. He fell hard, hitting his head against the wall of the pit even as the wolf was at his throat. Draga's hands grabbed desperately at the animal's back.

Dizziness roared in his ears, and for an instant he went limp, not knowing where he was. Then he remembered and tried to curl his fingers into the fur on the back of the wolf so that he might shove the beast away. But his fingers and arms had gone weak. He could not get a decent hold. Terror and near-panic ripped through him as he felt the animal's head rooting savagely upward beneath his beard. Any moment the teeth would sink into the soft skin of his neck, then jerk back as the snout buried itself in bleeding tissue, burrowing deep for the jugular and then, finding it, taking hold and ripping out his throat.

He tried to scream. No sound would come. He lowered his head and attempted to wedge the wolf away with his chin and jaw, but it was no good. The animal had him. The world was growing dark. The wolf was killing him. He would never have his moment of glory. He would never be lord. Never. Never...

Those standing upon the rim of the pit stood stunned. No one breathed. No one moved. Except Balor as he leaped into the pit. He did not think about doing it. He simply leaped and grabbed the wolf from behind about its neck with his bare hands and pulled. Back. Back. Gripping with all of his strength as somehow he straddled the beast, and they both fell sideways into the mud.

His grip tightened. He pressed. He squeezed. He felt the raw, savage power of the wolf as it strained and fought to break his hold. But he would not let it be broken. He held on, pressing harder, tighter, remembering his fear when the wolf had stalked him so long ago upon the distant moor. He felt no fear now. The little boy of the past was gone. Somehow the power of the beast was rising within him, transforming him. He was a man now, as savage as the wolf as he twisted the beast's neck until its snarls became whines and the whines became whimpers, and suddenly there was a deep, wrenching crack from deep within the neck of the beast, and the animal tensed, went rigid, spasmed against death, and then went limp as the breath went out of it; and slowly, so very slowly, the pulsebeat ebbed, and Balor could not feel it anymore.

Suddenly there was cheering. And hooting. And Gar and Donn were dragging him from the pit, and he was sitting, stunned, watching as they went down to haul up Draga.

"Is he alive?" Balor asked out of a daze.

It seemed forever before the answer came.

"Aye, and so he is...and only because of you, Balor the Lucky!" The comment came from Nia, along with a good, hard slap of approval on his back.

And in a while he and the redbeard sat together, before a fire that the others had made, and they brought the wolf up out of the pit and told him that by right it was his, but he demurred, saying that it was Draga who had gentled the beast and made it possible for him to kill it.

The redbeard did not speak for a long time. His throat had been lacerated, albeit not seriously, and his ankle was badly sprained. Although his friends packed it in mud and wrapped it in bracken fern, the pain would not be cooled or eased, so they left him alone to brood over it.

The hours passed. Soft, rainless clouds swept in from the sea to obscure the sky and hold captive the warmth of daylight. In the light of torches Balor skinned and gutted the wolf, still amazed, and somehow inexplicably disturbed by the fact that he had killed it, and with his bare hands. He brought the head to Draga and told him that the pelt should be his by right, but the redbeard waved him away as though the offering offended him. The youth stood close, not understanding his uncle's mood, attributing it to the pain of his injuries.

"It was wonderful," he said, wanting to cheer the redbeard, "the way you leaped into the pit. . . ."

Draga glowered. "And fell flat on my ass, with the wolf atop me? And would have died had not a boy come to my rescue? Ooh, yes, wonderful indeed . . ."

Balor drew a breath and exhaled softly. "I'm sorry," he whispered, and would have walked away had not the redbeard called him back.

"No. It's I who am sorry, Balor. I wanted that kill. I wanted it badly."

"You'd have had it but for the mud. Any man can trip. Next time you'll make the kill. And easily. As easily as you could have killed Nemed if they had only let you have the chance."

The redbeard reacted as though he had been slapped. He stared at Balor, his face contorted with frustration until, slowly, his features relaxed and he smiled. "Come, Balor. Sit with your old uncle. You do bring a man luck. You've saved my life this night. What would you have as reward?"

The youth shrugged, embarrassed. "Nothing . . ."

"Nonsense. Name it and it shall be yours. By clan law."

Now it was Balor who reacted as though he had been slapped. He stared. Then, without a moment's hesitation, he said, "I would have your daughter Dana as my woman."

16

Thus were the strands of the net that would ensnare him thrown out around him. He, Balor the Lucky, who had leaped into the pit unarmed to save his uncle's life by slaying the white wolf, was too young to know that luck often proves a heavy burden for those who must walk among others who have not been blessed by it, and that envy is the most bitter and dangerous of poisons when allowed to ferment within the hearts of power-hungry men.

That night they called him Wolf Slayer and lay their hands upon the bare skin of his forearms so that they might absorb some of his luck. When the cold wind rose to breathe upon them from across the miles of open moor, Gar and Donn and Nia built the night fire high. All but forgetting their loyalty to Draga, they served Balor as though they were his lackeys, doting upon him as they put the uncured, roughly scraped pelt of the wolf across his back as a robe of honor. It stank of blood and death, and he wore it with newfound pride, basking with pleasure in the knowledge that he had slain the heart of his boyhood terrors and in the attention and deference paid to him by those who, only hours before, had treated him as though he were an unwelcome member of their company. He did not see the resentment in his uncle's eyes or the hatred in Mael's as the pug-nosed youth hunkered close to the redbeard, loathing Balor for having done what he had not dared to do.

Dawn came up brazen. The day followed, with Balor feeling bold. Dana was to be his! By law and with Draga's consent, although the redbeard had taken all of the long night to consider his request and had not agreed to it until they had broken camp and were preparing to move on.

Mael was furious. "You can't be serious! Balor's not yet a man. He has not completed his Year of Trial. He has not endured the Rite of Passage. By law he is forbidden to speak for a woman!"

Draga shrugged. He said benignly, "Nevertheless, he *did* risk his life when he thought that mine was in danger. He *did* slay the wolf. And so by yet another of our laws, he may by right ask of me what he will."

The redbeard's words further riled the youth. "There'll be trouble over this, Draga. Mark me! I am not the only rightful suitor who will not happily stand aside for an unproven boy. He can't break the law without stirring up a controversy in the council, I promise you that! I don't care what he's done, or that he's your nephew, or if he is the chieftain's son!"

"Now, now," soothed the redbeard consolingly. His words were rough scrapes of sound issuing painfully from his bruised throat. He rose with difficulty, hobbling on his splinted limb and using his stave as a staff as he went to Mael and slung an arm paternally around the young man's broad, meaty shoulder. "We must not speak harshly of Balor the Lucky. As you have said, Mael, it is a matter for the council. Who are we to trouble ourselves over the intricacies of the law? If Balor wishes to spurn the traditions of the clan, who are we to say nay to him? We'll leave that part of it to old Munremar. He is the Wise One . . . the arbiter of law and justice."

Something turned in Balor's gut at the mention of Munremar's name. He stiffened, sensing that somehow he had been led onto dangerous ground and must be wary . . . but of what? "I've spurned no clan traditions," he said, suddenly defensive. "I've only asked for that which may be mine by right of law—according to what you have led me to believe, Uncle."

Draga grinned. His teeth gleamed white amidst the red sprawl of his beard and the down-curling ends of his mustache. "Of course, my boy!" His tone could not have been more conciliatory. "And so I have conceded to your request! You *did* leap to my assistance—although I did not ask for your help and would surely have slain the wolf myself had you not interfered—yet you risked your life to save mine. If you would have my daughter as reward for your bravery, how could I say nay to you? Yet as Mael contends, if there is dissent over the matter, you must be willing to come before the council to state the righteousness of your claim."

Quicksand. Balor sensed it rising all around him, suffocating him in an invisible mire of bewilderment in which he would surely be drowned if he did not leap away to safety. Surely he must be imagining it! Draga was his uncle, his friend, and if now he suddenly claimed that he had not needed Balor's help within the pit . . . well, he was entitled to a man's pride; Balor could understand that and had no wish to rob him of it. They both knew the truth, as did those who had witnessed it. No one could deny that he had willingly put his life at jeopardy for the sake of another. That was the fact that counted. So he responded with a deference he sensed was necessary to bolster his uncle's self-worth: "It was your bravery that inspired me, Uncle, and so I will gladly come before the council to speak for my reward. Surely you shall stand with me?"

"Of course! Of course!" replied the redbeard lightly, as though he could not imagine how Balor could have thought he would do otherwise.

Mael was smoldering. He glared at Draga. "And what of your daughter? Is Dana to have no choice in this?"

Draga clucked his tongue with admonishment. "If Dana were to have her choice, I doubt if she would name a man at all. But she is a good and gentle daughter. And when the time comes, she will do what I tell her to do."

The next night they joined the main body of the hunting band. They sat around a fire, which smoked for lack of dry wood, and watched the flames rise and dance in a soft, fair-weather wind. Luck had been with them all, despite the fact that several of the men had seen bad omens: an owl flying by daylight, a raven's feather lying on the track ahead of them. But all had come to naught. The clansmen were tired, satisfied with the way the hunt had gone for them, and were glad to be returning home. Solicitous of Draga's injuries, they nonetheless teased him about having been rescued by an adolescent, even while they praised Balor for his bravery until his face flushed red with self-conscious satisfaction.

He did not have a chance to mention his request for Dana, nor did Draga or any of the others, for Tethra was hot to tell them all of how Fomor, following instinct, had led his own group of hunters to the base of the tor. There, expert tracking had allowed them to come upon a deep, low-ceilinged cavern running far back into the hollow of the hill. From the feral scent of the place, it had evidently been a denning site for generations of wolves, and this season had been no exception. Led by Fomor they had gone deep into the earth, which strangely smelled of the sea. It was almost as though the lord had known the way, and soon they had come upon a family group of animals, taking them unaware, provoking them into an attack as both the male and female rallied to protect their yearlings and newborn cubs. According to Tethra, never had wolves fought more savagely, but the hunters had come away unscathed, with fine pelts, satisfied by the knowledge that if they were to judge from the size and ferocity of the male wolf, he might well have been the leader of the entire winter pack.

Gar looked at Balor, startled. "You said that there would be wolves there. Do you remember? You said that it was where you would go to make your lair if you were a wolf."

Silence settled. All eyes shifted to Balor. He was ill at ease with their scrutiny; there was something sharp about it, resentful, as though they wondered why a boy should possess the same insight as their chieftain when they, grown men and experienced hunters, did not. Confused by their sudden change of mood, he felt the need to soothe it, to be drawn back into their fellowship once again. He shrugged amiably. "It seemed likely to me . . . the tor being on high ground and all . . . 'Twas hardly a foretelling that any one of you might not have made."

But they had not made it. *He* had. They grumbled amongst themselves. Donn shook his head, challenging Balor's modesty. "No. It was more than that. You had a funny look about you when you spoke the words . . . like you *knew*, and you were ready to lead us there if we hadn't mocked you."

"It's not so strange. He *is* his mother's son." Draga spoke guilelessly, in the tone of a conciliator; yet there was an edge of underlying insolence to his words as he looked at Fomor and added: "And bold she is when it comes to telling us all that she has the Sight—the enchantress's eye—not that she ever sees anything for us but doom!"

Fomor's brow came down in anger. "And yet here we sit, alive and well, with our hunt a success despite all of her portending. As for me, I would not be so quick to say that the youth—whom *you* have named Balor the Lucky—has the Sight. Rather would I say that he has paid attention to his lessons on tracking. You would have done well to listen to him—you might have come upon the wolves at the base of the tor before I . . . and your ankle might not now be turned . . . nor would Balor the Lucky wear the skin of a wolf that should have been yours."

Draga flushed to his hairline, but it was Mael who spoke, his voice booming like a bittern's. "One must wonder, my lord, how much longer his luck will hold if he keeps on breaking the laws of the clan every time it suits him to do so." With that he told the entire gathering of Balor's asking for

Dana as his reward. He smirked, satisfied to see that Dana's suitors among the hunting band were not about to stand passively aside while their prize was given to a mere youth, no matter how daring or lucky that youth had proved himself to be.

Silence fell like a shroud. A murmuring went around the circle of men. They all looked at Balor, measured him, weighed his worth, and found it wanting. A moment ago they had been his friends. Now, suddenly, they were his judges, and with a start he remembered the night long ago when they had sat around him in the firelight of the council hall. So they sat now. And now, as then, he was afraid of them.

"Is this true?" demanded Fomor angrily. "Have you dared to speak for a woman before your Year of Trial has passed and you have endured your Rite of Passage?"

Balor gulped. His mouth had gone dry. "Yes," he said. "It is true. Draga has told me that it is my right by law."

"A man's right! Not a boy's!" roared Fomor. He was on his feet glaring, not at his son, but at his brother. "You know the law! What is this then? Have you deliberately provoked the boy into breaking it?"

Draga shook his head amicably, gesturing outward with his hands. "I have provoked nothing. The boy risked his life to save mine. I merely informed him that as reward he might ask a boon of me. How was I to know that the lad would ask for Dana?"

Boy. Lad. Balor chafed against the words.

"No *boy* could have slain a mature wolf with his bare hands!" he proclaimed. "No *lad* would have had the courage to leap unarmed into that pit to save the life of a kinsman! And no *boy* would have asked for Dana!" He looked his uncle straight in the eye. "You told me that I might ask for *anything.* Name it, you said, and by law it would be mine!"

Draga shrugged. "And so it shall be, my boy, if the law allows."

Fomor was clearly stewing in the rising juices of his anger. "The law shall not allow it. You must take back your request, Balor."

"I will not!" He forgot his fear and vented his righteous indignation. He looked at Dana's suitors. "When the wolf had my uncle by the throat, why did you not leap to save him? He is *your* friend . . . *your* ally. Then *you* might have asked for

Dana. But you all stood by. You, Mael, and Gar, Nia, and Donn—you *all* stood by. It was *I* who acted! And because of that I say that I am more a man than any of you! The council will affirm my right to claim reward from Draga, for the Twelve Winds know that I have earned it!" With that, he rose to his feet and stalked away from the fire, wanting to be away from them all.

No one, not even the chieftain, called him back.

It was not until much later that Tethra followed. He found Balor sitting cross-legged in the darkness, brooding as he flung pebbles viciously into the night. For a long while they sat together in silence, then Tethra said softly, "Let it go, Balor. There'll be trouble—deep, black trouble—if you insist on bringing your claim before the council."

"I have killed a wolf with my bare hands, Tethra. I am not afraid of trouble."

"Well, you should be!" Worry showed in Tethra's hazel eyes. "We've been friends for a long time, Balor. And as a friend I tell you this: Dana is a man's prize, and you *have* broken the law by asking for her. If you insist on bringing the matter before the council, you'll be putting your father in an impossible position. To prove his impartiality he will have to defer to Munremar when it comes down to a final arbitration, or the clansmen will accuse him of unjustly taking sides. And you know that nothing you say or do will make the Wise One sympathetic to your cause. He hates the very air you breathe."

It was the truth, but Balor did not want to give it credence. To soothe his own doubts he said, "More than half the men within the holding would have Dana as their own. If I wait until my Year of Trial has passed, she will be given to another."

"So be it then. By the will of the Fates, she is not for you."

Balor bristled. He remembered Dianket softly speaking the same words only days ago within the house of the healer's son. He did not want to hear them spoken by another, so he said sharply: "When we were boys at Point of Ale, Tethra, I learned that the Fates are what men make them. Luck is a gift given only to the bold. My uncle has said that I have won the right to speak for Dana. So speak for her I shall. I am not afraid. Draga shall stand with me."

"Will he? Even though he knows the trouble it must bring for you?" Tethra pursed his lips and shook his head. "I don't

like the stink of this, Balor. I'd not trust your uncle if I were
you. I've been watching him for a long time now, and I've
been listening to him tonight. I warn you, that man's tongue
could snare a fox." He reached out and plucked at the
reeking, white wolf skin that lay over Balor's shoulders as a
cloak. "Or a wolf... whichever is unwary."

They approached the holding in the red glare of sunset,
with the chieftain riding at the head of the hunting band.
They reeked of sweat and blood, of pride and uncured pelts,
and as they rode and jogged forward, with the heads of the
slain wolves garlanding the necks of their horses, their differences were put aside in the excitement of the moment. They
sang the songs of hunters, and although Balor kept his
distance from the others, he too sang and felt the thrill of
arrogance when Dathen took up the horn that had been
brought for just this occasion, trumpeting their victorious
return.

The people of Bracken Fen came out to greet them,
Munremar at their head, brandishing his staff of office as
aggressively as a warrior carries his spear into battle. The
women raced forward—through dogs, tame geese, and goats—
to festoon their men with garlands of welcome, offering
babies up into the arms of returning husbands, while children
skipped and danced and looked up at their sires and brothers
and uncles with open adoration.

Mael made certain that word of Balor's request for Dana
spread through the gathering. One moment the crowd was
congratulating Balor for his bravery, the next it was condemning
him for daring to break the law. Munremar's eyes fixed him
like the talons of a hunting bird questing deep into the flesh
of its prey.

By the Fates, Balor decided, let them all grimace and
growl at him! If Dana was all that he wanted, why should he
settle for a lesser prize? All they seemed to care about was
the fact that he had bent the law a bit. The law! He would
never understand why it always seemed to be in his way, like
a branch thrown in his path so that he must invariably trip
over it and lose whatever race he set himself to win. The law
should serve men, not intimidate them! He would *never* take
back his request! He would put it before the council as

bravely as he had faced the wolf in the pit. Then they would see that he *was* a man and would have to deal with him as such.

The bloodstained sinew of his brow band suddenly felt tight. He ripped it off, loosing the wild, uncombed masses of his pale hair. He shook his head defiantly and drew up into his nostrils the raw stench of the uncured wolfskin he wore proudly over his shoulders. He could feel the power of the white wolf running out of the skin into him. Or was it the power of his own virility rising in him? Yes! It was the latter. He *was* the firstborn son of the Wolf. And he was a man at last. It was time to let others see it.

With a howling yip of insolence he gouged his knees into the belly of his sorrel and whipped the animal into a gallop, urging it forward through the startled assortment of onlookers, looking for Dana amid the throng, wanting her to see the full measure of his boldness. Surely no other man within the holding would be willing to risk so much for love of her. But he did not see her. He saw Elathan gaping in shock at him. He saw Fomor glowering, shouting after him. He pretended not to hear. As men stood aside and women grabbed children out of his way, he saw Morrigan looking unnaturally grim as he passed her in a cloud of flying earth thrown up by the sorrel's unshod hooves. Had she called out to him as he passed? He could not be certain, nor did he really care.

With Balor urging it on, the horse cut a reckless path through the labyrinthine earthworks that encircled the palisade. The sun was well down now, but there was enough light to throw deep shadows between the embankments. The sorrel's hooves cut through them. Suddenly it seemed to Balor that something huge and threatening crouched in the shadows ahead, waiting. . . .

The sorrel sensed it too. It reared up, panicked, but Balor's thighs—a man's thighs—tensed and gripped the horse's sides. The horse whinnied and pranced in place, salivating and wide-eyed, but the rider was in control now.

All feelings of elation bled out of him as he sat rigid on the sorrel's heaving back. He was in a lake of shadow, between the inner embankment and the palisade. He thought of the white wolf trapped within the darkness of the pit, and his emotions whirled like leaves caught in the eddying force of a waterfall as an inner voice seemed to thrum a single sharp cord within him.

Beware, Wolf Slayer, do not go forth so boldly.

He looked up. Huldre stood looking down at him from the watch platform high above. Had she spoken? No—the warning had come from within. But her eyes had been on him. Those pale, ice-blue eyes. As always he was repulsed by her intrusion into his thoughts. He hated the realization that it was possible for her to trespass at will into his very soul.

He put up his fist. "Today we of the hunting band return to you triumphant, woman! Your omens of doom were wrong!"

Even in the bleak, shadowing hour, neither day nor night, he was struck by the fact that she was, as Dathen had described her, as ethereal as a marsh mist. Yet there was nothing fragile about her, no softness at all. Her skin was translucent, unmarred by the tracks of time, and her hair was as thick and white-blond as a young girl's. She stared down at him out of her strange, cold eyes, and suddenly he felt as small and vulnerable as a little boy lost and alone upon the wild, dark moor.

"Beware, Balor," she said. "This day is not yet done. Tonight the Planting Moon shall rise. And Munremar—as well as I—has seen blood in his sacred fires."

She turned away then and was gone. Like a mist on the bog tattered by a rising wind. As though she had never been there at all.

17

No one would have disputed that there was magic in the light of the Planting Moon, but later Balor would wonder if there was not madness within it as well.

Preparations for the rituals and sacrifices that would soon take place had been complete for days. Nothing might take precedence over them—not tales of the hunters' glory, not admiration for the many pelts ready for curing, not even the council, which must soon be called to determine the legality of a youth's hotly contested claim. All must wait, for on this night the earth would come alive. Tonight the Goddess, Mother of All, would rise up from the Otherworld. Tonight the Twelve Winds would do her homage as she opened her womb to take the seeds that would nourish the life of man, while above the moon would watch and grant the blessing of fertility to all living things.

Darkness came down quickly, and once it fell, all speech was forbidden lest someone inadvertently offend the spirits that would walk the earth this night.

And when darkness came, the youths who had entered their Year of Trial were brought into the House of Youth, which had been raised for them outside the palisade. It was a small, round structure, consecrated by the Wise One, the chieftain, and the elder males of the clan. From this night on the youths would pass the dark hours within its confines until, at the end of their Year of Trial, on the night of the Planting Moon, it would be burned in a ritual symbolic of the death of their youth. Half its ashes would be thrown to the Twelve Winds, as an offering to the spirits of their nomadic, warrior ancestors. The other half would be sown into the earth, along with seeds planted in the light of the Planting Moon, as an offering to the Mother of All.

Beyond this Balor and the other youths knew no more about the mysterious ceremonies that would culminate in their Rite of Passage into manhood. Munremar looked askance at him for bringing disharmony to the night, but the Wise One dared not speak his thoughts until the dawn, although Munremar would have kept Balor from entering the House of Youth, for in the fading moments of dusk he had clearly stated that no youth accused of a law-breaking must be allowed to enter a sanctified place. Such a judgment would have delayed his Rite of Passage for a full turning of the seasons. Dana's suitors had allowed themselves a muted cheer, but it was short-lived, for Fomor reminded them all that the youth had risked his life to save a kinsman. No act could be more respected by the traditions of the clan MacLir. To penalize Balor without a proper conference and consensus would be an affront to those traditions. So it was decided: Tonight, with the rising of the Planting Moon, he must go with the others of his age into the House of Youth, and whatever dissent existed between them must be put aside. Balor would come before the council on the morrow, when the issues could be properly dealt with in the light of day.

And so it was done. Excitement more intoxicating than the special mead that had been prepared for them, more nourishing than the ceremonial cake that was given to each of them, filled those within the House of Youth. Balor ate his ceremonial cake, a large, flat round biscuit made of flour ground from each of the grains that would be planted this night. Ritual demanded that each youth break his cake into twelve pieces, one for each part of the world out of which the Twelve Winds blew. When he had eaten he poured himself an extra portion of the mead of enchantment, the potent mead of dreams from which he would not awaken until the Planting Moon had risen and set. On this night he was neither boy nor man. He was as a seed, unplanted. He was the future. He was something yet to be.

The hours passed, and Balor awoke in the darkness, hot, tense, restless, and drenched in sweat. He had dreamt of wolves and had seen himself running with them, as furred and naked as an animal, across wild moorlands, beneath falling stars; a wolf himself, white and scarred and leader of the pack. Now the room seemed close, suffocating with the bodies of the other youths sprawled about. They snored and sucked air like drunken old men. He sat up, staring at them out of the darkness, for a moment wondering where he was, why he was not in the roundhouse with Dianket sleeping close by; then he remembered and felt a pang of pity for his friend. Dianket would never be fully accepted as a man of the clan MacLir even though, Balor was certain, Dianket would be a better man than most of these youths sleeping around him.

He stirred, ill at ease. Although it was night, it was not dark outside; light entered the room through the uncovered doorway. Flickering firelight, it bathed him in red and orange and gold. He backhanded sweat from his brow, wondering why he was awake while the others slept. It must be an omen of some sort; everything that happened on this night would be prophetic.

He rose. Barefoot, naked to the waist, clad only in a simple twisting of smoothly loomed wool tucked low at his hips, he went to stand in the doorway to cool himself, to breathe deeply of the fresh night air.

What he saw was forbidden to his eyes. He knew that at once, yet could not bring himself to look away. Was he still under the mead of enchantment? Perhaps he was still dreaming, imagining the entire scene that burned itself into his eyes.

From where he stood he could see the gate in the palisade. It was open, throbbing with the light of uncounted torches as, beneath the full moon, the men and women of the clan MacLir walked solemnly through it with garlands of dried wheat about their heads. They chanted a sound as low and deep and purposeful as the voice of a river running black and sure in the depth of night.

His nostrils tensed, then expanded. He could smell the torches. He could hear the sound of drumbeats and whistles from the distant fields. Deep within him the sound of the chanting seemed to entwine with his own pulse, and he could feel the dull, hot throbbing of the mead of enchantment working in his brain, rousing heat in his loins and belly, causing his mouth to go dry. Slowly, not knowing that he moved at all, he left the House of Youth behind him and walked out into the night beneath the light of the Planting Moon. It was forbidden for him to do so. He did not care. This was his dream. He could roam as he pleased within it. There were no laws to bind him here.

He paused beyond the earthen embankments, beyond the bogs, in the shadow of a great, low-branched oak. He could see the fields clearly from here, the dark earth transposed to shimmering silver in the moonlight. A great fire had been kindled. Even from this distance, he could feel the heat of it as the Wise One, clad in his ceremonial robes, stood before it with his arms raised in benediction. Slowly the men and women of Bracken Fen came to him, a procession of light and sound, until they formed two concentric circles surrounding the fire. Male and female. A sacred ring, symbol of life everlasting.

Balor found himself looking for Dana, then remembered that virgins were secluded upon this night unless they had named a man and had chosen to be mated beneath the Planting Moon; otherwise their presence might offend the Goddess. Tonight the womb of life was open to the forces of Creation. There were no children here. No infants. No elderly save the Wise One. Pregnant and lactating women stayed closed and quiet within their houses, as did the infirm.

Tonight was not for them. It was for the young; it was for the fertile; it was for life itself.

Balor held his breath. The world had gone silent. The chanting had stopped abruptly, as had the music. Munremar offered up a litany of praise and supplication as animals were led forth for sacrifice. Young, prime, they were precious and perfect offerings, heavily sedated so that they would make no protest when their throats were opened. One by one they dropped, and their blood was collected in the great, gleaming gold Cup of Life before their bodies were tossed onto the bonefire and the air grew rank and sweet and pungent with the stench of burning hide and horn, flesh and fat. In the light of the pyre the Cup of Life was passed around the circle from one man to another, who drank the blood until it was drained and the chieftain raised it high, turning it thrice dawnward as the women and men removed their garlands, woven of last year's wheat, and tossed them into the flames as a sign of offering and continuation.

Now the men took up their heavy plows. Each woman touched a torch to the fire and lighted a man's way as slowly the male-guided plows opened the feminine earth to take the masculine seed of life.

And so it was done. In the dawn of the next day the ashes from the bonefire would be spread to nourish the newly planted crops. But now as Balor watched, entranced, the men and women of Bracken Fen danced and laughed and coupled freely on the ripe, rich land. And if in the months to come a child came forth from its mother's womb resembling a man other than her hearth mate, no one would make mention of it. It would be a gift of the Mother, a child of the Fates.

Balor turned, suddenly startled. He was no longer alone in his dream. Morrigan had come to stand beside him, her upturned face a shimmering reflection of the moon, surrounded by the wild black fall of her hair.

"I've been looking for you everywhere," she whispered. "I must talk to you."

The mead was working heavily on his mind. Her words seemed to be coming from far away. He heard them, but their meaning was lost. He looked down at her. In his dream her eyes were lakes of moonlight. He stared into them and nearly drowned in depths of shivering silver. He could see the pulse in the vein at her temple, steady, as fast as the drumbeat coming from the fields, in perfect cadence with the pounding of his own heart. A deep, slow heat began to rise in him. "It is forbidden for you to be here," he said, and wondered if he spoke at all, or why. It was not necessary to speak in a dream.

"And for you," she replied, "doubly dangerous. Balor, you must listen to me."

He *was* listening. Wasn't he? Had her mouth always been so moist, or was it a trick of the dream and the mead? Had she always held it so, with her lips parted? And why was he kissing her? Kissing her until the breath went out of them both, and he felt her arms go up around his neck and knew the hard, throbbing heat within his loins for what it was.

In the darkness, in the flaming glow of the sacrificial pyre, beneath the light of the Planting Moon, he took her down onto the earth, and there, in a dream of heat and trembling, he lay with her in the soft, new grass beneath the great, sheltering oak.

He heard her whisper "I love you, Balor. Be gentle . . . I do not want to be afraid." The words irritated him. What was rising within him had nothing to do with love. And he could not have gentled his actions any more than he could have reversed a storm tide, for that was what he was experiencing. Savage, thrusting, it was as exhausting as rage, and when it had passed, it was more satisfying than anything he had ever known or imagined.

Sweated, breathless, he seemed to fall blissfully downward from heights of impossible pleasure into sudden, black, mindless sleep. When he awoke, only moments had passed, yet it seemed that he had slept for hours; mead-induced dreams could do that to the mind, twist it and turn it and lead it onto pathways that seemed more real than reality itself. Drums were still beating upon the distant fields, and the air was filled with the scent of smoke and flame. Yet his senses barely reacted to them; they were of reality, and he was still enmeshed in his dreams. He closed his eyes and allowed himself to drift, deeper, warmer, into a sweet, all-encompassing limbo of body and spirit.

"Tell me . . ."

He opened his eyes. Morrigan lay close against him, propped on an elbow with her cloak drawn over them both. He could feel its texture against his skin and the contours of her body, hot and soft against his own, even through the thin, finely worked doeskin of her tunic. She smiled at him. Shyly. Tremulously. As Dana would have smiled. *Dana*. Why was she not with him in his dream? It was Dana he wanted, not Morrigan. But even as he wondered, his eyes were on Morrigan's lips. Such moist, generous lips. It was impossible to refrain from putting his own over them in a kiss; a man's kiss this time, with no innocence to it.

She drew back and the full, silver face of the moon lighted her face and swam in her eyes. "Tell me," she whispered again.

"Tell you what?" The sound of his voice seemed to jar the dream. His mouth felt cold without her lips to warm it. The sense of equilibrium was passing; he wanted it back again. He reached for her, impatient, aware of the heat rising in his loins again, hungry now for what he knew would ease it. Beneath the cloak his hand moved along the sleekness of her bare thigh, edging her tunic upward.

Her hand stayed his. "No, Balor. First you must tell me that you love me."

He sighed, annoyed. Even in dreams there was someone ready to define the limits and conditions of a man's taking of what he desired. "What has this to do with love?" he asked.

"Everything," she said. "With me to love you, you have no need for Dana."

A dull ache sprouted at the back of his head. He reached up to rub it. "It is Dana I desire," he told her emphatically. He did not think twice about hurting her feelings; that was not possible, especially in a dream.

"Even now?" she queried softly.

"Especially now!" he snapped nastily.

She sat upright, pulling the cloak away from him, drawing it up about her shoulders. "She will never love you as I love you, Balor."

If the words stunned him, he gave himself no time to consider his reaction. He saw himself sit up as he spoke his thoughts to her without any attempt to gentle them. "And I could never love you as I love her, Morrigan!" He stared at her, suddenly amazed. There were tears in her eyes. Tears! He had not thought it possible. Now he *knew* he was dreaming. He frowned, discomfited by the look of sadness that had come to her face, by the unsettling feelings of remorse that stirred within him when he realized that he had put it there. Since when had he cared about Morrigan's feelings?

The darkness of the night was thickening. Balor looked up, chilled. It was a bad sign, a dark omen, for the Planting Moon to be shrouded in clouds. He was cold now, aware of his nakedness. Gooseflesh was pricking him, and suddenly, with a flush of disbelief and embarrassment, he knew that he was not dreaming. He was wide awake, and he stared at Morrigan, aghast, realizing what the mead of enchantment had allowed him to do.

His head was pounding—another gift of the mead. He put up his hands and pressed his temples with his fingertips, not able to look at the girl as he said, "What has happened between us . . . it should not have been. You should not be here. It is forbidden. You must go back to the holding. Quickly. Before you are seen."

She stared down into her lap. Her breathing was shallow, quick; she fought to withhold her tears and succeeded. There were more important things than her own tattered feelings to be considered now. Her throat was constricted as she struggled to speak. "Tomorrow, when you are summoned before the council, you must prostrate yourself before the elders. You must beg their forgiveness. You must tell them that it has all been a mistake. You must tell them that you did not mean to break the law. You must not ask for Dana."

He looked at her now, angry. "What I do or do not do is no concern of yours, Morrigan. You have made no claim upon me this night. Tomorrow, I *will* ask for Dana. I have won the right, and I am sick and tired of others trying to force me to change my mind!"

Slowly she looked up to meet his eyes. In the darkness her face was a shadow surrounded by the deeper shadows of her hair, yet somehow, he could still see the tears within her eyes, and the sadness.

"Do as you will, Balor the Lucky," she said, her voice taut with her efforts to control it. "But know this: If you ask for her, your luck will be forfeit, for you will have fallen into the snare that my father and your uncle have set for you—a double snare—designed for you *and* the chieftain, if he can be provoked into falling into it for your sake."

"You don't know what you are talking about!"

"I have drunk no mead this night, Balor. My head is clear. I have come out to warn you. When darkness first fell, when the people of Bracken Fen went to their houses to ready themselves for the rituals of this night, my father went to the council hall to gather the implements he would use for his ceremonial magic. Draga was there... waiting. Although it was forbidden, they spoke. In the darkness. Before the sacred altar. They did not know I was there. They spoke conspirators' words. Your uncle would be lord, Balor, at any cost. And tonight he has manipulated my father into supporting his cause against the chieftain at tomorrow's council."

"I don't believe you! Draga would not stand against Fomor. He would never cause a king-making!"

Her eyes narrowed. "The Fox is clever, Balor. He will maneuver others into doing it for him. He has been working toward this day for years, always so quick to question the chieftain's will, to criticize his decisions, to condemn him for any failure, insidiously planting the seeds of sedition within the holding so that when at last they take root and flower, they will seem to spring up spontaneously, without any assistance from him at all."

Balor stared, memories crowding his head, confirming her accusations, yet he shook his head, not wanting to believe her.

"You should not have saved his life, Balor. You should have let him die, for I have heard him speak of how he will use your act of bravery against you, as a weapon to be hurled against your father. He intends to say that it was conceit, not selflessness, that goaded you to take on the cloak of a hero. He shall say that were it not for you, he would not have been injured, for it was your bravado that prompted him to leap into the pit, and that he would have killed the wolf had you not prevented him from doing so. He shall suggest—and pretend to hate to do so—that perhaps you are, after all, a bringer of bad luck. My father will quickly agree and remind the clansmen that you have always been unlucky, that the moment you were born your father decided to lead his people into the fens, where so many have suffered and died from privation."

"They tried to call me a bringer of bad luck years ago and could not succeed. They will not succeed this time either. Fomor will not let them."

"How will he be able to stop them?" The question curled upward like smoke on a windless night; direct, heedless of all obstacles. "Rumor has swept through the holding that on the hunt you willed Draga to fall into the pit, and that you knew where the king of the wolves would be. *Knew*. As though the soul of the beast walked within your skin and guided your thoughts to his lair. Draga and my father will insinuate that you, as the spawn of the white-haired foreign witch, have the powers to enchant us all. They shall recall how *you* were sheltered by the Standing Stones and were guided by a falling star to a sacred place, not for the good of the clan, but to mark you as one apart from it. Munremar truly believes that you have the Power, Balor, a power that will someday surpass his own. He fears that sooner or later you will displace and dishonor him. And so he is your enemy, Balor, as is Draga."

"Draga is my friend!"

"Draga is no man's friend but his own. Tomorrow, when you come before the elders, he *will* stand with you. And when he has encouraged you once again to scorn the laws of the clan, my father will suddenly be beset by a Vision. He will rise, and dark omens will pour from his mouth like vermin fleeing a burning house. They will make you seem like a wound festering in otherwise healthy flesh. Munremar will recall all the many times that you have broken clan law, and then he will demand your life, Balor—as is his right—for the good of the clan, lest the elements turn against us once again and we will all perish for your sake. The chieftain shall stand against him. Disharmony will prevail in the assembly. And then, if all goes as Draga has so cleverly and patiently plotted, a vote will be called for. Many of the young men are loyal to the Fox these days—many of the men lust for Dana. It does not take the Sight to know that Fomor could not carry the vote. Nor does it take the power to know that he would never stand by and watch you buried in a bog as a bad-luck bringer. The moment he defies the will of the majority, a king-making will be called for. Fomor cannot stand against so many men. He and the few who remain loyal to him shall die. No doubt Draga will be named lord in his place. And under his leadership all of Fomor's house shall be slain—this Draga has sworn to my father—so that the Wise One may sleep well in the night, his power and place within the clan undisturbed and undisputed."

"I don't believe a word of it! Not a—" He stopped midsentence, suddenly aware of being watched. The intruder had made only the slightest sound; yet Balor had heard it and turned to see a dark silhouette amidst the many low, age-gnarled branches of the oak, well-hidden by the dappled black pattern of the leaves. Sensing danger, Balor slowly rose, reaching for his loin wrap and donning it as his eyes searched the darkness.

"Law breaker..." A smug voice snarled out of the shadows.

Even before he stepped into the pale, thin light of the moon, Balor knew his identity.

"Mael..."

"Aye. Did I not warn you to watch your back?" He smiled viciously. Balor could see all of his small white teeth gleaming. "I told you I'd have your head. When the council hears of this, they'll take it for me. I won't even have the pleasure of winning it for myself. Pity. But then, a man can't always have things his way, can he, Balor the Not So Lucky?"

Anger stirred within Balor. He could feel it coiling like a serpent, setting itself to strike.

Mael clucked his tongue as he observed high clouds obscuring the moon. "Look at that, would you? Rain clouds. The Wise One will say that they are bad omens for the newly planted crops. But with you around, how could we expect anything else?"

Balor was shaking. He could feel his fists clenching and unclenching at his sides.

"Let us see," drawled Mael provocatively. "How many laws have you broken tonight? Leaving the House of Youth... that was one. Witnessing the sacred rituals of the Planting Moon... that was another. And then there's this...." His small, sharp ferret eyes shone in his face. They narrowed and swept to Morrigan, appraising her with lewd and not unappreciative speculation. "Your father's been hiding you away in men's garments too long, girl. There's many a man who'd look at you with interest if they knew of the soft, ripe secrets you keep hidden."

She was on her feet, whirling her cloak around her, glaring at Mael with her lips pulled back from her teeth and her eyes full of dark fire. "What sort of moldering newt takes pleasure in spying upon others! And how dare you call Balor unworthy, you leering, snout-faced maggot from the bottom of a manure pile! If you had a man's bone of passion in you, you'd be off in the fields now, setting your pig's seed into some unwilling furrow, for surely not even a moldy teated sow would lie with you by choice!"

Mael's smile vanished. The small eyes went cold and hard, yet there was heat in them—the heat of too much mead. "I'll show you what I'm capable of, you black-haired spawn of a fen whore. And when I'm through you'll know what a man can do. You'll beg for more, but there'll be no more. Not for you, not once I tell the council of how I found you here in the light of the Planting Moon, speaking lies against the Wise One and whispering blasphemy against the gods of the clan, rutting with the law breaker and conspiring with him to bring down upon the clan MacLir the wrath of the Twelve Winds!"

"Munremar shall see you dead if you speak against me!" she threatened, her voice full of confidence and contempt.

"Will he? I think not." He smiled again, more viciously than before. "He is an ambitious old man. He'll not save you, for the only way he could do so would be to implicate himself in Draga's plot to win the chieftainship away from Fomor." He began to move forward slowly. "He'll name you liar, for his own sake. Tomorrow you and Balor shall lie together again, this time forever, buried alive in a bog. And if the chieftain offers protest—as we have planned—he will be slain for daring to stand against the will of his clansmen. Draga will be named lord, and Munremar shall have greater power than ever before. And Dana shall be mine!"

"Never!" The word came out of Balor, as full of warning as the growl of the wolf he had slain in the pit. He thought of that now, and somehow the thought was calming. His anger was gone. He was no longer shaking. His mind was very clear. "You will tell the council nothing of what you have seen," he said.

Mael snorted, looking him up and down as he paused before him. "And who's to stop me?"

"I will stop you."

"Ha!" exclaimed Mael as, without warning, he backhanded Balor brutally across his face with the full power of his closed fist and forearm.

Caught off guard, Balor took the full impact of the blow and whirled aside, falling, stunned, pain exploding in his jaw and temple as light flared and consciousness threatened to slip away.

"Now watch while a man gives this whore's spawn a taste of something to make the night worthwhile."

Morrigan tried to wheel away from him, but he was on her like a bear, growling, ripping at her cloak with one hand, taking her hair in the other as he jerked back her head so that her face might take the bruising impact of his kisses. Her fingers gouged his face. She could feel her nails piercing his skin and raking deep, but he was impervious to pain; he only gripped her tighter, suffocating her with the invasion of his kisses.

Balor stared, squinting to win back sight and focus while light and sound filled his head, then faded, leaving him to fight against the blackness that threatened to overwhelm him. Slowly he managed to get to his hands and knees, shaking his head, working his jaw, testing to see if it was broken. He could taste hot salty blood in his mouth. Then, as his vision cleared, there was something else. It was the bitter, vile taste of rage. He saw Mael gripping the girl, saw him kissing her and forcing her back; he heard the muffled moans of her smothered protests as she fought for breath and tried to fend off the outrage of his hands. Her cloak was gone and his fingers pulled back her tunic, baring her breasts to his trespass as he bent to browse fiercely, deliberately hurting her, biting her until his mouth was bloodied and she cried out, gasping in shock and pain as he took her down and set to rape her.

Balor did not hear the cry of outrage that came from his throat; later some would say that they had heard a wolf howl in the darkness of the ebbing night. He rose and flew at Mael, attacking him, leaping forward as he had leapt upon the wolf within the pit, grabbing Mael about the neck, straddling him and jerking him back, rolling sideways with him. Balor's knife arm came down across Mael's throat and his free hand closed about Mael's wrist, pressing. Pressing. Until the body within his arms lay still. At last he released it and in a daze rose to his feet, shivering violently as Morrigan knelt and tested for signs of life in the crushed throat.

It seemed an eternity before she looked up. Even before

she spoke the words, he had known what they would be. "You've killed him, Balor," she whispered.

The events of the next few hours would haunt Balor for the remainder of his days. Carefully, making certain that they were not seen, they carried Mael's body to the bogs. Under cover of darkness they weighted him with stones and dropped him into a well-marked quagmire. As clouds obscured the moon, they watched him disappear, while the wind whispered in the bones and raven feathers that were strung on the warning signposts. It was the only sound.

It was very late. The fire on the distant fields had died. The celebrants of the night of the Planting Moon slept in mead-induced abandon beside their plows or in the meager privacy afforded by shrubs and outcroppings of stone. They would not be roused until dawn.

Cold. Balor had never been so cold. He tasted the muck of the bog in his own mouth, felt it on his skin, smelled it within his nostrils.

Morrigan, standing very close, looked up at him, saw the desolation on his face and suffered it with him. "It might have been us there in the bog if he had lived to betray us to the council."

"I did not mean to kill him." The words seemed to come from beyond himself, from somewhere far away, out on the distant moor where wolves ran wild and free—killers like himself. The thought struck him violently. Again he shivered.

Morrigan slung off her cloak and reached up to put it about him. "Come. We must return to the holding. You must be back within the House of Youth before dawn. No one must know that you have been away from it. No one will suspect what has really happened. Drunken men have been lost in the bogs before, Balor. Many have never returned. Their bodies have never been found. No one will ever know—"

"That I have killed him."

Morrigan's face twisted with revulsion. "He asked to die," she said flatly.

He saw nothing, heard nothing. It was as though he had somehow gone down into the bog with Mael, leaving his own body to stand as an empty shell upon firm ground.

Morrigan was still speaking, plucking at his arm to draw his attention. "Balor, you must not linger here. Those within the House of Youth must believe that you have passed the night with them. Don't you understand? Give them no cause to name you law-breaker, and you will foil Draga's plot!"

He heard her words dimly now. He looked up at the spring sky. Spring. A time of hope. A time of new beginnings. But the wind that had risen from out of the moors was a winter wind, devoid of hope, whispering of endings.

The wind spoke to him with the voice of Munremar, and he heard and understood its words.

It was as though he stood within the council hall—alone, surrounded by firelight, while the eyes of his clansmen circled around him, judging him, condemning him. He stood like a captive, passive, knowing that there was no way to undo the netting he had lain so well for his own entrapment.

You have broken too many laws, Balor, son of Fomor.

Aye.

You have defied the traditions of the clan MacLir, Balor, grandson of Manannan.

Aye.

You have slain one of your own kinsmen, Balor, firstborn of the white-haired witch.

Aye.

You have lain with a virgin without sanction of the clan. Your eyes have wantonly beheld rituals forbidden to them. Your tongue has blasphemed against the gods of your ancestors.

Aye. And aye twice again.

The acceptance of his guilt made him shiver yet again as he realized that, despite Morrigan's uncharacteristic optimism, Draga and Munremar would spring their trap whether he spoke for Dana or not. Everyone knew that he had been a habitual law breaker since boyhood. Before how many witnesses had he dared to ask for a woman before his Year of Trial was over? And how many had heard him spurn the chieftain's command to take back his request? Even if the redbeard did not learn the truth about Mael's disappearance, the omens of the past few days and hours would all be on Draga's side. Had not the hunters seen an owl flying in daylight, and had they not discovered a raven's feather upon the trail? Omens of change and death. And now clouds veiled the face of the Planting Moon, a cold wind chilled the newly sown seedlings, and a man was lost to the bogs. Clearly the world was in disharmony. No one could deny that Munremar had warned them all that Balor was an element of imbalance, that he should not be allowed to enter the House of Youth until he had come to judgment. Now he would say that if the clan were not purged of the youth, he would become Balor, Bringer of Disaster.

The full realization of the extent and complexity of his uncle's betrayal settled upon him. It was difficult for him to believe, even now—and yet he did believe. How many had warned him? Dianket. Dathen. Tethra. He should have listened. Now it was too late. If he asked for Dana, he would die. If he did not ask for her, he would still die. If the lord stood to defend him, they would die together. And if the lord chose to abandon him to a fate that he had brought upon his own head, then he would die alone.

"Balor . . . have you heard a word I've said? You must get back to the holding!" Morrigan was scolding him.

"I can never go back," he said. Like the white wolf within the pit trap, Balor knew that he must escape or die.

She would have gone with him. She would have forsaken everything to be by his side, but he wanted no part of her. He told her to go home. He told her to look to her own safety and allow him to tend to his own fate, but Morrigan was not one to follow anyone's will but her own. She told him that he was a fool if he thought that he could simply run off naked and unarmed into the night. He must have food, clothing, weapons, and a plan of some sort. Where would he go? What would he do? She told him that his odds were better if he stayed and faced the judgment of the council, but he knew otherwise and would hear no argument from her.

He stood staring off into the darkness, knowing that there was no alternative to flight. Reality roared in his head as he saw his future beckoning to him, a black, featureless road into the unknown. Then a thought buoyed him. He actually smiled. He would go west, toward the distant sea. At least there his destiny would not be dictated by Munremar. He would be free to make his own luck among the friendly fisherfolk who dwelled along the shore. And this time he would spin the fabric of his life correctly, with caution, trusting no man.

So he ran back to the holding to gather his clothes and weapons and enough food to allow him to put a good distance between himself and Bracken Fen before he was forced to take time to hunt. Perhaps his clansmen would decide to pursue him. Or maybe they would be content to assume that he, like Mael, had fallen prey to the spirits of the bog. He could not be certain what they would think when they found him missing, except, perhaps, good riddance. He knew only that home and hearth, kith and kin, would soon all be behind him. He would be alone.

The thought was terrifying; it was best not to ponder it. With a harsh word to silence Morrigan, he continued on toward the holding, jogging along the well-known bog tracks. The girl kept pace with him and proved an asset, informing him that they would have no trouble slipping past the sentries because before she had left the holding to search for him, she had drugged their night's portion of mead with sleeping powder. A precautionary measure, it had allowed her to slip past them unseen. No doubt they would still be dozing at their stations.

It was as she promised. As they passed through the open gateway the sentries at their watch posts were lost to dreams. Balor and Morrigan stood together for a moment in silence. He was grateful for her ingenuity, but he wanted no part of her now. He whispered to her to go home, and when she glared up at him defiantly, his expression made it clear that he would tolerate no argument. She would only be in jeopardy for his sake. He did not want that for her. She had already risked too much for him this night.

He watched her disappear across the compound. Somehow the sight of her small figure being swallowed by the night disturbed him much more deeply than he wished to admit.

The night was ebbing rapidly now. His jaw ached cruelly where Mael's blow had found its mark. As he lay his fingers soothingly against his throbbing cheekbone, he found his way carefully to Dianket's little roundhouse.

Sure Snout, delivered of her pups and curled with them in a basket close to the hearth, lifted her head and whined a soft greeting. The sound woke Dianket. One look and Dianket knew that something was wrong. Balor, quietly sorting through his clothes and weapons, told him what had happened while he stared, not wanting to believe, yet knowing that it was all true. He did not speak; there was nothing to be said. There could be no alternative. Balor must go. Grief-stricken, he rose and stood wrapped in his bedskins while the dearest friend of his youth readied to walk out of his house and life forever.

Balor, now clothed in his sturdiest traveling clothes and most serviceable boots, slung on his bow. His quiver of arrows hung strapped across his back. He had his dagger, his ax, and a bag of flints at his belt. Without hesitation he took up his old cloak, then lifted and handed the skin of the white wolf he had slain to Dianket.

"Here. Take it. I promised I'd bring you back a fine pelt. Keep it. Wear it. And remember me."

They stood in silence. Dianket accepted the skin and clutched it tightly for a moment, then returned it. "You must keep it. And *you* must remember: The spirit of the Wolf is in you, Balor. Walk safely in its skin. When you are gone, know that your father shall hear of this. Draga shall not be allowed to spin more of his treachery. I shall see to it. This I swear to you, Balor, on a kinsman's honor. And someday you shall come back. You'll see. You *shall* come back." It was the sort of assurance that one comrade gives to another on the eve of a battle from which neither has much hope of returning alive. It was a lie, and they both knew it as they clasped one another in a savage embrace.

Morrigan entered, dressed for traveling and carrying a pack of food for the journey. Once again Balor told her that she could not come with him. She flamed with temper and told him that she would do as she pleased, and only Dianket's gentle counseling persuaded her that she could be more useful to Balor if she remained behind. Perhaps she could convince the clansmen not to go after him. She begrudgingly handed her food pack to Balor and promised to inform the people of Bracken Fen that she had dreamt of Balor in the night—a dream in which he had been summoned to the Otherworld by the spirits of the bogs. After all, she *was* the Wise One's daughter. She would be believed. But then sadness touched her. Balor was leaving. She could not bear it.

She ran to him, embraced and kissed him with a ferocity that stunned him, and only when Dianket had pulled her away did she look at Balor and speak her heart to him. "I love you," she said. "Remember that. Always."

Confused by the emotions her kiss had roused, he turned and without another word went out into the night. But the fragrance of her wild, black hair and soft, tawny skin was in his nostrils, and the moist sweetness of her lips lingered on his mouth.

He sought the deep shadows of the ebbing night, painfully aware that the darkness was thinning. He would have to move quickly if he was to be out of the holding before dawn. Soon life would begin to stir. Munremar would call for a council. He must be long gone by then.

The growing sense of loneliness caused him to pause, for it piqued a brutal awareness that to be alone in the world, without kin or clan, was to be vulnerable to the forces of Creation. Since Time Beyond Beginning man lived within the sacred Circle of Life in order to survive—sheltered and nourished by those of his own blood. But now he was outside that circle. If he survived, it would be to live among strangers. Never again would he see his mother or father, his sister or brother. He would never complete his Year of Trial. He would never endure his Rite of Passage. He would never be named a Man.

And all because the Wolf refused to be a Wolf and the Fox was biting at his heels, hungry and impatient to leap into his skin and usurp the glory of his name.

"Draga..." He spoke the Fox's name aloud, and his knife hand strayed to his dagger. As he thought of his uncle's treachery and betrayal, he knew what he must do for the sake of his honor.

Later he would wonder if somehow the madness of the mead had not returned to twist his thoughts, but now he felt sober and clearheaded. He began to move, stealthy and silent, with a purpose inspired by a new and deadly intent, toward Draga's roundhouse.

The redbeard's injured ankle had kept him from participating in the rituals of the Planting Moon. No doubt he lay sprawled upon his bedskins, drunk, sleeping heavily as he dreamt of blood and power. It would be so easy for Balor to slit his uncle's throat, and with such skill that the women and children would not stir. He would rouse Dana gently, and she would come willingly away with him. Or would she? Dana adored her sire and would be innocent of any knowledge of his schemings. She would never forgive Balor for taking her father's life, let alone flee with him into the unknown.

He paused. Draga's elkhound had seen him. It lay on the walkway before the doorway to the redbeard's roundhouse. Its head went up. A low, deep growl rippled at the back of its throat, a warning to Balor that if he advanced so much as another step, the dog would bark, alerting its master to danger.

Balor froze where he was. He could feel the hard, hot haft of the dagger within his curled fist. Somewhere within the fens a bird cried, and the dog rose to its feet, his ears back, tail tucked. The growl was louder now, and the voice of reason counseled Balor imperatively: Run, fool! Now! Before it is too late!

Yet he stood unmoving, twitching with frustration as he stared at the roundhouse of the redbeard, knowing that sooner or later, by one ruse or another, the Fox would rule in Fomor's place. Although he was unworthy, Draga would take up the great battle sword of the Wolf and be lord.

The sword . . .

Balor had forgotten about the sword of Partholon, the sword that had taken the head of Manannan MacLir, the sword with which Fomor MacLir had taken vengeance against Nemed MacAgnomain, the sword with which he had become the Wolf of the Western Tribes.

Retaliator.

The name slid along his consciousness like a blade, drawing the blood of resolve. The elkhound sensed a change in the youth and stepped back, cowed. The time had come, Balor decided, to claim the sword as his own, to take it from the battle chest, where it had lain hidden for too long. With Retaliator to grant him its power, he would gladly flee from the wretched confines of Bracken Fen. He would become a warrior. He would ride on the back of the Twelve Winds as was his birthright. He would seek out Nemed MacAgnomain and take the man's head and avenge the blood of his ancestors. As Star Gazer had predicted, a new Wolf would rise out of Albion. With the sword Retaliator within his hand, *he* would be that Wolf. He would go forth boldly. He would be afraid of nothing. And as Dianket had promised, he *would* return to Bracken Fen. He would come as a conqueror. He would see Draga buried alive in a bog. He would take Dana for his own. He would make those who had been disloyal to his father quake with fear before he struck them down. And then at last, with the holding burning behind them, he would form a new clan, and once again it would be as it had been ordained since Time Beyond Beginning. The men of MacLir would be as wolves upon the earth, roaming at will, the masters of all who would dare to stand against them. Balor would lead them, as he had been born to lead them, and the Wolf of the Western Tribes would run at his side, proud to grow old in the shadow of the new Wolf, who had sprung from his loins.

It was a glorious vision. For a moment it was more intoxicating than the mead of enchantment. And so it was that Balor went to the roundhouse of the chieftain.

In all of the vast space of the room, all was darkness save the soft, glimmering red lake of coals. Balor paused at the entrance, holding the weather baffle aside, listening for the sound of those within, but to his relief he heard no one. Little Bevin had evidently been left in the care of one of the older women, and Elathan had probably gone to pass the night with a friend of his own age. Only the dogs were left to greet him. He was an old friend; there was no need to bark.

Balor moved forward across the room to the far wall, where the lord's battle chest stood covered by the cloth of worn sealskin. His future lay there, locked within that chest, and he had very little time if he was going to claim it.

How easily the skin slipped away, how smooth was the wood of the chest as he reverently lay his splayed palms on the lid. The touch of it thrilled him. In daylight the copper braces would be as green as the sea, the leather strapping the color of good, aged mead, the wood variegated, all the colors of the earth of Albion. And how easily the straps were undone by his probing fingers. The hinges opened without a sound of scrape or protest. The lid came up as though it were eager to open.

With his heart pounding in his ears Balor squinted downward into the battle chest, willing the darkness to yield vision to him. And so it did. Through a mist of shrouded blue and gray, the last shredding remnants of the night, he stared at that which was forbidden to him.

But the sword was not there.

There was nothing visible within the chest but a heap of old skins and woolen rags. He drew back, disbelieving, then leaned forward, his hands rummaging, desperately searching until cold fire seared his knife hand and he drew back, cut to the bone and bleeding.

He sucked at the wound. It was a long, nasty gash on his index finger from the knuckle to the nail. A hasty winding of rags drawn up from the chest stayed the bleeding. There was little pain now; the pressure of the cloth relieved it, as did the excitement that had taken control of his senses. His hands went down into the chest again, threw out the rags and accumulation of old animal skins—and there, with no scabbard to hide the glory of the blade, the sword lay gleaming.

It was all and more than he had ever imagined. The hilt was of gold inlay over the dark muscle of the bronze; there were stones in it: carnelian, the color of congealed blood; emerald, clear and as dark a green as long, curling storm waves; amber, like beads of honey warmed in the sunlight; and jet, as black as the belly of clouds born of the North Wind. The haft itself was without ornamentation, smooth and wide, designed to fit within the palm of only the largest of men. But it was the blade itself that drew and held Balor's awe. It was a burnished sweep of pure power. Flawless. Massive. Double-edged and tapering to a rapierlike point. It could be used for slashing or impaling. It was an instrument of death. A warrior's weapon.

The thought stayed his hands.

This was the blade that had slain his grandparents upon distant Tory Isle. This was the blade that had taken Manannan MacLir's head. This was the blade that had decapitated Partholon and made a slave of Nemed MacAgnomain. This was the sword of Fomor MacLir, Wolf of the Western Tribes, warlord and master of the clan MacLir.

And he was Balor the Unlucky, an unproven, callow youth. He was not worthy of such a blade.

The thought cut him as deeply as the sword had slit his finger. Indeed, it was as though the sword itself had rejected him.

He drew back, alert to the sound of voices across the compound. The people of Bracken Fen were beginning to return to the holding. He had no time to waste. Quickly he reached for the haft of the blade with his knife hand, but the hand would not serve him. It had gone numb and weak, and he could not move his thumb at all. He stared, shocked to see that the rag was black with blood and dripping, darkening the blade. His good hand went down, curled about the haft, pulled back, and to his shock, could barely lift the sword. In all of his days he had never imagined that it would be so heavy.

He stood shaking. The numbness in his hand had turned to pain. He released the sword and pressed his wound with his uninjured hand.

The voices were coming closer. The dogs were listening, tails wagging, and Balor could see them clearly now. The sun was rising. It would be difficult to leave the roundhouse without being seen. It would be all but impossible to get out of the holding.

Unless he went now. This moment. Unless he left the sword and fled for his life before the blood that was welling out of him robbed him of the energy to do so.

And so he went, and swore that he would not be afraid as he fled into the fens and left his youth behind him, along with his father's sword and his shattered dreams of glory.

BOOK III

18

The cliffs of the island rose up out of the deep, blue waters of the Aegean Sea, as tawny as lions, and as dangerous. The island's summit was a broad, flat expanse of cypress-shaded gardens, dominated by a magnificent, multistoried, whitewashed estate. It stood fortresslike, built to the very edge of the cliffs above a clear deep-water cove. There were ships there. One large, lean vessel, its black and red sails folded upon its deck, lay anchored to a long stone quay, which jutted out into the cove from a pale strand of sandy shore. Several smaller vessels were beached there, each with a blazon of red and black running wheels painted both starboard and port of its bow.

The dwarf Coman looked down from his perch atop the wall that rimmed his mistress's private rooftop garden. Men and women and a few older children had begun to gather along the beach and quay far below him. He knew what they had come to see, and his heart quickened with expectation. He gave a little sigh of pleasure, glad that his mistress had left the island, glad that once again she had fought openly with her husband. Were she here, luxuriating in her summerhouse, he, Coman, as a mere slave—albeit a pampered one—would surely have been deprived of this roost of honor from which he had long hungered to view the sport that would soon take place in the cove below him. Indeed, were she here, it was doubtful if such sport as this would take place at all.

The rim of the wall upon which he lounged, lizardlike, was wide and flat, a safe enough place to sun himself above the world and the vast distances of glass-smooth sea; if he thought of falling straight down into the waters that licked the seawall, it was not a contemplation that disturbed him. If anything, it gave him a distinct thrill of danger, a sensation that sweetened the moment for him. Propped on his elbow, the misshapen dwarf peered over the edge of the wall. Curiosity overtook him: He plucked up a small, honeyed orb of fruit from the ornately painted, fire-glazed clay bowl he had brought with

255

him from the kitchen, and dropped the fruit, watching, fascinated, as it fell. And fell. And at last hit the water with a small explosive sound, sending liquid splashing and flashing upward in the sunlight. It sank briefly then popped to the surface, where it lay bobbing gently as rings of disturbed water radiated outward across the surface of the cove. The dwarf could see sharks rising from the green, clear, sun-filled depths to examine it.

There were always sharks in the cove. Coman smiled to himself as he saw them rise to test his offering. How beautiful they were, like the sharks he used to watch from the headlands of his cold and distant homeland. Long and sleek, as deadly and shining as silver daggers, they moved and turned in the water with the same exquisite grace as the snake dancers who had performed before his master at last night's meal.

The memory of that dance, like the awareness of the dizzying height at which he rested, thrilled him. Naked slave boys, lean-hipped, with taut, spare-muscled torsos, had danced with adders—as did slave girls, barely women, with firm, newly mounding breasts, nipples as hard as seashells, and painted the wanton red of crustaceans drawn up out of boiling water at a feast. Their eyes had been outlined with black and gold and green to resemble the eyes of their serpents; their dilated pupils betrayed their use of the drug of courage. Their flesh had been oiled and they were sweet and rank with the scent of musk. Their dance had been perfection, the purest provocation of death, the use of the snakes a perversion designed to arouse lust for blood as well as passion.

Coman had beat a rising rhythm upon a little lap drum while the sound of flutes and whistles had melded into a delirium of sound to which the drugged dancers whirled madly and coupled and were stung again and again by the adders; until all but one slave remained unbitten, while the others twitched in slow death agonies at his master's feet.

The lord had been in one of the black moods of depression that he had suffered ever since returning from Point of Ale five years ago. It had been said by his retainers that it was due to the knowledge that an old enemy had died without his assistance, thus depriving him of the only great ambition of his life: to take vengeance someday upon those who had destroyed his people and made a slave of him. At night he suffered from dark dreams of frustration. For days he would brood. He would abuse his servants. He would tyrannize his wife the queen, driving her from him so that he might engage in the sort of entertainments that offended even her vicious nature as surely as they soothed his own.

The snake dancers had done wonders for the lord's disposition. He had risen to roar with delight, so pleased and excited by their display that he had called their master forward and kissed him. The man had stood, bereft and stunned. He had not expected his entire troupe to be allowed to dance to the death. No doubt he had imagined himself ruined. But the lord had embraced him, had given him golden bracelets from his own wrists and jeweled rings from his own fingers. The man left the court smiling, wealthy for the remainder of his days if he did not squander his fortune, and left the one remaining dancer—a beautiful white-skinned, pale-haired girl—to be a dazed victim for the passions of her new master.

That night, among the slaves and retainers of the house, wagers were made as to how long the girl would last and if she would go to the same fate as had been devised for all the young, pale-fleshed, white-haired girls whom the lord had purchased for his pleasure over the past five years, since he had returned from his journey to the far trading centers of the North.

Now, as the dwarf looked down to where the sea met the land, he saw a kitchen slave walk out onto the quay, a large crock tucked beneath his burly arm. The man stopped half-way out, knelt, and dumped its contents into the water. Even from his great height Coman could see blood spill out to stain the surface of the sea as large fish heads and scraps of meat floated outward. The kitchen slave rose and stood, shaking out the last blood and pieces of flesh from the crock, watching as sharks began to cruise close, curious, then agitated as they began to feed.

Coman grinned, triumphant. The entertainment would take place! The gift to the sea assured it. Below him he saw that faces had come to stare down at the cove from windows set into the seaward wall of the great house. He sat up, salivating. He crossed his stunted, crooked limbs and waited, watching the cove with eyes hot with eagerness. His hands pressed against the little hawk-shaped talisman, which dan-

gled from a braided thong between his tunic and his chest.
He never took it out, lest people see it and covet its power
for their own. Fervently he made a wish upon it: that the
entertainment prove to be all that he lusted to see. Then he
thanked whatever gods had placed the amber charm into his
hands, for surely his life these five years had been soft and
rich and sweet because of it.

The cove was green and still below him. He trembled with
anticipation. His vigil was brief. The lord, clad in a tunic of
pristine white, came out of the house and walked out onto
the quay. The girl was with him. She walked as though in
pain, tight-thighed with fear, naked, as white as the sunlit
walls of the great house. The kitchen slave joined them, and
the gathering of onlookers cheered as the girl balked and was
escorted against her will to the end of the quay.

Coman licked his lips and nodded. She suspected danger.
But she would have no inkling of her fate as yet. But soon.
Soon. And then the entertainment would begin.

Without ceremony they threw her into the water. The
burly slave stepped back while the lord knelt at the very edge
of the quay, waiting patiently for her to come up again. From
his perch upon the rooftop wall Coman could see her body in
the water, white and beautiful and bright, reaching upward in
desperation as she kicked and grabbed for the surface. Flailing
and gasping, she reached it and broke through, sobbing,
reaching gratefully for the lord's extended hands. He gripped
her firmly by the wrists. She waited anxiously for him to pull
her up. But he did not. He shifted his weight. Balancing
upon the balls of his feet, he bent forward slightly and began
to speak to her.

Coman saw her go rigid. He saw tension and then panic
have their way with her as, quietly, the man who held her
continued to speak softly. She shook her head violently. She
began to kick again, to flail her body in the water, screaming
words in a foreign tongue that needed no translation. She
screamed against what was to come. She begged to be
withdrawn from it. And slowly, as the crowd watched, silent,
and a child began to cry, the sharks began to respond to her
frantic movements in the water.

They came at her. First one. Then two. Then more. They
nosed. They struck. They tore. They feasted. And the girl
lived on while the lord held her wrists and watched the sea

churned to blood and foam. No one could have counted the number of sharks in the water. They were frenzied now. Snapping. Ripping. Rising from the water. Sliding over one another. While the girl's screams rose and then choked into horrible, gasping, garbled sounds that sent a thrumming race of heat and pleasure running in the dwarf's veins and loins. He rose, better to see the spectacle below. He could not get enough of it.

But the water was too fouled now. The lord had released the girl's wrists, lest he lose his own. With his right hand he reached out, and before the sharks could pull it down, entwined his fingers in the sodden, blood-pink strands of her hair and pulled back, rising to his feet as he did so. As Coman watched, transfixed with delight, the lord lifted the head of the girl out of the water. That, and a tattered neck and a few bits of torso, were all that was left of her.

The crowd cheered. The child screamed. The lord held the head of the girl high, turning as he did so that all might admire his trophy, but as his own eyes examined it, a sudden wave of displeasure turned the moment sour. The expression of terror was gone from the dead girl's face. Her pale blue eyes were glazing over. Her mouth was agape, fouled, with the tongue lolling and beginning to fade to blue from lack of blood. It was no longer a pretty face.

It was no longer Huldre's face.

In the end they were never her face. Although he savaged and killed her a thousand times through the flesh of others who resembled her, the pleasure was never complete. Nor could it ever be. She was dead, and the Wolf with her.

And he had not killed them.

He could never kill them.

Nemed MacAgnomain, the lord of Achaea, shivered with supreme frustration as, with all of his strength, he hurled the head of the dead slave girl away. It flew high and far before it scudded across the surface of the cove, like a stone flicked viciously outward by a bored and hostile youth, then it settled, bobbing like a pod of seaweed against the gentle surge of the tide.

Nemed glared at it, knowing that soon the tide would turn. It would carry the head away to some far shore, where it would rot on a distant beach. Birds would peck out its eyes, and what they did not finish, the crabs and flies would reduce to bone. For a moment, he wondered who she was and what her name had been.

But no matter. She was not Huldre. None of them would ever be Huldre. The enchantress from the Northlands was dead, buried with the Wolf in some godforsaken land, with her cursed amulet and the sword of Partholon. Lost to the world. Lost to the power of his hatred and ultimate retribution. And yet somehow it was as if her spirit watched him across the long miles between this world and the next, blighting his days, haunting his nights, weakening his manhood so that he was often shamed before his wife. Huldre taunted him, mocked him, and reminded him that, as she had vowed, hers had been the final vengeance. Her grip on his life was as strong after her death as it had been when she was his slave.

He frowned sourly, remembering how he had first seen her on a trading expedition to the Land of the North Wind. She had been the most beautiful creature he had ever seen. He had wanted her, but her people had refused to part with her on any terms; so his father, Partholon, had set his swordsmen loose to slay them all. All but Huldre. She had been a gift to Nemed, but he had never fully possessed her, even though she had been his to do with as he had wished all those years. He had never broken her spirit or cowed her will to hate him. And he had come to love her. All that he had ever won as a warrior had been for her; and she had thrown it back at him, uncaring, unforgiving, hating, all the while calling down the wrath of Donar upon his people. And when it had come, she had gone willingly with his conquerors, offering herself to the Wolf, lying with him willingly as Nemed had been forced to watch in chains.

Although the sun was warm on his back, he felt cold, as he always did when he thought of her. The cheers of the crowd intruded upon his thoughts. Or were they mocking him like the specter of the white-haired enchantress who would not die?

He turned and looked up at the wall of faces and beyond them to where Coman, the dwarf, was doing a jubilant dance on the very edge of the rooftop wall of the queen's private garden. What was the obsequious little toad doing there?

Coman saw that he had his master's attention. He preened and bowed, then straightened his crooked body as best as he could and raised his arms, unaware that the amulet had fallen free of the tunic and now lay exposed against the blue sheen of the cloth. "We thank you for the entertainment, lord!" he cried, saluting as broadly as he could. "In all of the Aegean there is none to equal it! Hail to the son of Partholon, Nemed MacAgnomain! May the world long tremble in awe of his bravery and power!"

Bravery? Power? Was the ugly little toad also mocking him? It took no power to feed a woman to the sharks. There had been no bravery intended in the act. It had been meant as a casual diversion for the crowd, as a release for his own frustrations, as a climax to hours of sexual gratification that he could no longer find with his aging, sag-bellied wife; indeed, since he had learned of the fate of the clan MacLir, he could find a man's release only with those who resembled Huldre, by humiliating and inflicting upon them the pain and terror that he could no longer hope to inflict upon her. And the queen was growing old; she was losing her taste for pain and her patience with Nemed. There were younger, harder-muscled men in the Aegean, who, for a golden bauble, would eagerly seek to please a rich old queen when her husband proved incapable of doing so.

His eyes narrowed at the thought. What was glinting at the dwarf's throat? Gold? Had the queen given gold to him? He was Nemed's man, his slave and jester and household spy. What gave him the confidence to lounge so boldly on the wall of the queen's private gardens? True, she had always had a penchant for collecting the odd and the ugly along with the bold and the beautiful, but would she choose to couple with a dwarf, and worse than that, would she reveal a master's weaknesses to his slave so that the toad might dare to mock the man?

When she returned she would be called to pay for such an insult. A curse on the wealth and power of her family! A curse on their ships and estates and investments! He had proved his worth a thousand times over. He would kill the hag and claim his rightful place as master of her domain. He should have done so long ago; even their sons had prodded him to do so, chafing under her suffocating dominion, reminding him that she had many enemies. Her own kin, business associates, slaves, and retainers would rally to him; weak men always chose to serve the strong.

The cove was still alive with sharks when he decided to kill the dwarf for having dared to mock him. The crooked little man could no longer be trusted, and he had long ceased to be amusing. Perhaps he would amuse the sharks? With a shout that would have put fear into a corpse long settled in its grave, he commanded Coman to come down from the wall.

The dwarf came to him. Even before he paused and bowed, quaking before his master, Nemed saw that the bauble about his neck was not made of gold. It was of amber—a small, fine, exquisitely clear piece of amber carved into the shape of a hawk in flight. He stared at it as though the sight of it had dealt him a mortal blow; there was only one such amulet in all of the world. It was Huldre's amulet. He would have known it among a thousand imitations. "By the Fates! How came you by this?"

Shocked to see that his precious talisman lay in plain view, Coman's hands flew up to shield it. " 'Tis just a bit of amber. . . . A worthless piece . . . a mere trinket from barbarian lands . . ." His words ran together like mice fleeing down a tunnel when they know that a snake is after them.

Nemed slapped the dwarf's hands away and ripped the amulet from his neck. "How long have you had this? Where did you get it? Answer me, toad, or you'll follow the girl into the cove!"

Stammering, too frightened and confused to do otherwise, Coman told him what he would know, half choking on the rising sense of despair that told him that his luck now lay in the hands of his master and that because of its loss, this moment was to be his last.

But the moment passed. And with it, to Coman's infinite relief, Nemed's anger vanished. He stood in silence, listening, speaking only to probe the dwarf for details. He wanted to know everything that he remembered about the pale-eyed boy who had cast the amulet away into the mud at Point of Ale, about his band, about the redbeard, and most earnestly he wanted to know about the giant in the horned helmet; about the man from the south who had called himself Scallatha. Without hesitation, sensing that it was to his advantage to do so, Coman told him everything that he knew.

Nemed weighed the words against his memories. Slowly he began to smile. It was a smile that touched his eyes and nostrils. His mouth quivered but did not part until, quietly, he spoke through a murmuring, ominous laughter.

"The Wolf lives. . . . The white-haired witch has not gone to her grave. . . . The boy with the pale eyes, he is their son!" His fingers curled possessively about the amulet. He looked down at his fist as though it contained the riches of all the world. "With this the Fates are mine to command. With this, I shall have my final vengeance. Once I mocked its powers, but I shall not do so again." Slowly his arm rose, setting a shadow between himself and the sun. "At last! The Eye of Donar is mine!"

The hawk made slow circles in the cloudless, milky blue expanse of sky above the stifling haze of Albion's marshlands far below it. Its broad wings were motionless as it allowed the wind to take it and carry it high and higher still, until it appeared to be no more than a tiny dark flaw upon the face of the sun. And then it was gone, as though it had fallen into the burning, white-hot eye of noon.

Balor looked away, scowling bitterly as he walked. Now that he had left the holding far behind him, the sun shone brightly above the fens, in affirmation, no doubt, of his decision to leave them. He looked up once again, searching for the hawk, feeling a sense of kinship with it as he wondered where the wind had carried it . . . and where the wind must ultimately carry him, for he too was drifting upon its strong, invisible currents, yielding to them, trusting them to be the guardians of his fate; surely they could forge his luck no more disastrously than he had forged it for himself.

For days now he had been traveling in the light of this new and misted sun, setting himself on a course designed to confuse and eventually discourage anyone who might be seeking to follow him. Once out of the holding he had gone forth boldly, heading straight through the bogs, circling the pasturelands, then doubling back to set yet another trail through the gorse wood, into the highlands, heading always toward the tor. If anyone followed, they would search for him there—and by the time they realized they had been misled, he would be far away, traveling in another direction entirely as he took himself deep into the marshlands, through vast stretches of shallow lakes and enormous beds of tall, shadowing reeds. It would be impossible to pick up his trail, for here, using the skills he had learned during his never to be completed Year of Trial, he had lain none for them to follow.

And so the days had passed for him. And the nights had come down cold and dank and full of vapors that weighted the air and fouled it with the stench of rotting vegetation, filling a young man's mind with images conjured up out of fear and loneliness. Far to the south and west lay Point of Ale. He would go there and in anonymity find a place for himself, laboring to earn his keep. And he would wait for Nemed MacAgnomain. And when Nemed came, Balor would kill him. In the name of Manannan MacLir, Balor would avenge the blood of his ancestors. Somehow—even though it might cost him his life—he would make that much of the shattered dream his.

That thought gave him the strength and courage to go on. He would sit shivering in the darkness, thinking of how he would kill Nemed MacAgnomain. He slept only in troubled spurts, dreaming always of the men of MacLir stalking him... of Munremar, waiting in the mists with his sacrificial dagger poised and ready... of Huldre, watching him across the miles, her eyes setting a lighted pathway through the mists, allowing Draga and his slavering elkhound to find him... and of Mael, always he dreamt of Mael, rising from the bogs to name him man-slayer.

Now he walked on, groggy from need of sleep, cursing the marshlands, understanding why his father had forbidden any man to venture into them alone and why no enemy had ever followed his people beyond them. Disconsolate, he wondered how many more days he must wander before he would reach the hill country that lay behind Point of Ale and the sea.

Ahead of him a break in the reeds opened out on to a narrow stretch of water. It ran riverlike between the reed beds. A sweet, cool wind, unencumbered by the stifling, insect-plagued confines of the reeds, dappled the water and blew softly toward him, giving heart to his weary body. Had he at last reached the end of the marshes? He hurried forward. With the reeds now at his back he felt renewed as he sloshed onward, noting that the water was decidedly cooler and clearer than the muddy brew in which he had been slogging for days. Then, without warning, the bottom dropped out from under him and he fell, floundering in deep water, his body buoyed and carried by a fast-running current. Gasping in shock, with his traveling pack weighting him down, he went under, panicked. He did not know how to swim, but swim he did, in a mad, pulling, instinctive stroke that somehow got him back to solid footing in the muck of the reed beds. He sat there awhile, dazed and breathing hard, realizing how close he had come to death.

He went on, keeping close to the reeds now, finding comfort in them, knowing that where they lay rooted, solid footing would be found. As the day wore on he did not slow his pace, but kept the open water in view, certain that it must lead him west to the sea.

Toward dusk the open water narrowed and then disappeared entirely. He cursed. The marsh stretched out on all sides of him, the reeds towering above him in the windless air as he listened for the sound of the deep-water current. It was gone. In his weariness he had lost it. Now there was only the heavy silence of the marsh, sluggish and thick and alive with the droning of insects as the little milky brown lake in which he stood calf deep bubbled about his feet.

But the lake was no lake. Too late he realized that he had blundered into a quagmire. He tried to lift his feet and could not. The water was rising about his knees. In a moment it would be about his thighs. Terror seized him. He imagined that he could feel Mael's hands closing about his limbs, pulling him down.

He screamed. Birds flew up in terror of the sound. A marsh deer broke from the cover of the reeds ahead of him. Its upraised tail was a banner guiding him to safety, showing him the way to solid ground. If only he could reach it.

In desperation he flung himself forward, splaying his body outward across the mire. Flailing his arms, he strained forward with all of his strength. His limbs came free of the muck with a hideous sucking sound as he sprawled across the bog, dispersing his weight as evenly as possible across the surface until, grabbing desperately for great handfuls of reeds, he pulled himself to safety and lay on his belly in the mud, sobbing, not like the man who he wished to be, but like the boy he thought he had left behind.

Night came down. He did not heed it. Exhausted, he slept there in the mud, dreaming of the red-hided deer that had guided him to safety.

"Donar . . ." he cried. "Donar . . . father of the Twelve Winds, lead me from this place!"

He awoke trembling, chilled to his bones. The mists of the marsh were like threatening spirits fingering him, while the sounds of night predators pricked the darkness and slurred upon the waters of the marsh. A nighthawk keened, a sharp and lonely sound that rent him to his soul. His uninjured hand rose to close about the amulet, which he had hurled away at Point of Ale. He recalled Huldre's words:

"Time shall name the fools among us, Balor. You have disdained and defiled the gods of your ancestors. You have thrown away your luck."

Memory of those words haunted him for days. He cursed himself for not having brought along a change of clothes; he had lost his cloak and his white wolf skin in the bog, and the remainder of his garments refused to dry. They steamed through the daylight hours, lying upon him like a soggy, sultry layer of extra skin, and they made his nights a hopeless misery. Balor alternately shivered against the cold and damp or shook against the fever that had begun to rise in him, the result of infection beginning to work deeply within his sword-gashed hand.

Now, as dawn awakened him, he was afire. His uninjured hand rose to loose the lacings of his tunic, but when the cold breath of the morning touched his skin, reason kept him from casting away his clothes entirely. He knew he must have warm garments to shield him from the elements, or he would die from exposure, as surely as he would die if he could not find sufficient food to nourish him.

Food. Again he cursed himself. He rummaged through his traveling larder. He had packed it quickly and carelessly. Except for a few strips of moldy dried fish and goat meat, everything had been ruined. His only consolation lay in the small pack of provisions Morrigan had planned to use for herself.

She had thought of everything. She had judiciously wrapped everything inside waterproof animal intestine: stacks of small, round hearth cakes; dried currants and bog berries pressed into balls of soft cheese and rolled in roasted grains; and long, slender slices of cured meats. She had thrust a bone sewing needle into a wadding of woolen thread. She had packed an awl, several flint blanks, and a delicate pair of copper tweezers. Small, separate pouches of waterproof leather contained bladder-wrapped samplings of the "magic" powders she had shown to him so long ago, on that night when he had discovered the secret of the hidden room above the altar of the Twelve Winds. Secured by a bone pin that could be raised or lowered through a series of eyelets fashioned out of leather, an additional bag contained medicinal items that Balor knew not how to use: dried herbs and roots, fungi and samplings of tree bark, the jaw of a squirrel, the skin of a marsh snake, a packet of cobwebs, a neat little stack of the dried skins of bats and toads, and a cowry shell. There were also a falcon's claw, a tiny bundle of seven twigs secured by a winding of sinew, a selection of feathers, broken bits of nutshell, and several flakes of mica.

Perhaps she had thought to pay her way in the world through the practice of sorcery? At least she had taken the time to plan. He had not—and now, as he picked at the last morsels of cheese and berries, he cursed himself yet again for not having eaten more sparingly over the last few days. Once this was finished he would have only what was left of his own molding rations.

He knew that he would have no energy to hunt. The fever was working deeply in him, and his misadventure in the quicksand had caused the gash in his finger to rip open. He should have stitched it when he had first left the holding, but even though he had the needle and sinew thread necessary to do the job, he had no stomach to stitch his own flesh. Instead he had packed it with mud and bound it tight. Now the wound was hot and swollen. It felt as though living coals had been wedged beneath the oozing, enflamed flesh. The slightest touch was an agony. He decided to let it be, convinced that, once out of the marsh and into drier, healthier country, it would begin to heal.

But the marsh stretched on and on without end. He walked. And walked. And still the reeds remained a wall, cutting off the wind and all hope of a view, which might grant a vista from which he could take his bearings. As the day wore on, the warm, humid light of the sun poured down upon him like heated honey, suffocating him.

He lay down to rest and could not rise again. Fevered sleep claimed him. He did not hear the sound of the sea lapping at the broad plain of the estuary to which only a few more dogged steps would have taken him.

19

"Wizard . . ."

The word trespassed into darkness. Searing pain followed. The darkness burst into flame, consuming him until mercifully the flame went out, taking the pain with it. He drifted in the darkness, in a silence as vast and all-encompassing as a night without moon or stars.

"Wizard!"

Again the word. Sharp. Imperative. But he could not respond. Once again the word called to him. He was aware of the darkness. And of a tiny fleck of light. Slowly the light merged with the darkness, and he drifted dreamlike until sound filled his senses with the welcome vibrations of a human voice.

"Come now, Wizard, you must drink this. All of it. Your fever has broken at last. You'll need a man's strength in you again."

The man was in his prime, which was all the compliment that could have been given to him. Within his seafarer's worn and tattered clothing he was scrawny, lean to the bone, muscular in the way of a woman, with slim wrists and broad hips and a face that some might have called pretty.

But there was no softness in his face. The features were as bold and watchful and wary as a hunting bird's. When he smiled, the weather-tanned skin about his eyes crinkled like the lines about an old man's eyes. But he was not old. There was youth and vigor in his smile, and he smiled often, revealing crooked teeth that were as white and pointed as the teeth of a young hound.

He had built a shelter within the dunes, which lay between the marsh and the sea strand—a makeshift tent contrived of two poles of driftwood over which he had secured a span of oxhide. Anchored in the sand, facing out of the wind, it was just large enough for two grown men and provided warmth and escape from the damp fog that now shrouded the entire coastline. A small, meticulously tended fire made of scraps and shavings of driftwood crackled on a bed of broken shells within reach of Balor's hand as he lay, still too weary with residual illness to move.

The man smiled his ragged smile as he hunkered over a V-based clay cooking pot, which he had buried up to its rim in the center of the fire pit. With sand and seashells piled close about it and the fire built all around, seawater steamed within it. Strands of kelp floated in the liquid, as did strips of peeled freshwater eel and a single marsh bird's egg. He had been feeding Balor from this brew, using half of a clamshell as a spoon. Now he appraised Balor, put down the shell, and ran long, strong, dirty fingers back through his mouse-brown, shoulder-length hair, which was cut bluntly across his brow.

"It is good to see you conscious at last," he said, speaking in three different dialects before finding the vernacular necessary to spark understanding in Balor's face. "I would like to know what sort of a wizard you are, to carry within your sorcerer's bag all of the elements of healing needed to tend your wound and cool the marsh fever . . . and yet to use none of them to help yourself."

Balor was too weak to reply.

The man grunted and rubbed his nose thoughtfully. "Sleep then. Grow strong. Call upon your powers to hurry the healing process. I'm afraid I've gleaned all that I can from the wreck of the ship that set me alone upon this damnable shore, and I must be away from this place as soon as possible." Introspection shadowed his sun-browned face. "By the stars, I wish that my companions had not all drowned. I wish that they were with me now. To be without kin or strongman in a hostile land where slavers are known to roam . . . it is a bad way to be. So mend quickly, Wizard, or by the stars, I shall be forced to leave you as fodder for the Fates!"

But the stranger did not leave him. For all his blustering, the man stayed and tended Balor, and although his manner was begrudging and his conversation minimal, his care was tender and solicitous. At night, when the cold, damp fog pressed down upon the world, he slept back-to-back with

Balor, wrapped beneath the same cloak, sharing his warmth with the fevered youth, waking him when his dreams grew troubled, to press a cool, moist rag to his brow.

As the days passed, Balor felt his strength return gradually. His fever disappeared. He slept well through the nights. His hand was cool again, for the stranger had cauterized the wound while Balor had lain in delirium.

Now, after changing the dressing yet again and packing the wound with cobwebs and a balm of his own brewing, compounded of ingredients taken from Morrigan's supplies, the man's deep blue eyes narrowed speculatively behind thick lashes. "It was foolish of you not to have taken care of this yourself... or is it customary among your people to pack such a gash with mud and then allow it to fester as though it were a cheese that might improve when the green rot sets in?"

Balor flushed defensively. "I have no people!" he snapped, regretting the words too late to recall them. In all their time together the man had chosen to reveal nothing about himself other than the fact that he had been shipwrecked. He had not given Balor his name, nor had Balor given him his; they remained mutually distrustful.

"No people, eh?" The stranger clucked his tongue. "A sorry state, that. Lonely, wandering the world with no kin to comfort you and no land in which you are ever fully welcome."

The words cut deep. Far off, the sound of gulls calling above the surface of the fog-shrouded sea recalled the sounds of young men laughing and taunting one another on the training field of home; Balor's heart ached unbearably as he thought of the holding and longed for all that he had left behind.

The stranger watched him like a curious bird, his head cocked, his eyes slitted thoughtfully. "You carry a wizard's bag, but you are too young to be a wizard. Your looks mark you as Northman, but your tongue speaks the language of certain warrior tribes from Land Beyond the Sea. I have heard it spoken there, and on Eireann, the Western Isle, but never in the fens of Albion."

Balor did not like the tack of the man's musings; they struck too close to the heart of truth. "And what would a seaman know of the fens of Albion?"

"Enough to know that you are no native to them." He

smiled obliquely, his eyes as hard and sharp as polished blue slate. "But no matter. Keep your confidences, as I have kept mine. In this bleak and hostile land where men prey upon one another, distrust is a virtue to be nurtured by those who would survive."

In the warm haze of midday, with gulls circling and crying above them, the slave ships came. Balor and the stranger watched them from the protection of the dunes, lying prone in the sand as they peered through the sparse, rough grasses that topped the sand hills. Of varying sizes, they were the same sort of craft that had been carrying men and women up and down this coast since Time Beyond Beginning. With broad, deep bellies to accommodate cargo, they had high, curving prows and sterns. They were of tanned oxhides, stretched and stitched over wooden frames. They carried no sail, but with the aid of a single steersman, the men at the oars could easily guide their vessels through the summer surf to a safe beaching.

This they did, until some dozen vessels lay like so many stranded whales. Immediately the crew began to drive their human cargo ashore. Young males, with a few girls and women among them, responded quickly to the cursing and prodding of men with whips. Disheveled and broken spirited, the slaves were only slightly less filthy than their masters, some of whom were beginning to scour the beach and estuary for driftwood with which they would build a fire for their night's encampment.

The stranger exhaled a barely audible curse as he went rigid beside Balor. "Look at that! One of them's seen my footprints! Come on, Wizard, unless you can actually work some magic to make those bastards disappear, we'd best get scrambling if we value our freedom!"

Without another word they scooted back from the top of the dune and raced to their encampment to gather what they could. They struck down their tent, scattered the poles, and buried the fire pit and anything else that could not be quickly carried away. With hastily gathered grasses they swept away all traces of their habitation and footprints as they fled into the marsh.

Nightfall found them hiding on a hump of fetid land deep

within the reed beds, with no cooking fire to warm them or betray their whereabouts to the slavers. They sat in huddled silence, with only the stranger's cloak held above them to keep the fog at bay. It settled down upon them like a broody hen, smothering the sounds of the night, keeping its secrets. It was so quiet that they could hear the fog condensing, dripping from the reeds like rain.

Time passed. Sounds, distorted by distance, began to reach them from the beach. The laughter of men. An occasional curse in an alien tongue. Bawdy songs bellowed off key. Hands clapping a strident, vicious rhythm. A woman's shriek. A man's cry of pain. Then moaning. And laughter again—the laughter of cruel and perverted merriment.

"They're drunk," whispered the stranger.

"I wish I were drunk," drawled Balor darkly.

Time passed. The fog grew as thick as clotted cream. They slept. Then Balor awoke, jabbed by the stranger's elbow.

"Listen!" The word was a command.

Balor obeyed. He heard nothing and said so.

The stranger made a little exhalation of impatience. "Of course you hear nothing. No sound at all. The hour is late. The slavers sleep, with their captives close beside them and fog shrouding the world. Now is the time to make our move!"

"Move? Are you mad? I know this marsh. It's full of deeps and quicksand. Besides, come morning the slavers will go their way. They'll not waste their energies combing the bogs for us when they already have all of the slaves they can carry."

"Of course they won't. They'll go, and they'll take their boats with them, leaving us here, stranded upon this cursed shore."

Understanding began to dawn. Balor wanted no part of it. "You *are* mad! The smallest vessel on that beach is designed to be rowed by four men!"

"So I noted. It is beached off by itself, well to the south of the others. We'll have no trouble stealing it, not in this fog, and the sound of the surf will mask the sound of our dragging the boat into the sea. By dawn we'll be miles away. With the two of us working together, inspired by necessity, we'll have the strength of four. You'll see!"

Balor did not want to see. Suddenly the marsh seemed a comforting place, and he had no desire to leave it. "I . . . I haven't regained my full strength yet, and my hand...it is not completely healed."

With a harrumph the stranger stood up and slung on his cloak. "What's the matter, Wizard? Have you no nerve?"

"I am no wizard!"

"Perhaps not. But *I* am!"

Balor gaped, too stunned to speak. The man had drawn a dagger...*Balor's* dagger, taken from his belt along with his ax while he had lain delirious with fever.

"Now you listen to me...." His voice was low and dangerous. "I am Cethlinn, firstborn of Cromm Cruach, who is high priest of the People of the Stone. I was shipwrecked on my way home from a sacred pilgrimage to the far northern island sanctuaries of my people, and it is imperative that I return to the Plain of the Great Stone Circle before the dawn of midsummer sunrise. That boat out there on the beach...it was meant for me, as I now know that you were meant for me—a gift from the hawk that guided me to where you lay dying. Without you to help me, I could not possibly hope to steal that boat. So rise up! You are my good fortune. You are Destiny's hand, and by the stars, you shall strike an oar with me this night, or I shall gut you where you stand!"

It occurred to Balor that he was taller and broader than Cethlinn, and that his skill with a knife was such that he could use it with either hand. Yet as he rose to his feet, his eyes on the threatening weapon, he said, "I owe you a life debt, Cethlinn. If this is the payment you would ask of me, so be it. I am honor bound to pay it. But I must warn you...this is a dangerous venture that you would set for us...and I have brought luck to no man."

The fog gave off a strange, gray light of its own. Cethlinn's eyes seemed to bore right through it as he looked Balor up and down. "No man, eh? Well, don't let that trouble you. The past is past. The future is yet to be. And with me things shall be different for you. That much I can guarantee!"

Luck was with them. They had no trouble stealing the boat, which had provisions and bladders of fresh water—enough for four rowers—stored under the plank seats. By dawn they were miles away, rowing in a soft, sure swell that bore them swiftly through the fog toward the land of Cethlinn's people far to the south.

The hours passed. They rested often, so as not to unduly

stress Balor's hand; but he, as much as Cethlinn, was anxious
to put many miles between the slavers and their little craft,
and so they made good time.

The fog thinned and receded. They kept close to its edge,
ready to enter it at a moment's notice if the need arose to use
it as a camouflage; but they saw no ships or vessels of any
kind. Save for the occasional rookeries where seabirds or sea
lions crowded and called from the rocky coves and headlands,
the coastline along which they traveled was uninhabited.

And so the days passed for them. Cethlinn trailed a sinew
line from the stern of the boat, weighting it with one of
Morrigan's flint blanks and a hook he fashioned from a broken
seashell. Baited with strips of meat scraped from the mollusks
they pried from tide pools at each night's encampment, the
lure never failed to win them a fish for their evening meal.

Slowly, tenuously, a bond of trust began to form between
them, and although they kept their confidences one from the
other, gradually their defenses began to lower. Cethlinn
spoke freely of the People of the Stone, followers of a religion
he claimed was as old as the stars and as full of wisdom. He
spoke of great temples and monuments, of world-famous
centers of learning where men gathered to worship knowledge and to study the heavens. He spoke of the factions that
had begun to develop among the faithful—of mystic priests
who clung to the austere rituals of the past, and of more
liberal believers, like himself, who understood that in a
changing world a religion that remained inflexible must break
and fall as an oak before the gales of time.

The man's openness sparked a friendly response in Balor.
He told Cethlinn his name, and although he did not reveal
the identity of his clan or the reasons that had led him to
wander the marshes alone, he told him of the night he had
passed with Star Gazer, so long ago, on the cliffs north of
Point of Ale. Cethlinn listened intensely, his concentration so
keen that it put Balor on edge.

"Why do you stare? Is it so strange that I should have spent
time in the company of one of your people?"

Cethlinn's head swung back and forth in slow negation as
he sat dead still at his oar. "Describe him to me."

Balor shrugged and complied. "He was a scrawny old bird
dressed all in white. He talked circles round me, but he had
a way with horses that was pure magic. I doubt if I shall ever

forget him or the friendship he offered or the way he spoke about the great star we both saw fall into the west so long ago."

Cethlinn caught his breath. His eyes went round. Then he laughed. He slapped his thighs. Then he laughed again and shook his head as though he marveled at his own stupidity. "Of course! By the shadow of the circling hawk! I should have guessed!"

Balor was mystified by his outburst of enthusiasm. "What are you talking about?"

Cethlinn waved the question away and chuckled. "Time will tell the why of it, my fine young friend. In the meanwhile do not ask, for you would not wish to believe me if I were to explain it to you now!"

The miles fell away. The oars rose and reached, dipped and pulled. Their hands grew hard beneath the strips of rag they had wound around their palms until their blisters toughened into calluses. Cethlinn could not bear with silence. He filled it with whistles and songs. He spoke of the many marvels he had seen as an emissary of the People of the Stone, of bleak islands where no trees grew, of vast open lands where the earth never thawed and trees survived in miniature forests aeons old and only inches high. He spoke of floating islands of crystal drifting in frigid seas. He spoke of lands where, in summer, the sun never set, and the winter moon rose to light the earth at noon while cold fires trembled in the sky like multicolored ribbons whirling in the hair of dancing maidens.

At the command of his father, Cromm Cruach, high priest of the People of the Stone, he was to have brought home to his people a wizard of inordinate power from the Isles of the Sea of Mist, a man who was to be mated to Cromm Cruach's only daughter at the sacred festival of the rising of the midsummer sun. But disaster had struck on the return voyage. A great gray beast had risen from the depths of the sea, rammed their vessel, and capsized it. All aboard were drowned.

"Except the one who sits before you now," he said, bowing his head in the manner of one who expects to be congratulated for some hard-won accomplishment.

They lounged together upon a stony strand of narrow

beach. Cethlinn picked at the remnants of his portion of their evening meal and winked at Balor in the way of a conspirator.

"The Fates were against the venture from the start. But Cromm Cruach could not be convinced until he had seen the wizard for himself and judged his powers. Bah! The man was as I feared he would be—old and juiceless and as puckered as a fruit packed too long in brine. The daughter of Cromm Cruach shall not grieve for him. The mating was to have forged an alliance between the conflicting factions that have developed among the southern and northern peoples of our faith. It was Cromm Cruach's idea. His daughter wanted no part of it. Long ago she named the man whom she would have, and has waited for him, even though she has risked growing old as the years have passed and he has not come to her."

Balor sat cross-legged before their little fire pit, reknapping a damaged arrowhead. The work took all of his attention. He did not care about Cromm Cruach or his aging daughter. The conversation drifted as Cethlinn sensed his disinterest.

Silence settled between them. Cethlinn could not bear it. As he watched Balor smooth and sharpen the chipped edges of the flint, he said with open admiration, "You do that with the skill of one trained well to the warrior's arts."

"Aye, and so," conceded Balor, pleased by the observation, seeing no reason to deny it.

Cethlinn's brow furrowed with thoughtful speculation. "You carry an ax and a dagger, a bow and a snare net. Over the last few days I have seen you use each of these with equal and impressive skill. Yet about the contents of your wizard's bag you are obviously ignorant. I find this very strange indeed."

Balor felt that he owed the man some sort of an explanation. After all, they were no longer strangers, and Cethlinn *had* saved his life. So he told Cethlinn that it had been given to him by a friend and that he had not realized that it contained anything other than food.

Cethlinn raised a telling brow. "Surely, then, it was a gift of the Fates, for you would have died without it."

"It was you who healed me, Cethlinn."

"Yes, but only because the elements of healing were available to me." He puckered his lips thoughtfully. "We have a long journey ahead of us. I could teach you about these things so that never again would you be vulnerable to illness through your own ignorance."

"Why would you wish to share the gift of such hard-earned knowledge with me?"

"Among my people it is considered a sacred obligation to share our knowledge."

When the arrowhead was mended to Balor's satisfaction, he put it aside and together with Cethlinn spread the contents of Morrigan's medicine bag on the sand before the fire. He watched as Cethlinn rummaged through the items with interest, explaining how the various fungi and cobwebs and herbs and roots might best be used. At length, sorting through the bundles of twigs and feathers, he made a face of disapproval. "This friend of yours . . . her knowledge is admirable, albeit pathetically primitive."

Balor was amazed by his intuitiveness. "I do not remember telling you that the bag belonged to a woman."

Cethlinn shrugged offhandedly. "There is a certain feminine order to it. This female . . . would she be the one for whom you called when you lay delirious with fever? Would she be the one you love . . . the one called Morrigan?"

Balor was appalled. His face flamed. "Never! The bag was hers, but she is a dark thorn of a girl, and if I called out her name, surely I *was* out of my head!"

Cethlinn allowed himself a chuckle at Balor's expense as he looked at him out of eyes full of mirth. "It is often said, my fine young friend, that truth is more often spoken by a man when he is out of his head than when he is in it!"

Balor did not appreciate Cethlinn's sense of humor. He wrapped his arms vehemently about his bent knees and glared into the fire. "There *is* one whom I love, Cethlinn. But by the Fates, it is *not* Morrigan!"

Cethlinn's mouth puckered over his teeth, and he turned his attention back to the contents of the medicine bag, clucking his tongue with disapproval as he fingered the dried skins and bones with disdain before setting them aside. One by one, as Balor brooded in the firelight, he opened the little bags of "magic" powders, sniffed at them curiously, then probed them with a moistened fingertip, which he then carefully and tentatively put to his tongue.

"Cleverly mixed sorcery. Best kept far from the flames," he conceded as he set the little bags aside and began to speak readily of the healers among his own people, who performed medical marvels so advanced that they could open an ailing skull, perform delicate surgery upon the gray matter within it, then close the skull again, restoring their patient to full health and vigor within a matter of weeks.

Balor's mood had been soured by Cethlinn's talk of Morrigan. "What do you take me for?" he snapped nastily. "No man can open another's skull lest the life-force fly out, never to return! I don't believe a bit of it!"

Cethlinn was not offended. "Know this, my fine young friend—we who are called the People of the Stone are not like other priests and wizards. We are dedicated to the pursuit of infinite knowledge, and among us there are healers and soothsayers of such profound ability that, although there is no trickery to the work they do, many believe them to be wizards." He paused. He looked at Balor, and the fire that glowed within his eyes came from within him, not from the fire pit. "Our power is real, Balor. It lies rooted in our knowledge. It lies in our understanding of the nature of our fellow man and in our ability to predict the turning of the stars, the ebb and flow of the tides, the rising of the Black Moon, and the advent of the Dark Sun. As long as there is ignorance in the world, we shall have the Power... for a man who knows more than his brother, a man who can manipulate the fears and anticipate the needs of his brother, that man shall be *master* of his brother. Learn and accept this truth, and by the stars that hold the secrets of Creation, you too shall be a wizard... and master of the world—if you would dare to claim it!"

The next day they sighted the headlands of Point of Ale and at Cethlinn's insistence put far out to sea.

"These are dangerous waters for such small fish as we. Best we remain unseen."

Balor chafed at the oars and grew visibly restless with frustration as Cethlinn watched him with interest, asking if Point of Ale had been his original destination. Balor nodded in affirmation and added that when he had honored his life debt by seeing Cethlinn safely ashore in the lands of his people, he would return to Point of Ale to wait for one whom he would meet again, for vengeance's sake.

Cethlinn looked at Balor as though he had just discovered himself to be in the presence of an idiot. "Truly then, my fine young friend, you had better *be* a wizard who is as wise and wary as a wolf when you venture alone into that den of thieves. At Point of Ale there is no law for those who walk without men-at-arms to guard them or without bronze to give weight to the threat of their weaponry."

The advice disgusted Balor; it was as though his father had spoken through Cethlinn's mouth. Now, as in the past, the words implied cowardice. "And how do you know that I am not a wolf?" he snarled.

Cethlinn leaned on his oar. "Because wolves run in packs, my fine young friend. If they are to hunt successfully, they, as much as men, need brothers."

"I need no one!"

Cethlinn's eyes half closed as they took slow and rueful measure of Balor. "If you believe that, you are surely no wolf, my fine young friend. You are a fool."

Balor could find no words to equal the measure of his mood. Angrily he set to his oar. Cethlinn joined him. They rowed on in silence for a while, until the mouse-haired man felt compelled to fill the air with song. He had a light, pleasant voice. It soothed the passage of the miles.

Slowly the sun claimed the height of noon, and as the morning fog thinned to haze, they saw the stain of a red and black sail furled and full, bellying out on the horizon. Balor froze at his oar, staring, so full of memories that reality ceased to exist for him until Cethlinn threw the morning's catch at him. It was a still-twitching silver bass. It hit him hard across his cheek, stunning him.

"Row!" raged Cethlinn. "For your life, man, row!"

Shaking, Balor took up his oar. Together, working furiously, they turned the little boat hard into the troughs between the swells, risking the danger of being capsized, until distance claimed the other ship and it vanished shoreward.

Cethlinn glared at Balor from beneath a furrowed, sweated brow as they paused to catch their breath. "By the stars, man, do you care nothing for your life or freedom? Do you not know the colors of the house of Nemed MacAgnomain?"

"I know them." He rested heavily upon his oar, staring off unblinking into the distances that had swallowed Nemed's ship. And yet he saw the ship still, burned as though by flame into the fibers of his mind.

Cethlinn sat panting, hunched over his oar, his features congested with loathing as he too stared after the other ship. Then he motioned to Balor to pass over his dagger and the silver bass. Cethlinn began to cut slices from it angrily, in a rhythm that matched the fury of his words. "There must be a hundred vessels that fly the colors of that cursed house, and the shadow of Nemed's power sets the rats of dread loose within the belly of every man who justly hates him. But mark me, someday those rats will turn against him, for Nemed cultivates enemies as other men nurture friends." He paused. Slowly the rhythm of his breathing returned to normal, and he passed Balor several morsels of bass. As he chewed thoughtfully on his own portion, his eyes moved to rest upon Balor and his lids lowered in almost dreamy speculation. "It is foretold by the People of the Stone that someday a great lord shall rise out of Albion. He shall rise in days of darkness. He shall follow in the path of falling stars. He shall be a wizard and a warrior. And when at last he claims his kingdom, all men—even such tyrants as Nemed MacAgnomain—shall tremble before his might."

A bleak thought crossed Balor's mind. "Perhaps Nemed is the Mighty One," he said.

"No," replied Cethlinn, his tone emphatic. "True enough, he is master of a great and greedy pack of followers, whose loyalty he has purchased with gold. They carry the colors of his house upon their shields because they enjoy being reflections of his power and because they know that to do otherwise would be to invite the slavers' brand. But the Mighty One, he shall be a lord whom men shall follow willingly, warmed and strengthened by his power as men are warmed and strengthened by the sun. It is foretold that he shall spring forth from the loins of a wolf and shadow the sea with the wings of a hawk. His spear shall be the lightning bolt. His sword shall be both an answerer and retaliator for the Fates. His power shall spring from his mastery over all of the arts of man. Under his banner he shall unite the tribes of the great clan kingdoms, and his knowledge and wisdom shall be so vast that to the ending of Time itself men shall sing praises to his memory."

The words recalled Huldre's haunted, unwelcome prophecies. The coincidence was unsettling. Balor did not wish to heed it. "Surely, Cethlinn, you speak of a god, not of any mortal man!"

Cethlinn shrugged and shook his head. "But the gods *are* men, my fine young friend, cut from a different cloth, but men all the same, forged into greatness by the forces of life. Cromm Cruach has seen the Mighty One. And the daughter of Cromm Cruach has waited to be mated to him. Soon now he shall come forth. As a man. As a warrior. As one who is destined to become a priest of the Stone. Someday he shall take Cromm Cruach's place. And those who ally themselves with him shall become lords over all of the earth."

Far off toward the distant shore a horn sounded. No doubt it announced the arrival at Point of Ale of the ship with the red and black sails. Balor wondered if Nemed was aboard. The thought caused him to shiver.

"Unlike the aging daughter of Cromm Cruach," Balor said bleakly, "I am not willing to wait for a legend to come to life so that I might mate my desires with it. I have sworn a man's vengeance against Nemed MacAgnomain. When I have seen you safely to the shores of your people, I shall return to Point of Ale to claim it."

"If you go alone, you shall fail, as have all the others who have gone before you. He is wise. He is wary. He is heavily guarded. No enemy has a chance of getting close to him."

"I shall find a way. By the dishonored blood of my ancestors, this I have sworn: to take his life, even if it must cost me my own."

Cethlinn observed him shrewdly, cocking his head as his brows arched into the shaggy cut of his mouse-brown hair. "And beyond your dreams of vengeance, what else have you sworn to accomplish in your life?"

The question set dark fire to Balor's mood. It roused images of the past, of ruined dreams, of shattered ambitions, of the holding, so far away now, of friends lost to him forever. He saw Draga's face and snarled against the memory. "There is nothing for me but that. Vengeance against those who have wronged me."

Cethlinn's eyes narrowed. His white, crooked teeth chewed his lower lip with thoughtful speculation. "If all you seek is vengeance, then know now that your dreams are dark and shriveled things. Beware of them, my fine young friend, lest

in seeking to obtain them you lose sight of all that is truly
good and lasting in this life."

That night they made no encampment at all, but took turns
at the oars, guiding their little vessel as far from the waters of
Point of Ale as their stamina would allow. For two days and a
night they rowed thus, one keeping up the rhythm of movement while the other rested or slept. On dawn of the third
day they put in to shore on a broad beach rimmed all around
by sand dunes. Here they hid the boat, turned it belly down,
and propped up a gunwhale with a stone so that they might
crawl beneath it. Balor set a trap, and soon he and Cethlinn
were roasting small waterfowl, the fruits of his labor. Using
their boat as a shelter from the damp sea air, they slept, and
slept after their meal, confident that they would not be seen
or searched for in this bleak and uninhabited landscape. The
next day they were off again, refreshed by the food and sleep,
marking changes in the coastline as they savored the new
scent that peppered the wind. It was the fragrance of planted
fields and cultivated grasses. They drew it in and seemed to
grow strong from it.

"Soon now," informed Cethlinn, "we shall reach the country of the People of the Stone."

The days passed. Now and again from their boat they saw
fishing hamlets upland of the coves, with grazing animals
browsing in ill-tended pastures. Once, they saw a leather-clad
girl wading calf deep in the surf, a large, loosely woven
crabbing basket balanced on her hip. She was small and lean
and lovely. The wind lifted her long black hair, as currents
lifted the long, silken strands of sea grass, which drifted
within the sea.

Balor stared at her, suddenly stabbed by unexpected pain
and longing. The girl looked so much like Morrigan. Morrigan.
How far away she was from him . . . with her sharp tongue and
ready wit and sea-green eyes so easily transposed to soft and
liquid silver by moonlight. Morrigan. He almost spoke her
name aloud, but choked it back in time. Cethlinn was looking
at him, noting the way he eyed the girl. He blushed, annoyed
with himself as he forced his gaze away from the shore. He
tried to think of Dana. *She* was the one he loved.

They rowed on, traveling ever southward. Their bodies

were bronzed and hard from long hours spent at the oars, and their friendship deepened. They developed an easy camaraderie, which made the time pass quickly. Then, in the misted warmth of a hazed and languid summer noon, they shipped oars and stared landward. Cethlinn pointed to a tall, roughly hewn stone, which stood like a lonely giant upon the shore. He sat very still, breathing deeply to suppress his mounting excitement.

"The stone marks the way inland. To the east lies the country of the People of the Stone."

They brought the boat through the surf and rested it within a marshy estuary where bees busied themselves burrowing into masses of wildflowers and gnats droned like armies taking on the wind. Balor stood by while Cethlinn went to the Standing Stone and lay his hands reverently upon it. It was clear that he sought communion with forces beyond Balor's understanding; and it was clear too, that he found what he sought. As Balor watched, he could see the weariness flow out of Cethlinn as though the stone shared its strength with him. It was an amazing transformation. The lines about his eyes seemed to dissolve. He seemed years younger, pretty almost in the way of a woman as he stood smiling, as he might have done at a long-delayed and much anticipated reunion.

His face was radiant when he suggested to Balor that they turn the boat keel up so that it would not be swamped by a sudden rainfall before Balor could return to use it on his journey back to Point of Ale. Balor frowned and informed Cethlinn that he had no intention of accompanying him inland; once they had reached this shore, he reasoned, his life debt had been canceled.

Cethlinn harrumphed with righteous indignation. "Go ahead then! Leave me to make my way home alone across the long miles that lie ahead! With no strongman to guard me, I shall be vulnerable. But pay me no mind. Go on your way to seek your vengeance."

Cethlinn knew the knack of a woman's wheedling. Still, he spoke the truth, even if it was unwelcome.

They went on together. He was no fighter. But he had proved himself to be a friend. Although Balor itched to be on his way back to Point of Ale, he resolved to stay by Cethlinn's side. "But only until you reach the first village within the

jurisdiction of your people . . . or until you can join with a
caravan of pilgrims in whose company you shall be able to
find protection."

"So be it," said the mouse-haired man, hitching up his
traveling pack. "But should you decide to come all of the way
with me, I can promise you that Cromm Cruach shall be
grateful, as well as generous, to you."

This was a new and intriguing premise. "Grateful enough
to grant me gold? Gold enough to buy a bronze sword with
which to stand against Nemed?"

Cethlinn's eyes narrowed. "Cromm Cruach is a man of
peace. He shall tolerate no talk of swords. But ask life-
blessing at the moment that the rising midsummer sun stands
over the Marking Stone on the Plain of the Great Stone
Circle, and your reward may well surpass your wildest dreams."

20

They walked until dusk and slept until the first blush of
dawn. A full day passed before they saw conspicuous breaks
in the undergrowth, marking the hunting trails of man. Soon
they began to see signs of settled areas. Now and again they
would sight a man at work within a plot of planted earth, or
see the forms of women bent to gather herbs or kindling
while their children squalled and laughed about their knees.
Once, a dog came barking after them, and a man, alerted and
drawn from his plowing by the animal, cursed and waved a
stave at them.

Balor did not understand the farmer's unprovoked hostility
and wondered why they might not seek rest and solace and
perhaps a hot bath among these settled folk; but Cethlinn
warned that these were dangerous times in which men were
wise not to trust or welcome strangers. For the first time
Balor learned that not only Bracken Fen had been affected by
long winters and weather patterns that did not allow for
decent crops and pasturage. The skies over all of Albion—
indeed, over much of the northern world—had grown hostile
and unstable; and so, accordingly, had the peoples who

dwelled beneath those skies. Entire tribes had been displaced. They sought new territories, which they took by force. Those who could not defend against their predations in turn became predators: thieves and murderers, scoundrels and masters of survival at any cost.

But now the skies were warm and clear, and Balor and Cethlinn went on, finding it difficult to remember that only a season ago the weather had been foul, ruinous to crops, cattle, and men. At night they kept their fire small and as smokeless as possible lest it alert the human predators to their whereabouts. As soon as their food was cooked they scattered the embers and lay on their backs while Cethlinn spoke Star Wisdom, of an ordered universe that might be charted and understood. Balor absorbed the knowledge with such ease that Cethlinn paused and stared at him.

"Given time... and study... you could be one of us," he said.

Balor snorted. "A priest of the Stone? That is one thing that I shall most certainly *never* be!"

Cethlinn chewed his lower lip and eyed Balor. "If you live long enough, my fine young friend, you shall learn that nothing in this life is certain... except, perhaps, uncertainty itself."

Cethlinn was to be proved correct sooner than either of them could have imagined. The following day found them moving through deep woods, where they saw signs of recent large and small encampments: abandoned fire pits, broken shrubbery, areas of earth scuffed by the movement of human feet. Several times Balor paused, discomfited by the sensation of being watched. Although he saw no one, he kept an arrow nocked and ready, and advised Cethlinn to keep his dagger close at hand.

Twice they passed menhirs, tall, single upright stones around which sacrifices had been placed: small bowls of grain, a fat clay amulet carved to represent some sort of foreign female goddess of fertility, and, in a large earthen jug, a burned offering consisting of the broken, charred bones of a goat. Cethlinn scorned the ignorance of those who had left such primitive oblations, informing Balor that the stones were neither god effigies nor burial monuments; they were abandoned star markers, which had once been of astronomical importance to the priests who dwelled in small, isolated

farmsteads all across the northwestern world and as far south
as the isle of Malta.

Worsening weather patterns had altered the priests' way of
life. As clouds obscured the night sky with increasing fre-
quency, the old religion had begun to die. Converts were
rare. Those of the old way were now forced to dwell within
large communities of the faithful, safe behind walls and
ramparts. Slowly, in once-sacred clearings all across Albion,
woods and brambles were growing back about the isolated
marking stones. Multicolored lichens grew over them, covering the patterns that had been so reverently inscribed by the
ancients. Rain softened the soil that held them upright until
they sagged and fell. In time the Mother of All would take
them back into herself; in time, duff and debris would cover
them until, in millennia to come, those who would walk upon
the land would not know that the great stones had ever been
there at all.

Balor was glad when they put the stones behind them.
Something about them put him on edge, an aura of Other-
worldliness that was reminiscent of the stone circle upon the
moor that had sheltered a small, lost boy from howling wolves
and the stalking beast of his own fear, a circle that had existed
by night and had vanished by day. *Stones are merely stones,
rocks devoid of souls or spirits,* he reassured himself as they
walked. And yet in the shadow of the Standing Stones, all
things seemed possible. Even when they came out of the
dark woods and began to walk across broad expanses of open,
sunlit country, it seemed to Balor that the stones were
watching him. Several times he stopped and looked back, half
expecting to discover them marching after him.

All through the day the sensation of being watched continued to plague him. Even when Cethlinn began to point to
landmarks and informed him that tomorrow they would reach
the Plain of the Great Stone Circle, his mood was not
lightened. He kept looking back until, at dusk, they chose a
little grove of hardwoods in which to pass the night. They
cast off their traveling packs and built a fire over which they
began to roast the hares Balor had brought down earlier in
the day. For the first time in hours Balor relaxed.

Neither of them could have said just when the three
strangers appeared. They came so quietly, with no breath of
warning, that both Cethlinn and Balor knew instinctively that

they were up to no good. Big men and bold, they strutted about the fire, brazen fellows in filthy clothes. They talked loudly and joked amongst themselves in a language that Cethlinn wisely pretended not to understand; later he would tell Balor that it was a corruption of one of the local dialects, as crude and full of twists and turns as the minds of the three who spoke it.

"Be easy," he advised Balor quietly. "Play the fool, for they are of a mind to do murder, and they are better armed than we."

This was true. The men brandished long, serrated daggers of deadly sharp, unpolished, and unclean copper. A man would surely die from infection if not directly from wounds inflicted by such weapons. They had staves and bows at their backs and axes at their belts as they hunkered down, uninvited, close at each side of the fire. Without hesitation they began to help themselves to the half-cooked hares. When Balor moved to protest, one of them knocked him flat while another rose to kick him. Once. Twice. And once again. He gasped and rolled away, nauseated with pain and shame and anger as his assailant laughed and gave him yet another kick, this time to his backside. It took him a few moments to catch his breath and clear his head. When at last he rose, it was with his ax in one hand and the dagger Cethlinn had returned to him in the other. The interlopers seemed unconcerned about his threat. They gnawed at their appropriated meal. They laughed and pointed at him. One of them gestured him forward. Another drew his own ax. Only Cethlinn's cool head kept Balor from leaping out at them in bold acceptance of their obvious challenge.

"You cannot stand against all three of them, Balor. And I could not fend off even one of them alone."

Slowly, not taking his eyes from the interlopers, Balor lowered himself until he sat crouched, balancing on the balls of his feet. These were strong, cruel men. If he sprang at them, he would have a knife in his gut and an ax in his back before his own weapons could do much damage. Then they would take their time with Cethlinn, killing him for pleasure if they decided not to make a slave of him. Balor's eyelids lowered as he observed them. One wore a golden ring in his nose. Another wore silver loops at his ears. The third wore both, plus a rounded leather helmet. He had an ugly, flattened

nose, which looked as though it had been smashed with a
cudgel. Like his companions, he snorted with pleasure as he
gnawed at his food. Blood and juices and half-rendered fat ran
into their excessively greasy beards. They sucked at their
fingers and wiped their hands in their long, matted hair.

Slowly darkness claimed the hour. Balor did not move. The
strangers made no attempt to take his weapons from him.
They carried bladder flasks of mead and drank deeply, offering to share none of it with their unwilling hosts. They sat
very close to the fire, feeding it with kindling and cut wood
that Balor and Cethlinn had earlier piled close to the fire pit.
They kept a roaring fire to ward off the chill. Their faces
shone with grease and cruelty. Their eyes grew blurred from
drink, dangerous with a hunger that caused the hairs at the
nape of Balor's neck to curl. He had seen that look before—in
Mael's eyes before he had set himself to rape Morrigan. They
belched and loosed wind, laughing as they did so, cracking
the last of the bones of the hares between their teeth, sucking
marrow noisily and licking their lips with a slow, sexual
provocation.

"They'll make their move soon," said Cethlinn through a
strained grin, behaving as though he discussed nothing of any
more importance than the weather. "Perhaps if we make a
run for it, both of us at the same time, we might stand a
chance of escaping them in the dark. It's worth a try. If they
get their hands on us, their deeds will be an affront to the
dignity of life itself, and before they make an end of us, we
shall think of death as a mercy."

But Balor knew that it was no good. From the way the
threesome eyed them, this was exactly what they were
anticipating. He was not certain of how or when the idea
came to him, he only knew that he was feigning a yawn,
stretching languorously, as though he had not a care in the
world. His stomach growled, as he had hoped it would. He
grinned at the sound, like an idiot, blank-faced and tittering.
He rubbed his belly to indicate hunger, then slowly got to his
feet. The intruders tensed. They watched him suspiciously as
he told Cethlinn what he intended to do and what Cethlinn
must do if the ruse was to work. Grinning like a mind-
blighted oaf, he backed away from the fire pit and bent to
scoop up Morrigan's medicine bag. Once again, although the
girl was far away, she might save his life.

One of the brigands jumped to his feet, but Cethlinn gestured him down again, speaking in the tone of a conciliator, signing broadly with his hands that Balor was mindless and only sought food within the sack. The men had drunk enough mead to dull their judgment. They glowered, suspicious only until Balor began to pluck willow leaves from the bag and stuff them ravenously into his mouth. They were dry and bitter, but he made a good show of it, nibbling on them with relish as he came back to the fire. He was terrified. He wished that he had made a run for it while he had the chance, or had charged them boldly after they had kicked him. But to run or to stand and die like a warrior would leave Cethlinn alone to face a fate that would have no mercy in it. And he could not abandon a friend who had saved his life. Irony swept through him. If he and Cethlinn were to see another dawn, he would have to play the fool, as Fomor had once done in order to save Draga. As he knelt and put on his best idiot's grin, for the first time he understood that sometimes it took more courage to play the fool than to leap forward in a hero's skin.

The willow leaves were causing him to salivate. He was so frightened that he was very near to wretching as, summoning all of his courage just to keep smiling his dullard's smile, he rummaged in the sack again and came up with one of the little bags that contained Morrigan's "magic" powders.

Let this work, he implored. *By the Fates! By the Twelve Winds! By the Eye of Donar and all of the bright stars by which Cethlinn swears! Let this work!*

Slowly, fighting to keep his hands from shaking, he loosed the sinew tie and dipped his fingers into the little bag. Pinching up a fingering of powder, he put it to his lips and pretended to sample it with ecstasy. As he had expected, one of the interlopers growled with impatience and reached greedily across the flames in an attempt to snatch the bag for himself. But before his hands could grab it, Balor opened it wide, turned it upside down, and flung the powder into the blazing fire. It flared the moment the powder came in contact with it, exploding with a roar into a white-hot tower of incandescence. Cethlinn, with one of the strangers sitting close by, gave the man a sudden, brutal elbow jab that sent him toward the flames just as Balor kicked out, sending earth and fire flying upward into the faces of the two would-be murderers. In seconds the grease in their beards and hair caught fire. They rose screaming, beating madly at the flames that now had their heads blazing like torches. As their stunned comrade stared in horror, they whirled, blinded, and fled maddened by pain and terror into the darkness as the night was suddenly filled with the cries of birds panicked from their roosts by the screams of death and the stench of burning flesh and hair.

Dazed, the remaining interloper rose. With his ax in one hand and his dagger in the other, he stared with disbelief at the young fool who had transformed himself into a towering avenger and was circling around the fire toward him, menacing him with an ax and a dagger of his own. The man frowned. There was no question that the youth could use his weapons; but in hand-to-hand combat, hesitation could often be more deadly than any blow. And the youth had not chosen to hurl his ax. So without warning, the interloper threw his. It flew, tumbling in a deadly arc, finding its mark before the youth could leap away.

Cethlinn screamed as the force of the blow nearly knocked Balor down. He spun around, stunned by the impact as the ax bit deep and at an angle, shattering his right clavicle near the shoulder joint. He looked at his injury and could not quite grasp the enormity of what he saw. His arm and shoulder hung limp and useless at an impossible angle, and he dropped his ax.

Cethlinn charged the man, leaping on him with fists clenched and pounding. The man slapped Cethlinn aside, to tend to later. Now he was savoring Balor's reaction to the injury, convinced that the youth was useless as a fighter. He smiled. He would gut the youth now, rip him from sternum to crotch and leave him to meditate the complexity of the coils of his own intestines. After what had happened to his companions, the youth deserved to suffer. It would take him days to die.

Slowly, threatening with his dagger, the man began to advance. He saw the youth's left hand rise to close about the haft of the ax that was imbedded in his shoulder. He saw no danger in the movement. It was the brigand's last mistake.

The ax left Balor's hand with all of his weight behind it. It came out of his shoulder with a vast, sickening wave of pain that nearly dropped him to his knees. But he would not fall. He was in shock, but with his last reserves of strength he threw the ax with a power that came from some deep, inner core of resolve, as Fomor and Draga and the men of the clan MacLir had taught him to throw it: like a warrior son of the People of the Ax.

The weapon entered the man's head at the apex of his brow, directly above and between his eyes. It split his face as it buried itself haft deep in his brains. He was dead before his body had the grace to fall and cease its twitching.

Balor was cold. Cethlinn had built up the fire, but it did not warm him. The mouse-haired man tended Balor's wound, assuring him that with proper care the bone could be set and the muscles mended, and in time they would support the weight of his arm. The ax had just missed a major artery; a little closer to the neck and Balor would have bled to death. Still, he was bleeding heavily, and Cethlinn knew the wound must be cauterized before he left to bring help from his people.

"There are fine healers on the Plain of the Great Stone Circle at this time of the year. But you are too weak to travel, so I must bring them here to you."

The brand was put to his flesh. He leaped in agony before he fainted. When he awoke, Cethlinn was gone. The fire was out. The fire pit had been buried and all signs of their encampment had been wiped away. He lay in the little grove of hardwoods, hidden beneath a camouflage of leaves and branches from the eyes of potential scoundrels. Somewhere not far off, a nighthawk keened and wolves howled balefully. He thought of the three men whom he had killed this night. Where were the two he had burned? What had Cethlinn done with the body of the third? The killings had been necessary, yet as when he had slain Mael, he felt no sense of satisfaction; indeed, he felt as though a part of him had been lost with the lives he had taken.

Would he feel so when at last he took the life of Nemed MacAgnomain? Would there be no thrill of elation, no surge of triumph? A bleak thought crossed his mind. Perhaps he would never have the chance to find out. Perhaps his dream of vengeance was now shattered along with his collarbone.

Perhaps, despite Cethlinn's assurances, he would never regain the use of his arm. Perhaps in his race to return home
in time for the rising of the midsummer sun, Cethlinn would
never return. Perhaps he had left him here to die like a
wounded wood rat within a nest of sticks and leaves.

Through pain and weariness and worry he looked up
through the meshwork of branches and into the vastness of
the star-filled sky. No stars fell to trace an omen's path. The
heavens were as cold and desolate as his soul.

They came for him at noon, on lathered horses, for they
had ridden hard and far. Balor saw them as one views figures
standing at the far and misted horizon of a dream—men and
women in white and a leader advancing toward him upon a
great pale horse. The animal was as white and glistening as
new snow on a frozen pond, as huge and lean and powerful as
the monoceros of his boyhood dreams. The man astride the
horse sat with the authority of a lord, tall and clothed from
head to toe in a vast sweep of cowled cloak, which hid his
face and swept back over the horse's rump to its fetlocks. A
woman rode beside him on a small mare the color of mist.
Distance claimed her face. She was clad in white, like the
others, and there was a garland of blossoms and fern upon
her head, softening the fall of her straight, shoulder-length,
mouse-brown hair. She slid from the back of her horse and
ran toward him, in a simply cut, carelessly belted garment of
fine, thin summer linen, which did little to conceal the
contours of the body beneath it. She came to him on bare
suntanned feet and hastily drew away the branches through
which he viewed her.

He knew then that he was dreaming, for the woman's face
was Cethlinn's face, cocked to one side, blue eyes squinted
with worry, white, crooked teeth biting hard into the lower
lip. Yet another familiar face peered over her shoulder—bald
and wearing a single earring of lapis lazuli, with a pale jaw
shaded by a heavy growth of close-shaven black beard. The
face belonged to the healer who had once given Balor the nectar
of the poppy and stitched his head so long ago at Point of Ale.

The man frowned and pushed the woman away. "Stand
back, daughter of Cromm Cruach, if you would have me tend
the man!"

Bold, sure fingers probed his wound. He cried out and heard the woman scold the healer in a voice that was distractingly like Cethlinn's; but Balor did not find the similarity strange—he decided that Cethlinn was the woman's brother, perhaps her twin.

"Be easy with him, Keptah! He has lost much blood!"

The man made low mumbling sounds of annoyance. "If it is fated, he shall be healed. If it is not fated, he shall die. I will do my best for him, woman, but time shall tell the truth of the destiny you claim awaits him."

"He is the one who has been foretold. So tend him with a gentle hand, for I have not waited for him all of these long years and brought him all of these long miles to lose him to your bumbling!"

The words struck Balor almost as deeply as did the pain of the healer's ministrations. He gasped and nearly swooned as the man's hands worked within his wound.

"Bumbling?" Keptah glared at the woman over his shoulder, then turned back to scowl into Balor's torn flesh as his fingers continued their work. "From my homeland along the river Nile, to the isles of the Aegean and the distant Northland of the barbarians, I am famed for the 'magic' I work with my hands! But I am only a man, and you must learn that, no matter how you would wish it, Cethlinn, you cannot direct the Fates!"

Balor bolted upright despite his pain and weakness and slapped the hand of the healer away as he stared at the woman, wide-eyed and gaping. "*Cethlinn . . . ?*"

The white teeth chewed the lower lip. The blue eyes sparkled with familiar, secretive merriment. Strong, long-fingered, suntanned hands rose to take the garland from the mouse-brown hair. "Aye, and so, my fine young friend!" Cethlinn reached out and placed the garland upon Balor's head. "I am Cethlinn, firstborn of Cromm Cruach, daughter and only child of the lord of the Stone. And so you see, I am indeed a wizard to have kept my secret from you for so long . . . although many a time I wished to tell it, yet feared that if you knew my gender we would both be more vulnerable to the dangers of our journey."

Balor lay back, his mind in shock as well as his body. The physician eyed him drolly as he shook his head. "Beware of her, young man, for she has ambitions for you that may well amaze you."

Cethlinn smiled her white, crooked-toothed smile. "It is he who shall amaze *you*, Keptah! When you have healed him you shall see that he *is* the Mighty One, and while he regains his strength, he *shall* become a priest of the Stone . . . the one who has been foretold. The Fates have chosen him. I have chosen him. I am his woman now."

This was too much for Balor. "Over my dead body!" he roared, fighting off a wave of pain and weakness. He tried to stand.

Keptah restrained him. "Calm down, else your words speak prophecy!"

"Here, here, what is this?" A voice warm and mellow and strangely familiar intruded into the scene as the shadow of the man who had ridden the white horse fell over them, blocking off the light of the sun.

Cethlinn looked up at the tall, cloaked, faceless form who stood looking down. "Look at him, Father. Tell me that he is not the one whom you saw long ago in northern lands!"

Slowly the hands of the tall, silent form in the white cloak reached up to move back the cowl until it fell away to reveal the face of Cromm Cruach. Balor felt the world slip out from under him.

The lord of the Stone smiled. Star Gazer smiled. "Took a wrong turn in the road again, did you, lad? Well, don't look so shocked, old friend. Did I not tell you long ago that it does a man little good to plot his own charts where the will of the stars is concerned? Cethlinn is right, you know. Destiny marks us all. It chooses us. And like it or not, it shall have us all in the end."

"It shall not have me!" replied Balor, straining against Keptah's grasp.

Star Gazer raised his hands tellingly. "But it already has, my old friend. It already has. . . ."

And so it was that Balor, grandson of Manannan MacLir, firstborn of Fomor, Wolf of the Western Tribes, and kinsman of the People of the Ax, first came to the Plain of the Great Stone Circle. He came on a litter, drugged and unconscious, carried along an ancient road, across an ancient land where, amid fields of wheat and flax and barley, the ghosts of long-dead races whispered in the wind while their corpses slept, sealed and serene within vast circular burial mounds of chalk now green with summer's grass and starred with wildflowers.

He came as night was falling, and was kept drugged so that he slept and healed under Keptah's watchful ministrations even as the midsummer sun rose over the sacred Marking Stone, sending its light spreading across the plain and into the circle of trilithons, where those who were consecrated to the priesthood were bathed in its life-giving warmth, which affirmed their power and guaranteed order to the universe for another year to come.

It was full daylight when at last he awoke. He was in a huge, barracklike, timbered longhouse, which served as a hospital and residence for the healers who had come from all parts of the world to refine their art upon this sacred plain, where men could live and study in peace, dedicated to the most holy pursuit of knowledge. It took Balor a few moments to orient himself. He lay on a raised sleeping pallet, and save for other patients who moaned in their own private miseries behind screens of woven wickerwork, he was alone with Keptah. The Egyptian sat close at Balor's side on a low three-legged stool, mixing some sort of highly aromatic unguent in a lap mortar. It was the slow, dull scrape of the stone pestle, rubbing and turning, that had awakened him; beyond the walls there was the sound of ceremony and celebration. The room was thick with the scent of medicinal smokes rising from fire pits at each end of the longhouse.

"I'm afraid you've missed it all for this year," informed Keptah, allowing the pestle to come to rest within the bowl of the mortar. "But next year, if the Fates allow, you shall stand in the sacred circle with Cethlinn as your bride. Cromm Cruach has said that it shall be so . . . if you prove yourself worthy."

Balor stared, wondering hopefully if this was a nightmare. But slowly, as Keptah resumed work on whatever substance lay within the mortar, the oily, spicy smell roused by the pressure of the pestle cleared the last mists from his drugged mind. The moment was real enough. And awake or asleep, the thought of Cethlinn as his bride was worse than any nightmare. No matter how hard he tried, he could not reconcile himself to his companion's true gender. How could he not have noticed that Cethlinn, over all of their many weeks together, had remained unfashionably clean-shaven without once finding the need to razor his face? How could he not have wondered why the "man" had refused to strip naked to bathe in the surf or tidal pools or freshwater springs as he had done whenever circumstances had allowed? He closed his eyes. The depths of his own stupidity were beyond measure.

Keptah seemed to read his mind. He chuckled. "Do not judge yourself too harshly. Cethlinn can be devious and unpredictable. But she's not so bad once you get used to her. And they do say that an older woman is good for a young man. Between now and next year you'll come to see the advantages of your union with her. And surely there will be many a man who shall envy you for it."

"I will not be here next year!"

"No? Are you a betting man?"

"I am!" he replied hotly, and tried to rise even though his shoulder, indeed his entire right side, ached with a deep, all-pervasive pain. He had been bound into some sort of heavy, elaborate splinting, which immobilized his arm and held it fast across his chest. But it was not this that had prevented him from sitting and swinging his limbs over the side of his pallet. It was the tether on his right ankle. It was a braid of heavy thong, attached to a copper anklet that had evidently been welded about his ankle while he had been asleep. It was joined to another ring of copper, secured to the frame at the foot of the cot. "What is this?" he demanded, giving it a yank even though he knew that it would not come loose so easily.

"It is a shackle," replied Keptah, averting his eyes.

Balor's temper flared. "I know *what* it is! But *why* has it been put on me? I am not a dog in need of leashing. Nor am I a captive who must be hobbled in order to be kept in place. Take it off me at once!"

"That I cannot do." There was regret in Keptah's voice. His eyes went back to Balor again, dark and steady and filled with apology. "It was done at Cethlinn's command. You are her property now. You had best get used to it, young man. You are now a slave to the People of the Stone."

21

Autumn came to Bracken Fen. The fens burned with color. The sun lazed in a soft blue sky, and except for brief, occasional, nourishing rains, no clouds formed to shadow the earth. Truly, it was said, now that Balor was gone, the weather was as it had been when Fomor MacLir had first led his people to conquer the holding and begin a settled life; it affirmed the rightness of his rule and, to the continued grumblings of Draga, gave no ground to dissatisfaction.

Life was good. Peace was as sweet as the chieftain had promised it would be. Never had the people of the clan MacLir reaped a more abundant harvest. Never had the grain sheds been so full of stores. Never had bees gathered pollen so abundantly this late in the season, nor had the wild hives and domed skeps of twisted, tightly bound straw yielded so much honey to the eager makers of mead. Babies grew fat. Children grew strong. The old felt their infirmities lessen under the warmth of the lingering sun while the young men clashed in sports of combat upon the training field, vying with newfound enthusiasm for status and approval in the eyes of Dana and other prospective mates. And when at last the sacrificial fires of the season's end were ignited, never had the pyres burned higher or hotter, nor had the cattle and live-stock been driven through the ceremonial rings of flame with greater zeal. The men and women of the clan leaped through with their beasts, joyously celebrating the continuation of the Circle of Life, drinking deeply of the mead of summer's end—a heady, highly alcoholic brew distilled from honey, wheat, herbs, and fruit pulp, it warmed them with its dark, golden glow as they piped on whistles carved of swans' bones and beat on pottery drums that they broke at will, grinding them into the earth as they called down the spirits of the Twelve Winds to guard them in the long days of the dark half of the year to come.

Munremar watched them. In his ceremonial robes emblazoned with the whirling patterns of flame, he stood beside the chieftain on the high palisade and knew that in the fire-shot darkness all who passed below would see him as the All Knowing, Wise One, who saw all things in this world and the next. It was what he wanted them to see. He stood as tall as his slender frame would allow, puffing himself up within his pale, flowing garments, savoring the feel of the fire-fragrant wind as it fingered back through his thin white hair and long, gauzelike beard and mustache, knowing that it added to the illusion of greater size. Next to Fomor MacLir, all but the tallest and broadest of warriors would seem small. Yet tonight Munremar, as high priest, was an extension of the larger man's power; he basked in its reflection. If he had had feathers, he would have ruffled them; indeed, his skin prickled with pleasure at the thought. And if the wind grew stronger, with only a little more mead to bolster his sense of self-esteem, he would fly out into the night, borne upward on the invisible wings of his own smugness.

His eyelids, stained red with madder and outlined in blue woad, flicked up and down at the images of the whirling dancers. How like children they were! So easily manipulated. So gullible. So wantonly forgetful of all that had gone before. The endless rains. The blighted earth. The sickness. The death. But *he* had not forgotten, nor had he neglected to keep the kindling of fearful remembrance banked and ready to be ignited within them. If the days turned dark again, it would be in his best interests to be able to remind them that he had warned them that it might be so . . . unless they were generous with their sacrifices. . . . He smiled, visualizing the offerings they had placed before the altar of the Twelve Winds: beakers of mead and honey, jars of grain, sacks of flour, cages of fattened fowl—all in gratitude for the good fortune that had come to the people of the clan since Balor had disappeared. And all for the Wise One, who had warned them for years that it was the firstborn son of the lord who had been the source of their misfortune.

His white brows came together over the thin arc of his raptorial nose. His smile deepened. The white-haired enchantress had dared to prophesy disaster. But in the sacred smokes *he* had seen that disaster would fall upon *her*, through the loss of her firstborn son. Now the clan prospered despite her presence. Her omens had been discredited. She rarely spoke these days, and when, in the nights, she sometimes walked the palisade, mourning for her lost son and keening for his return, as many pitied her as made the sign against evil. The old man's lips twitched like small, pink larvae writhing within the cobwebs of his beard and mustache. He had seen to it that she was tolerated. If the dark days came again, it would be good to have someone to name as scapegoat for his own inability to control the Fates.

His eyes sought the lord. Fomor MacLir had changed in the last months; he seemed to cast a shadow upon all who came near him. Munremar could see the fine veins of silver that had begun to intrude into the gold of his hair and beard, and there were lines about his eyes that had not been there before. In the trembling firelight he could see the battle scars upon his bare upper arms, no longer raised and purple with newness as they had been in his youth, but as white as runes carved into granite. He wore the golden collar and elbow-high wrist guards, which ceremony demanded of him on such a night as this. Power moved within him as surely as deep, irrepressible currents run beneath the surface of the restless sea. The old man shivered, touched by it. The lord had made him feel small again. He was glad when one of Fomor's broad hands rose to rest upon the copper-studded leather of his baldric. There had been weariness in the movement, a weariness that was always with him these days. Balor's disappearance had all but sapped the joy from his life.

"My lord," Munremar counseled softly, "this is not a night to brood. You have led us out of the long days of darkness. You cannot continue to mourn for Balor. He is gone. You must forget him. It is not as though he was your only son. And you can make more."

The tawny head moved. The green eyes fixed the old man with a sadness that made his bones ache with empathy. "Aye. I have Elathan. And little Bevin. And Huldre is again with child. It may well be that she will present me with another son. But the birth of one child cannot replace the loss of another. Each is separate. Unique. Irreplaceable."

The Wise One chose to make no comment. Although Fomor was a good and generous father, there had been no doubt that Balor, his firstborn, had been his favorite. He had searched for the youth as though possessed, following his tracks with a determination that refused to yield to common

sense. It had soon become obvious that Balor had deliberately laid his trail wolf-wise and with great cunning; by the time
its true direction had been ascertained, it had been impossible to follow. Yet Fomor had followed. He had searched until
at last his kinsmen had persuaded him that his efforts were
futile. The youth had vanished. And perhaps it was for the
best, for whatever had prompted him to leave the holding
had also caused him once again to disdain the laws and
traditions of the clan. Had he been found, he would have
been called to judgment before the council. Had he been
found, he would have been asked to account for the whereabouts of Mael. Like Balor, he too had vanished. But unlike
Balor, he had left no trail to mislead those who would go in
search of him. It had been no secret that the two youths had
been at odds over Draga's daughter. They had openly come
to blows and had exchanged life threats. Perhaps Balor had
slain Mael on the night of the Planting Moon and then fled
for his life, for he must have known that it would be forfeit as
penalty for such an offense. *Perhaps*. The word found no
sympathy with the lord, even though the evidence against
Balor had been overwhelming. If he had not taken Mael's
life, by leaving the House of Youth he had wantonly profaned
the night of the Planting Moon and taken on the role of Law
Breaker. By consensus of the council, spurred on by Draga, it
had been agreed that Balor be named as one apart, kin-
wrecked, forever outside of the circle of the clan, a dead
man, with no right to trial if he dared to return.

A tremor had gone through the chieftain when the results
of the voting had been placed before him. The Stones of
Choosing—white for life, black for death—had been laid
upon the altar of the Twelve Winds, one by one, as each man
within the hall came forward in his turn. All of the stones had
been black. All save one—Fomor's stone.

For a long, terrible moment, he had stared at the stones,
and when at last he had spoken, the words came out of him
like a death rattle. "So be it, then."

Ashamed but not repentant, his men had looked away. The
youth had chosen his own destiny, but the expression of grief
on the chieftain's face had been that which no man would
wish to see upon any but his worst enemy. It was as though
something in the lord had died. They had all pitied him. All
were fathers. All knew the love of a sire for a firstborn child.

Only Draga had chosen to press him, behaving like a serpent, nosing a wound, seeking to strike and rouse pain twice. "Your consent as chieftain binds you to take his life... with your own hand... as our law decrees. But I wonder, Brother. If he returns, could you do it when, in the past, you have placed his life above the good of us all?"

An uneasy murmuring had risen in the hall. In the fluctuating lamplight Draga had stood tall and tense. His eyes had glowed—fox eyes, bright and hungry, wary but unafraid. There had not been a man in the room, including the chieftain, who had not known that the redbeard was savoring the moment, attempting to rouse the lord to a display of hesitancy, which would betray an inner core of weakness to his clansmen.

Munremar would never forget the look that had come to Fomor's face. The broad mouth had flexed and curled downward. The green eyes had gone as hard and dark and unforgiving as the black Stones of Choosing.

"I will take his life, Draga, with my own hand. As surely as you will someday force me to take yours if you continue to challenge me."

"*I?* Challenge *you?*" cried Draga. "Surely, Brother, you misjudge me!"

"No, Brother, surely I do not."

For one brief, thoroughly disconcerting moment, Munremar had wondered if Fomor had known of Draga's plot against him, and of the Wise One's part in it. But no, consolation had risen to soothe him. He had been certain that only the Twelve Winds knew of the words that he and the redbeard had exchanged on the night of the Planting Moon. He had been equally certain that Draga would never repeat them; to do so would betray his own treachery.

The old man had drawn in a little breath to steady himself as the sons of Manannan MacLir had glared at one another in a battle of wills. In the end it had been Draga who had turned away, muttering that his brother had wronged him.

Now, as Munremar looked into the eyes of the chieftain, he saw that the pain of that night still lingered within him. Perhaps it would always be there, as much a part of him as the aura of power Draga had coveted and failed to win.

The sound of song and shouting, of drumbeat and merriment, rose in the darkness. Munremar gestured outward. "Look, my lord, and listen to your people. They call to you to

join with them in their celebration. You have won this night
for them. As I have foretold, the days of peace and plenty
have at last returned to Bracken Fen."

Fomor observed the scene below him. His face was expressionless. "Aye, and so." His tone was desolate. "For as long as
the weather holds. For as long as the mead stays free of mold.
For as long as the stores last. For as long as memories of
summer serve to warm the people at their winter hearths.
For as long as I can keep the restless hounds of boredom and
dissatisfaction at bay." He sighed, a rasp of bitter acquiescence. It was like a low, lost wind wandering the summer
night, lonely and in search of a storm cloud in which to bury
itself. "Peace ... plenty ... aye ... at last I have won this for
them. But can it last, old man? Can I make it last?"

Dawn rose to find the bracken brittled by the first touches
of frost. In the days that followed, it blushed deep red in
response to the chilly nights and the diminishing light of the
ever-shortening days. To prevent overgrazing of the pastures
and possible starvation of their animals during the dark half of
the year, the people of the clan MacLir worked to thin their
herds. They reveled in the cattle killings as great gatherings
of ravens circled and swooped to scavenge, and the men, and
youths who were enduring their Year of Trial, displayed their
strength and daring at contests of bull baiting and vaulting,
stripped naked and armed only with daggers before the
charges of deliberately enraged bulls. They had trained for
this for months. The women and girls and elderly gathered to
cheer on their men. Many were gored, but none seriously.
All took pride in their wounds, knowing they would
make scars to envy.

Everywhere within the holding hides were being scraped
and stretched to cure. Meat was being smoked, salted, and
hung to dry. No part of the slain animals was wasted. Bladders and intestines were cleansed and oiled so they would be
kept supple for their many uses. Horns were stacked and
stored for future use as beakers or, if cracked, as buttons and
a thousand useful sundry articles. Bones were broken and
boiled into marrow broth, which all drank to gain energy
while they worked. Blood was quaffed and mixed with gruel
to be baked into dark, nourishing cakes, which would be

stored and used as sustenance throughout the depths of winter when other provisions grew short.

The people of the clan MacLir sang as they worked. The old songs. And the new. About days gone by. About days yet to come. They praised their chieftain. They brought offerings to the Wise One, for surely he had been correct when he had warned them long ago that it was the firstborn son of the lord who had brought the dark days of suffering to the fens. With the youth's disappearance, order and balance had been restored to the people of the clan MacLir.

"Balor." Morrigan spoke his name aloud with longing as her eyes followed the flight of a hawk as it swooped and rose and swooped again over the fenlands. She had come out from the holding to escape the stench of the winter kill and the increasingly worrisome attentions of old Falcon. He seemed to be everywhere that she went within the holding these days. He watched her with newly appreciative and unmistakably hungry eyes. She shivered to think of him and knew all too well what his attentions and unbounded generosity to her father portended. What he saw in her, she could not imagine, for her wild nature and sharp tongue had discouraged all other suitors, as she had intended. Not that her father would force, or even encourage, her to name a man; he had come to depend upon her far too much.

In the long, thin light of the ebbing day, she had walked far, but the sweet, hot scent of blood and hides and curing meat lingered in her nostrils. It nauseated her as she paused beneath the great, sheltering oak and drew in deep, steadying breaths of clean air. It drove back the sickness that had come close to overwhelming her. She came here often these days, secretly, to be alone with her thoughts and memories. Here she had lain with Balor. Here she had watched Mael die. Here, on the night of the Planting Moon, her life had been changed forever. Her dreams and hopes had been broken and smashed as completely as the little crockery drums had been ground into the earth on the night of the harvest celebrations. And no one knew. No one at all. Nor dared she tell them.

She had told Dianket the truth about Balor's disappearance and Draga's plot against Fomor, and she had begged her friend not to tell the chieftain. Fomor was already wary of his brother, and she knew that if Draga were accused and unable to clear himself, he would name Munremar as his accomplice and the old man would be slain or cast out of the holding to wander the fens or moorlands, alone and helpless until he died.

She shuddered. She could not bear to think of it. No matter what he had done, he was her father. She owed him a daughter's loyalty. Dianket had conceded to her will, but not easily. He still brooded over the loss of Balor's companionship. He rarely came to the Wise One's roundhouse these days, but kept his own company and seemed to find pleasure in winning patients away from the old man. Morrigan could not blame him. Despite his youth, many found confidence in his gentle handling of their ills. They called him Healer, as they had once called his father, and without assistance from Munremar—whose sham and showmanship as a physician he despised—he earned his own bread, and many luxuries had begun to come his way from those whom he had given cause to be grateful for his skills and advice.

Morrigan scowled. Dianket had won the attention of several widows, who openly vied with one another in the hope of winning a place at a young man's hearth, and now he had no time for her at all. Where had they been before Dianket had begun to work independently of Munremar? They had clucked their tongues behind his back, rejecting him for his crippled limb. They had offered him neither friendship nor food nor the makings of a fire from their own miserable hearths. But now they gave these things happily. She had told Dianket that the widows were hypocrites, caring not for him, but for his newfound status. If he continued to welcome them into his roundhouse, he would regret his kindness to them. He would have no time to himself, to pursue his art, to continue the fascinating experiments that had already resulted in new or improved cures.

She had warned him that he must send them away. But it was she who had been sent off.

His eyes had grown stern and anguished. "You are a woman grown, Morrigan. Go away, if you are my friend, and tend to your father's hearth fire. Already there has been talk about us. It must stop—for both our sakes. Would you have me branded as a Law Breaker for the sake of your visits? I am a cripple, without a man's rights. If it should be thought that

I have taken them with you, a virgin, I could be slain for the offense . . . and surely no man would want you if it were thought that you have been more than a friend to such a 'man' as me!"

"I want no man but Balor!" She knew that she had spoken sharply, but did not care. Dianket knew her heart.

"Balor is gone. You must forget him."

"Shall you forget him . . . he who was the dearest friend of your boyhood?"

"Never. But I would not wish him back again. If Balor returns, he dies . . . and that would be more intolerable to me than his absence."

Her right hand now flexed against the oak as her left hand lay protectively over the tight, hard span of her abdomen, where the fetus now lay like a tender new fern uncurling within the ripening loam of her womb. Until this moment, although all of her body signs had clearly spoken to her of the child's presence, she had not been certain that it was there. But now as she watched the hawk circling above her, the child leaped with life and rippled boldly against her palm, as though it would fly from her womb to join the raptor in the sky.

A little thrill of pleasure ran through her. And of fear. Her gift from the Mother of All, the fruit of the night of the Planting Moon. The flame of forbidden passion had ignited the spark of its life, between a virgin and a youth not named a man. The child of Balor, bringer of disaster. A child who would not be welcome in this holding. A child who, by clan law, would be ordered cast out beyond the palisade walls to become food for wolves.

She shivered. She could not let it happen. As long as the child lived a portion of Balor would be hers to love, to cherish, as she could not now ever hope to love and cherish its father. Tears welled in her eyes, but she blinked them away. Tears would accomplish nothing, except, perhaps, to betray her condition to others. Now more than ever she needed to be strong.

She drew in a deep breath and stared off across the hills. The hawk was no more than a tiny dark speck against the fading blue of the sky. Far off, she could see the solitary figure of a man, limping slowly across the land. Dianket. Out gathering herbs, no doubt. Her heart filled with warmth. For a moment she thought: *I shall go to him, tell him. He is my dearest friend. He shall take me to his hearth, and together we shall raise Balor's child. Only the Twelve Winds shall know our secret.*

But no. She remembered his warning. If the clan thought that he, a cripple, had fathered her child, he would be severely punished, perhaps even slain, and the child would suffer the same fate as Balor's infant lest it prove unlucky to the clan.

Again she shivered. The warmth within her went dark and cold. She felt trapped by laws, traditions, and ignorant men's superstitions. She did not believe in luck. She did not believe in magic. Yet even as she thought these thoughts, a thousand tiny, formless doubts rose within her, like bats winging up to mock her from out of the dark cave of her own fears and ignorance. They bit at her resolve, twisting and turning as their wings beat a whispering warning within her brain. *Do not be so certain, Morrigan, daughter of Munremar, child of Anu. The magic you doubt is real enough, and luck is a gift of the Fates . . . a gift that you now carry within you—for Destiny's sake, not your own.*

A voice distracted her from her thoughts. For a moment she was glad, relieved to be called away from them, until she saw old Falcon striding toward her, waving and calling out her name.

"Morrigan! My dear child, my dear, sweet child! I thought I saw you slip away. Why do you linger here alone, so far from the holding? Do I dare to imagine that you have been waiting here for *me*?"

Impulse told her to run from him, but she did not. She stood her ground. "I am not a child," she said as the old man came close, panting through his smile, tremulous in his eagerness to please her. He was a good man, and kind. There was not a soul within the holding who did not care for and respect old Falcon. Yet this knowledge did not console her as she realized for the first time that the words she had spoken were the truth.

She was not a child. She was a woman. And if the child within her was to live, she knew what she must do. "Yes, Falcon. I have been waiting for you," she said, and put out a hand to him in invitation as she knelt and began to untie the shoulder lacings of her dress.

*   *   *

Dianket worked in silence, busily gathering the last herbs of the season before another frost destroyed their medicinal value. Herbs to heal, to dull pain, to stanch the flow of blood; herbs for elixirs and poultices and unguents. They had become like old, reliable friends, growing always where he knew he would find them.

Along with Sure Snout, Balor's canine companion and now Dianket's own best friend, he worked his way across the far pastures and paused only when his back began to ache. His leg always pained him, so he never stopped for that.

Slinging off his gathering basket, he stretched and leaned on his crutch as the dog took after a sleek lop-eared hare, barking hysterically, as though she had never seen such a creature before. Dianket smiled. Sure Snout's enthusiasms amused him. She behaved like a pup, not like a matron. He admired her for that. Still, life had taught him that it was best not to press beyond one's limitations.

He rubbed his aching limb and caught sight of a tiny lizard scurrying off among the grasses at his feet. Half of the reptile's tail was missing, but a lumpy knob protruded from the stump, and Dianket knew that flesh and bone and muscle were somehow miraculously rejuvenating themselves. A gift of the Fates to lizards, but not to men. He frowned. Were he a lizard, he would strike off his offending limb and grow another. He would look forward to being whole again, a *man* of the clan, not a lonely outsider forever denied his heart's one true desire—Dana.

Even the old men were vying for her affections these days, plus youths who a season's turn ago had been boys, as well as those who had more than one woman already to tend their hearths. Soon she would choose one of them, and he would stand aside and watch, facing a future that would allow only aging widows to cosset him. His mouth curled down. Everything Morrigan had said about the widows was true: They had begun to make nuisances of themselves, intruding into his life when he least sought to welcome them. They were forever wishing to tidy his house, rearrange his belongings, or meddle in his vitally important experiments. One woman had even gone so far as to loose the captive voles and vermin that were central to his growth as a healer—because, she had explained, they fouled his house and spoiled her appetite for the meals she had brought for the two of them to share. He had tried not to be angry; she had not understood his ways. Indeed, few did, save Morrigan and Munremar and Balor.

But Balor was gone; Munremar was aloof toward him these days; and now that Morrigan was a woman, their friendship must become, by necessity, a thing of the past. The thought saddened him terribly. He missed her encouragement and lively curiosity. Still, for both of their sakes, he was not sorry that he had sent her away, as he would send away the widows when next they came; he would rather live alone and keep company with only his patients and his dreams.

A soft wind stirred. Dianket lifted his face and stared into it. Sometimes he fancied that he could see the wind—but reach for it, and it was gone. Stand into it, and it could bend a strong man in two or bring a woman to her knees or send a child sprawling. Often it seemed as though the wind was with the world as breath was within a man, and he had come to wonder if the wind were not the breath of Creation itself, the ultimate determiner of the laws of life by which all things were bound.

If only he could grasp it! It would then be his to command. It would reveal to him why the sun rose always out of the east, and where the moon went on the nights when it vanished from the sky. It would tell him if the stars were, as his people believed and he sincerely doubted, the distant torches of nomadic wanderers lighting their way across the fixed pathways of the heavens. It would tell him how bats and owls could see their way by night, and why the gift of flight had been given to them and not to man. It would tell him why the seasons changed, what caused green succulent seedlings to spring to life out of dry, dead pods, how yeast came to leaven the mead and bread pots, how mold found the grain within the sheds and why it flourished in damp weather and withered away in dry. It would tell him why disease blighted some men and not others. It would explain to him why the fragile webbing of a spider could often prevent the corruption of flesh if packed into a wound, and why hot urine, when used immediately after expulsion from the bladder, invariably proved a more effective cleansing agent than water.

The wind whirled around him, making a gentle mockery of his endless wonderings. Had he always been so full of questions? He could not remember. He only knew that he could not hope to know it all. He could only hope for small revelations, which in turn might lead to larger and more important ones.

His eyes strayed out across the land, and he sucked in his breath, startled by that which he had never thought to see.

Strangers were approaching the holding.

They came on horseback. Slowly. Three men and a smaller figure mounted on a pony. Sure Snout ran to them, snapping and snarling at their horses' fetlocks until one of the riders maneuvered his mount into a kicking position. A hoof struck true, and the dog ran back to Dianket, yipping.

He could see them clearly now. Men in simple, foreign-looking garb. The watchmen in the hills had spotted them too, for the warning horns were sounding, answered by the beat of the sentry's drum from the palisade. The sounds prickled beneath Dianket's skin, yet he stood his ground. There was no use trying to get back to the holding; his crippled limb would never get him there in time to avoid a confrontation. The men were nearly upon him now. If he tried to hurry away, his leg would deprive him of any semblance of dignity. Besides, he had his crutch to use as a stave if the need arose, and his dagger. A little surge of excitement rippled through him. He could use his weapons with a skill that would surely amaze his clansmen. Balor had taught him well, but he had not known until this moment that he was no coward to shrink back in fear of a potential enemy—even when he was outnumbered four to one, and by men on horseback.

The strangers came forward with their knife arms raised in the universal sign of peace. The riders who pounded out through the gateway of Bracken Fen made no pretense of returning the sign. They were fully armed, and the sight of them thrilled Dianket even as it must have sobered the strangers. Both groups reached the healer at the same time. He looked up at them, feeling out of place and vulnerable without a horse or true weaponry to grant him height and a fighting man's chance. He held his hardwood crutch poised in both hands, ready to do battle if it came to that.

"Hold now and turn away." Fomor MacLir's command was spoken in a tone that allowed no debate. "Strangers are not welcome in this land."

The horses stamped restlessly. It was nearly dark now. Sure Snout leaned, trembling, against Dianket's good leg.

The smallest of the strangers stirred upon his pony's back. "What clan is this that would withhold food and shelter and refuse hospitality to peaceful travelers in need?" There was righteous indignation in his tone. Dianket was impressed by how easily the man had adapted himself to the use of the language in which he had been "greeted."

"No clan deserving honor in the world of men, and that is the truth," replied Draga, scowling at the chieftain. "If we refuse hospitality to these travelers, Brother, we shall be shamed forever before all men who once honored the name of the clan Mac—"

"Hold your tongue, kinsman!" Fomor's words snapped like a whip.

Dianket looked up at them. He could feel the tension in them, strung as taut as an overstressed bow. The redbeard glowered on his big sorrel, so close at Fomor's right hand that the chieftain's stallion shook its great black head in protest and whinnied, biting out at Draga's mount. Its sharp cry of pain affected the other horses. Lomna Ruad's mount danced in place. Dathen's shied to one side. It was all that the others could do just to speak quietly to their animals, assuring them of their riders' mastery of the moment.

"How come you into the fens?" queried Fomor warily. "There is no established trade route here."

A dark, swarthy-faced stranger replied in a voice slow and fumbling with accent, "We seek new routes. We would have much to offer to those who would deal with us . . . but as you can see, robbers have stripped us of our wagons and our goods. We were lucky to escape with our horses and the clothes on our backs. Others in our party were not so fortunate when we ventured south of the Great Glen. We have wandered ever since, seeking the sea and a way back to our own land and people."

Fomor sat his stallion in contemplative silence. Then: "The Great Glen is far to the north. The sea lies to the west. Why travel south if you seek the shore?"

"The coast is hostile to travelers these days, beset by pirates and brigands. It was rumored that the fen folk were a kindly race, bound by the laws of hospitality that make brothers of men who would have commerce with one another in peace. And it is also told that on the southern shore there are trading centers where honest men may seek passage to far lands."

Dianket could smell the horses and men pressing close about him. The tension of the moment had not eased; if anything, it had grown more pronounced. He could see distrust on Fomor's face. The green eyes were narrowed. The mouth was set. Even in the ever-thickening darkness Dianket could see that he had come out from the holding wearing his sleeveless, well-worn working tunic, which was rank with the stench of the recent cattle killings. He wore no jewelry to mark his rank. Yet no man could have doubted that he was in the presence of no mere herdsman or farmer. This man was a battle lord. The scars upon his forearms were inscriptions clearly read by any man whose flesh had ever felt the bite of a blade or the sting of an arrow. Fomor MacLir reeked of power.

But the strangers did not question why such a chieftain was here, in the wilds of the fens. They sat their mounts, as affable as lambs. "One night is all that we desire," said the smallest member of their band. "One night is all that we shall need."

Dianket winced. The little man's voice had a subtle, oily quality underlying its deference. Fomor had heard it too. His head went up, alert to danger.

Draga was oblivious to it. "Your hesitancy shames us, Brother! We are honor bound to receive them. Think of how our women and children would relish the tales these peaceful travelers could tell in exchange for food and a warm fire and directions to the sea. By the Twelve Winds, they shall never let us hear the end of it if we turn these good men away!"

A muscle high at Fomor's jaw worked visibly above the line of his beard. He did not trust these strangers. But Draga was right; he was bound by tradition to honor their request. Yet if these men discovered the identity of their hosts and left the fens to tell of it, there was the chance that Nemed MacAgnomain might learn that five long years ago he had been tricked at Point of Ale. And the Raven would come for the Wolf, with all of his weapons of bronze and the might of his armies.

The chieftain eyed the strangers and knew what he must do. "*One* night," he said, conceding with obvious reluctance as he turned his gaze to ever-faithful Dathen. "Ride back to the holding, you and my brother. Inform the people that their lord *Scallatha* shall host guests beyond the walls of the palisade this night."

Dathen understood at once and nodded, but he had not yet reined his horse about when Draga protested loudly.

"*Beyond* the walls?"

"Aye, and so, Brother, or would you have these good and peaceful travelers blighted by the sickness that besets our holding?"

"Sickness?" pressed the third stranger, suddenly wary.

"A terrible thing," affirmed Fomor. "It is a curse of the fenlands. Linger here long and you are certain to get it. Entire clans have been wiped out by it in the past. It comes to a man innocentlike. A slight flush of the face . . . a tingling at the back of the neck. Then comes the palsy, trembling in the hands, and a roaring in the ears. The mouth goes dry. The gut begins to spasm. There's a bloody flux from the bowel. Then the pustules appear. Nasty little devils, behind the ears, in the crotch, up the nose. Green, oozing boils. Painful, they say. But once they come, the end is near. There's no escaping it. It comes with a fever that turns a man black. Then he's gone. *Phfft*. Just like that." He waved one hand upward, and as he lowered it, all saw the unmistakable trembling of his fingers.

The strangers stared. Without a word they began to rein back their horses. They thanked him. They said that perhaps, after all, they had best seek food and shelter elsewhere. They turned their mounts, and the men of the clan MacLir watched them go. It was a while before they allowed themselves to laugh. Only Draga found no amusement in what had transpired.

"Is this how it is to be, then? Each time strangers come to us, are they to be turned away by lies and guile? Are we never to know the world again? Are we never to know the joys of trade, or engage in conversation with any but our own kin? By the Fates, if this is to be the way of it, then Nemed MacAgnomain is right when he believes that we are dead. For dead we *are*. And worse than that! For at least a corpse goes into the darkness of its burial barrow with honor, but we have been deprived of even that!" Without another word he whirled his mount around and galloped back to the holding.

Dianket would always remember the moment for reasons uniquely his own. Not because of the vehemence of Draga's words; he was used to the redbeard's challenges and outspo-

ken dissatisfactions. Not because of the tactic Fomor had used
to turn the traders away from the holding. No. The strangers
had ridden into the wind, their cloaks swirling back. The
small man upon the pony had been the last to turn his horse
away. The little animal had circled, and Dianket saw the
cruelly misshapen limbs of its rider. Curled up and back
against the pony's belly, they were no longer than a toddler's
limbs. Dianket stared, knowing that the man could not
possibly walk normally upon such pathetically stunted, ill-
formed limbs. A surge of empathy and a healer's natural
curiosity made Dianket sorry that the strangers had not been
able to stay. He would have liked to have had a chance to
study his deformity. Such men were rare in the world. And
Dianket had never seen a dwarf before.

22

Balor stood at the entryway to the House of the Sick in the
settlement of the People of the Stone. The late autumn sun
was as soothing as any of Keptah's potions. He did not know
how long he had been in this place. He only knew that he
was slowly regaining his strength and that life on the Plain of
the Great Stone Circle was unlike anything that he had ever
imagined it would be.

There were buildings everywhere: barracklike structures
for guests and sojourners, longhouses for priests and scholars
and neophytes, and little huts of wattled wicker scattered
here and there for those who preferred to dwell alone.
Although the majority of the pilgrims who had come to attend
the festival of the midsummer sun had gone, many still
lingered to participate in star studies. Those who could not
find accommodations on the plain itself camped at the edge of
the surrounding forest along the broad, cool arm of the river
Avon.

From where he stood, Balor could not see the river, the
forest, or the temple, which stood alone. Sacrosanct, raised as
though upon an island, it stood serene, undisturbed except

for the priests and neophytes who alone were allowed to enter the Sacred Circle.

But there was nothing serene about the scene that lay before Balor's eyes. Even priests and scholars must eat. Sojourners must be entertained. Beyond the House of the Sick there were noise-filled avenues of merchants' stalls and the inviting smells of open-air markets, bakeries, and butcheries. Indeed, he thought, doing his best to ignore the weakness that forced him to lean against the timbered wall and wince against the pain of his tightly bound, still-healing shoulder, it reminded him of Point of Ale: foreign, fragrant, foul, and fascinating.

But as long as he was kept as a captive he would not allow himself to appreciate the nuances of the place. Although he was fed and cared for, cosseted like a pampered pet, he remained sullen and surly, ever watchful for the opportunity to escape. Even if his wound were not yet fully healed, he was determined to go, fast and far, not looking back. He dared not look back, for to his increasing consternation, he was finding it more and more difficult to maintain his desire to leave. True, he was kept shackled to his bed each night. True, he was viewed as a curiosity by many, and with open resentment by those who doubted that such a callow youth as he could possibly fulfill the dimensions of the role that Cromm Cruach and his daughter claimed would someday be his. Mighty One, indeed! The doubters echoed his own feelings: He would never make a priest; he would never consent to be consecrated; he would never squander half a lifetime amassing the knowledge and wisdom that were prerequisites to any man who would become lord of the Stone, successor of Cromm Cruach. And never, *never*, would he consent to be Cethlinn's man, no matter how she insisted that, by the Fates, this must come to pass.

He drew in a breath, and with it came the taste of sunlight, the fragrance of hot bread and spitted meats. A thoroughly pleasant and unwelcome feeling of well-being swept through him. Life *was* good here. Already he could flex the fingers of his right hand without feeling pain, and there was an occasional hot, maddening itch deep within his shattered clavicle—a sure sign of healing, according to Keptah. The physician had assured him that in a matter of months his shoulder would be fully healed. Months! Soon winter would be upon the land.

Travel would be difficult, if not impossible, for a man alone in
unfamiliar territory. Perhaps it would be best for him to
accept the hospitality of the People of the Stone until the
spring. He would be well then, and strong. Then he could
take them off their guard, and, when they no longer expected
him to flee he would do so, before he was seduced by
Cethlinn and her people into forgetting that he had made a
vow that bound him more tightly than any shackle. As long as
Nemed lived, he, Balor, was bound to hunt him, to find a
way to take his life, for vengeance's sake, even if it must cost
him his own.

The days passed. And the weeks. Slowly Balor felt the
return of youthful vigor and a resurgence of his natural
inquisitiveness. With the Egyptian physician Keptah as his
watchdog, he began to make brief sojourns across the plain,
exploring the life-style of the many who visited here. All
sojourners were welcome, regardless of their clan, land of
origin, or colors of the house to which they claimed fealty.
Food was plentiful, free to those who had no means to buy it,
and reasonably priced to those who did. Sacrifices of grain
and animals and gold from the wealthy were commonplace.
Many volunteered to work the fields or to tend to the
thousand tasks required to maintain a harmonious existence.
There was always enough bread to fill a man's belly and
always enough meat to grease his beard thoroughly. Women
sang sweet songs in the encampments, for according to the
tenets of the People of the Stone, gender was no obstacle to
individual achievement and could not be used as a measure of
one's worth.

Here life was safe, easy, disturbed only by the occasional
divergences of opinion that set those of the old and new ways
at odds with one another. Those of the old way, like Cromm
Cruach and the elders, preferred the austerity of the ancient
traditions; if Star Gazer were to have his way, the merchants
and hawkers would be banished from the plain and only true
believers would be welcome. Those of the new way, like
Cethlinn and the majority of the younger members of the
community, sought to increase the dwindling number of
converts through a more liberal interpretation of doctrine.
Yet whatever their differences, there was one point of univer-

sal agreement among them: Peace among the faithful must be maintained at all costs. No weapons were tolerated; all pilgrims and would-be priests set aside their arms before putting foot upon the Plain of the Great Stone Circle.

Soon the flaming leaves of the hardwoods within the forest brittled and fell. The days grew short. The majority of the pilgrims left to return to their homes, enriched by the knowledge and blessings they had obtained in the shadow of the Sacred Circle.

One night, when Keptah put up the privacy screens of woven wicker and sought sleep upon his own pallet within the House of the Sick, Cethlinn came to Balor. She stood in silence close beside his pallet until awareness of her presence roused him from sleep. When he opened his eyes and looked up at her, she allowed her long robe of white winter wool to fall away. She was naked in the darkness, but moonlight invaded the room through the smoke holes at the apex of the roof. Balor saw her clearly. All of her.

She had changed in the past weeks. It was difficult for him to realize that the opulent woman who stood above him and the ragged, scrawny fellow who had saved his life in the reeds were one and the same. There was nothing even remotely masculine about the Cethlinn who was with him now. Her hair was longer, worn clean and loose, fragrant with sweet herbs, as was her body fragrant and soft and redolent of musk—a scent that stirred the man in him, despite the fact that his arm was still bound tightly across his chest, despite the fact that he had sworn that he wanted no part of her. He told her to go away, but she stood still and let his eyes have their fill of her. By the stars she swore by, by the Twelve Winds and the Mother of All, he could not make himself look away.

She drew back his woven blanket. He was naked. She smiled, infinitely pleased by the sight of him.

"You *are* the Mighty One," she observed, and as she joined him on the pallet, balancing her weight so that she would not stress his shoulder, she touched him, moved on him so that he could feel the heat of her breasts and belly. His mind went black and blank with need, and with his one strong arm he drew her down and arched to meld with the violent rhythm of her full acceptance of him.

Later, half exhausted by the pleasure and release to which

she had brought him, he lay sweated in the darkness, awakened by the dull, deep pain in his ankle where the shackle had bruised him and rubbed his flesh raw as he had strained against it. Cethlinn lay on her side, close against him. The movement of his shackled limb had roused her from her dreams. With one long, gentle finger, she traced the contours of his brow.

"Swear to me, Balor, as you would not before . . . swear to me by the gods to whom your people swear that you shall not go from my people until the sun rises over the Marking Stone on the dawn of the midsummer solstice. Swear this and I shall have the shackles struck from your ankle and declare you to be a freeman, bound only by the honor of your word."

How well she knew him. His word would bind him more surely than any shackle. And yet she had asked only that he swear to stay. She had not asked him to vow that he would consecrate himself to the Stone or to stand with her as a man swearing the life-oath to a woman. He spoke his thoughts, and she smiled, drawing his hand to her breast, moving, deliberately arousing need in him again as she caressed his manhood.

"The Mighty One must come consenting. . . ." she slurred, guiding him to what would pleasure them both. "I have waited a lifetime for this. When summer comes I shall need no shackle to hold you, Balor. You shall stay with me. You shall become a man of the Stone. And gladly."

Never, he thought, but did not speak the word as he entered her. "Until the rising of the midsummer sun . . . until then . . . I shall stay with your people. On the blood of my ancestors, this much I shall swear."

Winter settled cold and bleak upon the Plain of the Great Stone Circle, but Balor was not chilled by it. He lived with Cethlinn within her small, oblong house of timbers. As she had promised, the copper ring had been struck from his ankle. His arm, no longer bound, rested in a sling across his chest. His shoulder was healing rapidly, although Keptah mockingly cautioned him about avoiding excessive nighttime exercise. The physician drolly commented that such activity, in moderation, could prove efficacious, since exercise was known to stimulate the flow of blood and would surely help to heal and strengthen injured tissue.

Time was proving him right. He was growing stronger every day, as was his relationship with Cethlinn. They were friends again, and lovers, although he knew that he was not in love with her. That was an emotion reserved for Dana. Always and forever for Dana. He often dreamed of her, yet always the dream would fragment. Dana's golden hair would become dark and wild, as black as any raven's wing. Her gray eyes would become green lakes with moonlight shimmering in them. Her face would become Morrigan's face. And it was Morrigan's image that stirred him, roused the man-need in him so that when his arms reached out for Cethlinn in the night, it was Morrigan to whom he made love.

Thankfully, there were distractions that kept visions of Dana, Morrigan, and homesickness at bay. Not only distractions in Cethlinn's bed, but in the House of the Sick, with Keptah and the physicians whom he had come to admire. Throughout the year, regardless of the weather, people came to seek their cures. Their knowledge was extraordinary. Balor requested to be allowed to assist them. With only one good arm there was not much that he could do, but he was eager to observe, out of a legitimate and genuine curiosity and desire to learn. He knew that had he been in Bracken Fen he would have died from the catastrophic injury that had felled him, and often he thought of Dianket's shattered leg and wondered if, under the Egyptian's care, the limb might not have been healed and straightened.

He and the bald, brown-eyed Keptah became good friends. He learned that Keptah had taken up with the People of the Stone five years before, when he had met them at Point of Ale. Disgusted with the living conditions there, he had abandoned a thriving practice so that he might dwell among those who offered him the peaceful surroundings necessary to pursue his research and to expand his skills and knowledge as a surgeon. Unlike Munremar, Keptah looked for a disease's causes and cures. No chanting for him. No sacred smokes. No mistletoe wafted above a patient's bed. No crying to the Fates that the victim was simply unlucky and therefore beyond a cure. Keptah and the master physicians allowed Balor to observe them and even agreed to let him witness a surgical procedure that amazed him.

A little girl named Macha had been brought by her father, Gorias, to be treated. She was a tiny, dark-haired, pretty little thing despite the terrible swelling that caused one eye to bulge out. She suffered from body-wracking headaches, which drove her to fits. The healers among her own people upon the far island had declared that she was possessed by spirits; they had gone so far as to suggest that she be "given" to the bogs, staked down and buried with her throat cut, lest the spirits that wailed for their release into the Otherworld through her somehow infect her entire clan. Bereft, her father, a foreign trader and warrior who had settled among them, had taken her away. They had traveled for weeks in the ever-increasing cold, in the hope that she might be cured. Balor, remembering how Munremar had sought a similar fate for him, had felt a particular affinity toward the child. And she seemed to take an immediate liking to Balor and held his hand while she was given the nectar of the poppy to drink. She fell asleep on his lap, comforted by him as though by a longtime friend. It was his youth that soothed her, Keptah said, carrying the little wisp to a long table where, as Balor watched, genuinely affected, the physicians gathered to shave her tender skull and open it by means of an intricate boring and wedging procedure, which they called trepanning. He had watched, awestruck, trying not to be sick, as he waited for the poor child's life-force to fly from her body; but it had not. Instead, Keptah had cut away a small dark mass from the convolutions of gray matter, which, he explained to Balor, was her brain. The source of her thoughts and memories, the wellspring of her every movement and very being. The dark matter was a tumor, a growth of alien tissue, which he compared to mold on bread. It had been pressing upon her brain, distorting the muscles of her eye, and creating the headaches and body spasms, which in time would surely have killed her.

Now she was recovering. Balor came to see her each morning. She smiled at him and spoke to him in a foreign language that needed no translation; it was the language of one who would be a friend. Each day, he volunteered to bring the little girl her morning meal of marrow broth. As he sat with her and made certain that she drank it all, she reminded him of his little sister, Bevin, and he would ache with homesickness even as he marveled at the procedures that had made her well again. For surely, he thought, it was the gift of *true* healers, the result of their patience, of their love for their fellow man, and of their never-ending quest to learn that made him wish that Dianket and even Munremar were here—if only so that Keptah and his fellow physicians could put the Wise One in his place and expose him as an arrogant, self-righteous manipulator who was of no value to anyone but himself.

As his strength continued to return to him, Balor found time to spend with the priests, learning from them of Star Wisdom as it was taught by the People of the Stone. They would go out at night along the raised, boulder-lined avenue that led to the great temple. The massive trilithons—which reminded Balor of gigantic stone doorways, with two upright megaliths and a third, like a lintel, lying across their tops— rose against the star-spangled sky, and in their shadow, under the tutelage of the priests, his mind absorbed enthralling concepts. Even though he did not wish to interrupt his teachers, he found himself so full of questions that he had to give vent to them or explode from the sheer heat of his enthusiasm. His probings amazed them, for he was obviously grasping complexities of theories that they had needed years to understand. They would stare at him in the darkness. And he would stare back. Although his feelings confused him, he sensed a kinship with them, a bond deeper than he had ever experienced with any member of the clan MacLir, with the exception of Dianket.

The realization was as unsettling as it was unwelcome. These were men and women of peace, passive folk. Peace! Had he not come to despise his father for his pursuit of it? Was it not a state of being that he could not, and would not, abide? How could it be that he had considered peace to be a coward's refuge for Fomor MacLir, yet found it to be a calming, understandable quality here? What was different? Balor wondered. And how long dared he remain before he forgot the vow of vengeance that bound his honor and his life?

Snow fell. And fell. Silent. Sweet. In the curl of his good, strong arm, Balor carried little Macha out to see it. She was bundled in furs, bright-eyed now. Her little hand reached out to catch the falling flakes. Her bandaged head tilted back so that she might savor the feel of them upon her cheeks. She licked them from her lips and smiled, hugging the young man who held her.

"Good!" she piped.

"Good!" he echoed, pleased that she was learning to speak his language, even as he was attempting to learn hers. It was a game they played to pass the time; to his surprise he found that he had a gift for it. It amused him, as it did the little girl and her father, Gorias, who claimed that he had never seen a man learn another tongue so quickly.

"Is true. This place . . . is magic. Wizards dwell here. And you . . . is said you be mighty wizard . . . make fire out of air . . . slay three by magic . . . fight with either hand. You young . . . be strong soon. Stay. Not go like some say you want go. You be great wizard in this place. Do good. Make magic. Heal many."

Deep within the forest beyond the river, wolves called, and the child's father cocked an ear toward the sound. He shivered. He had come out from the House of the Sick, where Keptah had provided him with a pallet beside his daughter's. He was not dressed for the cold and blew steam into his hands to warm them.

"Listen," he said. "Wolves. Many wolves in woods now. Maybe dark days come again. Winter stay. Men grow restless. Become wolves." He rubbed his palms together; they were chapped and dry and made a silken, slipping sound. His small, dark eyes held on Balor's face, earnest and intense. "You stay this place. Wolves not eat you here."

"I am not afraid of wolves," replied Balor.

The man measured him and blew into his hands again. Worry walked his rough features. "When snow stop, I go back to my home on Far Island. I tell many of magic worked here. I am lord. Warrior. And trader of big reputation. Many do as I tell. Many owe me life debt. Men of Fal. Men of Findias. Many. We come in spring. I pay back healers . . . pay back priests for Macha's life. Men of my tribe. Men of other tribes. We guard. No wolves come here, or we skin with swords!"

"Swords?" The very word excited Balor.

The man saw his reaction. "You know swords? Know use? Be magic in wizard's hand." He measured Balor's right, sling-bound arm, then nodded and smiled to show big, broken teeth with a great carnelian glinting where his left eyetooth should have been. "East of this place, in holy places where stones stand, I, Gorias, see wolves eat priests. For gold. For grain. Kill all. Time pass, bad men, they come here to Plain of Great Stone Circle. But I say no! Not happen here! In spring I come back. With many swords. I teach you. You be great wizard . . . mighty warrior with sword in hand!"

"Good!" piped little Macha again, still reaching out to the falling snow, unaware of the meaning of the words her father had just spoken. She leaned close to Balor's face, putting her cheek against his. "Good?" she queried, desiring his affirmation of her enthusiasm for the falling snow.

He nodded, but his eyes were on her father's face. "Good!" he said, and slipped his arm from the sling. His right hand reached out to Gorias. "In the spring you come back. Bring swords. Gladly shall I learn from you!"

BOOK IV

23

A cold wind bent the backs of the cypress trees. The great, whitewashed house on the cliff tops glistened in the winter rain. Below it the sea was gray, its surface riled by the storm. Huge, kelp-thickened combers surged and broke against the seawall. In the cove the water was milky with sediment stirred up from the bottom by troubled currents, as along the shore men labored to beach the battered vessel that had just managed to reach land. Its red and black sails, down now, were tattered. More than half of its oars were broken. Its crew was haggard with exhaustion—all but the misshapen little man who leaped onto the stony beach and hobbled up the stairs to the house.

Unshaven, unwashed, and soaking wet, Coman was oblivious to the elements. He threaded his way along familiar, labyrinthine corridors, demanding to know the whereabouts of his master. He quickened his pace, ignoring the stares and greetings of retainers and slaves, until at last he came to the guarded doorway that opened into the quarters of his lord. Imperiously he commanded the guards to announce him. Imperiously they ignored him until, shaking himself like a wet hound, with his stunted limbs spread wide and his hands splayed upon his hips, he informed them that those who impeded the progress of one who had news of the whereabouts of the Wolf of the Western Tribes had best think twice about the results of their actions.

The twosome needed no further prodding. They knew that the dwarf had been long away, sent with others as a spy to seek out and identify the Wolf; and they knew too that against all odds and in record time the little man had come home in the dead of winter, at the height of a howling gale. The smug glow of triumph in his eyes told them that he had succeeded in his mission. They stared down at him, glad, not for him, but for themselves. Now Nemed MacAgnomain would be stirred from the dark and murderous mood that had been upon him since he had sent out his spies. He would cease his endless pacings and the abuses of his servants. He would be inspired anew to pursue his old adversary, and all of the plans he had been formulating over the past months would now come to fruition: He would ready his fleet; he would gather a great force of men.

Throughout the Aegean and all along the trade routes of the civilized world were many a lord dependent upon trade and indebted to Nemed MacAgnomain for past favors and considerations. Such men would send arms and mercenaries to fight for any cause to which Nemed would set them. In return he would cancel their debts and grant them lucrative contracts, which would ensure their future loyalty. And then, since he was born to a warrior's life and often chafed against his role as a merchant prince, Nemed himself would lead the quest and, if all went well, return a gentler man for having at last cleansed his soul of the dark ghosts that had so long haunted him.

With shared but unspoken enthusiasm, the two guardsmen turned and drove curled fists hard against the door. It opened, just a crack. The face of a slave attendant peered through. They informed him of Coman's desire to enter. The door closed. Then opened wide. Coman, bristling smugly, stalked through it like a lord.

Above him the rain beat a gale-force rhythm on the outside tiles of the roof. He did not hear it. Before him the luxurious room was ablaze with the multicolored magnificence of mosaic floors and frescoed walls and ceilings. He took no note, for he had seen it all before, many times, and his mind was afire with visions of the reward that must soon be his. He strode forward, dripping pools of water as he went, approaching the couple who lounged upon gold-gilt couches atop a broad dais at the far end of the room. So Queen Arakhne was here. He had not expected her. She was a gaudy, painted shadow, robbing the moment of its brilliance.

Still, he refused to be daunted. "Bid welcome to your loyal servant Coman! I return to you from a far island, bearing news of the one you seek!" His voice rang out, loud and bold, as though sounding off brass. The room seemed longer than he remembered. Three wide, tiled stairs led up to the dais. When he reached them he paused and prostrated himself. It was the queen, Arakhne, who commanded him to rise; but instead he wiggled up the stairs on his belly to place a kiss upon her extended foot. She expected this of him. Indeed, she would be displeased if he neglected to perform what had become an obligatory ritual of humiliation. Her shoe was of some sort of exotic leather, dyed orange with saffron. It smelled unpleasant from the colorant, the dampness of the day, and the perspiration of the foot within it. He tried not to grimace as she pressed it upward against his face, allowing him a second kiss as he mumbled the necessary exclamations of delight until, to his amazement, he felt his shoulders being gripped by hard, strong hands. Nemed had risen, jerked the dwarf violently upward, and set him on his feet.

The master of the house leaned down to him, still holding his shoulders. "Say what you have come to say!"

The dwarf's reply came out fast and furious, tumbling over the terror that his master's temper never failed to arouse in him. All sense of smugness vanished until he focused upon the amber amulet, which was visible at the throat of the lord. It calmed him. It returned to him the sense of purpose that had filled his days with images of glory ever since he had set sail from the coast of Albion. "You sent me to find the lord whom you believe to be the Wolf of the Western Tribes. To Point of Ale I journeyed. And listened to rumor. Others in your employ followed their leads southward. I convinced several others to come with me to the north, deep into country where no man would ever think to seek the Wolf. And there, after days of wandering, after many a night spent in miserable fen hovels and makeshift encampments, we saw vast circlings of ravens upon the far horizon, a sight common over winter kills made by settled herdsmen. So we sought the land beneath the circling birds and discovered a holding far from where any men were known to dwell." He paused. He saw the black fire of excitement rising in his master's eyes. Instinctively he stepped back, frightened by it, but the hands upon his shoulders tightened, held him, shook him.

"Go on! What else? What did you find?"

"A great holding, lord. Built on high ground where the marsh country ends and the highlands begin. There are bogs there, but there are places where the land is good. Pastures have been cleared, and fields, and upland there is good timber. The settlement itself could easily house a thousand men and their families. And it is no wattle-walled encampment of mud-wallowing fen folk, but a palisaded, earth-mounded fortification—a warrior's domain, built as though its residents *expected* an attack. Yet we could not get close, for we were not welcomed by those who came out to us. Big men. And many. Ruddy haired. No small, dark, peaceful natives common to the fenlands, these men came out to us armed with daggers and axes, with slings and bows. But I saw no bronze, lord, no swords!" He saw the effect that this bit of information had upon his master and smiled, relaxing as he went on. "They used a ruse to send us away. They said there was sickness among them. But they lied. I saw no strain of grief or mourning upon their faces. Only watchfulness. Only wariness. Only the faces of men who guard a secret. A secret that I, Coman, took away with me and now offer to you! They should have slain us. For even if he had not called himself as 'Scallatha' with his own lips, I would have recognized him. Such men are not easily forgotten. The redbeard who challenged you at Point of Ale was with him. The Wolf of the Western Tribes lives, my lord. And in the spring, when the seas are calm and you have gathered your ships and your forces, Coman shall lead you to him!"

A tremor went through Nemed MacAgnomain. The scar that marred his handsome, black-bearded face was always white and bloodless; now his features were equally as pale. He leaned closer to the dwarf. "And the woman . . . the white-haired enchantress . . . was there sign of her?"

The dwarf felt his bladder spasm. For a moment he was not certain if he could control it. He cursed himself for not having taken the time to relieve himself before rushing forth to claim his reward. He tensed against his need, sweating despite the sodden garments that clung to him. He wondered if he should lie about the white-haired woman. A lie would make the moment safer, but it might turn back upon him later. "I saw no pale-haired woman, although she must be there if she still lives."

Again a tremor went through Nemed. His hands relaxed upon the dwarf's shoulders as he rose. His right fist curled about the amulet. The color returned to his face as his fingers flexed and whitened over the talisman. "She lives. . . ." whispered Nemed. "I *know* that she lives. . . ."

Coman's limbs were crossed as he fidgeted like a child embarrassed to express its need to use the household latrines. "But not for long, eh? Not now that Coman has found her for you! Did I not promise years ago that I would bring you luck? I ask only to see the pleasure that my efforts have won for my lord . . . and excuse to take my leave now, for the baths after my long and arduous journey!"

The queen swung herself into a seated position as she raised her arms to adjust the curls of her elaborate, overly hennaed coiffure. The skin between her elbows and armpits sagged and swayed, much like sleeves. Two long, tendinous limbs extended forward beneath the fall of her heavily embroidered dress of gold-threaded wool. Like her shoes it was a deep saffron; her favorite color. It made her look as sallow as an old bruise. Her brown eyes, outlined in kohl, spitted the dwarf with open annoyance. With a sick, sinking feeling, he knew that she saw right through him to the bones of his greed. She sneered at him, wanting him to know that she considered him below her contempt.

At last her glance moved to Nemed. "We have many contracts to fulfill when springtime gentles the seas—lucrative contracts. And tribute to collect from those whom we have long labored to bring to submission for our own gain. This Wolf has become an obsession with you, Husband. To seek him out in Albion will take months of precious time spent better elsewhere. Would you risk our ships and profits on the word of a newt? And if, in fact, the newt speaks truly, a Wolf who cowers in the cold, miserable fens cannot be much of a wolf at all, nor could there be much satisfaction to be found in his death." Her head went up imperiously. The wattling of her age showed beneath her chin. "I, Arakhne, say that you shall not waste the resources of our house upon such imprudent ventures. You shall not take our ships or ignore our prior commitments. I forbid it."

The lord stood unmoving. His eyes were fixed, focused inward, on the past and the future. Slowly his wife's words drew them into the present. They found her and held, fixing her with a look that caused her sallowness to turn clam white. "Do not stand against me, woman. I shall have my ships. And I shall have my Wolf. Whatever the cost, it shall profit me."

She rose, unwisely, to face him down. "You forget your place, Husband . . . a role that I have deigned to allow you to fulfill because your youth and barbarian temperament has pleasured me. *Has*. You are not as young as you once were, Nemed. Indeed, you are not the *man* you once were. I,

Arakhne, am mistress of the royal house of Achaea. And I, Arakhne, *will* tell you what you may and may not do!"

Coman stood transfixed as Nemed's expression changed. He had seen this look before. Always it thrilled him. Always it frightened him. Perhaps it was the fear that made the moment so sweet—a pleasure that he could find only when danger and death were near. He knew that the relationship between his master and his mistress had been strained for years. Now it oozed into purulent hatred, like a boil pricked by a silver lancet as Nemed, smiling, drew his wife into his arms and whispered to her in the tone of a lover.

"Arakhne . . . Arakhne . . . you are a dry, ugly, foolish old woman who has taxed my patience far too long. . . ."

Coman would never be certain exactly what killed her, the snap of her spine as Nemed bent her backward or the brutal twist of the strong, lean hand that crushed her throat. Her eyes bulged. Her mouth gaped. The dwarf was so excited by the sight of her death that he was unaware that he had lost control of his bladder.

Slowly, tenderly, Nemed eased his wife's corpse onto the couch upon which she had recently been reclining. He looked at her with disinterest. At the far end of the room the one slave in attendance cowered at the door. The lord gestured him forward. The man was a mute. Arakhne had always been cruel to him. It was known that he disliked her almost as much as he feared his master.

"Your mistress . . . the life-force has left her . . . a shock of some sort. . . ." Nemed's voice seemed sincerely saddened as he removed one of several rings from his fingers and offered it to the mute. "For your loyalty and silence . . ."

The man grinned as though his master had intended a joke. He bowed and took the ring, nodding his assent to silence, not certain of how to behave. Nemed's brow rose. "You may go."

The servant backed away, still grinning and nodding. Rain pummeled the roof tiles as though it wished to force entry through them. The smile returned to Nemed's face.

Coman stammered, "Her heart . . . it must have been her heart. I have heard her complain often . . . a pity too, that it could no longer serve her as loyally as I, Coman, have and would ever serve my lord."

Nemed threw back his head and laughed. He eyed the

soaring vault of the frescoed ceiling, gesturing to the storm raging outside. "Soon a rain of blood shall come to the fens of Albion. With you to lead me to him, soon the Wolf and all of his kindred *will* die, and the white-haired witch will be mine—again and forever!"

24

They were drunk. Dathen and Lomna Ruad and Fomor. It was very late. They were the last of the celebrants to linger in the sweat house. Again they toasted the birth of Lomna Ruad's newest son; indeed, they drank to all of the new sons and daughters who had been born—or soon would be born— to the people of the clan MacLir as a result of the magic of the night of the Planting Moon. Even now Huldre was in labor, and they had heard the crones who were mistresses of Woman Wisdom say that Morrigan, old Falcon's woman, was ready to come to her travail, even though by the girl's own reckoning she should not be near to term. The men laughed about that and toasted old Falcon, commenting that the old adage still held true: A first baby could come at any time; the others took the full passing of nine moons. They sat naked on plank benches in the hot, dark, herb-scented smoke and steam of the room and passed around the nearly empty bladder flask of mead, congratulating themselves on their virility as they took loud, proud note of the fact that they had managed to outlast all of the younger bucks at their merriment.

They sang songs and slapped each other on the back. Outside, snow was falling quietly in soft sievings that covered the world gently and made all things seem clean and new. The weight of the snow, piling higher and higher on the conical, thickly thatched roof of the sweat house, insulated the room beneath it.

Inside, it was very hot. Huge clay crocks of water, heated by warming stones, which the men drew from the fire pit and dropped into them at intervals, stood along the walls and sweat as copiously as the men. Condensation dripped from the roof beams. It formed a light, beading rain. Fomor squinted up at it, and in his drunkenness he found it exceedingly funny that rain was falling inside instead of out. He toasted the rain. He toasted the snow. He toasted the winter and the night and the water in the crocks and the coals within the fire pit and the smoke and steam in all of the sweat houses in all of the holdings in all of the world. Then, feeling magnanimous, he toasted the world, and the heavens above it, and the Twelve Winds, and the Mother of All, and all of the mothers of Bracken Fen, be they human or animal. Satisfied, he put back his head and laughed at his slurtongued grandiloquence. A great bubble of a belch rose up in him. He loosed it and was impressed, for it had been a grand belch, fully worthy of a salute. He toasted it, and the others drank to it and conceded that it had been the most magnificent belch that they had ever heard. They made a contest of trying to top it and ended convulsed with laughter, weak with glee, gasping and backhanding tears from their eyes.

Dathen could barely catch his breath as memories, ripe and ready, sparked more laughter. By the Fates, it was good to laugh again, and to hear the lord laughing as careless as a youth beside him. "Do you remember. . . ?" he asked, and spoke of their boyhood, of past pranks and jokes and jests made at one another's expense, of friends they had gotten the best of, and girls and women too. Lomna Ruad recalled an egg-gathering expedition, with the three of them sent off by Manannan himself to gather seabird eggs from the cliffs on the northwesternmost shore of the far island. He recalled how they had secretly taken mead with them, so that they had been drunk when they had roped up and rappeled down the cliffs, dangling hundreds of feet above the sea, meaddrunk as only idiot boys would have dared to be on such a venture. They had gathered eggs from nests built on ledges and crevices along the soaring cliff face, placing them not in their baskets, but hurling them back and forth at one another until they were slimed and yellowed and so slippery with yolk that they had barely managed to climb back up the ropes to safety.

"By the Twelve Winds, those were good times!" exclaimed Dathen.

"Aye," affirmed Lomna Ruad, "as these are good times now!"

Fomor looked at them and nodded, very drunk and very

happy. He rose and with a wooden dipper ladled up hot water from a nearby crock. He poured it over his head and savored the feel of it as it ran down his face, through his beard, over his back and chest, belly and genitals. Somewhere, far off beyond the holding, a lone wolf howled to the moon, which stood full and unseen above the winter snow clouds. He always thought of Balor when he heard the cries of wolves, but now another cry pricked his thoughts and drew his full attention. It was the sound of an infant's first cry— bold and strong and full of life's promise. His beard split with a smile. Huldre's labor had evidently ended practically before it had begun. He was not surprised. This had been a particularly easy pregnancy for her. He had no doubt that she had come through the delivery little the worse for the wear of it, nor did he doubt that the child would be fit and strong; for not one of the infants conceived upon the night of the Planting Moon had been stillborn, nor had a single woman died or suffered unduly during childbirth.

The dark half of the year was upon the land, but despite the recent arrival of snow, it was proving to be as mild as the omens Munremar saw in the sacred smokes. The stores within the sheds seemed inexhaustible. The people were relaxed in the safe, serene caul of the winter, and even Draga seemed somewhat pacified by the role to which Fomor had set him in hopes of soothing his dissatisfactions. He had named the redbeard master of arms and placed him in charge of the fortification of Bracken Fen. Draga had warmed to the duty. Under his supervision the great, circling embankments were nearing completion, sentries kept winter watch from the palisade and at various strategic positions across the fens and highlands, and the men of the holding were encouraged to hone their skills in the ancient arts of weaponry despite the short days and the unlikelihood that any enemy would ever come to Bracken Fen in the dead of winter. Fomor gave him his head, allowing him to organize frequent games and competitions lest boredom infect the men of the holding as it had once infected the redbeard and brought him close to a dangerous rebellion.

But now all seemed good between them. Draga still grumbled now and again; yet it appeared that the winter had gentled him, as his newly assigned activities put a new purpose to his life. Fomor's smile deepened. He was glad to be on good terms with his brother once again; they had been antagonists for far too long. Once again he dipped the ladle into the crock of steaming water and poured it over himself. "Aye," he said, "these *are* good times." And for the first time in many years he knew that he spoke the truth.

Draga awoke to the sound of the newborn's cry. In the darkness of his roundhouse the pain awoke with him. It was always with him now, as loyal as his women. The thought made him snarl as he lay unmoving, alone upon his bedskins. He could see the dark mound of furs, beneath which were his children; there were five of them here now, dreaming close to the wicker walls of the storage alcove—all boys, save one, a jumble of legs and arms and red-thatched little heads. The women had gone to keep the birth vigil, leaving his morning crock of mead close by. It was a widemouthed beaker brimful of brew. He reached for it, exhaling against the pain that movement brought. He lay on his side, brought the beaker close to his mouth, and slurped from it, knowing that for weeks now the women had been secretly adding some sort of medicinal herb. He had tasted the difference immediately—a slight hint of bitterness that had never been there before— but he had feigned ignorance.

He could not have faced the day without the mead. Whatever they had used, it was stronger than the oil of willow, which he had been using until Eala had noticed its absence from her shelf of stores. She had accused Uaine of taking it to rub upon the gums of her teething son; too much of the oil could prove harmful to infants. But Draga could not have enough of it or of whatever it was that they were mixing into his mead. He blessed them for adding it to his portion and cursed them for knowing his need of it. He saw the knowledge in their eyes. He sensed it in the solicitousness with which they overlooked his impatience with his children. He felt it as he lay upon his sleeping skins and knew that they had been cushioned by extra layers of bracken and heather mattressing. Women. Curse them for their kindness. Curse them for their pity. It unmanned him.

He lay in the darkness brooding, cursing the night because he lay awake in it, unable to sleep. Since the pain had come to him, winter nights seemed endless. He, who had once loved the dark half of the year as he loved any challenge, now cursed the cold, which congealed his breath before his face and brought the scent of illness to him—a taint of fevered sourness that he had never known in his youth. He refused to believe that the Twelve Winds he had honored all his life would now seek to blight him. Not Draga! Not the one who chafed against the unnatural life to which Fomor had led them; a life of peace that was, by its very nature, a blasphemy against the Twelve Winds.

Peace. The word was as sour as his breath. The night was very quiet. He listened to the silence. The newborn infant had ceased its cries. Fomor's child. He hoped that it had died. No—he hoped instead that it was ill formed, a creature to be exposed, placed outside the palisade as fodder for predators. *That* was what he wished for his brother's child. It was what Fomor deserved. Too many things were going his way lately. Indeed, *everything* was going his way! Draga scowled. He cursed his brother, his brother's newborn child, his brother's women, and all his children, especially Balor. By the Mother of All, most especially he cursed Balor. Had he not disappeared, Draga's plot to secure the chieftainship for himself would not have been spoiled. He would be lord now. He would be master of the clan MacLir. By the Fates, he hoped that the youth was dead!

The silence of the room settled upon him, the sort of quiet that came only when snow fell. Like everything else it served the chieftain. It was gentle snow, a snow in which children would dance and through which cattle could browse. Draga cursed it.

He reached again to tilt the mead crock to his lips and gasped loudly against the fire that broke loose within his bones to invade the muscles of his back and the sockets of his shoulders.

"Father! Are you all right?"

The question came from his eldest son, five-year-old Lorcan. He stared through the darkness at his sire out of a face as spangled with freckles as Uaine's. Draga told the boy to go back to sleep, but not before he explained himself with a lie.

"I was dreaming of the Days of Glory. I saw myself in battle. With you, a man, beside me. We fought with swords. Together we slew our enemies. I cried out. A victory cry as befit a true son of the People of the Ax."

The child listened. His father often spoke such words to him. Whoever these People of the Ax were, Lorcan was glad that they were confined to the realm of the redbeard's stories. They seemed a reckless, restless lot, always on the move, and Lorcan was happy in Bracken Fen.

"You must remember always that you are a grandson of the greatest battle lord of all! Manannan MacLir!"

Lorcan yawned. Manannan MacLir... He imagined that the man himself must have resembled the chieftain. No man could be more impressive than his uncle. Beyond the round-house, from across the holding, the baby began to cry again, and Lorcan listened, distracted by the sound. He liked babies. He yawned again. He was still sleepy.

Draga watched the boy lie back and wiggle down among the skins, sighing softly as he sought sleep among his siblings. *By the Fates*, he thought, *he will be a man to be proud of someday*. Then his thought turned. No! He's a man doomed by the lord's absence of ambition to be an ignominious cowherd and mud wallower. That is what all of my children must become—including Dana.

No wonder the girl refused to name a man! There was not one within the holding worthy to win her. In another place, in another time, when the men of the clan had been sea raiders and warriors, a girl like Dana would have won for her sire her weight in gold at any bartering. Not cows. Not baubles of bone and bits of copper and sacks of grain. Not sheep. Not geese. Not stink-teated goats. But swords. And gold. Dana would have been a chieftain's woman. She would have worn the trophies of a thousand conquests. Slaves would have bent to her every command, and everywhere she went, men and women would have cowered in fearful awe of her and known that she was Dana, the daughter of Draga, son of Manannan MacLir, warlord of the People of the Ax.

He twitched against an agony of frustration and wanting, then lay very still, thinking. He could not have said just when the idea came to him, for it came fully formed, a gift of the mead. He sat upright, oblivious to the pain. Inadvertently, in his excitement, he tipped the crock. It rolled over. The mead spilled out of it, warm against his bare thigh and buttocks as it began to seep through and beneath his bedskins. Why wait upon the impetuosity of the Fates when he had within his power the ability to turn them to serve his own ambition? He heard the cries of the newborn infant, of his brother's child, and he thought of all of the babies that had been born since the night of the Planting Moon, all signs of his brother's success as a lord. Lucky children. He exhaled a snort of a laugh. Lucky for Draga! His mind filled with thoughts about oils and other herbs, all efficacious when used in small amounts, dangerous if misused—but especially Eala's warning that too much willow oil could prove deadly to infants. . . . Woman Wisdom. He had never paid it much heed until now.

It was a girl. Elathan hurried to the sweat house to inform his father that both mother and child were doing well. Despite his shaggy winter cloak, he was numb with cold. By his own choice he had spent the last few hours sitting on the plank walkway outside of the chieftain's roundhouse. The old crones who had come to assist his mother with her delivery had sent him out, and he had gone gladly, for tradition demanded that males keep well away from such female mysteries. Yet he had been determined to stay as nearby as he dared. He knew that the crones disliked and distrusted Huldre. Although Mealla would be with them, and big, kindly, motherly Blaheen, it made him nervous to think of the old hags with his mother at a time when she was so vulnerable.

The old women had seemed to read his mind. They had clucked their tongues at him and called him a silly boy. Huldre was the chieftain's woman, and they would be as mad as she if they did anything less than their best for her. Besides, they said, had not Munremar proved that it had been the firstborn of the lord, and not his white-haired woman, who had been the source of the clan's bad luck? Why should they wish to harm Huldre? They told him to be off, advising him to pass the night with a friend, as his little sister Bevin had been sent off to do.

He had not obliged. With two friends—Badger and Fox Foiler, his father's dogs—he had kept his vigil, seating himself cross-legged upon the planks beneath the overhang of the roof, as close to the entrance as they would allow. If anything went wrong, he would be there; although just what he could do, he was not certain.

The women who came to stand birth vigil had ignored him.

They were mainly the older women of the clan, chatting and gossiping among themselves, clustered close against the cold. Custom prevented them from entering the house until the child was born, cleansed, and accepted by its sire. Virgins were not allowed to attend a birth lest, if the infant be stillborn, their wombs respond sympathetically and be barren ever after. Nor were there pregnant women in attendance, for everyone knew that the sight of another female in labor, or even the sound of her cries, might inspire the unborn to come forth prematurely. So it was that Elathan had been surprised to see Morrigan enter the group of women. They shouted at her and drove her away, for she was great with child and by venturing so near to the house had put herself and her baby in jeopardy. She had muttered something about having forgotten and quickly retreated.

For a long while Elathan had stared after her, troubled. It was not like Morrigan to be forgetful. He had wondered if old Falcon was aware that she had gone out. She lived with him now, sharing his little roundhouse with his grandson, Rinn. It was strange to think of Morrigan as anyone's woman, even though the scandal that her relationship with old Falcon had caused still stirred the tongues of every gossip within Bracken Fen. Witnesses had seen them coupling beyond the palisade, and long before that old Falcon had pursued the girl with such open ardor that, given Morrigan's wild and unpredictable nature, gossips had whispered that it was no surprise that the girl should be with child by the old man. Falcon had been severely fined for taking a virgin without the consent of her sire, but the chieftain had a soft spot for the old man and had allowed the union, even though the Wise One had seemed loath to let Morrigan leave his hearth. Now that the girl was great with child, Munremar had become so anxious about her welfare that his magical powers were temporarily drained; he conjured no magic smokes or fires above the altar of the Twelve Winds.

Elathan had thought about this as he had sat with the dogs and watched the snow fall softly in the dark. He wondered what Balor would have made of it. The pain of missing had risen in him, and he had wondered if it was always like this when one sibling lost another—like the pain that was said to follow an amputation, a lingering sensation that somehow the lost member was still there. He had wondered if the feeling would ever go away.

In that moment the newborn had announced its arrival into the world, and he had been roused from his musings by Blaheen. She had towered above him, fat and beaming, announcing the child's soundness and gender as though she had given birth to it herself. A girl. Another daughter for the chieftain.

Now, as Elathan approached the sweat house with the news, the two terriers close at his heel, there was no doubt in his mind that his father would accept the child. No infant had been exposed since the years of darkness, and then only because they had been malformed. Their own sires had denied them, as was their obligation, for to suffer such a child to live would be an affront to the Fates, which had marked it by its abnormality for death. And no one would ever knowingly risk offending the Fates.

Except Balor.

By the Mother of All! How he wished that he could stop thinking about his brother. Munremar had been right about him. He *had* been bad luck. Now that he was gone, the clan prospered. But by the Twelve Winds that swept the world and had driven Balor from the fens, Elathan missed him and would give anything to have him back again.

The oxhide that covered the entrance to the sweat house moved as a big, perspiring hand pulled it to one side. His father peered out at him.

"Well?" pressed the chieftain. "Have you news for me, or is that baby I hear bawling not my own?"

The lord was drunk. There was laughter in his voice and eyes. Elathan gulped and stood tall. "You have a daughter, my lord. She is perfect in all of her parts. Her mother is well. The women have assured me that all is in readiness for you to—" He was not allowed to finish the sentence, for Fomor reached out, took hold of Elathan's cloak, and jerked him into the sweat house.

He stood in smoke and steam as the lord declared to Lomna Ruad and Dathen that they must offer a toast of gratitude to the Twelve Winds for the life of his newborn child. The men were naked, and Fomor slung one huge, bare, sweat-slick arm about his son's shoulder and pulled him close in a bear hug of open affection as Dathen rose from the plank bench, grasped the bladder flask of mead, and raised it high with both hands. "To the newborn daughter of the MacLir! May she know a long life!" The flask came down and went into his mouth. He drank, sucking, for the bladder was limp with near emptiness.

Elathan watched as the flask was tossed to Lomna Ruad. He was on his feet, facing the youth squarely from across the smoldering fire pit. Elathan tried not to notice that the man's genitals were nearly as flaccid as the mead container; but then, Lomna Ruad was as intoxicated as Dathen and Fomor and as relaxed from heat and sweat and the herb-scented smoke, which caused Elathan's head to tingle. "To the daughter of the MacLir! May she be fruitful!" He lifted his flask and drew off his portion.

Now the flask came to Fomor. He loosed his hold on the youth and raised it. "May she dwell in peace!" The flask came to Elathan, and he hesitated, aware that the others watched him and waited. Never before had he been treated as a man by them. He was giddy and flustered with delight. He did not know what to say.

Fomor watched him. He was pleased by what he saw. Elathan was fast becoming a man. He would not be as tall as his brother, but he would be broader, in the way of the men of the clan, and would have their coloring. No one would ever be able to point to him and accuse him of being one apart from his kinsmen as they had done with Balor. Balor. The old hurt flamed. But no. He would not allow himself to yield to it. Balor was the past. Elathan was the future. He would salve the hurt with that and be glad for it. "Go ahead," he said to the youth. "Make your blessing, my son."

My son. The words took Elathan's breath away. They had always been reserved for Balor. For the firstborn. Elathan recalled all of the times that Balor had eclipsed him in his father's eyes. But now Balor was gone, and this time he would not come back. For the first time Elathan was glad.

He raised the flask. He formed his toast. One for his lips. One for his heart. *May he never return,* he thought ferociously, his emotions a turmoil within him as he spoke the blessing. "May my newborn sister know all that we have wished for her!" But when he put the flask to his lips, the bladder yielded dryness. Although he sucked upon it and probed it with his tongue, twisting it until liquid pearled up through its skin, all that entered Elathan's lips were the dregs.

It was nearly dawn when at last Fomor took his new daughter into his big hands. They were steady. A brisk walk across the compound from the sweat house had sharpened his senses and dulled the effects of the mead. The women who were in attendance said they did not think that they had ever heard a girl-child cry more aggressively. He agreed, holding her out, laughing aloud with pure delight at the sight of her. The women had cleansed her and scrubbed her free of caul and blood, but she was still red of skin and hair and temperament, as ruddy and rowdy as a summer grass fire. She did not cry out melodiously, as fair-haired little Bevin had done; she bawled until her belly went drum tight and her face flamed crimson. She kicked her little legs and beat her tiny fists at him. Mealla leaned close and shook her head, smiling as she said that the child cawed like a raven. Fomor did not disagree. Indeed, he took a sire's prerogative and named the child that. Babh. Raven. And when Blaheen protested and reminded him that the birds were carrion eaters, he countered by telling her that they were also wise and clever, and always they were survivors. She could not frame an argument to his reasoning, nor did she try as he knelt and tenderly kissed Huldre's damp brow. He held the child out to her, a sign of his acceptance.

"Here, woman. Give her suck. Perhaps your breast milk shall cool the fire of her temper."

She did not move. She lay pale and weary, cleansed by the women, and covered with a blanket of finely joined wolfskins to keep her warm against the chill of the room. The blank look that he knew all too well was in her eyes. Where was she now, he wondered. In the past? The future? Somewhere far away, in a world of her own mad conjuring, in the place where she had taken refuge ever since she had learned of the traders who had been sent away. She had cried out that they should have been slain. Her hands had plucked at her throat, clutching at the amulet that was not there. She had run to the palisade and climbed the stairs to stand in the wind, staring out across the miles, keening like a wounded bird. In a fury of impatience he had forced her down and had commanded

Mealla to keep her confined within the roundhouse lest, once again, her behavior turn others against her.

Now he stared at her and wondered what had happened to the fierce-eyed, beautiful young woman he had stolen from Nemed MacAgnomain, to Huldre of the North, who had come to him willingly, who had stood bravely by him in battle in the days when he had fought to unite the tribes under his leadership. She had known no fear then. She had not questioned his will then. She had not trembled against war or danger. He had been Wolf of the Western Tribes, and she had wiped the blood of battle from his sword with her hair until the pale strands had gone as red as Mealla's tresses. His clansmen had marveled at the sight of her, and to this day he was certain that his kinswomen had never experienced such envy.

But now, although she was still more beautiful than any woman had a right to be without offending the Mother of All, she stared blankly into the shadowed recesses of the lamplit room. She was unaware of his presence. She was uncaring of her infant. By the Fates, how could he continue to love such a woman?

He suddenly felt very tired. His head had begun to ache from too much mead. The crones had left the room; he had not noticed them go, nor had he heard them tell the women who had stood birth vigil to go. The lord was tired, they said. It was late, they said. Come back and ogle the baby tomorrow, they said.

Mealla knelt beside him and pulled back the furs that covered Huldre, exposing her breasts. How beautiful they were still, as firm as a young girl's, but full, with the nipples round and ripe and ready to offer nourishment to the infant. That much she would give to it, thought Mealla, but not love. Never love from Huldre for her children. What sort of a woman was she? If only she could take Huldre's place—to suckle, just once—to give life, just once!

Mealla nearly cried as she took the infant from the chieftain's hands and put it to Huldre's breast. The Northwoman did not refuse the child; she simply did not react to it. Until suddenly little Babh saw to it that she was roused from her lethargy. The baby wriggled. She burrowed like a badger, fiercely, digging with her tiny fingers, gouging with her knees, sighing and sucking and smacking with ecstasy until a barely sprouted milk tooth bit deep, and Huldre winced, blinked, and cried, "Ouch!" The blankness disappeared from her eyes as she stared at the baby.

"You are going to have a hard time ignoring this one," said Mealla, rising, turning away as she moved to her own pallet lest she be shamed by her tears.

Despite himself, Fomor laughed.

The color was seeping back into Huldre's face. She looked at the baby and frowned. "She is not pretty."

"She is better than pretty," said the lord. "She is strong."

Huldre's eyes closed. The weariness of childbed rose up to claim her. She sighed, drifting into sleep as she mumbled, "You were strong once. You might have been lord of all the world once."

Mealla had put out the tallow lamps. A sign that it was time for rest. The room went dark. Fomor could hear her settling herself beneath her sleeping skins. Slowly, carefully, as silence surrounded him, he rose and stood looking down at Huldre, not wishing to wake her. The infant, its hunger satisfied, had fallen asleep, soft and warm and milk-sweet against her breast. Tenderly he bent to touch the little red head, then drew the wolfskins close over the sleeping mother and child.

I am lord of all the world, he thought. *And all the world that matters is here in Bracken Fen. Someday, Huldre, perhaps you shall understand. It was nothing for me to be a warrior. It was easy for me to kill. With a sword in my hand and a battle cry in my mouth, it took no trick to lead men out for blood and glory and gold. But to lead them here, to bring them to a life of peace through which they and their children might dare to dream of future generations instead of the certain but glorious annihilation that awaited us as bronze-poor warriors . . . ach, Huldre, if you had but a portion of the Sight you claim to have, you would know that this has taken all my strength, all of my power. Now, at last, I am the Wolf. For I am wise enough to be content, woman. And there is not a warrior who could match me! For I have won the greatest battle of them all. I have learned how to survive. On my own terms.*

Within the darkness he heard the soft pull of Mealla's breath, sensed that she was awake, and knew what she must be feeling now. He went to her.

"My lord . . ." she whispered as he drew away the bed skins and, undressing, lay down naked beside her.

"Always," he affirmed, and kissed away her tears as he lamented that the seed of his life refused to take root within her.

She touched his mouth with her fingertips. "I am content," she told him. "You *are* my life, Fomor MacLir. Always and forever I ask for nothing more than to live and lie with the Wolf—in peace or in war, it matters not. You are my lord. It is enough."

And for a long while, within the winter dark, she made him know that *her* love, at least, was unconditional.

25

Days passed. Icicles dripped and sparkled in the light of noon as Donn and Echur charged one another like rut-maddened stags. The force of the impact stunned them both. They paused, breathless and dizzy, balanced and braced, heads together, arms locked.

Donn, sturdy and stocky, was not as tall as Echur, nor had he a warrior's reach; but he was quick on his feet and a master at coming at an opponent—fast and low, using leverage to full advantage—be it man or beast. He heard the older man's low exhalation of pain and surprise as his head butted upward, bruising bone and breaking flesh. Echur's blood ran down the side of his face. Hot. Thick. Donn thanked the Fates for having given him the gift of a hard, thick skull, and although the impact had scrambled his brain a little, through his whirling thoughts he hoped that Dana had taken note of who had won the charge.

There were always contests going on among those men not occupied with the herd or the endless everyday chores of life within the holding. Sometimes the challenges were organized events; sometimes, as now, they were spontaneous. This one had started when Dana had come out of her father's round-house to sit with her mother in the sun. It was a warm, windless, lovely day, and the two women had been taking advantage of it, talking quietly, taking turns grinding grain in a large lap mortar. Many women and girls were similarly occupied out-of-doors, but it was Dana who had won the unasked-for attention of a small group of men at the flint worker's shed.

Oblin the Stonecutter had started it innocently enough. He had commented that Dana's beauty grew more remarkable each day, so much so that even an aging old knapper thought of her in the night and grew as hard as his flints, much to the delight of his woman who, as a result of his newly roused ardor, had sought a tonic from the young healer. They had laughed at his boasting and followed it with boastings of their own. Crude and elemental, it soon grew antagonistic and loud. Soon they had won the attention of everyone within earshot, including Dana.

When she had looked toward them, Echur had preened and claimed that the girl had deliberately sought his eye. Donn had disputed his statement, saying that she would have no interest in a fading, flatulent fool whose manhood was as flaccid as the skin sagging from his elbows. Echur had roared in protest, saying that Donn would, of course, know all about flaccidity, for it was common knowledge that the only time he knew a man's rising was when he was secretly sucking nourishment from his mother's paps. That had done it. They had flown at each other's throats, and no one had been surprised to see blood flowing.

Dana rose quickly and fled into the roundhouse, an angry Eala at her heels.

The older woman caught her by the wrist and jerked her to an abrupt halt. "They battle to please you, Daughter! You cannot turn your back upon them!"

The girl's face was drawn and very white. "But they do *not* please me! I cannot bear to see them fight! They were friends a moment ago, and now, because of me, blood has been spilled."

"Bah!" snapped her mother, not wanting to hear more. "Men love to fight! If it upsets you, Dana, all you have to do is accept one of them and become his woman."

Eala released Dana's wrist. The girl drew it close and rubbed the red welt her mother's fingers had left. "I do not want any of them." She went to the hearth and seated herself upon the broadest of the curbstones, absently lifting the prodding stick and poking at the coals until they roused up red and began to smoke. She and her mother were alone in the house. Draga was off somewhere beyond the palisade, and Uaine had gone out earlier with the children, joining with a small group of matrons to share child-watching while they worked on their sewing.

Eala, her eyes narrowed, came to sit beside her. "Dana, we must talk about this again, you and I. You are well past the age when most girls begin to bear children. You cannot put it off forever."

"Why?" The girl did not look up. "I am happy here. Father has said that I may stay as long as it pleases me. Am I no longer welcome at your hearth, Mother?"

"It is not a question of your being welcome!" exclaimed Eala, frowning. The redbeard had always indulged the girl. Of course, it was difficult not to. Dana herself was happiest when pleasing others. Sometimes Eala wondered if there were not something wrong with the girl. To be so kind... it was not natural. "Dana, there are two women and five children in this household. I should think you would be happy to go to your own hearth, where there would be less work and a new man to spoil you."

"I do not want a man."

"Nonsense! How are you ever to have children if you do not take a man?"

The girl looked at her mother. *Let her understand. Please. Let her see it in my eyes so that I do not have to speak words that will hurt her. I do not want a man because I do not want the seed of his children in me. I have seen it with the animals ...blood, pain, and tearing. And look at you, Mother! With each child you grow older, closer to death. I can see it in your face, in the gray of your hair, in the color of your cheek. You age. And I do not want to age. I do not want to die!*

Eala waited for the girl to speak, but evidently she had no reply, so Eala said impatiently, "Dana, a woman is made to take a man, and a man is made to give seed to a woman. This assures the future."

"I do not care about the future." Dana felt sick and knew that her mother saw it in her face.

The statement angered Eala. "Ach! I should have known!" she cried, as usual misreading her daughter's reaction. "Look at you! As white as a corpse! Do you still brood over the

memory of a boy? Is Balor the reason you will not name a
man? Forget him, girl! He is dead most likely, and good
riddance, I say!"

"He was my friend."

"Then *be* a friend to him! Bury his memory! And let his
soul go to the Otherworld in peace so that we may get on
with our lives in a like manner!" She paused, lips pursed, and
considered her daughter. "Now you listen to me, girl," she
continued emphatically. "Even as we sit here blood is being
spilled over you. By clan law if you do not name a man soon,
the chieftain shall force your father to do it for you. Draga
does not like to be told what to do by his brother. The two of
them have been getting along fairly well these days. You
would not wish to be the cause of trouble between them,
would you, Dana?"

By the Fates and the Mother of All and by the stars they all
swore by, Balor wondered if the studies would never end.
Long, black hours of study, and not once in all of those hours
of that cold, clear winter, did he truly wish to have it end.
The study *was* peace to him, *and* challenge, a wondrous,
incredible filling of mind that sometimes made him laugh
aloud with pure joy. He was a dry and empty vessel, and the
mead of knowledge was being poured into him. Yet it did not
fill him! He grew to accommodate it, and for each new
question answered, there was another to be asked. On and on
forever. Like the stars.

Now he knew that the earth was a huge, spinning sphere in
a vast dark sea of sky, like the moon upon which it cast its
shadow. Earth! Before he had come here it had been only the
bogs of Bracken Fen, plus the marshes and moors and
highlands beyond. And the stars had been nomads carrying
torches across the face of infinity. Now he knew that they
were *worlds*, and suns, all bound together in a wondrous
pattern, which Cromm Cruach called the Harmony.

"Understand the Harmony and you shall understand your
place within the stars, my boy."

He stood and craned his neck and stared and stared until
he was drunk upon the endless stars and darkness and vast
seas of textureless infinity.

"No man can understand all that," he said. "No man's mind is big enough to grasp it."

"Man has been born to understand. For this understanding he exists. With this understanding he shall someday walk among the stars and know immortality amidst the infinite."

"Riddles. Always you speak in riddles. Infinity . . . you say that it is endless . . . but everything must have an end, and always there is a horizon, and somehow, somewhere, death must come to all things."

"No, Balor. There is no death. There is only change. Endless change. And beyond each horizon a new beginning."

And so the days had passed, and soon they initiated him into the study of star and earth alignments, of sun and moon risings, and, indeed, each day *was* a new beginning. Never had he felt more alive! The concepts were as staggering as the applications, and as fascinating. With them he began to understand how the priests of the Stone were able to predict the Black Sun and the Shadow that Eats the Moon, as well as the rising and lowering of tides and the lengthening and shortening of the days as the seasons turned in cadence with the movements of the heavens. His studies became as much an obsession as his need to work vengeance against Nemed MacAgnomain. He could not spend enough time on them.

"You shall burn yourself out . . . like the stars that fall," cajoled Cethlinn as she called him to other studies.

He lay with her within her timbered house when the snow filled the sky. He laughed with her and made love to her and slept with her . . . and dreamt of Dana dancing in a golden aura, amid falling stars. And of a hawk wheeling above endless marshes. And of a vast, bleak moor lighted by a huge and glaring sun. No—not a sun. It was the Eye of Donar, watching him across the miles. And in the center of that great, burning eye, the figure of a girl, a black-haired girl, called to him out of yesterday. *Balor!* Then a wolf howled in the wood beyond the river, a lonely, echoing sound taking him back across the miles between now and then.

He awoke sweating. He sat bolt upright, with Cethlinn beside him. "The wound . . . it pains you?" she asked, leaning to kiss the scar tenderly.

"No." He lay back, drawing her down with him. "The cry of the wolf woke me."

"I heard no wolf." She nestled close and made small,

sleepy sounds of contentment as she fell easily back into her dreams.

For a long time Balor did not sleep. He lay awake. Listening. But the wolf did not cry again.

Morrigan's house, old Falcon's house, was snug and warm and piled high with winter snow, but no watchful husband paced the walkway beyond the hide-covered door, awaiting the birth of Morrigan's child. Old Falcon was dead. His bones now lay within the new little barrow not far from the cattle ring where he had spent so many hours of his life. His had been a gentle death, and not unexpected, a wandering of the soul one night. In the dawn Morrigan had awakened to find him still and lifeless beside her. He was smiling, his open eyes as clear and bright as a child's. Startled, she had leaned close and tried to rouse him, but it had been no use, and for a long while she had lain quietly with her head upon his frail, bony chest, thinking about their brief union. A sad, sweetly reverent nostalgia had pervaded her senses, for she had come to care for him deeply. He had been a good man, a gentle and undemanding husband once his initial man-need had been sated, and even that had been accomplished gently and with consideration. His pride in having been able to win a young woman to his hearth had been boundless, as had been his delight in her pregnancy. If he had suspicions that the child was not his, he never spoke them, and often he would place his hand on her swelling belly, feel the baby move, and speak of how good it would be to have a child in the house again. His grandson Rinn, a belligerent young man who shared the roundhouse with them, openly resented the old man's union with a young girl, but Falcon told him to be content or to seek lodgings elsewhere. Rinn was one of the many who contested for Dana and refused to name a woman until she had chosen a man, so Morrigan, for old Falcon's sake, had tried to make peace with him, but it had been no good. When the old man died, Rinn swore that she had sapped him of his life-force.

But she knew the truth. She had made Falcon happy. With the other women of the holding to guide her, she had prepared his body for burial. With a widow's genuine sadness she had arranged it within its barrow as tradition decreed, in a fetal curl. A little cap of leather covered the baldness that had always shamed him, and the sparse, white braids that grew from little patches of hair just above his ears had been plaited so they seemed thick and as luxuriant as they must have been in his youth. She had placed all of his favorite things around him, keeping nothing for herself. His favorite beaker, brimming with mead. A fine stone ax. A short string of cowry shells, which he had brought back, years before, from Point of Ale. A cherished copper razor, and two slim armbands of gold, which, she knew, Rinn had coveted for himself; gold was a luxury that the people of the clan MacLir were not likely to come by again. She covered the small, frail corpse with the finest bedskins he had owned and then, as Rinn had sucked in his breath but dared not protest lest the other clansfolk who had gathered around the barrow hear him speak his greed, she lay a long-bladed copper dagger atop the furs. It had been Falcon's most prized possession. It had been his in the days when he had earned his name as a navigator for Manannan MacLir.

The lord Fomor had stepped forward to honor the old man, saying he had possessed the eyes of a hawk, that he could see through fog and distance to guide his chieftain's ships to safe beachings in any weather. The chieftain spoke of the past, of the Days of Glory, of a life so alien to the ways of the fens that Morrigan had listened spellbound and felt the child stir within her womb as though it sensed its kinship with the chieftain and wished, although it was yet unborn, to claim its rightful place within the clan.

Sometime later, in labor, she realized that her child could never claim its rightful place. That it could never be. Never. This realization came through to her as the labor pain returned yet again. She tensed and cried out against it, then plummeted into an exhaustion that took her beyond herself, beyond the moment, beyond the pain and into a dark, welcoming limbo, which seemed to be carrying her away, out of the house, out beyond the holding, beyond the bogs and the winter-whitened fields and pastures, where the herds of the clan MacLir nosed through the snow in a never-ending search for what was left of the grasses beneath it. How light-headed she felt! How buoyant! After agonizing days of labor, how relieved! Beneath her closed lids she seemed to fly across long miles of dreaming and remembering, as though, somehow, she followed the flight of the hawk she had seen riding the thermals on the day when she had agreed to become old Falcon's woman and had lain with him so that he—and anyone who might happen to see them together—would later assume that her child must be his.

High. So high. I can see the past below me: children playing on a summer's green, taking turns riding a white pony, careless, happy children, laughing and dancing in the sun.

The hawk was taking her higher, so high that she could barely catch her breath. The air was thin and sweet. Below her now she could see the cattle ring and beyond it, the high pastures and the last of the wattled fences. She could see the brambled tanglings of the gorse, and the wild country, darkened by long arms of forest that intruded here and there into the bleak, wind-scoured moor, and for a moment, beside a ring of standing stones, she saw a shadow of a great beast lurking. A wolf? Yes. But what wolf could be so huge? Its dimensions seemed torn from the fabric of a nightmare.

The hawk flew on. So high now that she could see the sea and the marshes, mile after mile of reed-choked wetlands. Her heart stopped. Balor had fled into the marshes.

Balor. She saw him now. In a far place. Within a towering, circling wall of stone. Beyond it the shadow of the great beast crouched and waited, ready to spring. She could see it clearly now. It *was* a wolf. A white wolf.

Balor!

She tried to call out his name in warning, but there was no strength left in her to call. The hawk was falling from the sky. She was falling with it, turning, weightless, plummeting to earth. The vast blue sky of forever was going dark. Somewhere, far away, she heard a baby crying.

And then she heard nothing. Nothing. Not even the sound of the women keening for her death.

Dianket sat in shock. Blaheen stood before him, blubbering. The girl was dead. Her son would live. A small, dark scrap of a boy called Cian, in memory of his mother, for he had the look of her and of the ancient race that had dwelled in this land before the arrival of the clan MacLir. Cian. The Ancient. The very sound of it made Dianket feel old with grief. He

wondered if the child truly was the son of old Falcon or if, as
he suspected, Morrigan had found a way to bear Balor's seed
and, by so doing, had become yet another unfortunate recipi-
ent of his bad luck. She had been with him on the night of
the Planting Moon. The time of the child's coming pointed to
a conception worked on that night. But he had kept her
secret. He had kept all of the secrets that had transpired
under the light of that moon. Law breaking. Murder. Conspiracy to work treason. He knew it all. And would take the
knowledge with him to his grave. As would Morrigan now
take it to hers.

"Poor girl," sighed Blaheen. "The child was well formed for
such an early comer. But small. No one thought it would be a
difficult bearing. If only she had not gone so close to the
chieftain's roundhouse when the Northwoman was at her
labor. Surely that caused the child to come forth too soon,
and so her labor was long. Too long. It took the breath from
her body, and she was simply too weary to draw it back
again."

The words rolled over Dianket. His hands lay lax upon his
lap, upturned. Blaheen had left the weather baffle open when
she had entered. A cold wind had followed her. It moved over
Dianket's hands, filling his palms, and as it did, memories
stirred within him of the many times that he had witnessed
stillbirths among animals. Of the many times that a tiny
creature he had thought dead had been brought to life
by the rough, sure licking and prodding of its mother, as
though the breath of life lay within it, needing only to be
awakened.

He rose to his feet, staring, trembling with a rising excitement. "The wind! It *is* with the world as the breath is with a
man—or a woman. . . . It *is* the force of life."

Blaheen thought that he had lost his mind. Poor man. It
was not good to live alone. She was about to ask him what he
had meant, but he had a question of his own as he reached for
his crutch.

"How long has she been without breath?" His heart was
racing. "How long, woman!"

"Only a few moments. I came to you with the news first,
knowing that she has always been like a sister to you and—"
She stopped. He was gone.

He stabbed at the snow with his crutch, striding forward so

aggressively that twice he nearly fell, and everyone who saw him stopped to stare. A crowd had already gathered outside of old Falcon's door. Dianket could hear the moaning of the crones within and smell the stench of the Wise One's funereal smokes.

"Wait, you! Dianket! Stop! You can't go in there! It is forbidden!"

Hands reached to stay his movement. He slapped them away. *Death!* he thought, snarling at those who would stop him. *Why is death not forbidden?*

He backhanded the door-covering and strode into the room. The crones who had come to practice Woman Wisdom shouted at him to go away, and gasped in amazement when he, who was always such a pleasant fellow, ignored them and forcefully, hurtfully, elbowed his way between them. He stopped only when he stood before the body of Morrigan, where she lay upon the still birth-bloodied pallet. The sight of her almost struck him down. She was so still, so pale in the shadowed light of the room, with the smokes of purification silently whirling green and gray around her; they would aid her soul on its outward and upward journey. They would take her to the Otherworld. They would also cut the smell of blood. There was so much blood. There must have been hemorrhage. He had seen it before, often, with beasts, and had discovered a way to treat it successfully. He asked the women if they had packed the girl, and if they had used the herbs that were effective in stopping excessive blood flow. They said no. They said it was not done that way in the Mysteries.

Munremar stood opposite him, grieving, looming over the girl, holding the sacred clay vessel in one hand and wafting a branch of mistletoe with the other. But Dianket knew Munremar's limitations as a physician and had long ago guessed the truth that lay behind the priest's magic. And that truth now lay dead between them. Did he mourn for the girl or the loss of an invaluable assistant? *Who shall climb the ladder to your secret room now, old man? Who shall be the mouth of your 'spirit' voices and the eyes behind your visions? Is this what you have always feared? Is this why she was encouraged never to take a man? Or is this what you have allowed to happen because you guessed her knowledge of your part in Draga's conspiracy against the chieftain?*

The latter thought loosed rage in him. Only seconds had passed since he had entered the room. What happened next would live in the clan as legend forever, but it happened so quickly that those who witnessed it could barely react before it was done. Dianket hurled his crutch at Munremar. He leaped onto the dead girl's pallet and straddled her. He took her by the shoulders and lifted her, shaking her violently as he pressed the side of his head hard against her chest.

He strained to hear a heartbeat. There was none. He cursed in an agony of frustration and began to rub her arms, quickly, brutally, until the white, cool flesh grew hot beneath the friction of his movement. But still her heart did not beat. Still she did not breathe.

Someone had called for the chieftain. He entered the room, so shocked by what he saw that he froze where he was, still at the entrance, holding the weather baffle to one side. The wind blew into the house.

Cold. Strong. It parted the sacred mists. It touched the healer. But not only with its chill, for as he gasped against it, inspiration struck him, seared him as hotly as any lightning bolt. He knew what he must do.

He bent to the girl. With one hand behind her neck and the other beating a sure press of rhythm against her chest, he put his mouth over hers and began to breathe the wind of his own life into her.

The impact of Dianket's crutch had shattered Munremar's sacred lamp and sent his sprig of mistletoe falling to the floor. But he did not move. No one moved. They were too stunned. They stared. Not quite believing what they saw. Dianket curled over Morrigan in what might have been described as a violent, passionate rape of death. The moments passed. The sound of his breathing was the only sound. Even the wind was still, as though it waited upon the will of the man. And then, suddenly, there was another sound. A single gasp of breath. And then another.

"She lives!"

It was one shout. From every mouth in the room. Dianket had done battle with the Fates and won.

26

"No! I forbid it! No exceptions. Tell them that there shall be
no swords brought upon the Plain of the Great Stone Circle!"

"But Gorias has traveled many miles to return to us, as he
promised, Father. And he has brought others, who are grateful for past considerations and blessings. Repayment is a
condition of honor with them. They have come to offer us
their protection. Surely you shall not turn them away!"

"I shall and I must!" Star Gazer was on his feet. It was just
past dawn. He and Balor had spent the night together on a
rise of land above the plain. It had been a night of computations and study and good fellowship. The land around them
was sweet with spring—the damp earth was furred with the
green of new grass, the air was crisp but not cold, and gray
only because the sun had not yet risen to put the color of the
day into it. They had made their beds of soft, new ferns, and
only when the stars had begun to fade had they pulled their
woolen cloaks over them against the dew and slept . . . until
the sure, hard hoofbeats of Cethlinn's mare had awakened them.

Balor looked up at her, rubbing sleepiness from his face
with his fingers. Somehow he had known what her news
would be before she had spoken it. His reaction disturbed
him. He had looked forward to Gorias's return. But the
winter had been so short, so pleasant. He hated to see it end.

Cethlinn was clearly angry with her father. She was clothed
against the morning chill in a hooded robe of unbleached
wool. Her face flushed pink with frustration as she reined her
mount impatiently, holding the animal in check, yet inadvertently communicating her restlessness through the tension
of her thighs. Confused, the horse tossed its head and danced
in place. "I will not give them such a message. You speak to
them. They await your word. In the wood across the river."

"With the wild wolves, where they belong!" snapped Star
Gazer. "I shall not go out to them. I shall welcome no armed
warriors here. Gorias should have spoken of his intent before

he left. The man brought his daughter to us to be healed. She *was* healed. *That* was our compensation, to know that we accomplished charity in a world where there is scant little of it! If Gorias feels bound by honor to do more in the way of repayment, then let him come forth unarmed. It is spring. Many pilgrims wintered upon the plain this year. They have needs that must be met. Extra hands shall be welcomed at any of a thousand tasks. Much is to be done before the hordes of summer descend upon us. Too much!" His features were sharp, honed as though by a careless stoneworker as he gestured vehemently outward toward the plain. "Look at it! It reeks like a charnel house and echoes with the sounds and stinks of the very civilizations we would counsel man to abandon for the grace of simpler times!"

"You may be Lord of the Stone, Father, but you cannot will the world to turn backward!"

They seemed to have forgotten that Balor was present. Star Gazer moved forward and took hold of the mare's bridle, rubbing her muzzle and cheek to gentle her even as his words sought to gentle and persuade his daughter. "Cethlinn . . . Cethlinn . . . can you and those of the new way not see that half of those who linger here do so not out of love for the Faith, but out of fear of the future? I have seen them kneel to the Stones and kiss them as though the Stones were living beings capable of being bribed and pandered to like so many corrupt magistrates. And I have seen you, High Priestess of the Stone, encourage such behavior when you know full well that it would be better to see only a handful of true pilgrims gather here—a few who truly seek to understand—than to risk the corruption of the faith of the ancients for the sake of fools who imagine they can manipulate the forces of Creation with a kiss, a genuflection, and the offering of a few tawdry baubles!"

"Tawdry!" Cethlinn made a rude noise. "Have you forgotten the days of darkness, Father? I have not. This winter was short and mild, and the summer before it was long and sweet. But what of the future? We cannot yet predict the weather. And so I tell you that it is the gold of fools that will maintain our monuments and the life-style that allows us the luxury of a peaceful existence dedicated to the pursuit of knowledge. And it is the gold of fools that will buy us the manpower necessary to guard our sacred realms when those who no longer revere our faith seek to plunder our settlements if the days of darkness return."

"Never," he replied, and continued on with sarcasm. "You of the new way have made certain of that, with all of your carefully placed superstitious ramblings about how eternal life blessings may be granted to anyone who makes pilgrimage here to stand in the shadow of the Stones at the rising of the midsummer sun. What drivel! Life itself *is* the blessing."

"Of course. I know it. You know it. But you must also know as well as I that most men need their fables and their magic, Father. If they believe that the rising of the midsummer sun shall grant them life blessings, what does it matter? Who is hurt? They come to us. They imagine that we grant them what they need. Then they go, strengthened by their faith, most leaving compensation... making it worthwhile for all concerned."

His eyes narrowed. "I do not like such reasoning, Cethlinn. It stinks of expedience. The Fates cannot be manipulated by man or by high priestesses with tendencies to overstep their authority. I have been lenient with you and your followers. I tell you this not as your father, Cethlinn, but as Cromm Cruach, Supreme Lord of the Stone. Go out now to Gorias. Welcome him. But tell him to leave his swords with the wolves in the wood. The beasts are best suited to guard the weapons of the beast."

She looked at Balor, contemptuous and imploring. "Tell him how it is with the world. Tell him what you and I endured together. Perhaps he will listen to you... you whom he believes can be the Mighty One without a sword in your hand!"

"It is as she says," he said, rising. "My grandfather once believed as you do, Star Gazer. Long ago, before I was born, he set aside an island to be revered as a holy place. It was to be a place of sacrifice and meditation, a place inviolate, dedicated to the gods to whom my people swear. Each year he made pilgrimage there, and although he had many enemies, no man would come against him on that holy ground. Until one day an enemy arose who had no sense of anything more holy than his own greed. My grandfather, unarmed, was struck down. And of all of my people on that island that day, only my father and uncle and our wise man remain alive... to be haunted by memories that need not have been."

Star Gazer's eyes went small and sharp. "And your people... did they have their vengeance? Is that why you are now wandering the world with no kin to name as your own?"

The question cut him. "It is," he said. "But their vengeance was not complete. In my hands it shall be done and finished forever."

"Vengeance is never done, my boy. It is the beast in us, the wolf waiting to be roused . . . always, again and again, until in the end, when at last we consume our enemy, we find that we have also consumed ourselves. The Mighty One shall understand this. The Mighty One shall be a warrior of wisdom and for truth, and he shall need no sword, for although he shall come to his kingdom in days of darkness, he shall be a wizard such as the world has never known."

Cethlinn snorted. "We wait for a different savior, Father!" She reached a hand out to Balor. "Come. Ride with me. I have a message to deliver across the river, to the 'wolves.'"

Balor hesitated, waiting for Cromm Cruach to tell him to stay, but Star Gazer said, "Go, if you must. Each man must seek the truth in his own way. Whatever path he takes, it shall lead him to his Destiny."

Balor cursed him for his fatalism as he took Cethlinn's hand and leaped up behind her onto the back of the mare. They galloped across the plain, along the wide arm of the river until they reached the shallows and urged the mare forward. She plunged ahead eagerly, swimming across the deepest section, out toward the far bank and the dark woods beyond. Where the wolves were waiting.

He did not expect to be laughed at. Nor did he expect such a small and motley-looking group of men. There were no more than a dozen. They wore no wool, but only skins and leather; and if they had swords with them, Balor could not see them, nor were horses visible. They came out of the trees, Gorias and three others leading the rest, obviously subservient. Gorias carried a lance; a long lance, stone tipped, with the slender shaft bound in leather.

"Ho! Wizard! Again we meet! I, Gorias, promise, is so?"

Balor stayed on the mare as Cethlinn dismounted and to his amazement went directly into the embrace of the largest man in the group. He lifted her off her feet and swung her around, rousing laughter out of her as he put her down again and held her in his arms just that second longer than Balor would have allowed had the choice been his to make.

He was the biggest man that Balor had ever seen. Even

among the men of the clan MacLir, this one would be a giant. Shaggy, weather-brittled brown hair fell back over his shoulders to his waist, and his flowing mustache seemed as long and ill-tended. Broad-backed, big-bellied, he came forward on limbs as broad as mature pine trees. It must have taken an entire warren of rabbits to form the leggings that were cross-laced about his enormous calves, and the biggest ox that Balor could imagine must have died to provide his short, tight-fitting, tatter-edged tunic. He wore a massive belt, but it was not visible until he hitched it up and readjusted the weight of his enormous midsection. Balor was certain that he had seen mares full of foal that were not so swollen; but if there was fat on that great mounding, he could not see it. It was as taut as a war drum and carried in as belligerent a manner.

"Where are the swords? You said you would bring swords!" Balor asked Gorias irritably, loudly, in the tone of a command, but his eyes were on the man who held Cethlinn, hot and angry, wanting him to see in them the statement that Cethlinn was *his* woman now.

The man saw the jealousy and the anger in his eyes. He released Cethlinn and lowered his head like a bull set to charge. It seemed to Balor that the earth trembled beneath his feet as the giant stalked up to Balor's mount and looked the youth straight in the eye. He was *that* tall. And *that* close. Balor could smell his breath and see the flash of his strong, white teeth as he snarled with open hostility and spoke in the S-shhing dialect, which the youth would later come to associate with certain tribes from the northernmost reach of the Far Island, Eireann.

"By all of the puking injustices of all of the turd-brained lords in all of this world, Cethlinn! Is *this* what you have chosen to be the Mighty One after all of these years of waiting? Is *this* what your sacred omens and 'signs' have led you to when all along you might have had *me*? I'll not believe it! He's naught but a teat-sucking infant with cheeks as soft as a baby's ass! I doubt if his balls have even dropped yet! Come on, whelp, don't stare at me! Get down off that horse and let's see if you're a man under those priestly garments!"

The winter chill went through Balor as he met the giant's eyes. They were small, as black and polished as beads of Brittany jet. Equally dark brows formed a single, querulous storm cloud over the bridge of his high, wide, crooked nose, which had the look of having been broken more than once. So when the man reached to pull Balor from the mare, Balor felt an obligation to break that nose once again.

He did, with a sure, swift brutal smash of his left fist. He still favored his right arm, and his left was not quite so powerful, so the blow was not as strong as it would have been had it been dealt before his injury. Nonetheless he felt the crush of bone and cartilage as the big man, taken totally off guard, went back and down from the force of the blow. He landed hard on his buttocks, grabbing at his face and cursing as blood oozed through his hairy-backed fingers.

Balor stared, rubbing his bruised knuckles, resenting the pain the blow had brought to him, not knowing quite how to react. Cethlinn laughed at the giant's expense, as did his comrades and Gorias.

"Well," said she, "we know whose balls have dropped now, don't we! Or would you like to ask that question of my 'teat-sucking' baby again, eh, Findias?"

Her words embarrassed Balor. He had dropped the giant where he stood, but he *did* feel like an infant sitting there, with all eyes upon him and Cethlinn gloating up at him as though he were a prized offspring rather than her lover. These men *were* men—tried and hardened by the years. He could see it in their faces and in the way they carried themselves. Despite their rough clothing, there was assurance and authority and more than a little arrogance about them. He envied their years and experience, and wondered, given his luck, if he would live long enough to be like them. Thinking that he might as well start trying now, he swung his left leg casually over the back of the mare, allowing his ankle to rest across his thigh as he assumed what he hoped would be a posture of restrained and nonchalant dignity. It worked for a moment. Until the big man on the ground began to get to his feet and the mare nervously shifted her weight without warning. Then Balor fell off.

They sat in a clearing, between the woods and the river, while Findias, the giant, scooped up mud from the bank to pack onto his nose. To Balor's surprise, the man was not angry. He explained that after weeks of traveling with Gorias and listening to him rave about the assets of Cethlinn's Mighty One—a role he had long coveted for himself—he had been bound and determined to see what the youth was made of.

"If you had taken the insult, I would have been sorely disappointed in you and in Cethlinn."

"I am glad that you approve," she said drolly, coming close to see if she could assist him with his mudpack.

"I do *not* approve! The youth *is* a youth. After all of these years of waiting, Cethlinn . . . well, I would have thought that you would at least want a *man* in your bed."

Balor rose angrily, but the giant growled amiably and gestured him down. "You see! You're too quick to rise to your passions. That's the trouble with youth. No control. No experience. In battle or in bed. I said sit *down*, boy! Now, Gorias has told me that you would learn to fight with the long blade . . . that as a debt of gratitude for your kindness to his little girl, he has promised to teach you. But he has done better than that. Since I am a master of the long blade, Gorias, generous man that he is, has agreed to release me from a debt I owe to him only when I have taught you to handle this weapon. So while the others here are offering their arms to protect the People of the Stone, you and I shall be otherwise engaged, Balor. What clan did you say you came from?"

"I am not a boy. And I have not named my clan."

"Why not? I've never liked a 'man' with secrets. It usually means he has something to hide and can't be trusted."

"He saved my life at the risk of his own," informed Cethlinn. "And not for any hope of reward, but for honor's sake. He *can* be trusted."

"*Hmmph*. If you say so. Who am I to argue with the High Priestess of the Stone, eh? Only a man. Only a clan lord in my own country. Only a tried and proven warrior who has made pilgrimage to Albion every year in the last ten in the hope of winning her and the title, which now, it seems, shall be given to one more pleasing to her and to the Fates. Impossible to figure the Fates. Almost as impetuous as women! But who knows? After he's housebroken, in ten years or so, perhaps he might begin to show possibilities as a fighter. At least he knows enough to strike first when he's approached by a man with trouble on his mind."

Balor was on his feet again. Furious. "It shall not take me ten years to master the use of your long blade. Is that how long it took you? Seeing your size and clumsiness, I would not be at all surprised. But tell me, Findias, where *is* your sword? In your mouth perhaps, for surely it is big enough!"

The giant laughed, pleased to note that his remarks and jealousy had roused antagonism in the youth. He clucked his tongue, admonishing and provoking all at once, liking the young man despite himself. He knew that he had never had much hope of winning Cethlinn. Brawn and bravery were not enough. The stars had been against him from the first. She would have only the one chosen by the Fates. By omens. By signs. He eyed the young man. There was something vaguely familiar about him; he could not quite say what it was. There was good blood in him and good breeding. Better than most. Gorias had told him that it was said that he could fight with either hand, and like a demon. He had struck down three armed men single-handed, so Cethlinn had gotten safely home against all odds. Young, yes. But he was right when he said that he was no boy. There was a hardness to him, a resolve that was rare in youth. The dark brows twitched on the giant's forehead. His mustache followed suit as he pursed his lips and thought, *There is something about this lad, something deep in those strange, pale eyes, like a dark, cold current running beneath the surface of a warm summer sea, something of the haunted and pursued, as though a wolf ran at his back.* Yes. He had the look of one born to battle. Good reach. Good eye. Quick reflexes and good balance, if one did not count his slipping from the horse. It would be interesting to see how he handled a sword. But not yet. The youth *had* won Cethlinn, after all, and Findias's nose hurt miserably. He would make the youth squirm a while as penalty; he owed him something, even though he had as much as asked for the blow.

The swords had been left within a stand of hawthorn trees at the edge of the wood, lest the sight of them offend any People of the Stone who might have crossed the river with Cethlinn. The swords had been wrapped in Findias's huge, heavy cloak of sealskins and carefully camouflaged beneath a scattering of leaves. No passerby would have noticed them, and even if he had, it was said that the hawthorn, a sacred tree, would move to protect the swords, raising its roots from the ground to strangle anyone who might seek to take them. Nevertheless, Findias's brother Ogma had remained in the wood to guard them.

The giant's summons called him to join the others. He was young, and his looks clearly marked him as Findias's brother, although he had not half the giant's size, and the set of his even, beardless features betrayed a disposition as mild as the spring morning. He was glad to leave the shade, for although the flowers of the hawthorn made a pretty cover, they also made him sneeze. He carried the bundle of weapons out into the sunlight in his outstretched arms and deposited it gently, with obvious reverence, upon the ground within the circle of men who gathered to claim them. Slowly he unrolled the sealskin, and the swords relaxed from their bunching; they made no sound of metal against metal, for each was sheathed according to its owner's fancy. Thirteen swords. One for each man. And one more.

After attaching his own weapon to the loop at his belt, Gorias took up the last sword and turned to Balor. His carnelian eyetooth glinted red. "Here. Take! For you I bring. As gift of thanks. For friend of heart. Macha say you learn use from Findias. Make you great warrior. Then you come to island of Macha. Take her as woman someday!"

"Ha!" exclaimed Cethlinn, frowning, but obviously amused. "My people save her life and now she wants to claim my man as her own. She has a bold streak, that child!"

"It is natural for a child to seek out the company of another child," drawled the giant, his eyes fairly glowing with merriment at Balor's expense.

But it was Gorias who replied, not succeeding in his attempt to suppress a smile. "Balor is man to Macha. Not child. She say she share him with lady priest. Macha, she generous."

Laughter rippled among the men. Balor reached for the sword, and as he took it from Gorias, a rush of heat filled him. He stared at it, braced, expecting it to be heavy, as Retaliator had been heavy. But this blade had not the massive dimensions of his father's sword; it was not as long, nor was it as broad across the blade. But it *was* a sword, and it was *his*!

"Mine. . . ? Truly mine. . . ?" he asked, incredulous. He had expected the jewel-toothed man to return, and with swords; but he had never in all of his most audacious dreams imagined that Gorias would bring to him that which he most desired in all of the world: a sword of his own.

Gorias seemed to read his mind. His smile deepened as he inclined his head forward, assenting. "Yours," he said.

The blade was hidden within a scabbard of finely woven wicker laced over a protective frame of wood, yet Balor could feel the substance of the bronze within it. In his mind's eye he could see the darkly golden metal even before he withdrew it from the scabbard and held it up to the light of morning. Naked, honed and polished to a sleek and burnished sheen, it drew the light into itself even as it reflected it outward, searing Balor's eyes until they teared.

By the Fates, he thought, was Cethlinn right? Had the hand of Destiny driven him from the holding of Bracken Fen? Had the Twelve Winds struck him down, only to raise him up again amid the People of the Stone so that through them he might yet fulfill the dreams of his boyhood and the vow of vengeance he had sworn in his youth?

A fire was burning within him; the sword had ignited it. All of the soft, gentle memories of the long, peaceful winter he had not wanted to end were suddenly erased. He heard the rising wind. He felt it not as an external thing, not warm and sweet with the scent of hawthorn blossoms. This was an internal rising, a stirring within his soul that was as cold as the storm winds that had howled across the fens in the days of darkness. Somewhere, from so far away that the sound was barely perceptible, he heard the cry of a wolf. A single slashing cry, a tearing, a growling deep within him. He tensed, listening, but the sound was gone, leaving a gash across his awareness, a sense that somehow he was bleeding—hot, dark blood. It filled him with a sense of purpose and power. He could feel it burning in his eyes as he looked at Cethlinn. His hand curled around the haft of the sword so tightly that it ached, but the pain was pleasure to him as he held it out toward her, leveling it so that it pointed as though it were an extension of his arm.

"You have given me back my luck, woman. With this I shall fulfill my Destiny. With this I shall take the head of Nemed MacAgnomain!"

There was not a one of them who did not know the name or fail to react to it.

"You? A boy? Take the head of *that* one? Do it, and I *shall* accept you as the Mighty One!"

Cethlinn looked up at the giant angrily. "Do not encourage him in his folly!" Her eyes found Balor, spitting him with unexpected anger. "Even now . . . is that still the scope of your ambitions? Vengeance?"

"It is what I live for. I have made no secret of that."

She glared at him, watching as he tested the weight of the sword, balancing it, admiring it; his eyes glowed as though he held the world.

The giant was measuring him thoughtfully, nodding in unspoken appreciation of the scope of the youth's intent; yet he knew vengeance against Nemed to be a fool's ambition and said so.

Balor was sick of the mockery and criticism. He faced Findias and glowered at him. With the sword in his hand he felt no fear of the giant's great size. "I *will* take the life of Nemed. When the sun rises over the sacred Marking Stone on the dawn of the midsummer solstice, my promise to stay among the People of the Stone shall have been fulfilled. I *will* seek out Nemed MacAgnomain, even if I must search in every land and across every sea of the world. And when I find him, I *will* take his head. With this sword in my hand, no one shall be able to stop me!"

"Ha! The flea will scratch the dog to death!" laughed the giant, shaking his head. "You will not get near enough to him to slash out at his shadow before his guardsmen cut you down!"

"No? Try me!" Balor was drunk with confidence as he took the stance of one ready to parry a blow.

It was a mistake. There was a great, dark blur suddenly leaping out at him, and somehow his sword flew from his hand as the giant's blade swiped it away on the backstroke. Pain flared in his hand as his entire right side went numb. As he had felled the giant with an unexpected blow, so now the giant felled him. One moment he was standing, the next he was sprawled on the ground, stunned but unhurt except for his deeply gashed pride. It bled into anger as, shaking his head to clear it, he got to his feet, retrieved his sword, and protested that the giant had taken unfair advantage of his reach.

"Fair?" Findias turned the word as though it offended him to speak it. "If you would go against Nemed to kill him, you had best strike that word from your vocabulary. There is nothing fair in a death battle, boy. With Nemed there is only victory and death. Which one you shall win can be determined by the measure of your strength and resolve and the skill and cleverness with which you use your sword. If you believe that the Fates shall deal fairly with you, then indeed you are a fool!"

"Here, boy, stand to me. My reach is not as great as your own." The challenge came from one of the other men, a brown-haired fellow with a long, narrow face, a slim body, and eyes that shone without threat or mockery. "Go ahead. Try to take me. We shall see what you can do when you are more evenly matched."

The man seemed friendly, and Balor was certain that he could win, even though his arm still tingled from the force of Findias's blow. He could feel stress deep inside his newly healed clavicle. He shifted his weapon to his left hand and waited for a look of surprise to come to his challenger's face. When it did not appear, he knew that Gorias had told the man that he, Balor, could fight equally well with either hand. Balor smiled confidently and gripped the hilt of his sword tightly, as though it were a dagger, jabbing outward with it, bending low as he began to circle his opponent.

"I would not hold my weapon quite like that if I were you, Balor . . . your balance, it is all wrong . . . and the angling of the blade. No. No. Here, like this . . ."

Balor was not smiling anymore. His sword was flying again. Now his left hand was numb. The man had come at him with finesse. Balor stood staring at him, disarmed and gaping, blushing as red as a virgin caught naked at her bath, trying not to hear the laughter of others at his expense.

"Come. Try again. And this time follow the blade. Do not try to squeeze it to death." The man's name was Fal. His tone was as sweet as the hawthorn blossoms, but mockery was in his eyes now, as sharp as any of the giant's insults.

Balor snatched up his sword. He stood to the ready, summoning up all that he remembered of fighting technique as it had been taught to him on the training field of Bracken

Fen. But except for his brief and unfortunate encounter with Retaliator, he had never held a sword before, save in his dreams. In less time than it took to parry the weapon twice, Fal easily broke through his defenses and had the point of his own sword at Balor's throat.

"That is a *sword* that Gorias has brought for you, boy. Not a dagger, spear, or ax. You must honor it for what it is. Feel its balance. Follow it, do not lead. Listen to it as it speaks to your own flesh through its own."

"Aye!" hissed Balor and, with an unexpected feint back and to one side, put himself out of Fal's reach as he stood ready to challenge him once again. "I have told you. I am no boy! Come. I shall prove it to you now!" They came at one another, slashing and parrying. The air rang with the high song of the blades as they met and fell away and met again. Balor had the feel of the weapon now. He was following Fal's instructions. Cethlinn cried out in protest that the battle was too much in earnest, but the men who stood watching assured her that all would be well. They cheered for Fal and for the youth whose spirit and unwillingness to be cowed by defeat had won their unanimous approval.

"He *does* have the instinct," said the giant, then shouted to the youth. "Yes! Good! Well done! You learn quickly, by the Fates, you do!"

Gorias was nodding, excited and wishing to aid the boy whom he had armed. "Your blade is named Teacher. Forged for you. Learn. It will instruct. Yes! Like so! Do not trust eyes. Eye is treacherous. Eye can be fooled. Let the sword lead! You follow! Yes! Is so!"

Gorias's suggestions were well meant, but instinct, like any good blade, must be honed to sharpness. The sword Teacher was sharp, but Balor's instincts needed much in the way of refinement. He tended to work against the weight of the blade, and soon Fal's weapon hissed close beneath his ear, raising a long line of pearling drops of blood along the young man's neck. It was a minor wounding, a hairline slice that barely penetrated the skin. But Balor knew, as did those who watched, that Fal could have taken his head if he had so desired. His fingers reached up to probe the wound. He felt the warmth of his blood. Passion and pride and arrogance drained out of him with it.

Fal saw that Balor had been sobered. He nodded, satisfied.

He had sought to bring the youth down a peg or two. "You should know, boy, before you challenge the most feared and hated of all warlords, that I am considered to be no more than a mediocre swordsman. Nemed is a master, and his guardsmen are recruited from the finest fighters in the world."

Frustration and shame silenced him as Fal put his weapon into its scabbard and requested that Gorias and Findias give them a display of true swordsmanship. They did so gladly. Balor stood mute with awe, realizing what a fool he had made of himself. After all these months it seemed that he had changed little from the thoughtless, impetuous boy who had fled from Bracken Fen. Yes, he had won the weapon of his dreams, but it was useless in his hands; it was one thing to possess a sword, and another entirely to become its master.

27

They sat together along the wide arm of the river. The water ran before them, dark and cool, racing away toward the distant sea. Beyond it the sacred plain stretched away, green with spring, and they could see the great circle of trilithons rising in the distance, burnished gold by the morning sun.

They spoke of many things, Cethlinn and Findias the giant, and Gorias and Fal, and Ogma and Muri, a yellow-haired fellow whose short, ruddy beard looked as if he had scorched it. There were seven other men of Eireann whose names were unpronounceable to Balor. None was offended or surprised by Cromm Cruach's refusal to grant his permission for them to bring their weapons onto the sacred plain; they had assumed as much when he had not ridden out across the river with Cethlinn and Balor. Still, they were perplexed by his reasoning and spoke of recent raids on unfortified gathering places of the faithful, both in Eireann and Albion, and even as far away as those settlements upon the shores of Land Beyond the Sea, which had heretofore been untouched by the violence of the times. Sooner or later, they said, men who held no reverence for the ancient faith of the Stones were going to covet the wealth that accumulated on the sacred plain of the Great Stone Circle during the festivities accompanying the rising of the midsummer sun.

Many of the pilgrims left armed escorts camped along the river, but it was the opinion of the men of Eireann that unless they were prepared to fight in concert, these guards would be nearly as vulnerable as those they sought to protect. These were sobering words, and Cethlinn brooded as she listened. She was certain that only the fear of angering the spirits of the sacred Stones had kept the raiders at bay so far, but she was not so naive as to pretend that there were not men to whom monetary gain, taken by whatever means, *was* luck, men who held no faith in stones or stars or in any deity demonstrably less forceful than themselves. These were the men who haunted her dreams—dark, shadowy figures such as those who had beset her and Balor in the woods . . . men who took pleasure in spilling the blood of the unwary and the innocent . . . men who had multiplied and grown strong during the long days of darkness and now overran the earth in great, dark tides like rats flushed from an ill-tended granary at summer's end.

The thought made her shiver. She eyed the men of Eireann dubiously. She had expected so many more of them. "Twelve men. What can twelve men do if raiders should fall upon the plain in any great number?"

Fal replied enthusiastically. "Twelve men can be a beginning, and can convince others to join them. Twelve men with bronze swords are equal to three times that number without them! We shall be watchdogs for the faithful and see to it the guards who escort the pilgrims do not forget that they have come to protect, not to fleece, their masters. I have seen it happen. When the scent of greed taints the wind, men can turn on one another like hungry dogs, mindless of all meaning of honor."

He paused and swung his head back and forth as he rubbed his long, narrow jaw and fingered his closely clipped beard. "Is it any wonder that the spirits of the ordered universe have turned away from us in disgust? Upon the far shores of Eireann we implore the heavens to restore our good fortune to us, but even the Singing Stone of Destiny stands silent in its hidden glen. It sings no more, nor shall it sing until the Mighty One rises to unite the clans, to drive the foreign intruders from our shores. So it is that we have come to

Albion to serve the priests of the Stone, hoping to find the Chosen One, daring to wish that we might bring good fortune to ourselves so that we might share it with our people in Eireann."

His words were heady stuff, but Balor frowned, annoyed by their overtones of superstition, remembering his mother's legends and his father's mockery of them. "Stones do not sing," he said. "Nor, I think, do they grant blessings." He ignored the glare of the men of Eireann and was surprised to hear Fal agree with him.

"They do not if they are *ordinary* stones. But the stones that comprise the sacred trilithon of Albion are not ordinary stones, nor are the menhirs that mark the star risings through all of the northwestern world. And the Singing Stone of Destiny alone holds the echoing song of the beginning of the world; the voice of Creation is locked within it. It was the first stone to be raised by man. Through it the first lightning bolt infused the earth with the glory and power of the infinite. The man who raised the Singing Stone was also struck by the lightning. Its power is in his seed, sleeping through all of the generations. When the Mighty One comes— the one who has been foretold—the Stones shall know him, shall rise up to protect him against his enemies, and imbue all who follow him with their strength. And when at last he stands before the Singing Stone of Destiny, it shall sing a wondrous song to him, for it shall know and name him as kindred." He paused and took a summing look at Balor; a look that clearly found him wanting. "All deference to the good lady priest, boy, but I do not think the Stone of Destiny shall sing to you."

As so often happened these days, images of the past flooded Balor's vision, unsettling him. He saw the boy, the moor, the dark night full of sound and hidden terrors. He saw the white wolf stalking him in the darkness and the great, flaming star marking a burning pathway across the heavens—a pathway that had led him to the tor and the sheltering circle of stones beneath it, a circle that had not been there in the light of day. And now new images intruded—Huldre whispering in the night of enchanted islands and a stone singing in a misted secret glen of the menhirs he and Cethlinn had walked past through the dark and dangerous woods of Albion. And of himself, looking ever back, fighting the sensation that somehow the stones were watching him, following him, as though they wished to warn him against the dangers that had lain ahead.

The reverie was discomfiting. He was glad when Cethlinn's sharply voiced rebuke shattered it. "Think what you will, Fal, but time will prove the truth of my claim. In time, when he has become a priest of the Stone, the Singing Stone of Destiny shall sing for him. In time this youth shall prove to you all that he *is* the one who has been foretold. The signs, the omens, they all confirm it."

"Time! Signs! Omens!" Muri, the yellow-haired man, spat the word, then hacked up phlegm and spat that too. He sat hunkered down, balancing upon the balls of his feet as he rested strong, hairy blond forearms across his broad knees. "We are beset *now*. If we wait much longer for the promised Mighty One, when at last he comes forth to us—if in fact he exists—there shall be no clansmen in all of the islands of the Western Sea left to stand with him against our enemies, for we shall all have been slain or enslaved. My respects to you, Priestess, but this youth you bring out to us . . . he *is* a youth. No man of Eireann would follow him."

A low chuckle came out of Findias, but there was none of his usual merriment in it. It was full of memories and regret. "The men of Eireann follow naught but their own stubborn pride. I wonder if even the promised Mighty One could ever hope to unite the chieftains of the clan kingdoms of the far island. For surely the Wolf could not, and there were many who thought that he was the one foretold. Fomor, son of Manannan MacLir—now *there* was a man for you . . . a lord I would have followed into the black belly of the Otherworld without ever looking back."

The mention of his father's name set the ground reeling beneath him. He stared, dry-mouthed, tense as a runner set to sprint.

"You knew the MacLir?" pressed Fal, his eyes full of eagerness to know more.

"I saw him. Aye," affirmed the giant. "When I was a stripling lad brought by my father to the great clan councils. Never was there a man born to equal him. The great Fomor, avenger of Manannan, slayer of Partholon, warlord of the Western Sea. No man could stand to him. None in all the world."

Muri spat again; a long, clear arc of fluid that landed in the grass not far from Findias, knocking a beetle flat as it spattered. "He was a sea pirate like all the rest!" he said, making it quite clear that he did not share the giant's enthusiasm.

But the giant would not be cooled on his subject. "Aye!" he proclaimed. "Like his father, he was one of the greatest of them all! But since you are not a man of the coast, you do not know how it was in the days when he ruled from his stronghold upon the wild cliffs of Eireann and made Tory Isle a place of sanctuary. Where he conquered, there was justice. Those who swore fealty to him were allowed to remain lords in their own territories, for it was his intention to create a great confederation of the clans. He raided only trading settlements and the holdings of those who sided with foreigners against him. And for many years, by the Fates, it was rumored that the Mighty One *had* come, for the clans were being united. But after a while, the chieftains began to resent his overlordship. They began to fight amongst themselves. Like rabid wolves they were, slashing and tearing at one another, and at the back of the MacLir himself. In time he wearied of it. He took his great ships and unfurled his sails of green, Manannan's color, and sailed away with his women and his priest and all of his clansmen. He put his back to the warfare and endless strife of Eireann. Never again was he seen or heard from until, a few years ago, rumor came to Eireann that he and all of his clan had died of plague somewhere here in Albion." The disheveled head swung slowly back and forth. "By the Fates, he deserved better than that. But then, he had the woman with him—the white-haired beauty of the North—trouble she was to him from the first. So many men hungered to have her. Many a time I have cursed my own father's bones in his barrow, for he was one of those who, for want of her, spun rumors that turned the clans against the Wolf. But then, he should have known; he was warned when he took her away from the slaughter scene that he had made of the house of Partholon, that she was a Huldre...."

It was Balor who asked him the meaning of the word—the meaning of his mother's name—although he barely knew that he spoke the question. Somehow he knew what Findias's reply would be before he spoke it.

"A Huldre...ach...'tis a word from the far land of the

North Wind. 'Tis the name they give to certain spirits there—enchantresses, creatures of unnatural beauty. Of flesh they seem to be, but in truth they are born not of man, but of mist. Their home is in the cold, damp heart of the northern marshes, and when they rise like a cloud above the bogs, it is to lure men to their death. Bad luck, a huldre. A man who takes one as his woman, he takes death to his hearth as well."

Soon they broke out flasks of mead and sat around, talking and drinking and eating from their well-stocked traveling larder. Balor was not hungry, nor had he much of a thirst for their mead, but they forced it on him, and soon he was drinking deeply; the words Findias the giant had spoken concerning Huldre had deeply disturbed him. Balor the Unlucky... Balor, Bringer of Disaster... had he won those names because he was her son? Had Munremar been right after all? No! It could not be! She had not brought death to Fomor. She had not even managed to win that for Nemed, even though she would gladly have risked every man and woman in the clan to achieve that end. How then could she have brought bad luck to him? No. He had done that himself. All alone. Through his constant refusal to obey the laws of the clan.

The conversation of the men of Eireann drifted, and soon, once again, he was the butt of their jokes. They found his display of swordsmanship a great source of merriment. Two of them rose to imitate his ineptitude. After a while, staggering from the mead, he rose and asked Gorias to use his lance. With this lean, long, finely balanced weapon, he demonstrated a skill that impressed them all, even Findias, who then produced an ax and a dagger and a sling, each of which Balor used with equal finesse. Cethlinn was delighted as the men of Eireann loosed whistles and cluckings of admiration. In turn, each of them rose to match him in spontaneous contests, and at each he was victorious until Findias, thoroughly annoyed, came forth with a cudgel cut to his own dimensions. Balor could barely lift it, let alone hurl it. He conceded defeat, and the giant was mollified. Now Balor was on better terms with them all.

Later he would ask them what they put into their mead, for it seemed more potent than the mead of Albion. Soon his lips were numb and his head was reeling. He rose to stand close to the river's edge, breathing deeply to steady himself. Cethlinn came close to him and put a soft, sure hand upon his forearm.

"They will stand with you in time, when you have become a master swordsman, when you have become a priest of the Stone. All but one of the prophecies will have been fulfilled. You *shall* be proclaimed as the Mighty One, and the clans will unite under your name. Together then, if it is still your will, you can go against Nemed MacAgnomain. With their combined strength at your back, you will take his head and know the vengeance you have so long desired. But you must go together. The law of Creation will be against you if you try to go alone against Nemed."

He could feel the mead working deep inside him. His mind felt thick, his face flushed, and everywhere, from scalp to toes, there was a warm tingling sensation that made him feel very secure and very serious and, strangely, very prone to laugh. "I would keep the law. I have learned that it is unlucky not to keep it. I might yet prove to be lucky if I kept a law. Any law. Any law at all. The law of Creation will do. Yes. For a start."

She saw that he was drunk and smiled, taking full advantage of the moment. "Swear to keep it, then. Swear, by the law of Creation, that you shall be sanctified as a priest of the Stone, that you shall stand with me in the shadow of the sacred Marking Stone on the dawn of the rising of the midsummer sun as my man forever. Swear it, and I vow in return that in time all men shall kneel to you as the Mighty One, and the luck of all the world will be with us both!"

It was amazing how mead could make things seem so uncomplicated. He turned. The men of Eireann were staring at him. He frowned, trying to bring them into focus. "Is she right? If I were the Mighty One, would you stand with me against Nemed?"

"Aye, boy! If it was your will... if you were the Mighty One." It was Fal who replied, grinning out of his narrow face, his eyes as sharp as a civet's.

They were all grinning. One of them said that he hoped that Nemed lived to be a very old man so that he would be alive when the Mighty One was at last ready to come against him. Indeed, Findias added, they must all live to be very old so that they could stand with Balor when at last he learned how to use a sword.

They laughed. They all laughed, except Balor. The sun was climbing toward noon. The day had grown very warm. His head had begun to ache. The men's laughter buzzed in his head like insects. By the Fates, after all he had shown them of his prowess with a man's weapons, they still laughed at him. They still saw fit to humiliate him in front of Cethlinn. Later he would wonder just how he had allowed the madness to take hold of him. Perhaps it was the mead; he had never been able to hold his liquor. But more likely it was simply his own nature running wild, like the white wolf that howled in his dreams.

"I will show you," he said. "I will make you choke on your laughter!"

They watched as he went to the mare, mounted, and rode drunkenly across the river with Cethlinn at his back, her thighs pressed against him, her arms wrapped tightly about his waist. Together they galloped across the shallows and raced across the sacred plain toward the Temple of the Standing Stones.

And there it was done in a state of drunken rage. He leapt from the mare, and with a less than sober Cethlinn at his side, he strode past the sacred Marking Stone, down the raised Avenue of Processions, through the outer embankment, and into the flat expanse of the inner circle of trilithons.

Cromm Cruach was there, busy with his endless computations, marking off geometrical alignments. He had his little bundle of staking sticks, the long, knotted cord by which he kept track of his figures, and a long winding of string.

"What is this?" He eyed them both warily. "What do you want here, Daughter? The youth is drunk!"

Cethlinn ignored him. "Swear now," she goaded Balor softly. "Consecrate yourself to the priesthood of the Stone. Do it now."

He looked up. The sun seared his vision. Knives of light pierced him, blinded him, yet he moved forward, as though drawn by instinct.

"No, boy!" Cromm Cruch said. "Not until you are ready! Until you are sure! Not like this; you debase yourself and the Stones when you come to them like this!"

Balor did not heed the warning. He stood at the open end

of the circle of trilithons, reaching outward so that both hands made contact with the Stone, and beneath the light of noon he swore to the moon and the sun and the Twelve Winds, which had brought his people from Eireann to Albion in the days before his birth, that he would fulfill the Destiny to which the great white star had led him so long ago.

"I *shall* be the Mighty One! No man shall ever dare to laugh at me again! By the Fates, Time shall be my ally. I, Balor, grandson of Manannan MacLir, son of Fomor, Wolf of the Western Tribes, shall unite the clans of the Western Sea. Together we shall rise to drive Nemed MacAgnomain into oblivion! This I swear! This I vow: to fulfill my Destiny in blood . . . on the honor of my ancestors, in the name of the Stone to which I now consecrate my soul!"

Even before the last words were spoken, the wind that had risen in the wood beyond the river reached the plain, driving clouds before it. High clouds, as thin as mist, they shrouded the sun, turning the world gray and cold. Against Balor's palms the flesh of the Stone, only moments ago warm with sunlight, now went cold.

And far off in the distant hills wolves began to howl.

28

Once again the Planting Moon rose and set, and as the days and weeks went by, the fields and pastures surrounding Bracken Fen greened with promise. Yet today the dawn had risen red and cloud-shadowed, and as the day ripened, the sky had taken on the cold look of impending storm. But within the chieftain's roundhouse, Mealla and little Bevin paid no heed to it as they tended the baby, Babh, cleansing and rubbing her skin with soft, freshly picked ferns, which would later be discarded and burned in the refuse pits beyond the palisade. The lord had left the house just after dawn. Now that calving had begun, he and the other men spent most of their time with the herds. Elathan was with them. Since Balor's disappearance, when he was not occupied with the other youths of his age who had entered their

Year of Trial, he was always at Fomor's side, granting the chieftain the open adulation that Balor had once shown to him many years ago, before the fateful expedition to Point of Ale.

Huldre, as she always did when the lord was not there to stop her and Mealla was not paying attention, had left the house to walk the palisade to watch for signs of Balor, leaving little Babh in Mealla's care.

Mealla did not mind. She loved the baby as if it were her own. She smiled as she allowed little Bevin to swaddle the infant, taking the moment to put her work-roughened hands upon her hips, stretching back a bit to ease the stress on her lower back. The movement caused her breasts to ache, even though it was not yet her time to go to the House of Women to sit out her days of blood; indeed, she had missed her time now for two moons' passing, and only this morning she had sought out Blaheen so that the fat woman, so knowledgeable in the intricacies of Woman's Wisdom, might confirm her suspicion and tell her what she had so long desired to hear. And so it had been. At last! After having lived to savor over thirty-five summers, she, Mealla, first woman of the chieftain of the clan MacLir, was carrying her man's child; the child that she had despaired of ever bearing. How she wished that Fomor would hurry home! How she wished that he were here now, so she could share the news with him. For the first time in more years than she could remember, she felt young and beautiful and fully a woman. Surely it was yet another affirmation that the Twelve Winds were truly smiling upon his rule.

Little Bevin watched with delight as Mealla took up the baby and held her high, whirling her around as both woman and child laughed with unrestrained happiness. Bevin was glad to see them both so merry. She rejoiced with Mealla at the news of her pregnancy, and it was good to see little Babh laughing. The rowdy babe was no prettier than she had been on the dawn of her first breath. She was big for a female infant, slant-eyed, broad-nosed, furry-cheeked, with a swirling of tawny, reddish hair as brittle as that of a goat. But what she lacked in looks, she made up for in tenacity. Fomor *had* named her correctly. Everyone had agreed that, like the raven, she *would* be a survivor. Yet she had been cranky and colicky of late, so much so that Bevin was relieved to see her smiling.

So many of the babies seemed to be suffering from similar distress, and she herself had not been feeling very well. Often, after meals, her head ached, but it was such a mild ache that she had not complained about it, nor would she do so today lest she spoil Mealla's happiness. Besides, people were upset enough over the recent deaths of Dathen's baby and of poor, wattle-chinned old Enda, the stonecutter's woman. She had overheard Draga say to several of his companions that perhaps despite the continuing good weather and improved life-style of the clan, the Twelve Winds might be dissatisfied with the peaceful life to which his brother had led them. She had listened, angered and upset in some vague way that she had not fully understood. She had never liked the redbeard very much. He made her think of a sly, shiny-eyed fox, sleek and patient, waiting in the shadows of his den, watching for an unsuspecting mouse or unwary hare to pass by. Then he would pounce and eat his prey. And lick the blood from the ground and bury every scrap of bone and shaft of hair so that, when he retired into his den to wait for his next meal, his new victim would blunder into the same trap as the old. Of course, the fox was a clever creature and admired by many, but Draga made her nervous. She did not like the way he criticized her father behind his back. And it was unfair of him to suggest that Fomor was in any way responsible for the deaths of Enda and Dathen's baby. Had not the Wise One said that death was a natural portion of the Circle of Life? Nevertheless she had seen many faces looking furtively at Fomor as he stood beside the Wise One, listening respectfully as the priest officiated with much pomp and ceremony over each interment. And Bevin had sensed renewed restiveness drifting as a pall over the funeral processions, which had gone out to the barrow grounds, far beyond the palisade, upon sacred and consecrated land.

Often in the night, troubled by her headaches and unable to sleep, she would go out to look up at the stars. She tried to imagine them as torchlit processions of people in the Otherworld. There were thousands and thousands of wandering souls, Balor among them; he would be with Enda, and she would be holding Dathen's baby, and Bevin would smile, soothed by the thought of them together.

And often by day, when she sighted a hawk circling high above the land, she would wonder if Balor's soul had not returned to Bracken Fen, for surely she was convinced that when at last he returned to earth in the form he had chosen in the Otherworld, it must be as a hawk, so that he might at last soar high and live free and wild as he had never been allowed to do when he had dwelled among his own kind.

The knife went in. Hard. It pierced tunic and skin and muscle and would have gone straight into Echur's heart had Donn had his way. But the stocky, surly, younger man was not as tall as his opponent. He had misjudged the distance and had struck upward, as he had intended, but too high. The tip of his flint dagger struck Echur's sternum, sheared bone, and was deflected by it. Cursing, Donn drew the dagger down and would have jabbed again had Echur not stepped back. The wounded man's knees buckled. He dropped to a kneeling position, clutching at his chest, blood welling from his fingers. The expression on his face was clearly that of a man who expected to keel over and die any moment.

Donn looked down at him with disgust. The stupid fool! And he a man who had known battle in the days of glory! Surely Echur must know that had Donn pierced him with a heart-wounding, he would be in the Otherworld already. *A pity you are not*, he thought. *A pity there is not one less man to covet the fair Dana! By the Fates, shall she never choose a man? Does she take pleasure in the misery we suffer for want of her?*

They had just reentered the holding. They had seen Dana walking from the grain sheds with her little brother Lorcan, and when they had called out her name she had lowered her head and hurried her pace. The boy had looked back at them with a critical, why-don't-you-leave-my-sister-alone sort of frown. They chided him for it loudly, and she had stopped, turning to look at them out of those great, misty eyes. Any sort of a look from her was enough to set their hearts racing and their fevers rising. The other men who had been with them out on the pastures were filing through the open gateway behind them. They too spoke the girl's name and began to tease one another. Some of the comments were bold enough to make the girl blush.

"Is this how you hope to win me?" she cried, obviously distressed as, with one hand looped around her grain basket, she put her free hand on Lorcan's skinny shoulder and began to nudge him along ahead of her toward her family's roundhouse.

"Ahh, to be a boy again, and touched by the fair Dana! Truly, girl, we seek your heart and mean no offense," Echur called after her in a tone that was the essence of gallantry.

"I'll take *your* heart and serve it up to her on a trencher, old man, if you don't leave her alone!" Donn had said, squinting up at Echur belligerently, one hand on the hilt of his sheathed dagger at his belt, the other on the bridle of Echur's mount. "Get down from that horse, Grandfather, and we'll give the girl a show as to which of us is worthy to seek her heart—a young man like myself or an aging braggart like you—"

He had not finished the sentence before Echur leaped down at him. Dana screamed. The gathering herdsmen cheered, and in no time at all a crowd had gathered, dogs were barking and circling, and Echur was on his knees, convinced that he had been mortally wounded while Donn stood before him, menacing him with his bloodied dagger.

"Enough!" It was the chieftain's command. He had elbowed his way through the throng and now stood, with the healer at his right hand, staring at the cause of the melee. One look at the gray-eyed, golden-haired girl cowering next to Lorcan, her face wet with tears and pale with panic, told him what he wanted to know. His face was taut with anger as he told Dianket, who had been assisting him with a difficult calving most of the day, to check the extent of Echur's wound. A cursory look was all the healer needed. He informed the lord that Echur would live and be only little the worse for the wear of the wounding. The news did nothing to mollify the chieftain. His brows had met to form a single span above green eyes dark with controlled temper.

"You! Daughter of Draga! These men contest for you. Blood has been spilled between them a second time. Are you aware that this is so?"

"I . . . am aware. . . ."

"And are you aware that if death had been the result of this contest, the victor would then have had to pay the dead man's kindred his life-worth . . . the worth of all of the cattle and livestock and goods he could have been expected to gain for

hem during the span of his life? And if the victor could not
make this payment, then his own life would be forfeit by clan
aw?"

She tried to take a breath to calm herself, but it caught in
her throat. "I am . . . aware. . . ."

"Then I ask you now, daughter of Draga, before these
many witnesses—many of whom have also contested for you
and known the letting of blood in squabbles concerning your
name—to select one of these good clansmen as your own
before more blood is spilled for your sake."

She stared at him, and beneath the curl of her fingers she
squeezed the flesh of young Lorcan's shoulder so hard that he
squirmed and whimpered. She did not notice; she saw only
the face of the chieftain and knew that at last the moment she
had been dreading had arrived. She could not bear turning
away any man who might desire her, lest her repudiation
cause him pain and humiliation. Yet she could not bear the
thought of accepting any of them or lying with any of them; it
was the horror of that that struck her dumb now, with her
terror of childbirth.

"I . . . cannot. . . ." she whispered, and heard the murmuring
of resentment around her.

"So be it, then," the chieftain replied coldly. "In one
week's time I will expect your sire to come forth to me. He
shall name the man if you will not. Tradition will allow him
this prerogative. If he refuses to take it, then I, as chieftain,
will take mine. Let it be known that from this moment on any
man who bloods another in his attempt to secure your favor
will forfeit your favor. I have been lenient in this matter far
too long. I will not allow you to continue to be an element of
disharmony. You *will* be mated, girl. Tell your father that in
one week's time I expect to be given the name of the man
who will take you to his hearth."

Draga sat alone in the shadowed recesses of his roundhouse. He did not move as Morrigan entered. His hands lay
open and lax upon his thighs as he stared into the glowing
coals of the fire pit. He did not rouse himself to stir them,
nor did he relight the tallow lamp, which had gutted and
gone dark.

The young woman approached him slowly, upon bare,

silent feet as she held her infant close. The tiny boy slept peacefully in her arms; not even the cries of the crowd through which she had passed, ignoring the row between Echur and Donn, had disturbed him as she had crossed the holding to seek out Draga. She had seen him return from the far pastures, dismount, and hand the reins of his horse to one of the youths who had come to attend him. She had watched him stalk off, limping it seemed, to the bathhouse, and she had waited patiently for him to emerge and return to his roundhouse, and for Eala and Uaine to take the children out to the latrine before settling them in for the night. She had risen then and hurried to his dwelling, for she would not have much time before the women returned. She did not want them to hear what she must say to him; indeed, she would prefer if they did not know that she had been to see him at all.

Draga looked up at Morrigan as she spoke to him out of a shadowed face. With the last light of dusk blue behind her, she seemed to float upon the air like an apparition risen from a dream. Her voice reached out to him, so low that he strained to hear it, and then was sorry that he had.

"I have seen you in the night, late, so very late. I have seen you bending over the well shaft from which we all draw our water. Yes. I have seen you, Draga, with your little bags from which you empty something into the water after looking around to make certain that you are alone...."

He stared at her, speechless. He had been so careful, so very, very careful!

"For three days I have watched you. For three days now I have not drawn water from the well shaft, nor have I drunk from the water-storage crocks within my house. For three days now I have taken water only from the flasks I filled while gathering herbs beyond the palisade... and for three days now, my infant has not suffered from colic, nor has my head ached... nor has my breast milk been poisoned!"

He denied her accusation vociferously, but to his shock, she told him not to bother. She informed him that she also knew of the plot he would have worked with her father against the chieftain to further his own ambitions. She had kept her silence then, for her father's sake, but now she would not stand passively by knowing that he had begun to play new and dangerous games. He stared at her. He denied everything once again, saying that she was a foolish girl whose eyes had tricked her.

"It is you who are the fool, Draga. Do you think I am the only witness to your treachery?"

Now, for the first time, he was worried. It showed on his face. Even in the shadowed room he knew that she smiled.

"You must be careful in the future, Draga. Eyes follow your every move. You must learn to be content with your lot in life." The smile had left her lips. "If you would be chieftain, Draga, then be man enough to openly challenge your brother face to face, before an assembly of your clansmen. But know now that if you do, there are those who shall speak against your past deceit. And what would your kinsmen do to one who attempted to advance his own rank by nurturing dissatisfaction against the lord by putting them and their children at risk? Was that not your intent? To make us all ill, to see the weak among us die so that you could point to your brother and say that the favor of the spirits of the Twelve Winds had abandoned him?"

He was speechless. She had seen into the darkest recesses of his soul.

"Who are they, these other witnesses who would speak against me? Liars and defamers who would prefer to live in squalor under a passive lord? Spies who have forgotten that they are People of the Ax? Afraid to follow one who would lead them back to glory!"

"Glory? Is that what you have dropped into the well shaft, Draga, to poison their bodies as thoroughly as you would seek to poison their minds against Fomor MacLir?"

With no one in the room to hear him except the girl, he dropped all pretense. "Aye!" he hissed.

And she hissed back at him. "You are a despicable man, Draga, for truly you care only for yourself and, therefore, are not fit to rule over others!"

"Time shall tell the truth of that, Morrigan, but I warn you, though you may well bring me to ruin, know now that I shall bring your father to ruin with me."

"I think not," she said. "My father is an old man. I would not have him dishonored . . . but better that than to allow my son to live his life under the misbegotten leadership of a traitor who, in his lust to bring glory to his name, would lead his entire clan to ruin. So it is for the sake of my son that I come before you now, Draga. For his sake I warn you to be wise, for if I and my watching eyes see you at it again, be assured that I, and they, shall betray you to the lord and to the council. Your life shall be forfeit, Draga. And forevermore when your women and children speak your name, they shall remember with shame how thoroughly you have dishonored it . . . and them!"

Perhaps if Dana had not run weeping to him so soon after Morrigan had left him, perhaps if his anger had been given a chance to cool, he might not have committed himself to the course that would soon lead them all to such appalling tragedy. But he had been drinking mead all day, and when Dana came to him, with Lorcan behind her, his mind was still filled with Morrigan's warnings. Dana's tears shut out the rising sound of the wind. The roundhouse seemed to be closing in around him. Suddenly there seemed to be no order in the world at all.

Tremulously, in abject misery, Dana approached him and knelt at his feet. "The lord has sworn . . . with over half the holding looking on . . . that if in the passing of one week's time you do not name a man for me, he shall do it for you. He shall force me to be mated, Father! You promised that it would never happen. But it has. Because he is lord, and you are not, you can do nothing to stop it."

There had been no condemnation in her soft voice, only a sad, bleak acquiescence as she lay her head upon his knee, as she used to do when she was a little girl and would come to him to be consoled over an injury or sadness.

It was the truth. Fomor was lord. He was not. He could do nothing. Nothing. He rose, sighing against the pain that every movement brought to him. He would never be chieftain. He would never know the taste of battle. He would never have a chance to win glory to his name. He was condemned to be eclipsed by his brother until his dying breath. He could not look back upon a single time in his life when he had been master of his own Destiny, and now Fomor was depriving him of his sire's right to be sovereign over the decisions that affected his children.

It was then that the idea struck him. If he could not stand against his brother, if he could not be chieftain in Bracken

Fen before the bone blight reduced what was left of his manhood to rubble, he could do what he should have done years ago: He could strike out on his own. He could take his women and children and those few men whose loyalty to him was beyond question, and secretly, in the depth of night, they could leave Bracken Fen. Gar and Nia and Donn would gladly accompany them, especially if each were to believe that he had a chance of winning Dana at the journey's end. They chafed against the settled life almost as much as he did, and still spoke longingly of the foreign enticements to be found at Point of Ale. Now *there* was a place where a man could win the world for himself if he had a bit of luck on his side! And Draga *had* been lucky there, until Fomor had stepped forth to ruin his good fortune and shame him beyond measure.

He did not pause to think that a small, poorly armed band of travelers consisting of women, children, a bone-blighted would-be warrior, and three men who had never done battle in their lives would be vulnerable to the predators of the day. He thought only of his brother. Fomor had become the focus of his hatred, the enemy who sapped him of his pride and would now rob him of the last vestiges of his authority.

But he would not allow that to happen. A broad smile split his beard, and his teeth shone. Yes! By the Fates, he would leave Bracken Fen! Fomor would not force his daughter to take a man against her will! He, Draga, would *not* allow it! He would take Dana to Point of Ale. There she would have her pick of prospective mates: men of rank! Chieftains and merchants who would pay in gold for the privilege of possessing a girl of such extraordinary beauty as Dana.

Gold. The thought of it made him shiver with wanting. Gold to buy a new and better life, a life that would lead them southward into warmer climes, which would be kinder to Draga's bones and perhaps even drive the blight away forever.

He crossed the room quickly and backhanded the weather baffle. Large snowflakes, typical of spring storms, settled on the holding. The wind was out of the west. Experience told him that the storm would hold for hours. Tonight they would go! In the soft, secret silence of snowfall. By morning they would be miles away. By morning snow would cover their tracks and it would be impossible for anyone to follow them.

And by morning Draga would be a lord, a chieftain of his own band and master of his own Destiny at last.

29

By the thousands they came, although it rained and grew cold, making the journey hazardous for those who traveled from beyond the seas. Soon the weather cleared and warmed, and the Plain of the Great Stone Circle throbbed with life. Balor could not imagine the size of the crowds that Star Gazer said had assembled here in days gone by. He claimed that the throng that gathered here now was small in comparison. Soon all available space was spoken for upon the sacred plain, and large, rowdy encampments began to spring up across the river, gatherings of not only pilgrims and their escorts, but of entrepreneurs who could find no room, or welcome, on the holy plain itself.

Food vendors set up their stalls and built their fires. Soon flat, round hearth breads were baking on wide, charred griddle stones in smoldering beds of coals. Meat roasted on spits while caged goats bleated and fowl honked and called and looked their last upon the world out of panic-round eyes. Itinerant pimps strut indolently about with their painted, bangled whores. Hawkers of cheaply made, overpriced trinkets flaunted string upon string of amulets and talismans—fat, roughly worked, hippy little representations of the Mother of All, and crude replicas of the sacred Marking Stone upon which blessings would be asked on the dawn of the midsummer solstice. Jesters and dancers and professional gamesmen mocked and whirled and cheated the gullible with the well-practiced finesse common to their arts. And enterprising ferrymen, who had portaged small, leather-sided coracles many a long mile overland in the hope of turning a profit through the use of their vessels, happily rowed pilgrims back and forth across the river for only a slightly outrageous fee.

Balor moved among them as he had once walked among the throngs and stalls of Point of Ale. There was so much to see, but although he paused to examine the trinkets and observe the jesters and the dancers, it seemed as though he looked at the world through the eyes of a stranger. The bright luster of boyhood was gone, along with his innocence. He saw the whores for what they were, and recognized the glint of avarice in the merchants' eyes, and saw no beauty in the crudely made baubles that were offered at inflated prices.

He had changed since he had sworn his drunken oath upon the sacred Stones. The incident colored everything he did; it haunted and troubled him, for he saw it as more than the drunken posturing and blabbering of one frustrated by impossible ambitions. He had not only shamed himself before Cromm Cruach, but by naming his clan and sire, had compromised not only his own life, but the lives of his people. If the information fell into the wrong hands, if it came to the attention of Nemed MacAgnomain, might he not be sought out to confirm the death of the Wolf? And how had the son survived the plague that claimed his clan? Surely they would ask him that and perhaps demand that he lead them to the barrows of his people so that their death might at last be confirmed.

He could not bear to think of it. So he had told Cromm Cruach that he had lied to further his own ambitions, that he had claimed to be the son of the long-dead lord of legend in the hope that the men of Eireann would then volunteer to help him to fulfill his vow to take the head of Nemed MacAgnomain. The words had tumbled out of him in tanglings of desperation and desire to be believed.

Cromm Cruach had looked right through him. He had sent Cethlinn away. The two of them were alone, with the shadows of the great, circling trilithons falling gray upon them. "Do not lie to me, Balor. I have known your identity since that night long ago, upon the cliffs north of Point of Ale."

As on that night when they had stood together listening to the surge of the sea against the cliffs of the trading center, he put his arm paternally about the youth's shoulder and stood so still that, but for the movement of the wind in his hair, he might have been carved out of the rock of the sacred Stones. "The vow you have sworn on the sacred Stones outweighs all others, Balor. This Nemed... the forces of Creation shall devour such a man in time. If it is fated that yours shall be the arm to strike him down, then the Fates themselves shall place you in his path. But now they have led you to pursue a greater Destiny than men such as Nemed may ever hope to know. Drunk or sober, you have consecrated yourself to the Faith of the Stones. This vow cannot be undone; to break it would be unthinkable." He paused, measuring the haunted, troubled look on the youth's face. "You are one of us now, Balor, son of Fomor, Wolf of the Western Tribes. You must learn that with wisdom comes true power, for when my soul leaves my body to journey forth into the infinite, you shall take my place as Lord of the Stone. Then shall the foretelling be fulfilled. Under your guidance the clan kingdoms shall unite. They shall refuse to trade with such men as Nemed. He and his kind shall find no welcome upon our shores, and you shall be the Mighty One, ruling in righteousness as the Fates have led you to be. Surely, Balor, can you not be content with such a vision? Would you jeopardize it in your stubborn quest to take the head of one ignoble man?"

Content. The word was alien to Balor's nature. Yet now, as he looked off across the river to the great circle of trilithons, the feelings of restlessness fell away. He knew that Star Gazer would keep his secret, as would Cethlinn, until it served them both—and him—to speak it. A strange, thoroughly disconcerting sensation swept through him, so pleasant that he could not help but feel at ease with it. He *was* content! He thought of Cethlinn lying close beside him in the night, pleasuring him while the stars whirled away toward dawn above the roof of her warm, timbered house. He thought of the joy and hours of endless challenge he found in the study of those stars and of the many friends he had made among the scholars and priests who studied with him. He thought of Keptah, who had saved his life and miraculously restored the use of his shoulder and right arm. He thought of Gorias and the men of Eireann, of the sword Teacher they had brought to him from the Far Island, forged for him and brought forth in answer to all of his boyhood dreams.

How could he *not* be content? Each night he walked beneath the stars with Cromm Cruach and drank in the knowledge that was privy only to the People of the Stone, and each morning he crossed the river to hone his skill with the weapon of his dreams against the hard edge of the

instruction given to him by Findias, until his body raged
against the agony of fatigue. But this too brought pleasure to
him, for he knew that each day he grew stronger, wiser in the
way of the weapon and of the world, and each day the giant
drove him harder, begrudgingly conceding to his progress as
Cethlinn cheered and onlookers gathered to goad him, hoping to see him throw down his weapon out of sheer exhaustion and frustration. But he did not throw it down. He stayed
on his feet, battling until the weapon was whacked from his
hand or the giant said "hold." Either way he was satisfied,
because he knew that he was learning. He was seldom
bloodied now, and only this morning *he* had bloodied the
giant, opening a long, deep gash across his upper left arm,
which needed twice a dozen sutures to close.

"Well done, teat sucker," the huge man had acknowledged
as someone ran to fetch a healer from the other side of the
river.

Balor, sweated and trembling with elation, had bowed in
silent acceptance of Findias's compliment, knowing now that
the giant's worst insults came only from his loss of pride.

Now Balor's attention was drawn by the high, distant
keening of a hawk. He paused and looked up, shielding his
eyes from the glare of the sun with the back of his hand. Yes.
He could see the hunting bird clearly, the broad wings
motionless as it rode the thermals. He recalled the hawk that
had flown above him when he had been hopelessly lost within
the marshes. It had led Cethlinn to him and, by so doing,
had saved his life. It had led him to this place of refuge,
where the Fates had healed and strengthened him and had
opened vistas before him that even now amazed him. Could
the prophecy then be true? From the loins of a wolf, in the
shadow of a hawk...he had come forth to them. Could
Cromm Cruach and Cethlinn be right about him? Might he
dare imagine that someday he would be the Mighty One,
master of all of the clans of Albion, Eireann, and Land
Beyond the Sea? The thought filled him, as heady and
stimulating as a draft of mead quaffed too quickly. Huldre had
said that the world would be his someday. Perhaps she had
been right after all? Yes! It all made sense at last! Here he
would live as a priest. In time he *would* become Lord of the
Stone. And when at last his lineage was known and he had
honed his skills as a warrior to his satisfaction, no man alive

would deny that he *was* the Mighty One. They would unite under his banner.

Then, as he had vowed, as Dianket had promised, he *would* return to Bracken Fen, bringing with him the head of Nemed MacAgnomain. He would see Draga buried alive in a bog. He would take Dana as his own. He would make those who had been disloyal to his father tremble before he struck them down. And then the Wolf himself would bow before him, and in time a new and younger wolf would rise out of Albion.

A soaring sense of happiness filled him. *Yes,* he thought, *it will happen. I will make it happen! It may not be Star Gazer's vision for me, but soon it will all come to pass. And in the meantime, what can a few years matter in the scheme of things? I am young. Time shall pass quickly. And in this place I am content.*

Donn moved forward in silence, elbowing back the tall, thickly massed reeds that slowed his pace and caused the bare skin of his arms to itch. Silently he cursed the miserable marshland into which Draga had led them. How long had they been wandering, lost and probably in circles, since they had fled from Bracken Fen with their heads filled with visions of Draga's dreams of a better life? And how long had it been since the redbeard had become too ill to travel? They had set up a temporary encampment, and the women had set themselves to nursing the fever from their man's bones; but days had passed and he was worse, and Donn could count weeks since they had secretly left Bracken Fen during a snow-filled night. Weeks, and still they had not reached Point of Ale. Gar and Nia had been gone for two days on their search for the coast; he wondered if they had found it and were even now on their way back, or perhaps they were lost or drowned in a bog. Either way, other than Draga, he was the only man in their traveling band now.

Uaine and Eala were napping with their children after the midday meal. Draga slept too; drugged and muttering to himself in his dreams. Donn had eaten and drunk deeply of what was left of the mead in his traveling flasks, then had dozed awhile, fitfully, miserably. After that late-spring snow-

storm the weather had turned hot, humid, and close. Too
close for a comfortable, deep sleep.

The soft stirrings of the girl had roused him. He had
watched Dana through slitted eyes, feigning sleep as she rose
and crept from the encampment, tiptoeing lest she disturb
anyone as she made her way into the reeds along the little
trail that he and the others had cleared. He had waited, at
first thinking that she had gone out to relieve herself, but
when she did not return, he had known that she had sought
out the shallow little pond nearby and would be bathing.

Now he moved silently, stepping high and slowly so that
she would not be aware of his approach. Most of the ground
was under about an inch or so of water, and he could feel
liquid inside his boots, oozing and squishing beneath the
weight of each step. It was an unpleasant feeling, but he did
not care. He moved forward. Just one more step. Then he
paused and caught his breath. He could see the girl now.
Alone. Thigh deep in the pool. And naked.

At the edge of the reeds Donn's gaping mouth went dry.
There was no coolness in him. The rising pulse of man-need
heated him and caused his loins to throb and harden.

She stood, bending to scoop up handfuls of water, splashing
them over her body, sighing with pleasure as she turned her
face upward and felt the slightest breath of cool air touch her
skin. It was well past noon, but the sun was still high. How
strange to think that only weeks ago it was snowing! The very
thought of snow made her smile. She sighed and wished that
she were back in Bracken Fen, safe and secure, with the cool
flakes of winter drifting down, down, melting to cool her skin.
Her hands rose to gently trace the contours of her body,
drifting downward from her shoulders over her breasts, rousing imagined coolness until gooseflesh prickled and her nipples peaked and she shivered with delight.

"By the Mother . . ." he sighed.

The girl stared, startled by the sound of a man's voice. Her
slender arms folded across her breasts as she ducked down
into the water, wishing it were deeper and could cover more
than just the tops of her thighs. She told him to go away, that
she was not yet ready to return to their campsite, but he did

not move. He stared. He licked his lips like a hungry dog.
Something in his eyes frightened her.

He saw her fear and smiled. It excited him, made him
aware of her vulnerability. If he acted quickly, he could bring
her down quietly, without alerting the women to the fact that
anything was amiss. Once the thing was done, they would not
have much to complain about. Draga had all but promised
the girl to him, and had they taken the route along which
Fomor had led them years ago instead of taking the redbeard's
"shortcut" through the marshes, they would have been safely
to Point of Ale by now and Dana would already have known
the heat of his shaft.

His smile deepened into a leer of pure intent as he began
to move toward her. "You have been virgin far too long,
Dana...." He heard her gasp. He saw her start to rise to turn
and flee. He lunged at her across the small pond, and his
body stretched out as his arms encircled the girl. They went
down together in a great splashing impact, with Donn deliberately knocking her sideways as he rolled with her onto the
narrow, muddy embankment. He stifled her scream with his
kiss as she flailed beneath him, desperately trying to push
him away, but the movements of her soft, ripe body naked
against him only served to intensify his lust. He could taste
blood in his mouth—her blood...hot...salty. He had felt
his teeth tear her upper lip as he had claimed his kiss. He
held it now, smothering her into submission, depriving her of
breath as his tongue probed her own with a symbolic, stabbing ferocity that nearly drove him mad with need. One
broad, strong knee rammed down, forcing her limbs apart.
She was losing consciousness, growing pliable in his arms.
She was open to him now. Now he would pierce her. He
would bathe his manhood in the blood of her virgin womb,
and the only thing that might have made the moment sweeter
would have been if Lomna Ruad and her other suitors could
have borne witness to his triumph over them with her.

He did not hear the sound of those who approached him
from the opposite side of the pond, nor did he know that they
were there at all until a pair of strong male hands latched
onto his shoulders and pulled him off the girl. He expected to
see Draga, thinking that the redbeard had been roused by
the splash of the water and had come up out of his drugged
stupor to see to the welfare of his daughter. Even though he

was in the process of raping her, and even though he had not
forgotten that Draga was her sire, the thought of any man
having the audacity to interrupt another at the very moment
of penetration filled him with blind rage. He flailed back,
wanting to drop the redbeard where he stood.

But it was not Draga. It was a swarthy, curly-haired,
meaty-armed man in a soiled tunic. Behind him stood at least
six others, all in white, with short traveling capes of red wool
with some sort of circular black pattern woven around the
edge of each garment. They were dirty and unshaven and
armed to the teeth. And from the tips of two of their spears
the severed heads of Gar and Nia stared back at him.

A gasp of terror escaped from his lips even as his manhood
shriveled. He tried to get to his feet, but at least three of
them were on him, laughing at him, kicking him, forcing him
down, pushing his head beneath the surface of the pond.
Then one of them held it there with the pressure of a strong,
sandaled foot. He fought, but it was no use. His face was
being pushed down into muck and slime. He could not
breathe and yet could not help but try. Ooze filled his mouth
and went down into his lungs, choking him even as it seared
upward through his nostrils and exploded within his sinuses.
Pain came. Then blackness slowly filled him, but it did
nothing to erase the terror. He knew that until the very end.

Lorcan ran faster than he ever thought he could. He ran up
the trail that bisected the reeds, slipping and falling, but
rising and running again and again. *I must warn them,* he
thought. *It would be easy to hide here in the reeds, but I
must be brave. I must get back to camp and warn the others!*

He had gone to the edge of the pond, drawn there by the
sound of fierce splashing. It had awakened him, although no
one else had stirred. They all slept soundly. All except Dana
and Donn. They were gone. Together. And Lorcan did not
like Donn; he worried about the way Donn looked at his
sister. So he had risen and rubbed his eyes and gone to see
what had drawn them both away from the camp. What he had
seen had shaken him so deeply that he had been unable to
move. Donn, grappling cruelly with Dana, and strange men
emerging from the reeds at the far side of the pool. They had
the heads of Gar and Nia impaled on spears and, as he had

watched, stunned, they had drowned Donn and surrounded the prone, naked figure of his sister. He had not been able to tell if she were alive or dead. All he had been able to see were the heads of his kinsmen, blank-eyed and slack-jawed with dried gore coloring the hafts of the spears upon which they were impaled. It had been too much for him to absorb. After a moment, knowing that he was a small boy, not fierce enough to stand up to a band of armed marauders, Lorcan thought of his father. Draga could help Dana. Draga was the only one who could!

He had turned then, and he had run. He had not looked back lest the strangers be following him. There or not there, he could feel them at his back. The sweat of terror broke from his pores. It made him shiver as he ran, thinking: *I must get to my father! Draga is brave. Draga is fierce. He killed the sentry upon the palisade; he pulled him close and slit his throat from ear to ear so he could not betray our flight.*

Suddenly he heard a scream and stopped dead in his tracks. The sound had not come from behind him; it had come from directly ahead. It was Eala. A sharp, piercing cry of surprise and pure terror. One of the babies began to cry. He heard Uaine curse and shout at someone. Masculine laughter followed. And then Draga's voice, harsh and strained, demanding to know what the strangers wanted in his encampment and how they dared to upset his wives and children by their rudeness and the display of weaponry.

The answer came from all around. Lorcan hunched himself into a little ball, scooting back off the trail as armed men stalked by him, brandishing the heads of Gar and Nia, shoving a dazed and stumbling Dana ahead of them as the one who had held Donn's face underwater now carried that victim's severed head by its hair.

The women were on their feet, drawing the children close. Uaine had a dagger in her hand, and with her baby held in one arm, she menaced the interlopers with the other as they stared at her out of eyes as hot as sunlight, as black as bogs by night. They had thrown Dana to the ground. She curled in upon herself, with her arms wrapped about her knees and her head buried. Draga stood in shock, trying not to show the panic that was crawling upward from his belly to scrape madly at the back of his throat. If he opened his mouth to speak, it would escape as a scream to shame him. He held an

ax tightly in one hand. It had been jabbed through his belt
while he had slept, to keep it out of the reach of the children.
His dagger too was at his side. Sheathed. He shifted the ax
into his left hand and reached for the dagger with his right,
cursing the pain and stiffness that slowed his movements. He
must have winced, for the men murmured to one another,
and he knew with a sick, sinking feeling of despair that they
had sensed his weakness.

He counted fifteen men, all armed, and with swords. His
palms began to sweat even as his mouth went dry. The ax felt
slippery in his hand, and his fingers, stiff and clumsy, dropped
the weapon to the ground. He bent and snatched it up,
barely taking his eyes from the intruders, trying not to swoon
as the beast of pain broke loose within him. Then he stood,
fighting for balance, shaking his head to clear it, wishing
desperately that he had not drunk so greedily of Eala's
medicinal mead.

But it was too late for regrets. Instead he thought: *Now, at
last, you shall do battle. . . . And you shall die like a warrior
with a weapon in your hand!*

And perhaps it might have been. But the heads of Gar and
Donn and Nia were staring at him. And it struck him that
there was nothing glorious in their dismemberment, in their
blank and juiceless eyes settling back into their lifeless skulls
while tendons and severed veins and fragments of gore hung
from the ragged stumps of their necks. Indeed, as he looked
at them, he could feel the blood pulsing in his own neck, and
it occurred to him that he did not want to die.

It also occurred to him that perhaps the intruders had
already slaked their thirst for blood. The way they were
looking at his women bespoke another hunger. His mind was
whirling, his thoughts building a rationale, not for glory, but
for expedience. Why should he stand and fight to the death
when, in the end, the consequences to his women would be
the same? Perhaps then, when the strangers were sated, they
would go their way? Or the women might beguile them into
drunkenness and he could slay them while they slept? The
thought calmed him. If each of his women serviced five of
them, perhaps no one need die. Uaine had been a slave used
to serving the sexual gratification of men before he had won
her in the fighting arena north of Point of Ale, and years of
pleasuring him had made Eala pliable. And as for Dana, it

was a pity, of course, but no girl could remain a virgin forever, and she had been one longer than most.

Smiling deferentially, in the way of one who knows that the game is up and fairly won with the spoils inevitably destined to the victor, he threw aside his weapons and gestured outward with both hands.

He explained his reasoning as gently as he could to his women, certain that they would understand that he was only concerned for their welfare. He told Uaine and Eala to remove their garments, to yield passively to what must be inevitable.

Dana made small, whimpering sounds as Eala, weeping, began to undress, but for a long moment Uaine did not move, as all color bled from her face. She stared at Draga, unblinking, as disbelief slowly was transformed to rage and hatred within her eyes, and with a scream of loathing, she ran at him with her dagger raised.

He deflected her blow easily. She fell to the ground, the knife knocked out of her hand, but her baby still cradled, screaming, in the fold of her left arm. The other children were crying loudly, wide-eyed with fright and confusion as the strangers began to close a tight circle around them. Uaine rose to a seated position, her hair a wild red mane as she glared, snarling at the man who had drowned Donn. He had thrown the bleeding head aside with as much interest as he might have shown to any other carelessly taken trophy when another, more interesting prospect presented itself. To her shock, he extended his hand to her, inviting her to take it with a look that clearly stated his appreciation of her action against Draga. She took it, staring at the redbeard with contempt as she told him that he was not fit to live.

The statement struck deep, perhaps because he knew that she was right and could not bear the knowledge, so he met her stare with an equal measure of contempt. "And you, Uaine, are not worth dying for!"

She spat at him, and the men laughed, and for a brief, painful moment, he remembered the wild, spotted woman for whom he had been willing to risk everything at Point of Ale. It seemed a lifetime ago, yet she had not changed. But *he* had.

Dana screamed as one of the men jerked her to her feet by her hair. He spoke to his comrades in a foreign tongue as he pulled her to him, turning her so that her back was against him as he fondled her obscenely. Laughter, deep and hungry, rippled through the men as they began to respond to whatever Dana's tormentor was saying. Draga's eyes darted in his head. They were all looking at Dana. All. Even the man who had helped Uaine to her feet. He had stripped off his tunic and was advancing toward Dana, loosing his breechcloth. Eala was sobbing, half maddened by a mother's worst nightmare as she tried to make them understand that her daughter was a virgin.

"Take *me*! Take *me*, all of you! Come, I shall welcome you! Only leave my girl alone!" Frenzied, she threw herself against the man who held Dana, beating at him with her fists. He knocked her away with an impatient, brutal elbow jab that sent her sprawling, stunned.

One of the toddlers broke away from his siblings and ran to his mother, screaming. The child was an irritant to one of the men who had decided to mount Eala where she lay. He struck the little boy so hard that blood spurted from the child's nose and ears. He went down, neck snapped, face shattered, drowning in his own blood. The man took no note of what he had done as he began to sate his rabid passion upon the dazed Eala.

A terrible, expanding light burst within Draga's head. It was the blinding explosion of unbridled outrage. No! He could not consent to this! This was not what his expedience had been willing to bargain for. He shouted his protest. He stepped forward, bending to take up his weapons—and never saw the blow that struck him down.

It came from the dark, burnished bronze of the Achaean sword, which one of the men had drawn and held at ready. He had been standing close at Draga's back, so that when the blade struck it struck from behind, so well placed and clean a blow that the redbeard's head was severed before he was aware that the dismemberment had taken place. He felt no pain. None. For the first time in years. The last things that he saw as his head went flying were the reed beds scudding past, and the sky, and a brief, fading vision of the stump of his own body spurting out its life's blood into the muddy earth of the marsh.

Mud, he thought. He had fled from Bracken Fen to seek a life of glory. Only to die in the mud after all.

*   *   *

Minardos sated himself on the girl and then drew back, momentarily weakened by the outpouring of his passion. He stood aside and allowed the others to take their turns on her. As commander of this small group of storm-tossed seafarers, rank allowed him this privilege, obliging him to be the first to pierce the virgin. He knew his men well enough to know that they would come to blows over who would win the right of first blooding, so since it was his duty to keep the peace among them, he had done so without hesitation. The girl's beauty was remarkable, albeit pale and bland for his tastes; nevertheless, knowing that he would be the first to take her had excited him, and he had not come away from his obligation dissatisfied. In the hours and days to follow he would use the spotted, flame-haired woman for his pleasure; her fire aroused him, and he had ordered her bound and hobbled and swore that he would castrate any man who touched her.

"Nemed shall be angry about the virgin. He always reserves the fair ones for himself. If he finds out that you did not keep her for him..." The man beside Minardos let his words drift; further emphasis was unnecessary.

"Who shall tell him? You? Would you deprive yourself of pleasure for his sake, when he is miles away and would only feed such a girl to the sharks in the end? A waste, I say! I have been his master-at-arms for years and am weary of standing aside while he always appropriates the best for himself. Thanks to the unseasonable storm that struck us weeks ago, we are certain to reach the rendezvous at Point of Ale long before Nemed and the main body of the fleet, so why not pleasure ourselves awhile? These women shall fetch a fair price at the trading center. And who knows what sort of women we shall find when we at last join with Nemed to fall upon the hidden stronghold of the Wolf. In the meantime I say we take full advantage of what the Fates have placed at our disposal."

Minardos stared off to where Uaine sat huddled with the children. They were clustering round her, babes not much older than three, one of them holding a screaming infant. Although she was bound, the spotted woman was attempting to calm them, to keep them close, to make them look only at her lest they be further terrified by the ongoing degradation of Eala and Dana. The scene made him smile, for those who had bound her had half undressed her in the process, and she had fought them like a mountain cat all the way. Just looking at her caused the heat of renewed need to rise and harden in his loins. His smile deepened. It pleased him to know that although he was no youth, he could be ready again so quickly.

He began to advance toward Uaine then, and when he reached her, the intensity of the children's cries grew louder. He stood over them, feeling the power rise in him as he displayed himself for the woman. He wanted her to cower, to cringe at the sight of that which would soon so thoroughly impale her, but she did not cringe, nor did she cower. She measured him with steady, seething, contemptuous revulsion before she spat at him, as she had spat at the now-decapitated redbeard. Anger rose in him. It was for the sake of the children that she behaved so bravely. Impatiently he called back for someone to bring him his sword.

She understood what he intended to do. She blanched. She begged him for their lives. He stood immobile as she cringed before him, weeping, imploring. But when the sword was brought, he used it without hesitation. The children were of no use to him. And it gave him immense pleasure to know that not only his master Nemed knew how to make a woman scream.

Hidden in the surrounding reeds, Lorcan saw it all, too frightened to move. He wanted to attack the murderers of his father and brothers and the rapers of his mother and sister and poor, brave Eala. He wanted to be Lorcan the Fierce, for Draga's sake more than for his own. But if he attacked, he would be cut down. If he should be discovered, they would take off his head or drown him in the pool. So he remained hunkered down, motionless.

He was not certain when the first cool shadows of night touched him. Incredibly, he had dozed; he had willed himself into a state that had allowed him complete immobility, total obliteration of all that he had witnessed. But it came back to him now, in an explosion of terror and total recall, a thousand visions he could not bear to see. Perhaps he had dreamt them? He moved, carefully and quietly, making no sound at all as he peered back through the reeds again. Draga would be there, lounging by the evening fire, engaged in the gambling game he and Gar, Nia and Donn often played to pass the time. Eala would be putting a meal together while Dana entertained the children, and Uaine would be nursing her baby.

But that was not what he saw. And as he stared, a need to retch nearly overwhelmed him; but if he yielded to it, they would hear him. They would kill him.

And so he fled, backing off through the reeds, then turning and striking off at a run, pausing only once, to be sick, before running on again in blind, heartbroken panic. He was sobbing, choking in the sound lest someone hear him and take him captive and drag him back to share the death of his brothers and father and kinsmen. He ran. Night fell, and still he ran. He knew no fear of the stalking night creatures of the marsh. None of them could be more of a threat than the murderers from whom he fled. He went on, stumbling through mud, wading through shallows, and half drowning in deeps, until at last exhaustion claimed him and he curled up into a damp little ball upon a hummock of dry land and dreamt of the chieftain's son Balor, who had fled into the marshes never to return. And then, gratefully, dreamt of nothing at all until the light of dawn woke him and he looked up to see seagulls wheeling overhead.

He had come to the mouth of a narrow stream, which ran out of the marsh and into the sea. He stared, overwhelmed not by his first glimpse of the ocean, to which only a few additional steps had brought him, but by the realization of how close Draga had brought them to the coast. How beautiful it was! How the women and children would have exclaimed with delight in it. He wept then, remembering blood, terror, and death.

He headed up the beach and soon paused, brought short by the sight of several large ships. They lay high upon the strand, red and black sails down and wrapped upon their decks, while men in the same colors as the murderers lounged about, talking, busying themselves at various tasks. He did not allow himself to get close enough to see them clearly, lest they see him.

For two days he wandered southward along the shore. He did not know where he was going, he only knew that somehow he must continue on. He walked and walked and took what nourishment he could from the sea. Raw shellfish when he could manage to pry them from the rocks in the tidal pools, and seaweed, and small, bitter slugs that were easy to catch but so sharp-tasting and slimy that he puked them up even before he could fully swallow them.

It was hunger that brought him to exhaustion by the end of the third day. He sought shelter against the damp of the night within a clump of tall shore grass. He did not hear the travelers' shouts as they brought their ship through the gentle summer surf to a safe beaching. He did not smell the smoke of their fire. It was the scent of roasting meat that awoke him, but by then they were standing over him.

They were kind men, and generous. They saw the terror in his haunted eyes and gentled it with offerings of food and mead and a clean bedskin placed close to their fire. He was wary and untrusting, but in no position to either break away or refuse their kindness. He sat on the skin they gave him and ate greedily of the food they shared. Still, he would not let himself sleep, lest they slit his throat in the night. His downfall was in gulping the mead they warmed and served to him; sleepiness came then, and he cursed himself for a fool as he lay back, warm and soothed by the fire and the sound of their low talk. Their language was not totally different from his own. It filtered through to him, and slowly he relaxed, realizing that they would not harm him. They were pilgrims, bound for the southernmost shore of Albion and then inland to a place of sanctuary . . . the Plain of the Great Stone Circle, where they would ask blessings for their distant village by the light of the rising of the midsummer sun.

30

"You! Here! Only one week left to buy yourself a bit of luck to make your life wish come true when you stand in the light of the rising of the midsummer sun!"

The hawker stepped deliberately into Balor's path. He was a fat-bellied, hairy-armed seller of cheap amulets, which he displayed on a pole-mounted frame, twisting it back and forth in a manner that caused sunlight to glint upon his wares: talismans and amulets strung upon poorly cured, smelly leather thongs; chubby little female figures of clay, fat-bellied and as big-butted as the hawker himself, with tiny, faceless heads and round little breasts with nipples studded with painted granules of river sand, which the vendor swore were rubies from the Land That Burns. "Here!" he cried. "Don't walk away from luck, young man! Here's a charm to interest a man of your coloring! You'd be a Northman by birth, eh? And what Northman could pass up a chance to own a bit of amber? They say that the Eye of Donar, the northern god of thunder, is in each talisman. Aye, rub it against a bit of wool—"

Balor did not let him finish his sentence. He reached out and snatched the amulet, staring, his heart racing. Amber! Could it be? But no. It was *not* Huldre's exquisitely carved hawk-shaped talisman. This was a crudely shaped, ugly lump with a hole pierced through one end to allow an equally crude leather thong to be passed through it. But as he looked at it, images from the past came raging into his head: a young boy standing in the rain with a talisman of amber within the curl of his fist . . . Draga lying unconscious upon the ground with Nemed standing over him, leering, poised to strike him in half with his blade of burnished bronze . . . his mother, keening on the palisade . . . Morrigan standing beneath the oak with a child in her arms. *A child. Whose child?*

And then he saw Dana. Wondrously beautiful, she stood outside the holding, ankle deep in a small, shallow pool. A hand rose out of the water. Hideous, rotting fingers flexed, all bone and dessicated flesh groping for the girl's ankle . . . Mael's hand . . . risen from the bog to pull his beloved to her death. . . .

Balor gasped. This was no vision. This was memory, mired in guilt and homesickness and longing. Dana would have named a man by now. He could not bear to think of it, nor could his increasing fondness for Cethlinn ease his longing for her. Nothing could ever do that. Yet even now, as his nightmarish vision faded, in his mind's eye Dana's golden hair went dark, and her eyes shimmered like the surface of a lake in moonlight. It became Morrigan's face.

Morrigan! Why did she always intrude into his dreams? And why did he miss her so?

With a cry of anguish he hurled the vendor's ugly little lump of amber to the ground at his feet. "What sort of trickery is this! Liar! Charlatan! Do not try to foist your tawdry merchandise on me!"

The man flushed and squatted to snatch up the talisman. Others had turned to stare. He did not appreciate being made the target of the young man's defamations. Such a scene was not good for business. He stood up, turning the amulet so that all could see how it glinted, albeit dully, in the sunlight. "'Tis amber! See for yourselves! This mannerless wretch wouldn't know a bargain if it bit him!"

A small, wizened little woman stared at him, and warned, "Ee's the one in the priestess's favor. Some say ee's a wizard . . . burned three men up alive just by lookin' at'm. Be careful, lest ee put a spell on ye."

The hawker glared at Balor with a jaundiced frown. Life had long since taught him to know no fear of spells. What he *did* fear was a loss of business; so he fixed the young man with stern and reproving eyes as he pointed a fat, dirty finger at him. "Don't say I didn't offer it to you! Don't say that I didn't give you a chance! Throw away amber and throw away your luck! And me . . . offering it at such a reasonable price!" With this he turned away and stalked off, smiling as several would-be buyers followed close, snared on his well-placed lure like so many hungry, stupid fishes.

For a long while Balor stood among the crowd, shaken. Memories continued to surge within him. Yet surely, he told himself, they *were* only memories.

"Mead, eh?" A seller of brew ventured close. "Free to a man of the Stone."

He took the beaker and drank from it, making a note of the location of the vendor's stall so that he, as a novitiate, could reward the man later for his generosity. It was customary for those in his position to reimburse, not with cowries or trade goods, but with much coveted positions close to the Great Stone Circle on the dawn of the midsummer rising. The mead was rich and soothing. It sent his troubled memories ebbing away. He thanked the vendor and began to walk on. He felt better now and was glad to see Cethlinn coming toward him from a fruit-seller's display. She carried a shallow basket filled with fruit, a ring of crusty, seed-pebbled bread looped over one arm.

She had been looking especially radiant these past few weeks, and sought him out each day to share her midday meal with him before he went to the sanctuary to counsel with the other priests as they prepared for the rituals of the night. These were growing more involved as the sun moved closer and closer toward the solstice.

Tonight Cromm Cruach would lead the priests into the hills for the last of the presolstice meditations. As a novitiate, Balor would accompany them. It occurred to him that had he not been forced to flee from Bracken Fen, he would now be readying himself to endure the Rite of Passage that would have initiated him into full acceptance as an adult male of the clan MacLir. But the Fates had decreed that he would endure other rites. He would be accepted by a new people. He would be proclaimed as a man of the Stone, and he would strive toward a far greater Destiny.

As Cethlinn came toward him, smiling her white, crooked-toothed smile, he realized for the first time just how dear to him she had become. He linked his arm through hers and together they walked through the teeming encampment toward a quieter place along the river. The sun was warm, and the woman beside him was as fragrant and giving of life as the fresh bread she carried. *By the Fates*, he thought, *I am happy here!*

And Cethlinn's smile deepened as she felt his happiness. She held his arm and was glad that tonight would begin the ritual meditations that would culminate during the solstice ceremonies in his formal acceptance as a priest of the Stone. From their meal upon the riverbank they would go together to the sanctuary, and from that point tradition would forbid all conversation. They would give their thoughts to the stars, and she would see to it that no one told Balor the news that had begun to circulate through the encampments since the newest arrival of pilgrims: A great fleet of ships was heading up the coast, a raiding fleet, its sails as red as blood in the summer sun, with the black running wheel of the house of Nemed MacAgnomain shining like the eye of a raven, watching across the miles, searching out the hidden holding of an enemy whom all men thought long dead.

She looked up at Balor as they walked, and although she felt the shadow of uneasiness darken her mood, she would not yield to it. *If you knew that Nemed was near, you would leave me. If you knew his destination, you would break your vow to the Stone. Even though you are not yet ready, you would attempt to defend your own, and he would cut you down. And so I will keep you here beside me. I have waited all of my life for you, and I shall not let you go, Balor. In time. But not now. For my sake and for yours, but most especially for the sake of your child, whom I now carry, I shall not let you go!*

The week passed in fasting and meditation and solitude. And Balor sought a place far from the Plain of the Great Stone Circle, upon the softly shouldering hills. Today had been the last day of the bright half of the year. Tomorrow the sun would rise due east and set due west, and the light would be equal to the darkness for this brief breath of time before the world spun away toward its rendezvous with winter.

Now, as he lay back staring skyward, it was well past midnight, hours yet until dawn. The distant fires that burned upon the Plain of the Great Stone Circle had gone out. There was nothing to detract from the starlight. Balor drew in the sight of it. The night satisfied him, left him at peace with his thoughts.

Peace. The last few days had given him that. Somewhere along the line he had ceased to regard it as an enemy, as something to be sought after only by cowards like his father. Unlike his sire, he had not run from his Destiny. There was no question in his mind that someday he would be all that Cethlinn and Cromm Cruach had foreseen for him, all that his father might have been had he not turned away to pursue a less challenging path. But a man must breathe between heartbeats. He must pace himself. And peace could fill the interim well.

Balor half closed his eyes, allowing the starlight to filter through his lashes, and it fragmented into prisms. White turned to red and blue, to green and yellow, all incandescent. He pressed his eyelids gently with his thumbs. The colors swirled like galaxies across the endless vistas of his imagination, and it was as though he were a boy again, lying warm beneath his bedskins, dreaming of a golden plain shimmering beneath the stars while Huldre whispered to Fomor of distant islands and of stones that sang and of a mighty lord who would someday capture the fabled monoceros and ride out upon its back to become master of the world.

"Balor . . ."

The voice called him forth into wakefulness. He sat up, looking toward the east, where the first light of false dawn shimmered mauve above the horizon. A lone horseman was etched against the night directly in front of him. His hand extended toward Balor as his great white horse stamped restlessly and nickered softly.

"Come, Balor. Soon the sun shall rise. You must come forth to the Stones. The time has come at last for you to accept your Destiny."

It was Star Gazer. Balor came close and mounted, and they rode forth together in silence, down from the hills to the sacred plain, which would soon glow gold in the rising of the dawn of the midsummer solstice.

And so it came to pass that Balor, grandson of Manannan, firstborn of Fomor, Wolf of the Western Tribes, son of Huldre, daughter of the Land of the North Wind, stood within the Great Stone Circle. He came in a procession with other novitiates and the elders among the priesthood. He came with Cromm Cruach on his right and Cethlinn on his left, through a silent sea of watching thousands. Not a single torch or fire burned, but Balor could feel the flame of faith and expectation growing out of the dying night as the immense gathering of pilgrims waited for the dawn to be born.

He was weak and light-headed from hunger, yet never had he felt stronger, had his mind been clearer, his senses sharper. With the other novitiates he prostrated himself upon the sacred earth of the Inner Circle. Arms splayed, legs together, his head facing due east, he could see the distant Marking Stone rising against the thinning night between the trilithons before which he lay.

It was as though the weight of the infinite pressed down on the plain. Then slowly the chanting began. Low and sure, it was a rhythm with no tune, a sound that rose and fell as the sea rises and falls upon the land and as the land itself rises and falls over the molten core of the world. It was in the language of the Ancient Ones, of those who spoke the remnant history of ages before this age. In fragments it had come down out of antiquity to the priests of this day. Only they knew it. And yet Balor understood—not the words themselves, but the meaning beyond the words. The knowledge lay within his bones and blood.

"So be it!" he cried, and knew that for this moment he had been born. The Stones *had* walked upon the moor. The great, white brand of the falling star *had* called him forth. To this. He rose to his feet and raised his arms and threw back his head, so that as the sun rose he could see the last stars of night fading above him. He was united with them in that moment, and with the earth beneath his feet, a man of the light and the darkness, with the sun and all of the vast, whirling worlds enmeshed within the infinite harmony of Creation.

Slowly the crowd beyond the towering circle of trilithons began to dance as they chanted, like a vast, living sea of grass in motion, stirring and bending in the wind. And it seemed to Balor that the great Stones swayed with them. Impossibly, they moved. Impossibly, they leaned inward toward him. Impossibly, born out of the heart of the rock, a sigh was escaping from them, a deep, voiceless resonance.

And though no other man or woman save Cromm Cruach heard the sound, Balor heard it. The Stones were singing. They were welcoming and affirming his presence within their holy circle. He *was* the one who had been foretold.

"Balor!" Lorcan's cry struck out through the gathering. The priests and novitiates had left the Inner Circle. They walked toward the Marking Stone along the raised Avenue of Processions while the crowd chanted in the light of the fully risen dawn. Balor did not hear the boy's cry. He walked as though his soul drifted within his body. He had sworn the oath that would bind him forever as a priest of the Stone. He had stood with Cethlinn at his side to receive Cromm Cruach's blessing upon their union. He had stood content, knowing that there was nothing that he could ask of the Stones that Fate had not already given to him.

Then the boy cried out his name again. He recognized the child's voice even before Lorcan burst forward through the throng to run to him, to wrap slim, bony arms about his limbs and hug him, sobbing with the ferocity of despair. He lifted the little boy into his arms, momentarily disoriented, not understanding how Draga's son could be here with him upon

the Plain of the Great Stone Circle. Then the boy spoke
and the world turned back upon him. He could feel the sun
and the stars falling around him as, with Lorcan in his arms, he
left the procession of the faithful. With his back to the Great
Stone Circle, he began to walk through the gathering toward
the river and the encampment he had shared with the men of
Eireann. His sword lay there, hidden within the hawthorn
grove. Although uncountable eyes stared after him and a
restless murmuring rose from the gathering at the sight of his
defection, he did not look back. He knew what he must do.

"You cannot go! You have sworn upon the Stone to stay! In
the light of the rising of the midsummer sun you have sworn
it! The vow cannot be broken, lest you forfeit your luck
forever!"

The passion in Cethlinn's voice did not touch him. "Luck
has never been my ally, Cethlinn. I was a fool to think that
the Fates would grant it to me now."

They were across the river, in the encampment of the men
of Eireann, where Cethlinn had followed him. He strapped
on his wrist guards and attached the sheathed Teacher to the
loop at his belt. Lorcan stared wide-eyed at the weapon as
one of the pilgrims who had found the boy and brought him
to the holy plain demanded to know what attachment there
was between Balor and the youth. The pilgrim had grown
attached to Lorcan.

Balor explained that Lorcan was his uncle's son. "He may
stay with you if you would wish it, for he cannot come with
me." He looked at Lorcan and tried to erase the lost, hurt
look in his eyes. "You must understand. If there is a chance
that Dana and the others are still alive, I must try to find and
help them. You cannot come with me, Lorcan. It will be too
dangerous."

"And that it shall be, young man," affirmed the pilgrim,
"for these marauders of whom the child speaks, according to
his description, they wore the colors of the house of Nemed
MacAgnomain. We have seen dozens of that devil's ships at
various places along the coast. It is rumored that when
Nemed's ships join forces at Point of Ale, there shall be over
fifty vessels, with at least thirty men to each crew. You're
talking of nearly two thousand swordsmen all set to march

inland after an enemy whom we all thought dead. I'd not set myself in their path if I were you, young man. The women you speak of, best forget them. You haven't a chance of getting them back. Pity them, as you should pity the Wolf when the Raven comes against him unaware, for his death has been written for him in the stars."

Balor's world was reeling. He was staring at Cethlinn as though at a stranger. "Did you know of this?" He read the answer in her eyes. "You *knew* and you spoke no word of it to me?"

Findias, the giant, shook his head and exhaled a droll laugh. "Why should she tell you, eh? So her precious pet could run off to take the head of Nemed and lose his own in the bargain?" He clucked his tongue. "The real pity of it lies in the timing... if only there were time to sail back to the Far Island to tell the men of Eireann that the lord of the clan MacLir of the Western Tribes still lives. By the Stone, lad, that's a cause that would bring them together—to fight for the Wolf against Nemed. With the promise of the Wolf to lead them, we could form a fleet of ships such as the world has never seen! We'd take Nemed's head. Together we could do it! But now, with the fleet of the Raven already moving up the coast, it's too late. And mark me, unless the Wolf is aware of the danger, unless he can match the numbers and arms of those who shall come against him, all is lost for him."

When Balor spoke, it was quietly, almost as though the words came from the mouth of a stranger. "How came you to Albion, Findias, you and your companions?"

"By sea. In a fine, strong ship. Why do you ask?"

"And upon the holy plain now, among the thousands who have gathered to make pilgrimage, are there not others from your island and from across the far seas, men known to you, who also despise Nemed?"

It was Muri who came closer from where he had been standing by the river's edge. "Aye," he said. "And all have weapons with them, secreted within holy groves or back at the beach with guardsmen posted to watch their—"

"Ships." Balor finished the sentence for him. There was fire in him now, and tension strung as tight with purpose as a good bowstring. "How *many* ships would you say could be mustered to form a fleet to rally under the colors of the Wolf?"

Muri's eyes were afire. "As many as would match the ships of the red and black!"

"Perhaps more!" affirmed Gorias, grinning, his jeweled tooth sparkling sunlight. "And many are armed with the strong, sweet, deadly bronze swords of Eireann!"

"But we are not all as finely trained to the sword as are Nemed's men," reminded Ogma. "And many, like myself, have not seen much of battle."

His words did not cool Findias's ardor. This boy of Cethlinn's, he *was* an audacious and a clever brat; his words made so much sense that Findias wondered why he had not thought of them first. "And who would lead this great fleet of ships of the men of Eireann and the far seas, eh? You? Would-be Lord of the Stone? And how are we to find the holding of the Wolf, eh? By your 'wizard's' powers? Is that what we are to tell those whom you would have go against Nemed MacAgnomain?"

Balor felt strangely calm, strangely at peace. "You may tell them that Balor shall lead them and that he shall accept their wisdom and their will to win against a common enemy. You may tell them that I call them forth in just and righteous vengeance against those who have slaughtered my kindred and subjugated the lands of the Western Seas. You may tell them this: that Balor calls them forth to join forces with the Wolf . . . for I am his son . . . and I can lead them to his holding."

Cromm Cruach rode with them as far as the sea. The entire long way he was silent, as was Cethlinn, who kept her mare reined close to the fine white beast Balor had been given to ride. As they passed through land that was familiar to them both, Balor could feel Cethlinn watching him, reliving their journey through the wild country. They passed near to the place where they had been set upon by the interlopers. Balor found himself looking for signs of their bodies, but there were none. It was like trying to recall a dream, to make it begin again where one has left it. A year had come and gone, and the youth who had ridden away from the sea was now a man who rode toward the sea . . . with Cethlinn, his woman, beside him, and Cromm Cruach, Lord of the Stone, leading him away from all that he had come to love and cherish, from all that the Fates had led him to believe could be his. When they passed through the woods where the menhirs stood, he reined in his mount for a moment, staring at them, remembering how, so long ago, they had seemed to be watching him, following him and warning of danger. He drew a breath, remembering other stones and the sense of kinship he had felt with the infinite.

"It is not yet too late to go back. . . ." Cethlinn's voice was very low, devoid of emotion, yet somehow it hinted of words left unsaid, of feelings unshared.

He expected her to apologize to him, or explain why she had betrayed him for the sake of her own possessiveness. But he could never forgive her, and when she remained silent, he rode on. Nothing she could say could make him stay. She could never own him. Dana needed him. Bracken Fen was in danger. And Nemed MacAgnomain was at last in a position where he, Balor, might actually dare to go against him and win. The thought made him tremble.

. They were nearing the shore. He could smell salt in the increasing moisture of the air. The men of Eireann took note of it and began to sing a song of the sea. They walked, as did most of the many men whom they had convinced to join them. A few of the newcomers rode, for they had brought their mounts with them to Albion in ships large enough to carry livestock, many men, and huge cargoes.

Balor kept his horse's pace even. Soon they reached the coast, and it was as he remembered it. Herons browsed in a narrow estuary, and bees buzzed in the wildflowers while gnats droned like armies taking on the wind. He looked back and saw that his army was massing along the shore. It was not nearly so large a gathering as the men of Eireann, in their enthusiasm, had been certain they could bring together; but by the time the last horse and the last stragglers came out of the wood, Balor counted nearly two hundred men. And Gorias had assured him that there would be nearly twice that number when all of those who had been left behind to guard their vessels were accounted for.

So it was that these men of Eireann—and men from the far and near shores of Albion and Land Beyond the Sea—who had come together for the ceremonies of the summer solstice, were easily recruited to a cause dedicated to the destruction of such a lord as Nemed MacAgnomain, especially when

Cromm Cruach, the High Priest of the Stone, rode with those who had formulated the venture.

Balor had no plan at first, but with the combined expertise of the battle-proven men of Eireann, soon the way was clear in his mind. The Fates had opened the way for him when the storm had divided Nemed's fleet. According to the latest rumor the main body of the fleet was still making repairs somewhere to the south, near Land's End. Smaller groups of vessels had struck out northward from wherever the tempest had driven them. It was at these ships that those who would join forces with Balor and the men of Eireann would strike as they journeyed northward to the place where they would then travel inland to band together with the Wolf. Balor had told them that his father's holding was well fortified. He had not told them that the fighting men of the MacLir were bronze poor, or that disease had halved their numbers, or that the Wolf himself was now only a shadow of what he had been in the Days of Glory. Somewhere along the coast to the north Dana was held captive; he would not allow himself to think that she might be dead. He would find her. He would take her back to Bracken Fen, and there, with an army of well-armed men at his back, he would force his father to become the Wolf again so together they could defeat Nemed's forces and win vengeance at last in the name of the clan MacLir.

There were clouds in the sky when Balor said good-bye to Cethlinn.

"I shall never forget you," he said to her. "I shall always remember how you saved my life and shared your own with me."

They had dismounted. They stood alone, and the bond between them was as strained as it was strong. "You shall come back," said Cethlinn. Her hands reached out to his and held them as tightly as if she were drowning. She would not speak her secret. She could not. Not now. He would think that she was attempting to entrap him. He would not believe she was with child. Nothing she could say could turn him from his purpose now. "You *must* come back. Your Destiny lies here," she said, yet the words implored: Do not go. Stay. And deep within her a cold wind of foreboding stirred—he had turned his back upon the Stones; he had forfeited his luck forever.

Her father was watching her with quiet introspection, as he often did these days, and came over to join them. "None of us can ever go back, Cethlinn. We ride the winds of Fate. And from wherever we may stand in life, we can only go forward."

"Riddles again, Star Gazer?" queried Balor.

Both men were awash in memories. Cromm Cruach smiled as he echoed the past. "All life is a riddle, my boy. Someday perhaps we *will* puzzle it out. But for now it seems that once again Destiny calls us out onto different roads."

Clouds were gathering high above them, dark clouds stirred by high winds that did not touch the earth. Yet they chilled Cromm Cruach, for he saw them churned and transformed into wild and feral shapes, into packs of wolves, which leaped across the sky; and amidst the wolves, a hawk rode the back of the wind—not a hawk fashioned from clouds, but of living flesh and feather and sharp beak and watching eye.

Cromm Cruach turned to Balor and embraced him and knew it would be for the last time as he thought: *May the blessing of the Stone not have abandoned you . . . may the Twelve Winds be gentle at your back, for the world grows dark and wolves run loose upon the land. They call to you more strongly than does the song of the Stone. You must follow them. Your Destiny lies with them now, in blood and in darkness.*

31

They struck northward. Lorcan led them to the place where he had come out of the marshes to the sea. They saw no ships carrying sails of red and black, only long-abandoned campfires. Balor and a small party composed of Findias, Gorias, Muri, and Ogma went into the marsh to see if they could locate the scene where the rape of the women and the murder of the men and children of Draga's family had taken place. It was Findias's opinion that the women had probably been used and then slain, since women would only be a hindrance on a raiding expedition, and if the men were headed north to Point of Ale, they could buy their pleasure cheaply enough on the many whores and slave women available there.

He was proved right soon enough. The stench of decomposing tissue as well as the sound of feasting birds drew Balor's party to the site. They saw Eala's body right away, cruelly mutilated beside the bloodied corpses of the children. The decapitated body of the redbeard lay sprawled where it had fallen, unrecognizable, as were the others, save for their clothing. The predatory creatures of the marsh had done their work well. There was no sign of Dana or Uaine, or of the heads of the men, which evidently had been taken along as booty as well.

For a long while Balor stood over Draga's body as the others dug a grave for the corpses. His reaction to the redbeard's corpse was not what he had expected. He felt no satisfaction; what he felt was remorse. How strange to feel that for one who would have seen *him* buried in a bog to further his own ambitions! How strange not to recall the man's duplicity and wanton treachery, but to think only of his deep laugh and his bright, watchful eyes and the flash of his white teeth gleaming within the brazen sprawl of his red beard. How strange to remember only the good times, the mock battles when he had challenged the youths upon the training field, the sight of him stripped nearly nude as he and Fomor had come against one another in friendly clashes of staves or bouts of wrestling, when the power of his big, broad, red-furred body had been second to none except to the lord himself.

He thought of him now, as he had been on that night at Point of Ale when he had circled Creugas in the firelight and brought him down, laughing, posturing for the crowd and the spotted woman.

Uaine . . . where was she now? Was Dana with her? Were they alive, or had they been slain?

His eyes took in Draga's degraded corpse. No man deserved such a death. No man. Unless it was Nemed, or those who had worked this utter degradation upon Draga and his family.

"They'll have headed up the coast to Point of Ale," said Findias. "My guess is that if they didn't kill the women here, they've taken them along for sport and sale. Unless the women give them undue trouble, they're probably alive . . . but in what condition... well, we'll have to discover that for ourselves."

That night Balor dreamt of Draga rising headless from the grave, and he awoke, sweated, to feel the pitch and roll of the large, broad, deep-bellied ship of the men of Eireann. The miles slipped by, and soon the sky took on the dull, washed look of a cloud-covered dawn. They saw no ships other than those of their own fleet of followers. A wind rose with the morning. They raised their broad leather sail, and Balor thought of the grandfather whom he had never known, of Manannan MacLir, whose name meant Son of the Sea, and of the ships Fomor had burned when he had led his people inland to seek a life of peace within the lost, wild fens of Albion.

They made good time. Findias pointed out landmarks as they proceeded along the coast and told how the currents would run off each bay and headland. Balor grew curious. He asked him how a man of Eireann knew these waters so well. The giant laughed, as did the others aboard.

Muri spat downwind. "We are sea raiders when the fancy takes us, lad. Pirates, if you will. We plunder the coastal hamlets of Albion where the people are known to deal freely with such men as Nemed... for it is their willingness to trade with such devils that encourages them to linger in our seas, to beset Eireann when the mood takes them."

"Tell the lad what you wished on the Stone, man," pressed Findias.

Muri shrugged and massaged his scorched-looking beard. "I wished to come to Point of Ale one day with a great fleet of raiding ships filled with like-minded men, and that we might burn the entire place to the ground, all its foreign merchants with it. But not before I sacked it first, and loaded onto my ship all the fancies I could carry away without the risk of foundering in the crossing back to Eireann."

Balor thought of Point of Ale, with its narrow alleyways and buildings of wood and thatch; of Horsa, factor of the trading center, lackey to its mentor, Nemed MacAgnomain, prince of Achaea; of the ill-treatment he had received at the hands of the cloth merchant; of the slave women he had seen degraded; of the humiliation of his own people; and of how life throbbed there, as close and foul as maggots on unburied garbage in the refuse pits of Bracken Fen.

"Help me to find my kinswomen, Muri, and by the Twelve Winds, I shall personally light the torch for you to set to the place."

"I'll help you find them, dead or alive," Muri promised.

"They *shall* be alive!"

Again the man spat, only this time he did not turn his head quite far enough and pearls of saliva went back into his beard. He scowled and backhanded them away. "It might be kinder to wish them dead, lad, especially the fair one, if she was as gentle as you say."

They saw the crimson color of the sail before they saw the ship. It was beached high in the neck of a narrow cove. The sail was down and rolled upon the deck—a great, elongated mound of color. The tide was out, and the ship was well aground. Two men were aboard, doing repair work at the base of the mast, while a full dozen others stood at the water's edge, staring seaward. They held swords in their hands, as did the man who hunkered down by a large fire pit, his weapon across his knees. There were two women seated close together across from him—a blond and a redhead.

Had the choice been Balor's, he would have leapt overboard in his desire to reach them, but Muri grabbed him by his hair and told him to stay where he was. "There's an art to this, lad. Approach with your temper high, and you'll not live to learn it."

They stayed well out from the land, moving northward, showing no signs at all of putting into shore. For several miles they proceeded thus, until the men of Eireann were satisfied that no other enemy ships carrying the red and black sails were in the vicinity. Then, at Findias's command, some twenty men were put ashore north of the cove. They would approach the encampment of Nemed's men from behind while Findias and his own handpicked group of swordsmen would come in openly by way of the cove. They would present a facade of friendliness, traveling pilgrims en route home from the great gathering on the sacred plain to the south and wishing to share an evening's meal and a night's fire. By the time the men on the beach grew suspicious of their heavy armament, the women would be warned back and away and the twenty men waiting at their victims' backs would charge forward. Nemed's men would be slain and left to rot as they had left Draga and his people to rot.

The men of Eireann would savor what they deemed "a bit of battle sport" and claim the Achaean ship as their own, striking its markings even as they slashed its hated crimson and black sail; it would be powered by oarsmen until they could fit it with a new sail at Point of Ale. Balor's kinswomen would be saved, and vengeance and justice would be served.

Balor was refused permission to row into the cove with Findias and his men.

"If the women were to give any indication of knowing you," Muri explained, "the game would be up. The men would try to use them as a shield. They'd not get off the beach alive, lad. Take my word on it. I've seen it happen."

Balor glared at him, distraught, convinced that Muri lied merely to keep him from participating because of his inexperience. He said as much.

Muri shook his head sadly. "Many a long year ago my own sisters were stolen and I ran off alone to avenge them with a handful of young hotheads like myself. Swords we had too, from my father's forge, but he was taken captive with my sisters and could not warn us away from what we thought was valor. For days we stalked them, the men of Nemed MacAgnomain. We found them and burst to the attack. And my eldest sister—the one who still had a mind left after what they had worked upon her—cried out our names with joy. They cut her down where she stood. My friends and kindred were slain, and I was taken captive. For five long years I was a slave at Point of Ale. So do not tell me what you would do, boy! If you are the son of the Wolf, then *be* a wolf. Be wise, know when it is time for you to fight. Timing is half the battle."

Chastised, Balor did as he was told without further complaint, joining the group of men who would approach the cove from the land. It went exactly to plan. From his position with the others, lying flat behind a thicket of thick shore scrub on a steep rise of hillside directly behind the beach, he saw it all, and when at last he saw Uaine take Dana's arm and gently guide her to an inconspicuous spot well to one side of the fire, it was then that the rising thrum of rage began to beat in him. He could see the women's battered and swollen faces, and from within the wild, uncombed tangles of their hip-length hair that only partially disguised their nudity, their skin was blue from bruising. Dana hobbled, bent like an old woman, as Uaine's freckled arm tenderly circled her slender shoulders. The girl's eyes had the wide, blank look of one whose soul has wandered from her body. What had been worked upon her to reduce her to the broken semblance of a hag?

He must have made a choking sound of agony, for the man beside him lay a strong, firm hand upon his forearm. "Easy, lad, hold it in. Then let it go, like a storm of blood upon them. . . . Now!"

The signal had been given. Balor had missed it. It did not matter. His companions were raining arrows onto the beach even as they ran forward, howling—yes—like wolves. His own cry joined theirs, ululated in a high, shrieking wail that did not end when he came down upon the beach. He held Teacher in one hand and his ax in the other. Impossibly, they would tell him later, he used them simultaneously, whirling, dancing, maiming, and finding that his energy was without bound. He took no men's heads, nor did he dismember enemies . . . for these men were not men, they were not enemies, they were rabid beasts to be cut down without mercy. He laughed when they begged for it. He hooted when, disarmed by the force of his weapons, they turned and fled, and he leapt out at them and brought them down screaming. Several times he felt them at his back. He pitched them forward over his head or ducked and leapt sideways, and always, somehow, came away unscathed. Or so he thought.

When it was done, he did not know it until Findias's huge cudgel came against his back and dropped him to his knees. He sprawled, stunned, suddenly nauseated, looking up at those who surrounded him, but seeing nothing but red— thick, hot, red pulsing down into his eyes from the gash that had lain open his scalp and brow above his left eye. Slowly, dizzy now with exhaustion, he rose and wiped the blood away and saw the men of Eireann staring at him as though at a stranger. He was bleeding from cuts upon his arms and legs. Indeed, his entire body was red with his own blood and the blood of the men he had slain. His right arm felt oddly light, and for a moment panic struck him as he feared that he had severely injured it or even lost it. But when he looked, he saw that it was Teacher that had been ruined, broken in half; and still he had used it, although he did not know how.

"By the Fates, never have I seen the like," said Muri, so impressed by what he had seen that he forgot to spit before or after his statement.

"I tell you. People of Stone, they right! Balor, he be wizard!" exclaimed Gorias.

"Did I . . . kill . . . many . . . ?"

"Mother of the Twelve Winds, boy, save for the two near the ship and three more who tried to run past us into the sea, you killed them all." Findias had the look on his face that men who have seen visions are known to wear. "Ten men. *Ten* armed men. By the Fates, teat sucker, I'll grant Cethlinn was right about you. You *are* the Mighty One!"

The words went unheard. As did Uaine's when she came close, wrapped in a short cape, which one of the men had given to her for modesty's sake. She held it around her, standing tall and bold, defiant almost, as though her bruises and battered face were scars of some terrible battle she had courageously survived. Yet there was a hardness in her face that had not been there before. She was a woman who had seen her babies murdered and her man decapitated; she would not be the same again. Something in her had died with them. Yet she was alive, by nature a survivor, and she had seen vengeance served. There was solace for her in that. She lay a questing hand upon Balor's bloodied shoulder. "I shall stitch your wounds, son of Fomor."

"When I have seen Dana. Where is Dana?" She had left the beach. He could not see her anywhere.

Uaine's reply had the edge of unbearable sadness. "She is in the ship, hiding. Do not go to her, Balor. Not until you have rested. She . . . is . . . not the same as you remember her."

He ran to the ship; no one tried to stop him. He was aboard and practically on top of her before he saw her curled against the sail. She held something in her arms, wrapped like an infant. She rocked it. She crooned to it, a soft and careless little child's tune. It was a moment before she turned to look up at him. There was no recognition in the great gray misty eyes that stared up at him out of a face that was still beautiful despite the bruises and abrasions that discolored and distorted it.

"*Ssh* now. You must be very still. He is not well, you know. He needs his sleep." She smiled, then; that wonderful, radiant smile, which only Dana could smile. "Here. See for yourself how peacefully he sleeps. Soon he will lead us safely to our destination."

The covering came away. It was Draga's head.

For the next two days they beat their way into the wind, moving ever northward through long, deep swells under clouded skies. Several times they provoked encounters with ships carrying the red and black sails and traveling alone or in pairs. They surrounded these lone or paired ships, forced them into submission, took their weapons, and learned what they could of the Achaean's plans from the men aboard before they killed them all, threw them into the sea, and confiscated their ships. According to all that they could learn, a fleet of nearly fifty warships was following only several days behind. From an original gathering of some eighty vessels drawn from Nemed's personal armada and a dozen vassal lords, the violent sea storm had honed the fleet but had not broken it. The fleet was to rendezvous at Point of Ale and provision the army there for the march inland to the unsuspecting holding of Bracken Fen.

"But the Wolf will be wise to them, because we shall get to him first, eh?" said Findias. "Teat sucker knows the way to the holding and shall lead us there quickly!"

"Aye, I shall. But call me teat sucker again and you'll not live to see it."

They measured each other. The past days had changed them both: Findias, because he had seen a new and dangerous side to the youth who had won Cethlinn from him, and Balor, because the blood of battle and Dana's madness had hardened him and brought him to a disturbing and as yet undefined awareness of the man who was evolving out of the skin of the youth.

Findias's small eyes summed him as he observed him, not unappreciatively, for he remembered the youth as he had been on the beach of the cove when they had come to the rescue of the two women. "Balor . . . of the Mighty Blows, then. Shall that do for you?"

Coming from the ever-critical giant, the compliment was extraordinary. But Balor was looking off across the body of the ship to where Dana sat with Uaine, asleep in the curl of the older woman's arm, clutching the wrapped and hideous trophy that she would allow no one to take from her. "Nothing shall do for me, Findias, except the sight of Nemed MacAgnomain's head in a sack and the knowledge that his body lies rotting at the bottom of the sea."

Using a plan Muri had conceived, they stormed Point of Ale by night, in waves, from land and sea and from within. They had sent scouts ashore by day, and when Findias ignited the signal torch from his ship, these scouts went out about the trading center and killed the sentries where they stood watch. The night burned red, and stank of smoke and blood, and when it was done, the earth was scarred with charred and bleeding rubble, and those who had not been slain— servants and slaves and local peasants who were warned away and told never again to deal with foreign merchants who flew the colors of the red and black—wandered stunned and silent through the carnage.

Muri grinned and spat and said that no ships would be provisioned here again, nor would Nemed's men be able to find food to sustain them for their journey inland.

"They'll sack the nearby hamlets for what they need," said Findias, "but it'll slow them up a bit and buy us time to reach the Wolf and warn him to ready his pack for what is to come!" He turned to Balor, the light of bloodlust still hot in his eyes. "How many men does he have, eh? A thousand? Twice that? More? By the Fates, in days gone by they said that ten thousand followed in the wake of his ships! Ach! He must be lord over a great host by now, eh? Together we shall put an end to Nemed! Together we shall be lords of all the earth!"

Balor said nothing. They stood on the cliffs above the sea. A dawn wind pushed the smells of death and carnage back across the land. Behind him his men were still looting the rubble. Others had slaughtered cows and other livestock and had set them to roast on spits over huge fires. Now and again a woman's laughter rose from somewhere amid the confusion of activity. Laughter. Had the women laughed so with the men who now lay dead all around them? He thought of Dana and wondered if she would ever laugh again. Laughter was an obscenity in this scene. He turned and observed the smoldering ruin of Point of Ale. How many men had he killed this night? For vengeance's sake. Always for vengeance's sake. Why then did he feel so empty now that the slaying madness was gone from him? Where was the sweetness? Where was the elation that was said to come with thé winning of battle glory?

Glory? Was that what he now looked upon?

By the Fates, surely there must be more to it than this.

32

From all across the fens the horns of the watchmen of Bracken Fen sounded like frenzied stallions beneath the leaden sky. Two days before the column of riders and men afoot neared the holding, Fomor MacLir knew that they were coming.

"I tell you it's your son, my lord, riding at the head of a great hosting of men. He is much changed. Wound-marked and a man—no longer a boy. He sits astride a great, white horse, with a giant striding beside him. He says he comes to bring bronze to the men of the clan MacLir! Swords, my lord! And he brings back to us two of the women of Draga and bids me inform you that the Raven is flying and knows the denning place of the Wolf. What does he mean, my lord?"

It was one of the few times that Rinn's obsequious manner did not irritate the chieftain. He sat with his women as they tended to the makings of the midday meal. The smell of the meat-rich gruel was thick in the room, redolent of all of the scents that bespoke the benevolence of the summer fields. Elathan had been passing the morning with him; the two of them had been reknapping arrowheads. At the news Elathan nicked himself with his blade and rose to his feet, staring, his mind exploding with conflicting emotions. Happiness, rage, joy, anguish, all meshed into an impossible melding. He cried his brother's name aloud, wondering how it was possible to

love someone and loathe him at the same time. If Balor came
back, he would be a second son again. If Balor came back . . .

"Munremar shall demand his death!" exclaimed Mealla,
her face a mask of concern.

"Death . . ." Huldre's voice was barely audible. She had
been nursing Babh. She looked down at the sleeping child,
then her eyes drifted away, away across the smoky, shadowed
room, away to lonely, misted visions, which only she could
see. Little Bevin, sitting on the hearthstones playing with her
little leather doll, forgot her toy and shivered as slowly her
mother's eyes focused back into reality and a look of quivering
ferocity tensed upon her face. "Death . . . yes . . . I can smell
it. It is close now. Have I not warned you? Over the long
years have I not told you that I have seen him coming toward
us across the miles? *Mine* have been the true visions! Not the
conjured smokes and sparks of that wizened old man who
masquerades as a prophet in order to earn his keep and avoid
soiling his hands at a man's honest labor. But now you shall
know the truth! My son has returned . . . the Raven is
flying . . . and the Wolf can hide no more!"

Fomor dismissed Rinn, telling him to inform the men of
the clan that there would be an immediate assembly within
the council hall. It would be hours before Balor and his
hosting reached the holding. It was said that there were
nearly four hundred men with him, all of them armed. Four
hundred men! Were they coming as allies, or was the youth
coming home for blood? With only a scant hundred men
of the clan MacLir left after the years of darkness and
disease—and only half of them in their prime and fit for
battle—they would be at a profound disadvantage if taken
unprepared.

He suddenly felt very tired. He wished that Rinn had been
able to give him some word of Draga's fate and of how Balor
had come by two of his women. Two. Which two? By the
Twelve Winds, he hoped that it was not Dana. She was sure
to stir up trouble among the ranks again, as she had before
her father had taken her and the others and fled into the
snowstorm. He had never understood Draga's reason for
behaving as he had, but the man had not been rational for
some time. Fomor had sent out parties of trackers to find
him, but the snow had been Draga's ally, leaving no trace of
his little band. In time things had settled back to normal;

Dana's many suitors had contented themselves with other women or with the hearth mates they already had. Of all of them, the young healer, Dianket, had been the most visibly distraught. Strange and sad, for he had never had a hope of winning the girl.

And now Balor was back. Ach! It was good to know that the boy was alive! And how good it would be to see his son once again. But no. It would *not* be good. Had he not sworn to take his life if Balor returned? Aye. On the Stones of Choosing. Before witnesses Draga had forced him to swear it. Kill his son or die himself. Yes. Clan law was very clear about the punishment that must be meted out to those who broke oaths sworn upon the Stones of Choosing. Munremar would not allow him to forget. Not when the death must be Balor's. Since boyhood his firstborn's powers of precognition had put the old man's feeble talents to shame. Poor Munremar, to be born to the Wise One's role and to possess no wisdom—a cruel fate for an inherently cruel man. Fomor knew now that he should have exposed Munremar for the charlatan that he was years ago. But loyalty to his father's one-time servant, to one who had saved his life and guided him when he had first accepted the chieftainship, had long caused him to excuse the man's true nature.

He thought these thoughts as Mealla brought out the golden collar and placed it about his neck and shoulders. Had it always been so heavy? She helped him don the ceremonial leather baldric and handed him his twin jewel-handled ritual daggers and the magnificent long-handled ax that the lord of the clan MacLir held during all ceremonies in lieu of a scepter. Her hands were shaking. He lay the daggers and ax across his thighs and took her hands, knowing that she thought of the child that at long last was growing within her womb, knowing that she must be terrified of what was to come, especially now—good and faithful Mealla, who had been so satisfied with the peaceful life, who had raised another woman's children as her own and never complained, only supported . . . even now. "It shall go well for us," he said, consoling and assuring even though his heart was full of great, blank empty spaces where feelings of confidence should have been.

"Yes, with *this* it *shall* go well for us!"

Huldre had come to stand beside Mealla. She had given

little Babh into Bevin's arms, and while Fomor had been lost
in introspection, she had opened his battle chest. She stood
before him now, as she had stood so long ago, before he went
forth to battle. Her face glowed with the passion of excitement and resolve. Her arms were held out and down, and
across her palms lay the unsheathed magnificence of Retaliator.

"It is time, my lord. . . ." she whispered, and knelt before
him, proffering the blade.

He stared at it. At Partholon's sword. The sword that had
taken his father's head and cut the unborn child from his
mother's womb. The sword he had stolen to loose a tide of
vengeance, which even now swept back toward him out of
time. The Raven was flying. And he must become the Wolf
once again.

"Aye," he said, acknowledging that which could no longer
be postponed or denied: The days of peace were gone
forever. He took the sword from her hands and felt its weight
balanced across his palms. Retaliator. His eyes held upon its
burnished perfection as the substance of the cold bronze took
on warmth from his flesh. "It *is* time," he conceded, and felt
the long-forgotten sense of kinship with the sword rise as
power within him.

Huldre was smiling. For the first time since they had
settled within the fens, her eyes were clear. There were no
mists in them, no fear. "It *shall* go well with us now. The
Raven comes. We shall face him and slay him, and the Twelve
Winds shall be at our back. I can feel them rising to protect
us. With the Wolf to lead us, we cannot fail."

Her confidence was contagious. He could see it shining in
Elathan's face, and Mealla too seemed encouraged. Little
Bevin kissed Babh's fat cheeks and told her not to stir or to
fret—the Raven was coming, but the Wolf would eat him and
all would be well.

He kept the image of them with him as he walked out of
the chieftain's roundhouse to where the men of the clan
MacLir were assembling, fully armed, before the council
hall. The tension was palpable. They had been milling in
silence until he appeared, until they saw the sword at his
side. Then, as he watched, they cheered, crying out his
name. As Elathan beamed with pride beside him, they raised
their own weapons in a sign of consent to fealty, in a shrieking,

stamping, howling affirmation of their willingness to do battle in his name.

For a long moment he did not move. The great, black empty spaces expanded within him as he raised Retaliator and held it high. Their cheering intensified, and he thought, *You* are *children of the People of the Ax. This is what you truly hunger for, and whatever comes, you shall welcome it ...until the very end, when it is too late. Then you shall remember, then you shall lament the loss of all that I have won for you ...in peace ...without the sword.*

"Though I am not yet a man by rite and law, I would stand with you in battle, Father, and take vengeance upon those who have dishonored my ancestors and would now dare to come against my people!"

The fire in Elathan's voice was undeniable. No use now to try to quench it; it would only smolder with resentment and burst to flame in the end. "Against the Raven, against the forces of Nemed MacAgnomain, we shall need every hand before this battle is done."

They went forward to the council hall together. And Fomor was smiling as he thought of Draga. *Ach, little Brother, why did you run? It is a pity that you do not walk beside me now. You would be content at last, to know that you have won your way after all!*

They assembled all along the walkway of the palisade while horsemen, headed by the chieftain, rode out to stand massed along the ramparts of the earthen embankment in full display of weaponry. Those men who had swords stood in the first rank, giving the illusion that those behind them were similarly armed; but Fomor knew that Balor would not be bluffed. He knew that his people were bronze poor, so if the men of MacLir were going to impress the men who followed him, it would have to be by the ferocity of their look alone. So they had donned the blue woad and red madder, battle paint to make men look large and fierce and somehow more than men. And Munremar stood high upon the palisade in all of his feathered finery, looking like a skinny white bird, as Morrigan, with tiny Cian in her arms, stood beside him and said that he was a fool if he thought that Balor had come for any other purpose than the one he avowed: to warn his clan of impending danger and to stand with them against it.

Slowly Balor and his followers approached, with weapons sheathed and arms raised in the universal sign of peace. Huldre, standing on the palisade amid the press of the curious and the apprehensive, gasped with pride to see her son riding at the head of the great hosting upon a huge, white horse, with Dana riding against him at his back . . . and for a moment, she saw not Balor, but Fomor, as he had been nearly a lifetime ago, a warrior riding with a pale woman, carrying her boldly away from her enemies.

Then Balor spoke. He spoke loudly and clearly and with the authority of one twice his age. He spoke of all that he had endured since he had fled from Bracken Fen, and he spoke of the blessings he had been given by the People of the Stone, of how Lorcan had found him there on the dawn of the midsummer sunrise to tell him of Draga's fate. He paused then, and Uaine came forward and vowed that all that he had said was true, and an awed whispering went through the listening clan as they brooded over the terrible fate that had befallen the redbeard and his family. Then as they watched, the head of Draga was taken from a piece of red and black sail from one of Nemed's ships, and as Dana stared blankly, Balor held her trophy high.

"Behold the fate of Draga, son of Manannan, brother of the Wolf!" he cried. "Behold the fate of the clan MacLir if we do not now join forces against Nemed MacAgnomain with the tribesmen of the West who have come here with me to swear their allegiance to the Wolf!"

The silence that fell then was deafening. It was Findias, the giant, who broke it, eyeing the assembled men of the clan MacLir and counting their numbers as he felt a deep, sick feeling in his belly. Where were the thousands? Where were the wolves with whom his father had once run? Together with the men of Eireann and those who had come into the fens after ravaging Point of Ale, there would still be less than five hundred men . . . and Nemed would have close to two thousand! "Where is this Wolf?" he demanded of Balor, beginning to suspect that he had been manipulated to serve a cause he could not hope to win.

Then, as a solitary figure mounted upon a black stallion rode out of the ranks of men massed upon the raised embankment, the giant felt the color drain from his face as a vision risen from the past came toward him.

In a robe made of the skins of wolves taken in that fateful hunt when Balor had saved Draga's life and nearly ruined his own, Fomor MacLir rode out alone. And the power of all that he had ever been was more radiant than the gold of his chieftain's collar, more awesome than the sight of the fabled blade he carried unsheathed and held diagonally across his massive chest.

As he drew rein before his son and Findias, slowly, from beneath the wolf's head of his cloak, his eyes surveyed the giant and the men assembled behind him as if they were stubble he could rend and shatter and send flying before the Twelve Winds.

The giant's breath caught in his throat. Surely this man could be lord of all the earth if he only willed it to be so. Surely this man could bend them all to his command.

And this the chieftain did, quietly, in a deep, even voice, which was heard as a storm is heard whispering upon a far horizon. "*I am the Wolf. I am Fomor MacLir, son of Manannan, kinsman to the People of the Ax. If you have come to swear allegiance to me, then do so now, and together we shall break the forces of Nemed MacAgnomain, dividing his power among us, and as in Days of Glory, together we shall be lords of all the earth!*"

His power consumed their will. To a man they dropped to their knees before him as those who were mounted slid from their horses to do the same. Even Findias knelt and bowed his head in a gesture of fealty and absolute submission. There was no question or doubt in his mind now. Fomor MacLir had assumed the proportions of a god in his eyes. Under his command anything was possible.

And suddenly an epiphany came to Balor. His *father* was the Mighty One—mighty in his own world, on his own terms, with only his own vision to grant him the courage and will to lead. He had brought his people out of the bloodied turmoil of the world so that he might dare hold back the darkness for them for a little while, between the wars and ragings that other men called glory. The days of peace were gone forever. And he, who had so longed for this day as a boy, now mourned for it as a man.

*   *   *

They were allowed to enter the holding. Fomor watched them move forward. He held his horse back and told Balor to do the same. Uaine sensed his need to speak privately with his son and gently drew the mindless Dana from the horse and walked with her toward the palisade, where Dianket had appeared with Blaheen and several other older women. The girl was wrapped immediately into a loving embrace. The sight of Dianket caused Balor to instinctively knee his horse forward, but Fomor reached to hold him back.

"Your life shall be forfeit if you enter the circle of the clan."

Balor was stunned as Fomor explained all that had gone before and told him of the earlier council in which the Wise One insisted that the sentence not be waived at a time when the very fate of the clan might depend upon its chieftain's will to keep its laws.

"Law. Ever since I can remember, Munremar has always used the law against me."

"And always have you managed to fuel his animosity, to place yourself outside the law, even now, when you bring to us the gift of life."

The leaden sky colored the world, weighted the two men who spoke quietly beneath it.

"It is a talent I have," Balor said darkly. "Show me a law or an oath, any time, any place, and I shall find a way to break it."

A tenuous smile of irony moved upon Fomor's mouth. He extended a hand to his son. "Nevertheless, many have missed you, Law Breaker. Things have not been the same in Bracken Fen without you."

Their hands met. Locked. Held.

"Because of my actions your enemies approach the holding, Father. You should have listened to the Wise One long ago concerning me. I have brought danger in my wake. But I'll tell you this: We have taken many swords on our way here. You shall be well armed."

"Against how many?"

He could barely bring himself to speak; but the truth would be evident soon enough, and so he did not hesitate. "Some say as many as two thousand."

Fomor stared, stunned. "And you come to me with a force of four hundred? Do they know the odds?"

"They come to fight beside the Wolf, the one who was once the lord of the Western Tribes and shall be so again." A sense of renewed purpose was rising in him. Fomor had withdrawn his hand. Balor saw it rested upon the haft of his weapon. Upon Retaliator. His heart beat fast at the sight of it. "We shall be victorious, Father. You have designed the holding well; it shall stand indefinitely against a siege. And Nemed's men shall be ill supplied. They'll be raiding villages and eating off the land all the way . . . we saw to that en route." Balor told him then of what they had worked at Point of Ale, how they had burned all of the Achaean ships that had been beached there, and the sea boardings they had made on their journey northward. He did not know that he was shaking until his father lay his hand across his forearm.

Fomor saw the young man's eyes focus out of memories too ugly to hold. Their glance held. Quietly, Fomor said: "There shall be no siege, my son. The wolves are loose. The men whom you have brought with you, they will not sit content behind an embankment for weeks on end. As for our own kinsmen, Draga's lust for glory infected them long ago. They had their battle chests open and were boasting of past bravery and what they would do when they had a chance to prove their worth as warriors once again before your men were sighted from the palisade. Siege? They would as soon sit still for castration."

"But they cannot stand man to man against two thousand!"

"No. They cannot. But they can die as sons of the People of the Ax have always died in battle. Nemed's forces shall be victorious, Balor. And so I speak to you now, not only as your father, but as your lord, as chieftain of the clan MacLir. The watchmen out upon the land, they advise me that the Raven flies close behind you—two days, perhaps less. That can buy us both the time we need—time for me to formulate some sort of a battle plan, and time for you to take the women and children, the healer, and those among us with life-skills away from the holding, out across the moor, leaving no tracks by which any Achaean dog may later follow and come against you. Go to the tor. Take refuge there. When all has been finished here . . . if it is the will of the Twelve Winds, I shall seek you there. If I do not come to you, then do not look back. Go wisely, as the Wolf must go, Balor. You shall carry the future of the clan MacLir with you."

33

They stood amid the rubble of Point of Ale, and Nemed held the Eye of Donar curled within his fist as he stared inland.

"How far to the holding of the Wolf from here, toad?"

The dwarf stood carefully out of range of his master's ire. "A few day's march, my lord. Due east, then due north, then slightly west for the remainder of the trek."

"We shall half it—no, we shall quarter it."

Coman felt sick, but said nothing. Since they had seen the distant fires of the burning settlement upon the horizon, Nemed had driven his men without mercy. They had not eaten. They had not slept. They were beyond exhaustion.

The face of the Achaean twitched. There was unbridled savagery upon it as he turned and faced the great assembly of his men and spoke with the passion of one who is obsessed. "You have all seen the corpses and burned ships we have found on our voyage to this place. *Our* ships. *Our* comrades. Slaughtered by those who are in league against us and obviously intent upon joining forces with the one whom we are set to find and destroy."

A murmuring went through the exhausted men. Below them the sea washed within the cove where the bones of ships and men lay burned and stinking in the bleak, cloud-covered light of the day. Flies had come to feast, and birds had come to do battle, species against species, as they fought for remnant scraps of flesh and gore. Their caws and keens could be heard clearly. The men listened, sullen, and Nemed did not misjudge their mood.

"Those who have done this have done it to deprive us of supplies because they think us to be weak, dependent upon the things of the flesh. But I say that we are strong. We shall go forward. We shall not eat until we feast on the blood of the Wolf. We will quaff his mead and leave the bodies of his people for carrion. In the name of Minardos, in the names of all of those who have died in my service since we set sail from

Achaea, for every man who marches with me now without complaint, I offer a life's bounty in gold and slaves and land! So who is man enough to walk with me, to follow the Eye of Donar and not look back?"

He did not wait for an answer. He turned and began to stride out across the ruined land. To a man they rose and followed him.

And Coman the dwarf trotted behind, wondering why he was needed as a guide when the Eye of Donar seemed to be leading the man more truly than the light of the North Star; but then, even if he had been told to stay behind, he would have followed. Death walked in the wake of Nemed Mac-Agnomain's intentions, and Coman had always savored the stench and color of blood.

"But the lord has commanded me to stay! You cannot go! Tonight there shall be another assembly, a last gathering before the men make ready to do battle. They shall need my magic to strengthen them against the enemy!"

Morrigan heard the desperation in her father's voice. It did not touch her. Gently she lifted the traveling basket that carried little Cian and slung it onto her back. "Give them magic then! You are the Wise One, not I."

They stood within the snug little house that the girl had inherited from old Falcon. Rinn was off readying his weapons for battle with the other young men. The girl stood before Munremar, dressed for traveling and impatient to go. "You cannot leave," he implored. "Who shall make the magic for me if you go?"

He seemed so small and old standing before her, supplicating. If only the people of the holding could see him like this, they would not want any part of such a weak man's magic. She had been a good and caring daughter; but now at last she knew the full extent of his selfishness and found it difficult not to loathe him.

"For the last time I have fed my son the mead of sleep so that I might serve as your assistant and make your powers seem great. This afternoon, when you insisted upon holding the chieftain to the law concerning Balor—even though his firstborn son has come here at the risk of his life with an army of men to warn us of danger—I vowed it would be the last time that I would ever lift a hand to help you!"

"But Balor is unlucky! The entire clan knows that! It is he

who brought this calamity upon us. To welcome him back into the holding, to disregard clan law, it would be disastrous to us all!"

"No. Only to you. Because he knows you for what you are—a conniving, jealous manipulator who would see a man buried alive in a bog for the single crime of possessing gifts potentially greater than your own! And the sad thing about it, Father, is that you were never even wise enough to understand that Balor wanted no part of Vision. The last thing he would have sought in Bracken Fen would have been to usurp your role as priest."

He stood stunned. This hard-eyed, black-haired woman was a stranger. Where was the little girl who had been so malleable in his hands, ready to serve him? "Morrigan! Come back to me, Daughter. Balor shall bring all who follow him to destruction! He has been bad luck since first he moved within his mother's womb...and she, a huldre, shall lead you to your death!"

"Bah! You loathe her for the same reason you loathe her firstborn son, because she has the gift of Vision, and you do not! Well, now at least the holding will know the truth of her Sight, for *she* predicted this, and you did not!" Morrigan hefted up the bag of food and mead and items that others might find of need upon what might prove to be a long and difficult journey. "Pray to the Twelve Winds, Father, and to the Fates and to the Mother of All. Perhaps after all of these years they shall heed your supplications. Who knows what may happen when a man is forced to stand upon his own two feet and face the truth about himself? You may have powers that you have never dreamed of! But I am not under your will anymore. I have a son to think of. And I shall face the future with his father. It is time for me to leave my own."

The statement confused him. Had she lost her senses as well as her sensitivity toward her sire? "Old Falcon is dead!" he reminded her.

She had crossed the room and reached the door. She turned momentarily to look back at him, and this time she did feel pity for him, for he was bereft and pale and trembling. "Look with the eye of common sense, Wise One. Your other daughters shall see to your welfare now, for they are both still childless and have been commanded to stay behind to help the wounded when the time comes. But *this* daughter, this small, dark thorn of a girl has borne a grandson to the Wolf! This daughter has carried the blood of the great Manannan himself! This daughter has borne a son to *Balor*... and if the Twelve Winds should curse me for it, then I, Morrigan, shall curse them back! I am not afraid. I have been to the Otherworld and back again. I have seen death. Now I shall get on with my life. Free of you. And unafraid."

Yet she was afraid. She came out from the holding to where the women and children were gathering together for the trek to the tor. Dianket was there with Dana, who stood with little Bevin. The chieftain's little girl was mounted on Dana's white pony, and as Dianket held the animal's halter, Draga's daughter combed the little horse's long mane absently with her fingers, crooning to it, and speaking to Bevin as a child would speak. She looked up as Morrigan came close, and her eyes were wide and blank as she cocked her head and asked her if they had not met before.

"I am Dana. My father has brought me this fine pony from a far land. When I am a woman grown he shall bring me a great white horse with a golden horn upon its head. He has promised. But I am in no hurry. I do not want to grow up. It is better to be little. One cannot ride a pony when one grows too tall."

Morrigan saw the agony in Dianket's eyes and turned away lest she burst into tears.

"Morrigan..."

She knew his voice before she saw him coming toward her through the throng.

"Balor!"

And yet it was not Balor. The height, the coloring, even the face—these she remembered, but all were altered subtly, cruelly. The youth was gone. He was a man now. No longer wild, in spite of his tangled hair and soiled, tattered, battle-stained clothing, but tired... to his soul and beyond.

Slowly, not even knowing that she did so, she reached up to touch his face, even as his own hands gently touched her own.

"You... are not the same...."

The statement came simultaneously from them both.

"I have seen you... in so many unlikely places... always, you have been in my thoughts...." His words did not come easily. His eyes were lost in the cool green of hers as he remembered a night when they had been full of fire and moonlight. But now the coolness was soothing, and now, as then, without willing himself to do so, he was kissing her, and her arms were about him, and then she was crying softly as she cradled her face in the hollow between his neck and shoulder, and he heard her say that she loved him, and he knew, with a sudden shock and an absolute lack of reservation that he loved her too—so deeply that there was no way to tell her. He held her. He kissed her again and let his kiss speak for his heart.

Then he thought of Dana—and remembered that it was his love of Draga's daughter that had kept him alive across the long miles . . . and although it was true that Morrigan, unbidden, had been in his dreams as well, it was Dana who had always had his heart. Morrigan had taken a man in his absence. Dana had not. She had waited. For him. He was certain of that. And now she would need him. She would be his woman after all.

Slowly, reluctantly, he put Morrigan away from him and tried to smile as he said that she would always be one of the dearest friends of all his heart.

The stricken look upon her tear-streaked face touched him so deeply that he found it necessary to mask his feelings with idle small talk. "That powder you packed in your traveling case . . . it saved my life, you know! And the cakes too! Never was there anyone to bake a griddle cake like you, although I never said so, eh? A lifetime ago, it seems. And what's this I hear about you being a widow already? And a mother of a son? Not you! I'll not believe it of you!"

He could not understand why she was so angry, or why she so defiantly displayed her tiny, handsome, dark-haired son to him. He only knew that her fiery display was welcome. He could be comfortable with the old, argumentative antagonist of his youth.

"Who does he look like to you?" she demanded.

He looked. He shrugged. He told her the truth. "Like you. Did you make him all yourself?"

For a moment he thought she was going to throw the baby at him; instead she drew it close and glared. "He will name Falcon as his sire."

She walked away from him then, and Dianket, who had heard it all, came close and called Balor a fool, but had time to say no more.

Dathen came galloping up, reining in so hard that his horse whirled and screamed in protest. It was lathered and wet from what had obviously been a long run made at full speed.

"By all of the Twelve Winds, Balor, if you're to lead these people to safety, do it now! Nemed's forces have been sighted! And you were right about the rumors you heard—there *are* two thousand of them! By the Mother, go, man! Go now! For we haven't a prayer of holding them here!"

They went out across the land with Balor leading them, and never had it been more difficult to obey a command than it was for him to turn away from the battle that the men of the clan MacLir must soon endure. Yet he went, astride Star Gazer's great white horse, remembering a dream dreamt by a little boy in the mead-dark of long ago.

He was Balor, son of Fomor, chieftain of the clan MacLir. He was a tall, powerful battle champion like his father. But this was no unicorn upon which he rode. Nor was he master of the world.

And this was no dream. As the horse shook its enormous head, its travel-weary sides quivering against the weight of its rider, it was not the heat of power that ran in Balor's tensed thighs. It was the heat of fear. He was a man at last, with the full weight of a man's responsibilities upon his back. And he was afraid.

Huldre was troubled. She did not want to be here. This was not how things were supposed to be. Mealla grew concerned just watching her as they plodded through the gorse bushes. "What is it, Huldre? Is this not what you have always wanted—to run before the Twelve Winds and put Bracken Fen behind you?"

"Not without him."

"He has assured us that he shall follow when he has bought us the time to escape with the children."

Huldre stopped dead in her tracks. She could not bear Mealla's eternal optimism. She put her hands to her temples. The terrible, deep, aching drone that had so often plagued her was back, along with the whirling, cold mists, the savage mists that set terror to her heart and warned her to run...run...run or he shall find you...and hurt you again....

"Huldre?"

She gasped. Mealla's touch actually hurt her arm. Her right hand sought her throat, sought the amulet. But the amulet was long gone; the Eye of Donar lighted someone else's path. And through the mists she saw whose path it was. The Raven. Nemed MacAgnomain. There was no doubt. No speculation. He would be approaching the holding now. With two thousand men at his back and the Eye of Donar to lead him to victory. The Eye of Donar. *If I were to take it from him, he could not win. If I were to bring it to my lord, the victory shall be his, as it was so long ago when he stole me away from Nemed and slew the clan of Partholon and was Wolf of the Western Tribes.*

"Huldre, we must go on. Come along."

Huldre looked up. It was growing dark. A storm was growing within her, around her, sapping the light of day. *If I steal the amulet, I can—*

"Huldre, please. We have fallen behind the others. We must go on...the lord has *commanded* us to go on!"

"Yes. Of course. You go ahead. I shall be along. I want to catch my breath."

Mealla frowned. "You don't seem winded to me. And little Babh shall need nursing soon. Listen: She's bawling in poor Blaheen's arms."

"Tell Blaheen that I shall be along in a moment."

But she did not follow. She waited until Mealla was out of sight, then struck off back for the holding at a run. She did not know that Mealla trailed her, nor would she have slowed her step if she had. They had come a long way. And she *had* to return to Bracken Fen, and then run beyond it to seek out the Raven, to do this for Fomor, for if she could not—it occurred to her now, for the first time—she had no wish to live without him. The immensity of her love for him struck her, as thunder rolled in the distance in the direction of the holding.

But it was not thunder. It was the sound of an approaching army.

Panic overwhelmed her then. It set the familiar black emptiness rising within her. The whirling mists. The visions of blood. The memories of rape and pain and endless humiliation. She tensed against them. They were the maelstrom of terror. If she allowed the emptiness to take form within her, it would take away her sanity. There was only one way to stop it; she must outrun it; she must get back to the holding; she must seek out Nemed and strip the Eye of Donor from his neck or die in the attempt.

Misery rose with truth. Old Munremar had been right about her all along... her amulet had brought this tragedy upon them. She was responsible for it all. She and Balor. If only he had never been born. If only she had not goaded him into seeking his Destiny... if only... her breath caught in her throat as she saw him now, a man and a warrior, riding far ahead, leading his people as she had always known he must. Balor, a pale rider whom the men of the clan had once called Wolf Slayer.

"No!" she cried, and knew that the wolf to be slain was Fomor. "I shall give you back your luck!" she cried again, and did not care that no one heard her. She herself had heard, and that was enough for now.

She ran. She galloped, breaking out of the gorse and hurtling madly through the thigh-high shrubbery of the far pastures, weedy now with luxuriant summer growth. It stung her bare limbs, for she had hefted her tunic high, oblivious to pain, taking no notice of the branches that bloodied her as surely as any whipping would have done.

She ran blindly, her heart beating in her throat. She stumbled twice, but rose, her arms flailing at branches that seemed bent upon impeding her progress. She had reached the outer edges of the bogs, and had she paused to take her bearings, she would have seen how close to the holding she was now. Bowmen were visible all along the palisade and upon the rim of the outer fortifications of the earthen embankment. Beyond this, a great mass of mounted men and warriors afoot were massing. Even in the rain the crimson and black of the house of Nemed MacAgnomain was visible. But she saw nothing but the blur of the rain blowing suddenly into her face. The wind struck at her, driving her back. She paid it no heed, nor did she hear the screams of Mealla calling her to come back.

She ran on, leaping over mud sinks and wallows, slipping and falling, fighting for footing that half the time was not there. She ran until she was sweating. She ran until her gorge rose and she had to stop lest she be sick. She stopped, her muddied, bleeding limbs planted wide. She was shivering and sobbing and suddenly confused. Who were the men massed ahead of her? Armed men. And who was the horseman advancing so slowly toward her?

"Huldre! For the love of life itself, run!"

She wheeled. What was her hearth sister doing behind her? And was that not little Bevin approaching close at the auburn-haired woman's heel? Yes. Mealla was screaming for her to come back. Back where? The holding lay ahead.

The holding. There had been a reason for her run to the holding. Strange, her race across the land had driven it from her mind. Perhaps when she looked at it again, she would remember.

But what she saw when she turned brought other memories. The horseman had drawn rein before her. She stared up at him.

The black eyes of the Raven never blinked as he smiled and held down his hand to her. "We meet again, Huldre of the North," said Nemed MacAgnomain. "Look. I wear the Eye of Donar now. Come. Ride with me. We shall share its fortune. Now and forever."

What happened then was inevitable. In the gathering storm-dark, with Huldre a captive riding before him upon his horse—and little Bevin and Mealla taken by his men, Nemed paraded in the torchlight of the palisade, just out of arrow range, and demanded that the Wolf come out of his den to face the Raven, man to man, so that he, Nemed, could savor the pleasure of putting the slave collar around Fomor's neck.

"And the terms for my people if I do?" roared out Fomor from the heights of the palisade.

"Terms? You gave no terms when last we met, Fomor MacLir!"

"I had come for vengeance's sake, to win in blood the honor that your father deprived my own kinsmen of when he—and you . . . and all of your clansmen—came upon us at our holy sanctuary upon Tory Isle and struck us down unarmed! It was a vicious and blasphemous raid you and your sire led, defiling sacred ground, disemboweling a pregnant woman, degrading a man before his sons, and then hurling them into the sea to their deaths."

"You look well enough to me, Wolf!"

"Fight with me then, man to man, and let the outcome satisfy honor between us once and for all!"

Never. The word rumbled in two thousand throats, and in nearly five hundred more atop the palisade. But there was not a man in either camp who did not itch to see such a battle, and lust then for the greater conflict that must follow it.

It came.

Alone, his sword at ready, Fomor came out from the gateway of the palisade, with only Dathen and Lomna Ruad, fully armed, at either side of him.

Then, as now, Nemed's armed men formed a ring of watching, wolfish faces into which the fighting men of the clan MacLir looked down from the palisade and roared their lord's name in resounding affirmation of their faith in his power. They would swarm like hornets if he fell. They would rain arrows and spears, and many would die, even the women and child of the lord whom the men of Nemed had brought within certain range in the foolish hope that they might prove a deterrent to the MacLir warriors' wrath.

They met, as they had met before, and for a long while they measured one another as the hatred of a lifetime congealed within their hearts and made their blood run hot and fast until it burned behind their eyes and Fomor forgot that his women watched, and little Bevin with them, and all that existed for him was Nemed, slayer of Manannan . . . man-slayer . . . sadist . . . ruiner of dreams and lives and all that Fomor had worked a lifetime to build and secure.

It was easy to hate such an enemy, to want the satisfaction of killing him, even if his own death must also be assured. He began to circle slowly and did not know when he lunged forward. His blade struck bronze and rang, but not before it tasted blood, and Nemed cried out, more startled than stung. But he was bleeding, from a gash across his upper sword arm; it was a cut that would allow strength to be sapped quickly. Nemed would have to end this match before Fomor had a chance to end it for him.

With the slightest raising of a brow into the white snag of scar that marred his face, the signal was given. Fomor felt the blow come from behind almost at the same time that Echur, with a well-placed arrow, dropped the man who had given it. Nevertheless, the tip of the man's spear, bronze and honed to a killing edge, had slashed the back of Fomor's right thigh deep to the bone, ripping muscle and vein. The lord of the MacLir went down onto his left knee, half blinded by agony. Nemed leaped forward and swung his blade cruelly across Fomor's massive chest.

Mealla screamed, and little Bevin burrowed her head in her skirt, sobbing and terrified.

The Achaean's blade sliced back, with all of Nemed's weight behind it, but Fomor swayed and avoided the swipe that would have taken his head. He came up onto both feet, fighting for balance as, with his sword in both hands, he moved to the attack so aggressively that Nemed backed off, cowering and calling for assistance to the howls of protest from the clansmen of MacLir. The armed men in red and black hesitated, eyeing the bowmen on the palisade and the still-twitching spearman who had taken an arrow through the back of his neck after attempting to hamstring the chieftain.

But there was one among the throng of men in red and black who, by his small size, was less vulnerable to attack, for he could move beneath the limbs of his comrades unseen by those above on the palisade. With a bow and arrow borrowed from one who hesitated to use the weapon himself, Coman the dwarf stood beneath the protective bodies of his comrades, nocked an arrow, and aimed, smiling as he did so. He was a poor archer because of his stubby arms and misshapen hands, but the back of Fomor MacLir was an enormous target.

Struck through the heart by Coman's shot, Fomor stood a moment—long enough to name the Raven "coward" for all to hear. He dropped, like a great tree that has been cut in a forest. And when he fell, silence fell with him, and all who looked upon his lifeless body knew that something fine and honorable had been lost forever, and those who had felled him had been dishonored by the cutting down of so magnificent a life.

Even Coman felt it. He went cold and dropped the bow even as he felt the pale eyes of the woman upon him. Never in all of his life had he seen such eyes. He made the sign against evil and ran, scooting back and away from the carnage that was to follow.

No one knew how long the battle raged. Only a few managed to escape, to do Fomor's bidding—to set fire to the fields and slaughter his beloved cattle so that when the clan MacLir was destroyed, the Raven and his men would not feast off the holding they had brought to ruin. Every foodstuff and every sack of grain, every crock of mead and flask of water had been poisoned. This was the vengeance of the Wolf, after his death, and in days to come, when many of Nemed's half-starved warriors bloated and died of poisoning, when wolves howled on the distant moor, there would be those among them who swore to the Raven that it was the spirit of the Wolf himself laughing.

But this was yet to be.

Beneath the storm-dark the fighting raged on. Coman took refuge upon the ramparts. Above the heat of battle, in the smoking light of the torches that were fixed at intervals along the heights of the palisade, he could see it all. His loins grew hard with lust induced by the sight and sound of death. He pleasured himself. He danced in joyous celebration of the carnage. He whirled and pirouetted and balanced like a monkey that he had seen long ago at the trading center of Point of Ale. He walked upon the very points of the timber tops, feinting and slashing with an imaginary sword, stabbing at the torches with the small copper dagger that had been his reward from Nemed MacAgnomain for having discovered the whereabouts of the clan MacLir. He hooted; he jabbered. He was so excited that he failed to notice the movement of the pale-haired woman who had thrown herself across the body of the fallen Wolf.

The Wolf! He, *Coman*, had slain the Wolf! He put back his head and howled.

He did not see the pale form stalking him. Huldre trod as cautiously as she had once pursued overly avaricious mice that dared to trespass into the storage alcove of the chieftain's roundhouse. The child followed in her wake, wild-eyed with fright as the battle raged around her.

Coman did not hear her approach. He slapped his thighs

and clapped his hands and did not see Huldre ascend the
ladder as soft of foot and dangerous as a lynx.

"You savor the thrill of heights, I see?"

Startled, he nearly lost his balance as he wheeled to face
her. Her eyes were upon him, those pale, strange, unearthly
eyes.   Only now they were not blue—a sudden gust of wind
had risen out of the north, feeding energy into the torches.
The one immediately to his right flamed, and its color flared
red within the woman's eyes. Like the blood-red stone of
carnelian that glowed within the Eye of Donar, it burned
him. He gasped, suddenly terrified as he perceived her
intent.

"No!" he screeched, and slashed out at her with his dagger
as she grabbed him by the shoulders and tossed him up as
though he were an infant.

"I shall please you!" she informed him, turning him so that
he faced outward and found himself staring at the base of the
palisade, nearly twenty feet below. He squirmed and wriggled in her grasp, but she held him fast. "Look, Bevin! This is
the creature that killed your father. Watch and you shall learn
the best way for a toad to die!"

She flung him down hard. And when he hit she heard him
break, and watched him die twitching, impaled upon Nemed's
dagger. For a brief moment she felt better than she had
thought it possible to feel.

Below, beyond the palisade, the world spread wide before
her, and across that world the north wind blew from out of
the far country where she had been born. A storm was rising.
Great black banks of clouds were massing above the highlands. Below them a terrible darkness was gathering. And
into that darkness her children had fled, with Balor leading
them, as somehow she had always known he must.

A new Wolf would rise out of Albion. But the old Wolf was
dead. Never again would she feel the warm breath of his life
and love. Never.

Yet somehow she felt it now. It was a warm wind rising all
around her, combing back the long, moon-pale strands of her
hair. It soothed her, calmed her. It was the breath of her lord
and love, borne now forever on the tides of the Twelve
Winds, whispering to her not to be afraid.

A high, sharp sound pierced the moment. She looked up to
see a hawk wheeling upon the wind—a hawk the color of

amber. Circling and keening upon motionless wings, its eyes glinted red as they somehow caught the last traces of light from a sun that had already slipped below the western horizon.

"Donar!" She cried the name of the god and knew that, although Nemed possessed her talisman, the god himself was with her now. The world beyond the palisade suddenly seemed to burst into flames as it had long ago, when she had stood in this same place watching the men of the clan MacLir leave the holding on the dawn of the wolf hunt. She had seen the future then, as she saw it now. In flames and in darkness it was no future at all.

The din of the battle invaded her senses. A man's voice, Nemed's voice, was shouting her name angrily. And a child was tugging frantically at her tattered skirts.

"Mother! They are coming for us! Mother... I am afraid. I—Mother! Your face!"

Her hands strayed upward. She had not felt the wounds until now; the dwarf *had* slashed her, deeply, from temple to mouth and across again. She did not care. The wounds would have no time to heal.

Only seconds had passed since she had hurled the dwarf to his death. Soon Nemed would be at her side. He was on the ladder now, raging at her.

She knelt and quickly did what she had never done before and knew that she would never do again: She embraced her little girl ferociously, with a love that would have to last the child a lifetime—if she could buy enough time for Bevin to escape. "You must be brave, my little one. You must flee. Donar of the North will guide your steps, and the Twelve Winds will speed you on your way."

Savagely she kissed the little girl, then rose, ripped off her dress, hefted the child, and using the garment as an extension of her arm, leaned over the timbered wall and made Bevin understand that she must climb down and leap to safety.

The girl hesitated only a moment. She was afraid to go, but more afraid to stay. And surely her mother would follow.

Huldre did not follow. She reached back and tore a torch from its bracket. She stood her ground. Nemed was on the rampart now, the sword of the fallen Wolf in his hand. His body was wet with sweat and blood and his eyes were engorged with battle fury.

He stared at her, half blinded with rage. Fomor MacLir was dead, but *he* had not killed him, nor had he yet had time to mutilate his body, for the men of the Wolf had exploded into battle madness when their lord had fallen, and Nemed had been forced to fight for his life against them. He had not been able to retrieve the sword—his murdered father's weapon, the sword of Partholon—until the tide of the fighting had turned against the men of the clan MacLir. He had vowed to wrest that sword from the man who had slain his father, at the cost of that man's life. But a misshapen toad had deprived him of that privilege.

And the woman had taken the privilege of killing the toad. Alerted by one of his men to the scene on the ramparts, he had feared that she was about to hurl herself from the heights. Barely looking at the sword as he lifted it from the hand of the dead chieftain, he had raged at her to hold. He cared not what happened to her child. His men would kill her later, as they would find and kill all those who must have fled from Bracken Fen at the insistence of their lord.

Now all that mattered was the woman. Above all, her death had become the object of his life; her death at his hands. The ruination of her beauty, at his hands. The destruction of the world of the Wolf, whom she had chosen above him, at his hands.

He trembled at the thought of it. The haft of the sword was hot within his hands as his fingers flexed around it. It was lighter than he remembered, and not as well balanced as the sword he had tossed away in exchange for it. He held it out now, with both hands curled above the hilt. With this, the sword of Partholon, Huldre of the North would die. At his hands.

"The final vengeance is mine, after all," he said, smiling mildly. "Cast away the torch, Huldre. You cannot stay your fate with such a makeshift weapon against the great sword of Partholon. Your Wolf is dead. His holding will soon be in ruins. Your beauty will be stripped from you, and with this sword the life you have chosen to live shall be finished."

In the storm-dark, in the torchlight, she stood tall and unflinching. The wind blew her hair forward. He could not see her face, but the sight of her body was enough—the man-need in him stirred and swelled. Behind him several of his men had followed him onto the walkway. He heard their low growls of hunger for rape, their exhalations in affirmation of her beauty. But this rape would be his. And when he had finished, the blade of Partholon would rape her. His vengeance would be satisfied at last.

"Never . . ." The word came out so softly that at first it seemed to be only the hissing of the wind. "Your vengeance will never be satisfied. The Wolf is dead, but not at your hands. This holding was in ruins long ago. And my beauty is no longer yours to take."

Holding the torch with one hand, she stroked back her hair. She heard the appalled intake of his breath as he saw her wounds. She laughed at him.

Rage filled him again. At his throat the Eye of Donar grew suddenly hot, searing his skin. He reached up and ripped it from his throat, hurling it at the feet of the woman.

"You have haunted me far too long, Huldre of the North. Now I *shall* take your life!"

When he lunged with his weapon, she sidestepped the intended blow. She could feel the wind now, all around her. The Twelve Winds, Fomor's gods. A wolf answered the voice of the storm, and hearing its song, for the first time since she had come to Bracken Fen, Huldre was not afraid.

Nemed cursed aloud. He felt Huldre's eyes upon him as he dislodged the unwieldy blade from the palisade timbers and leveled it at her.

"A new Wolf shall rise out of Albion, Nemed MacAgnomain. His children shall eat of your bones. And I shall run with that Wolf forever."

"You shall not!" he roared, raising the sword to strike just as the hawk plummeted, striking its talons into Nemed's hand with such force that the sword fell to the walkway.

Huldre took the torch in both hands and held it outward, looking through the flames at Nemed. "The Wolf has tricked you once again, for it is he who howls last, and the sword you have taken is *not* the sword of Partholon. And my life was one with Fomor MacLir's . . . and by my own hand I now set my soul free to join him, for he shall be lord of the Twelve Winds forever, and wherever you go, he shall make a mockery of your name."

It happened so quickly, he could not stop her. She pulled the torch inward, embracing the flame even as it transformed her hair into fire. She breathed it in, standing a moment before she fell. She was not afraid. The Eye of Donar was in her hand, and Fomor awaited her with the hawk, upon the back of the Twelve Winds.

The storm came out of the north. It came across the Sea of Mists, with all the fury of the Twelve Winds at its back. The hawk flew before it, and seeing it winging above him, Balor followed. He knew where it must lead him. Night had fallen, but by the flash of the lightning, Balor saw his way. To the tor.

With the monolith towering above him, Balor led his people to shelter within the hollow of the tor, past a row of man-tall boulders that hid the entrance so completely that any man, not knowing that the cave was there, would never find it.

Yet Balor walked forward as though he had been this way before. Into the dark maw of the mountain, into the cave where his father had once tracked wolves, he led his people and knew that there would be torches waiting to light their way; Fomor would have left them. The Wolf *had* been wise, and wary enough to foresee a time when they would be needed.

There was the scraping sound of flints; the light flared. Dianket had ignited a torch and now held it high, illuminating the cave. As the women and children whispered to one another, Balor saw that they stood not within a cave at all, but in a wide, natural passageway that narrowed back into darkness as it ran on and on into the dark belly of the underworld. Far away, miles perhaps, there was a restless surging sound, like that of the surf crashing against a rocky shore.

Dianket came to stand beside Balor, listening. "What is it, Balor?"

"It is the sea," he replied, "the wide, dark sea." He knew in the way that Huldre would have known, with the Inner Vision. Her gift. Her power. He accepted it now and knew that when he led the others onward, they would find a deep sea cavern opening onto a rocky shore; and there in the darkness a great ship would lay waiting with green sails down and wrapped upon its decks, the one ship that Fomor MacLir had not been able to bring himself to burn. There in the darkness, amid the charred rubble of what had once been a great fleet, Manannan MacLir's ship *Wave Sweeper* lay waiting for the Wolf of the Western Tribes to return to the old way of life and to the Days of Glory. But the old Wolf would not return. A new Wolf was rising out of Albion. Balor trembled against the vision, hating and wanting it at the same time.

"You do have the power," observed Dianket.

"Aye, and so. But what sort of power is it, to have led me here, and to have brought my people such an end as this?"

"It is not an end, Balor," Morrigan said. "It is a beginning." She came very close. "It is the Circle of Destiny. Fate calls to a man, and he must follow. Your father knew that, yet chose to walk his own way. It was his decision to turn from the ways of his ancestors that marked the turning of your stars, Balor. A man must be what he has been born to be . . . and if he is a Wolf, then he must walk in the skin of a wolf or die."

Her words recalled his mother's words, spoken so long ago in the dark silence of the chieftain's roundhouse. He could not bear the memory, or its implications. "The Wolf is *not* dead. He shall come to us when he is victorious over the Raven. And if he does not, what makes you believe that I am fit to walk in his skin?"

Her eyes were steady in the torchlight. "You are his firstborn son. You must be worthy."

He left them then, and went out into the storm alone to climb to the summit of the tor, to stand facing into the wind, waiting for his father to come to him.

But it was Dathen who came, leading the survivors of the battle of Bracken Fen to safety. Elathan was with him, and Tethra. Before the storm had broken, Fomor had sent the young men out to burn the fields and slay the cattle, with Dathen to lead them to the tor when they were done; it had been his way to save the youths their honor, and to save their lives as well. They had come upon little Bevin cowering in the gorse wood and had brought her along. Findias came following in their wake, with a battered Muri and Ogma and only a handful of others.

"All the rest, dead. The Wise One sacrificed on his own altar. And the lord slain, by treachery."

Findias told the tale, and as he spoke, Balor stood at the edge of the tor where he had once stood with his father, and he wept. The wind blew hard and cold against him where once it had been warm and sweet in the face of a young boy who looked out upon the world for the first time and had seen naught but wonder and glory in it.

"Glory!" He hurled the word into the storm. He drew the much battered sword that he had taken as his own after Teacher had been broken. He loosed it from its sheath and whirled to break it against the hard granite boulders of the tor. It screamed as it broke, and the sound of its dying moaned long upon the wind.

"Would you run off now into the wild country? Would you guide your people to a new Destiny... of peace... where the ravens of the world shall never find you?" It was Dathen. Gentle, patient counsel. "The ravens always seek a man out in the end, Balor. It was a lesson the Wolf learned too late. Now the ravens own his world. *Your* world, and ours. Would you run away from them upon the Twelve Winds and never look back until it is too late? Or would you call upon the Twelve Winds to serve your will, to take what is yours in this world—not for vengeance's sake, but in the name of justice?"

"Words..."

"A man must start with something. A great deal can be built on words, Balor, if the foundation stones are placed correctly. The Wolf has put the remnant of the clan MacLir into your care, and into your hands—this..."

From the sheath at his belt Dathen drew a sword and held it out to Balor. And as Balor stared at it, all the world went round and back again as a sob of recognition wracked him.

"It is Retaliator... your father's gift to you. You are the Wolf now, Balor. With this you may dare to carve a better world."

Dathen placed the blade across his palms, and then, together with the others, left him alone with the sword. With his Destiny.

It was as heavy as the weight of all the world, and yet as the moments passed and the storm raged around him, it became strangely light. It balanced perfectly in either hand, as if it had been crafted for him alone.

For a long time he stood with the sword in the rain. Soon the Raven would bring his warriors across the highlands to the tor, but they would not find the people of the clan MacLir, for by then Balor would have led them to the sea, to the waiting *Wave Sweeper*, which with the help of Dathen and Findias would carry them southward, ever southward, until they found refuge among the People of the Stone. And there, from out of the loins of a Wolf, beneath falling stars, a new Wolf *would* rise out of Albion. Someday he *would* be the Mighty One. Someday Retaliator would taste the blood of the Raven. Someday. But not now.

Now the Mighty One was only a man—a young man. And he was too tired to wish to be a warrior. When the white wolf snarled at him out of the crack of a lightning bolt that stung the summit of the tor, he turned his back and walked away.

He descended from the height of the monolith and walked to the entrance of the cave. A baby was crying, Morrigan was waiting.

He walked toward her, Retaliator in his hand.

Author's Notes

This novel has been drawn from the lore and prehistory of Ireland, Scandinavia, and the British Isles. Contrary to the currently fashionable libel that the people of northwestern Europe were cave-dwelling savages who clothed themselves in vermin-infested animal skins while the cultures of Asia and the Near East basked in halcyon days of civilized splendor, carbon-14 dating of ongoing archaeological discoveries confirms not only the antiquity but the richness of those cultures that historians of Imperial Rome dismissed as "barbarian."

The great megalithic passage tomb of Newgrange in Ireland predates Stonehenge. And Stonehenge predates the pyramids of ancient Egypt. Approximately thirty-four centuries before the birth of Christ, the prehistoric sanctuary at Avebury, not far from Salisbury Plain, might well have been Europe's first university; its stone circle, composed of over one hundred monoliths weighing some forty tons apiece, was thirteen times larger than the sanctuary sarsen-stone circle of Stonehenge. Both were old when the civilization of Mycenae was new.

There is no real mystery behind Stonehenge. It was a great center of learning and religious celebration. It fell into disuse not because of magic, but because a religion and way of life built around star-gazing must have clear skies. For reasons we may never understand, sometime in the early Bronze Age the clear, dry skies over northern Europe clouded. The climate changed. And with that change a culture died.

Ancestors of the Vikings were raiding and trading in Ireland, England, and on the mainland of Europe since Neolithic times. Men of Eireann were fighting as mercenaries in foreign wars and engaging in an active gold trade with peoples from as far north as Ultima Thule and as far south and east as the Mediterranean and the Black Sea since the dawn of history.

Two thousand years before the Roman occupation of Judaea,

Stone Age physicians were routinely and successfully practicing the surgical art of trepanning in Denmark. Megalithic astronomers and mathematicians not only knew that the world was round, but taught their students that the atmosphere "lay around the earth as shell encompasses the egg." The Bronze Age was born in the Balkans at the same time that it was developing in the Fertile Crescent.

The people of northwestern Europe may not have possessed a written language, but their oral tradition has survived to this day, and despite what the Roman historians may have recorded, archaeologists have revealed that the "savages" not only wore more than the skins of animals, but used zippers to close their travel bags, manicured their fingernails, and possessed a good working knowledge of the loom. Their women and girls wore hair nets, donned miniskirts and cropped tops for summer wear, and had a taste for jewelry, both domestic and imported. Feather cloaks were popular among the clergy, and it might be noted that the ancient Greeks learned the art of soap-making from traveling "barbarians" from Celtic lands.

Wolves of the Dawn is based on the "wonder sagas" of Scandinavia and the Irish Mythological Cycle that many historians now acknowledge as "the earliest voice from the dawn of Western European civilization."

Balor, lord of the Fomorian sea pirates, was a real man, not a twisted, cyclopean devil as Christian myth has made him. With Cethlinn, crooked toothed and loyal to the end, he sired a daughter whose son was Lugh, the Mighty One, Master of All the Arts, Lord of Light, and principal deity in the great pantheon of Celtic god-heroes, along with Morrigan, the Great Queen. The ruins of Balor's prehistoric fortress still stand on the wild cliffs of Tory Isle, about seven miles off the coast of western Ireland.

Bronze was to Stone Age men what no other substance had been before. An alloy of copper and tin, it achieved a hardness and malleability impossible to be found in stone or softer metals. It was only natural that warrior societies would recognize its potential. The first swords were extensions of daggers and allowed the hand-to-hand fighter a new reach, a new power that was to change the face of war. In the first years of the Bronze Age, when most battle lords were still equipped with the weapons of the Stone Age, the first bronze swords must have seemed to be "magic" to spearmen and bowmen who had no idea how, or of what, a sword was made. The long sword was unknown to people of Neolithic times and did not fully come to form until steel was perfected late in the Iron Age, despite all of the long swords of steel shown in Conan comics and popular "barbarian" movies of today.

★ WAGONS WEST ★

A series of unforgettable books that trace the lives of a dauntless band of pioneering men, women, and children as they brave the hazards of an untamed land in their trek across America. This legendary caravan of people forge a new link in the wilderness. They are Americans from the North and the South, alongside immigrants, Blacks, and Indians, who wage fierce daily battles for survival on this uncompromising journey—each to their private destinies as they fulfill their greatest dreams.

☐	24408	**INDEPENDENCE!** #1	$3.95
☐	26162	**NEBRASKA!** #2	$4.50
☐	26242	**WYOMING!** #3	$4.50
☐	26072	**OREGON!** #4	$4.50
☐	26070	**TEXAS!** #5	$4.50
☐	26377	**CALIFORNIA!** #6	$4.50
☐	26546	**COLORADO!** #7	$4.50
☐	26069	**NEVADA!** #8	$4.50
☐	26163	**WASHINGTON!** #9	$4.50
☐	26073	**MONTANA!** #10	$4.50
☐	26184	**DAKOTA!** #11	$4.50
☐	26521	**UTAH!** #12	$4.50
☐	26071	**IDAHO!** #13	$4.50
☐	26367	**MISSOURI!** #14	$4.50
☐	24976	**MISSISSIPPI!** #15	$3.95
☐	25247	**LOUISIANA!** #16	$4.50
☐	25622	**TENNESSEE!** #17	$4.50
☐	26022	**ILLINOIS!** #18	$4.50

Prices and availability subject to change without notice.

Buy them at your local bookstore or use this handy coupon: